CatStronauts

SLAPDASH SCIENCE

CatStronauts
SLAPDASH SCIENCE

BY **DREW BROCKINGTON**

Ⓛ Ⓑ

Little, Brown and Company
New York Boston

About This Book

This book was edited by Russ Busse and designed by Ching Chan. The production was supervised by Erika Schwartz, and the production editor was Annie McDonnell. The text was set in Brockington, and the display type is Brockington.

Little, Brown and Company
Hachette Book Group
1290 Avenue of the Americas, New York, NY 10104
Visit us at LBYR.com

First Edition: August 2019

Little, Brown and Company is a division of Hachette Book Group, Inc. The Little, Brown name and logo are trademarks of Hachette Book Group, Inc.

The publisher is not responsible for websites (or their content) that are not owned by the publisher.

ISBNs: 978-0-316-45124-6 (hardcover), 978-0-316-45126-0 (pbk.), 978-0-316-45125-3 (ebook), 978-0-316-45121-5 (ebook), 978-0-316-45122-2 (ebook)

Printed in China

1010

Hardcover: 10 9 8 7 6 5 4 3 2 1
Paperback: 10 9 8 7 6 5 4 3 2

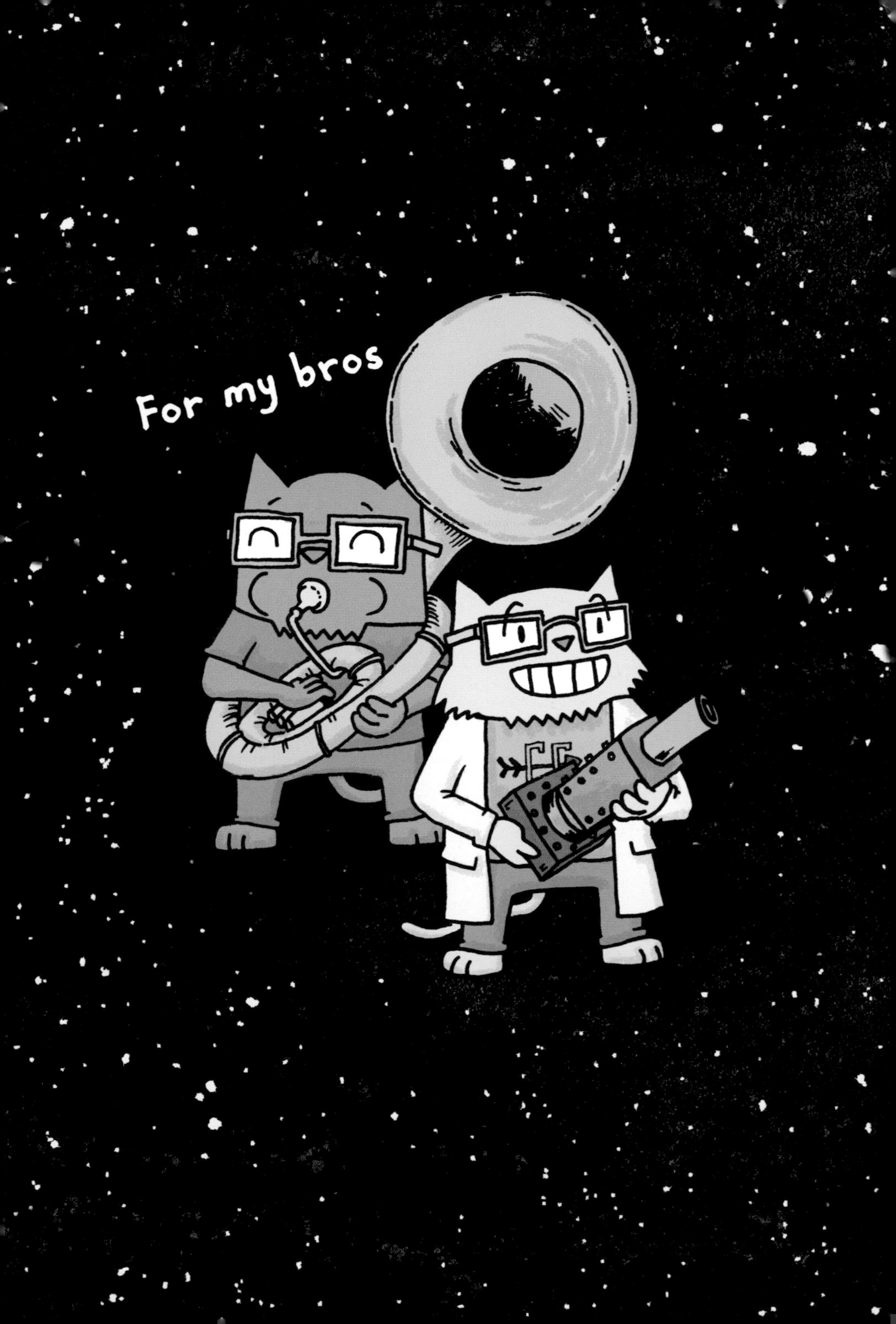
For my bros

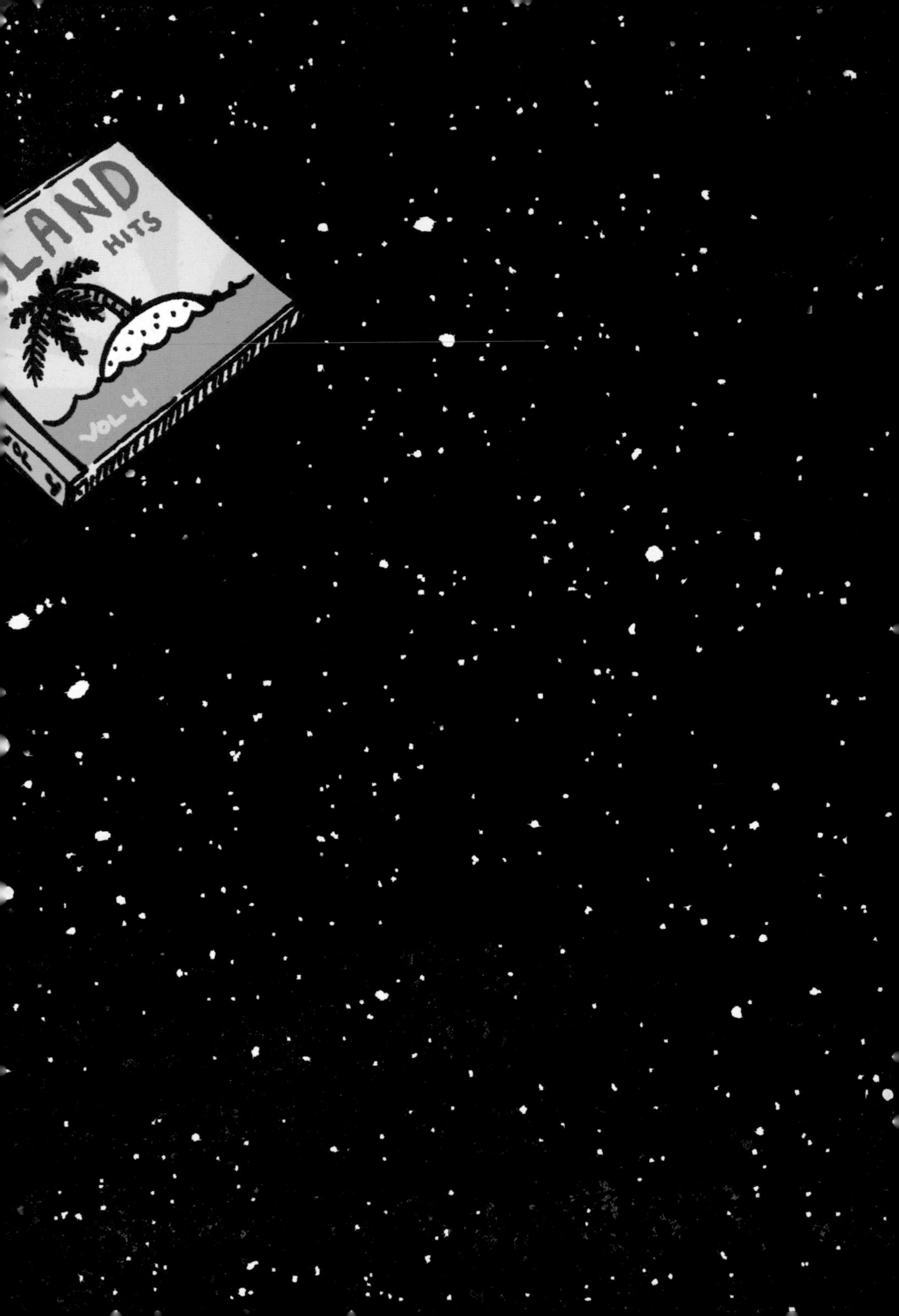
LAND
HITS
VOL 4

CHAPTER 1

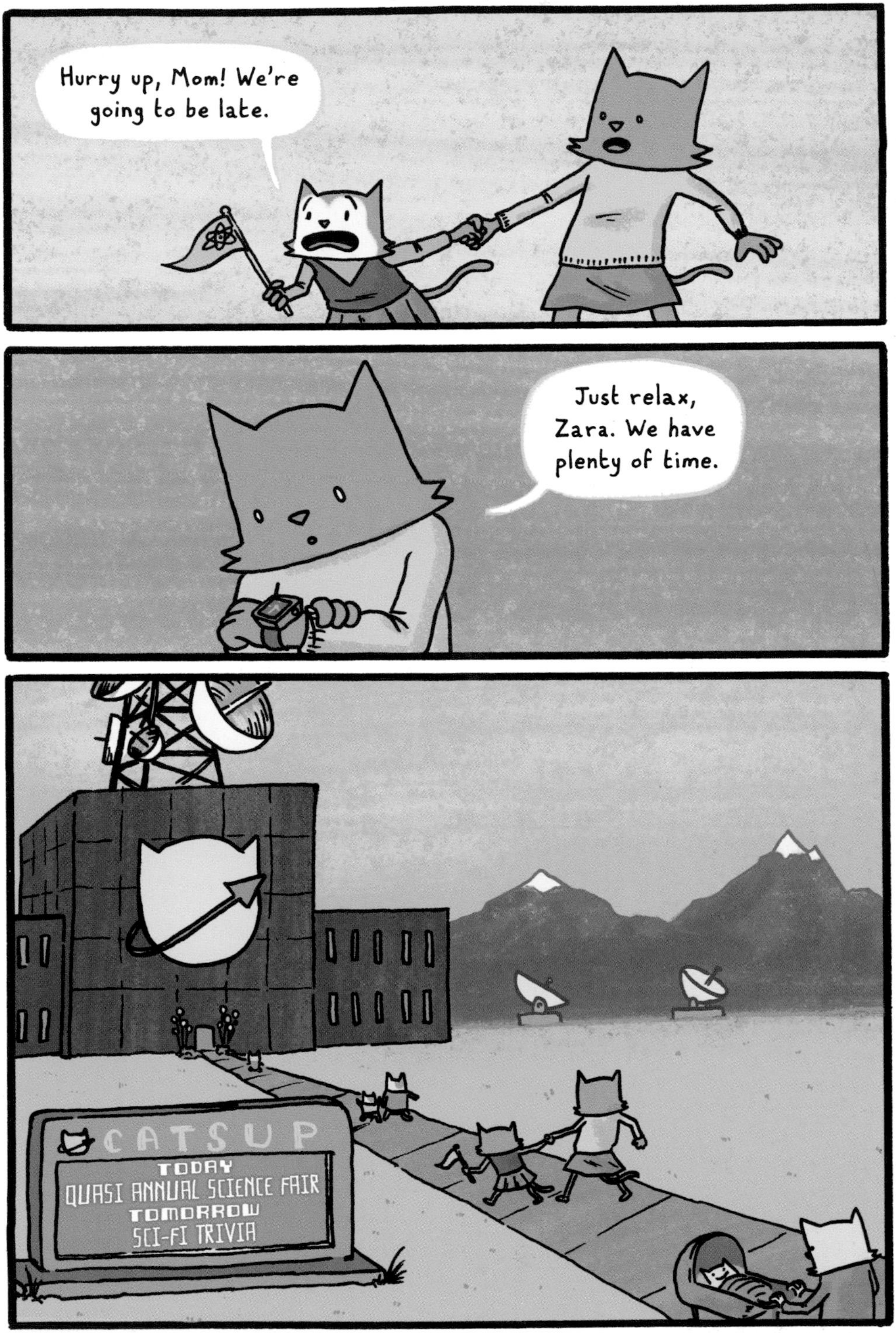
Hurry up, Mom! We're going to be late.
Just relax, Zara. We have plenty of time.
CATSUP
TODAY
QUASI ANNUAL SCIENCE FAIR
TOMORROW
SCI-FI TRIVIA

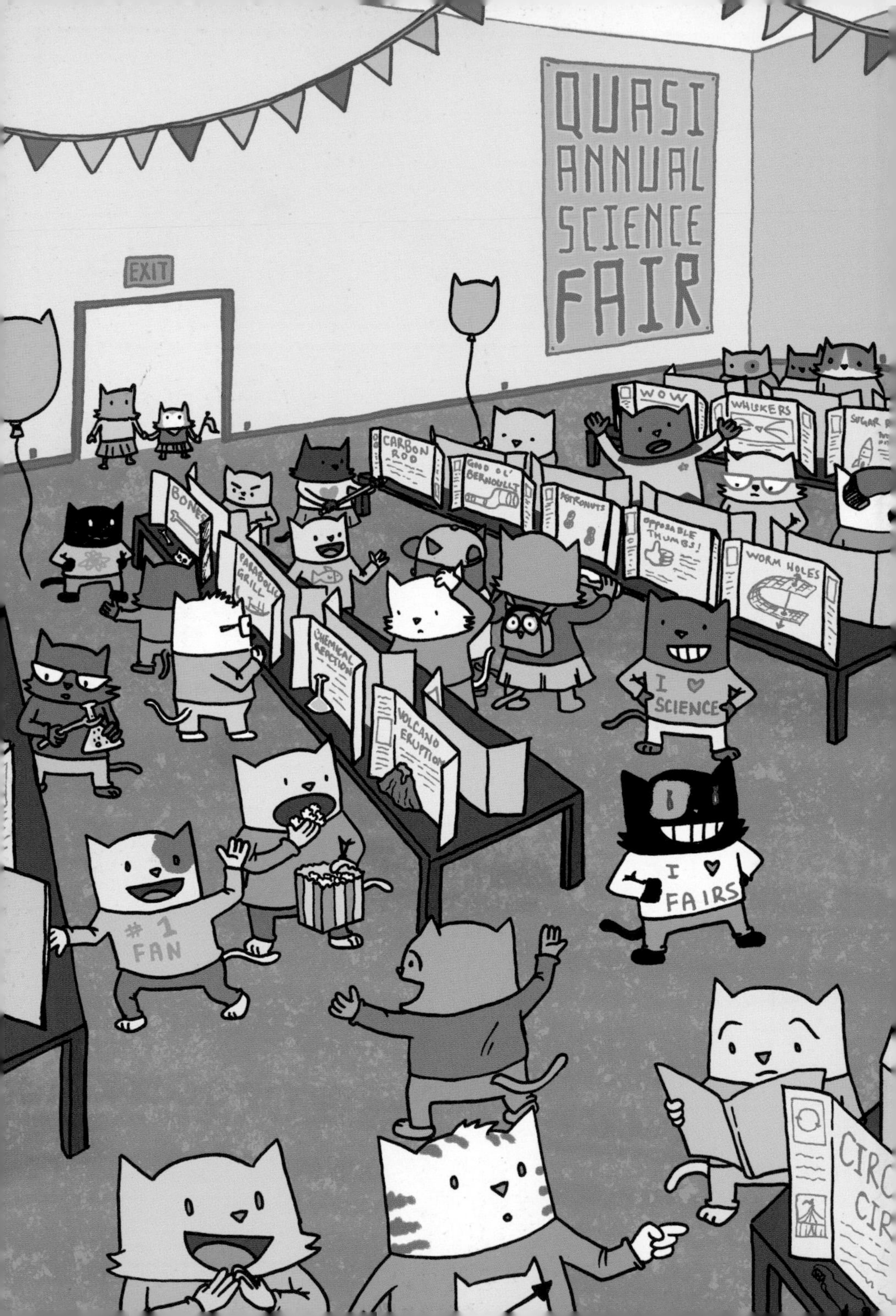
QUASI ANNUAL SCIENCE FAIR
EXIT
WOW
WHISKERS
CARBON ROD
GOOD OL' BERNOULLI
BONES
PARABOLIC GRILL
OPPOSABLE THUMBS!
WORM HOLES
CHEMICAL REACTION
VOLCANO ERUPTION
I ♥ SCIENCE
I ♥ FAIRS
#1 FAN

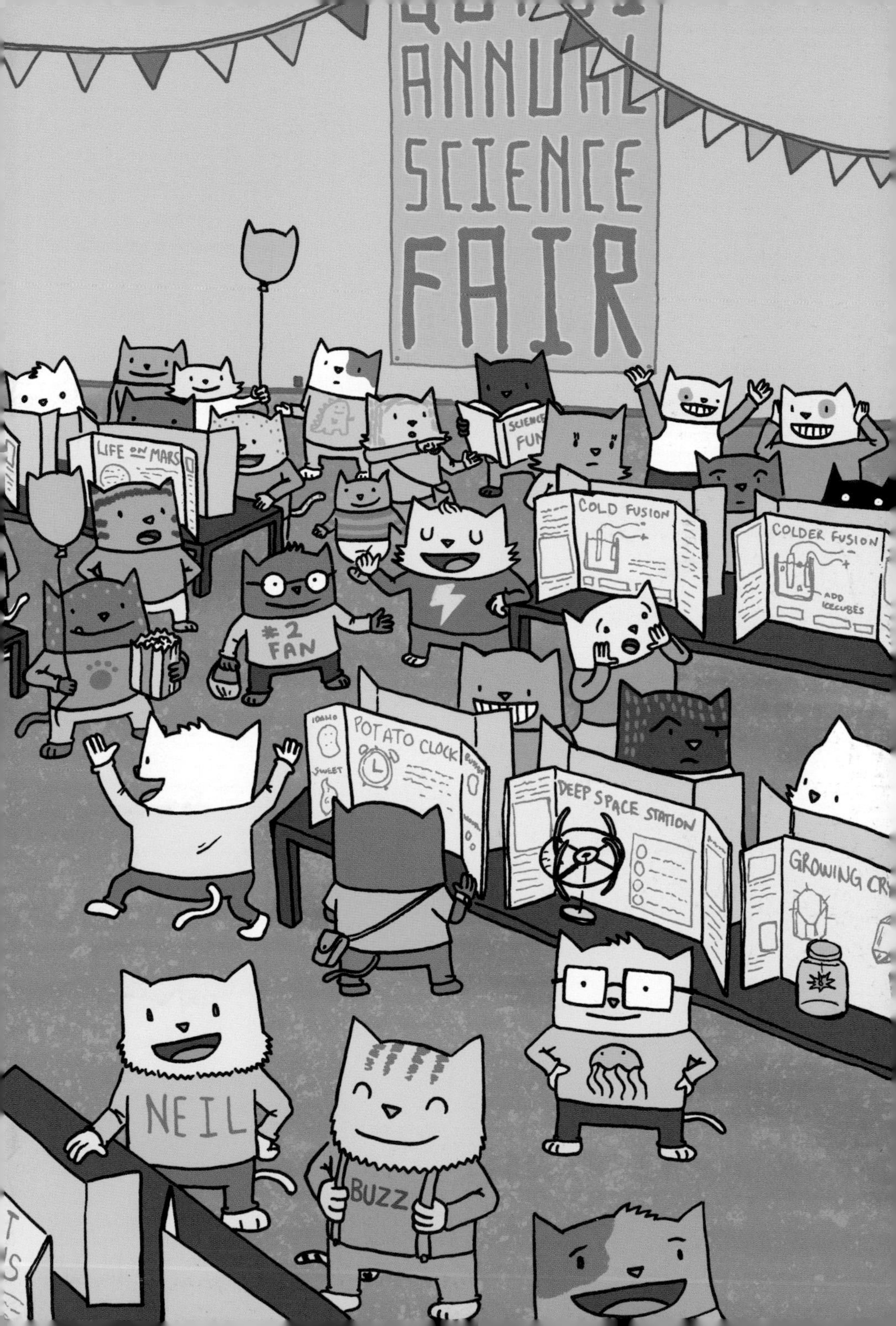
ANNUAL
SCIENCE
FAIR
LIFE ON MARS
SCIENCE FUN
COLD FUSION
COLDER FUSION
ADD ICECUBES
#2 FAN
POTATO CLOCK
IDAHO
SWEET
DEEP SPACE STATION
GROWING
NEIL
BUZZ

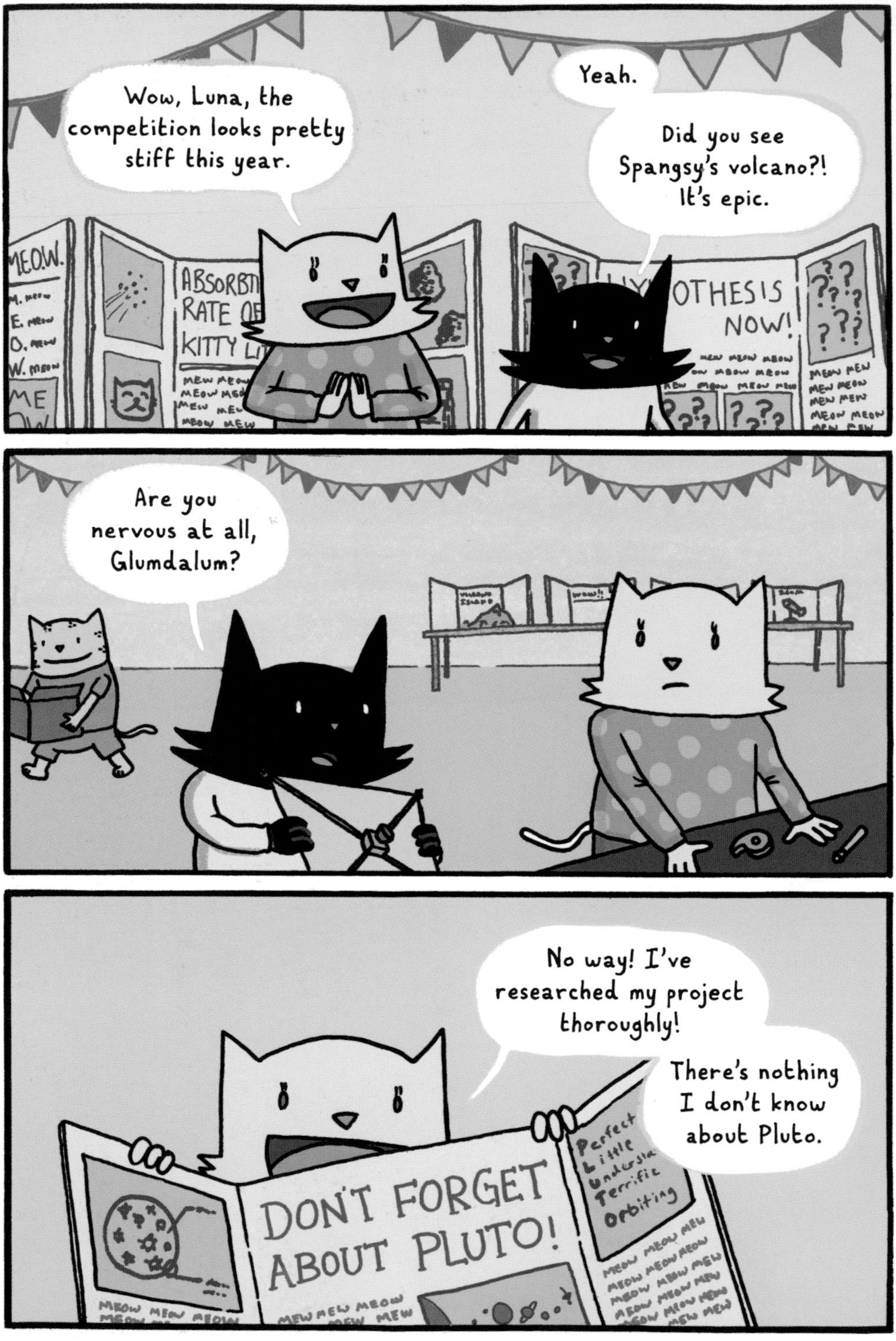
Wow, Luna, the competition looks pretty stiff this year.
Yeah.
Did you see Spangsy's volcano?! It's epic.
HYPOTHESIS NOW!
Are you nervous at all, Glumdalum?
No way! I've researched my project thoroughly!
There's nothing I don't know about Pluto.
DON'T FORGET ABOUT PLUTO!
Perfect Little Undersize Terrific Orbiting

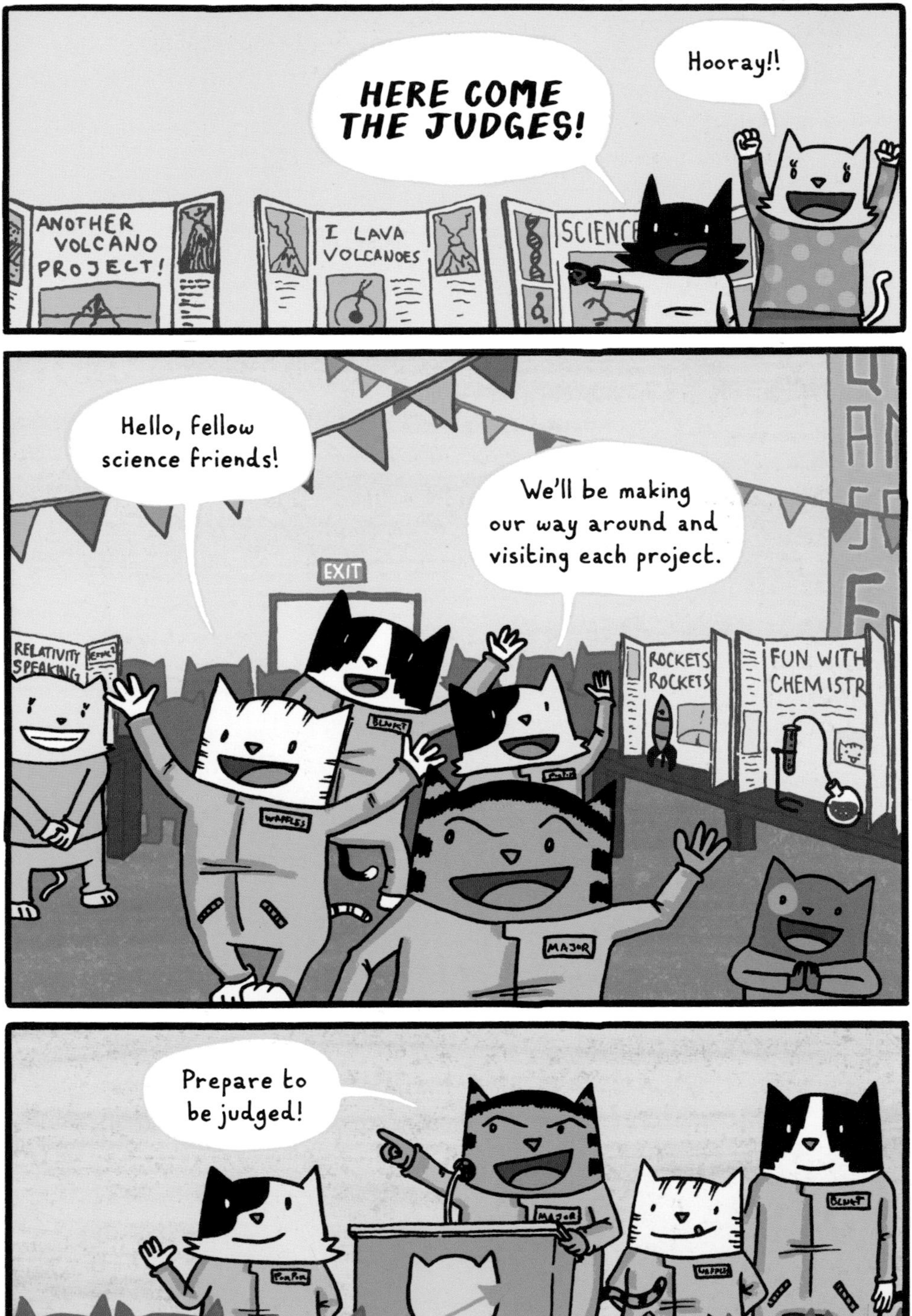
HERE COME THE JUDGES!
Hooray!!
ANOTHER VOLCANO PROJECT!
I LAVA VOLCANOES
Hello, fellow science friends!
We'll be making our way around and visiting each project.
EXIT
RELATIVITY SPEAKING
ROCKETS ROCKETS
MAJOR
Prepare to be judged!

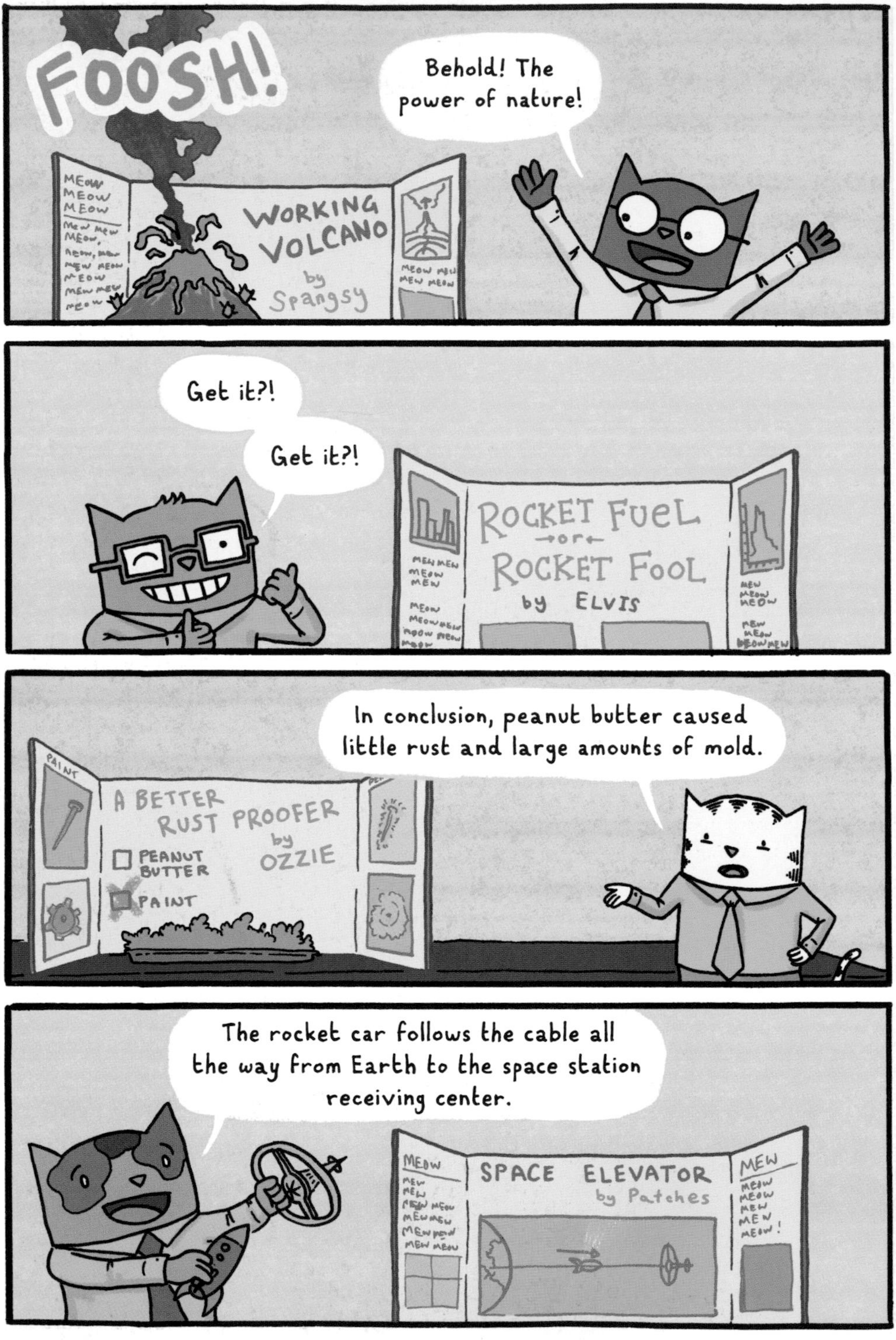
FOOSH!
Behold! The power of nature!
WORKING VOLCANO by Spangsy
Get it?!
Get it?!
ROCKET FUEL or ROCKET FOOL by ELVIS
In conclusion, peanut butter caused little rust and large amounts of mold.
A BETTER RUST PROOFER by OZZIE
PEANUT BUTTER
PAINT
The rocket car follows the cable all the way from Earth to the space station receiving center.
SPACE ELEVATOR by Patches

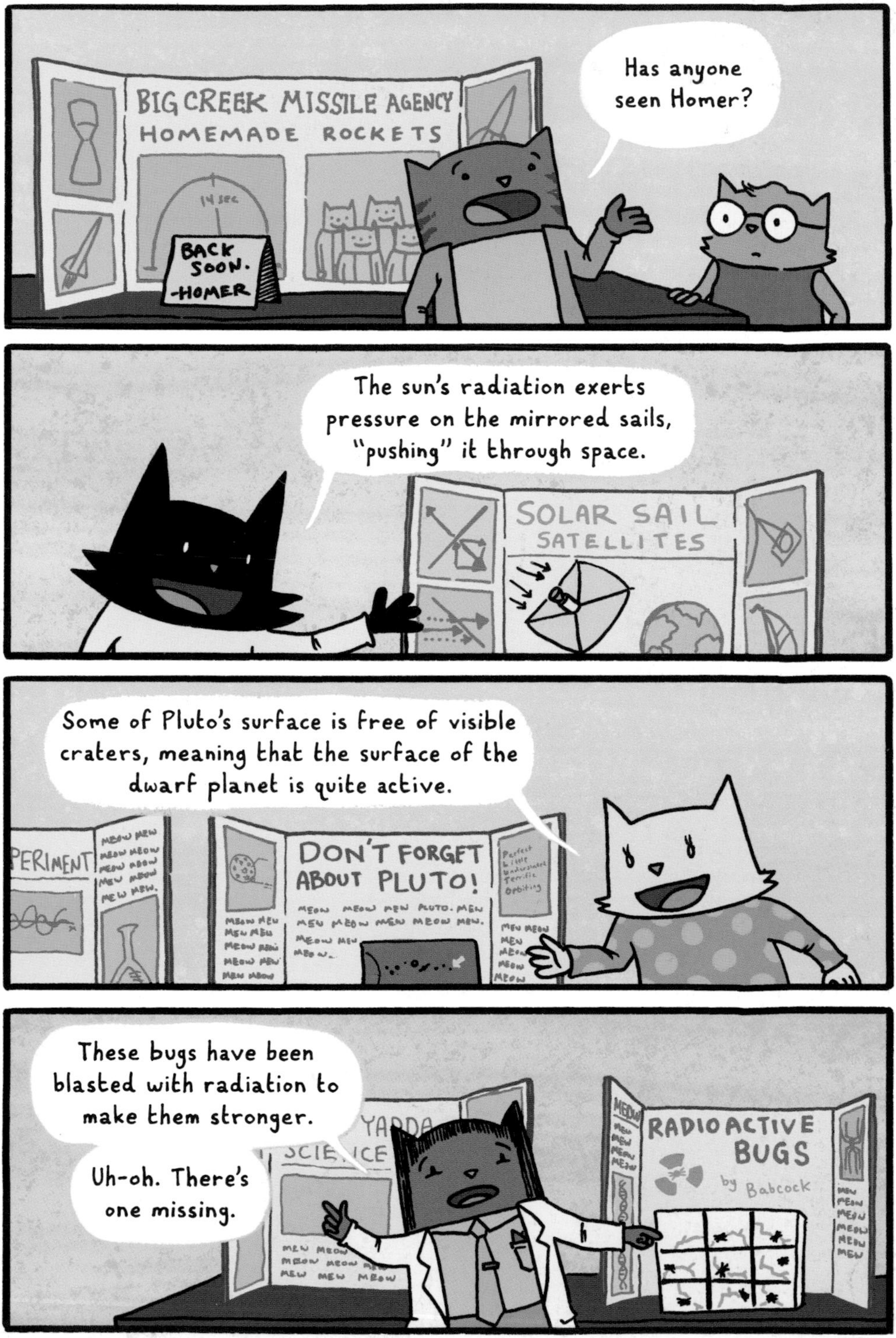
BIG CREEK MISSILE AGENCY
HOMEMADE ROCKETS
14 SEC
BACK SOON. -HOMER
Has anyone seen Homer?
The sun's radiation exerts pressure on the mirrored sails, "pushing" it through space.
SOLAR SAIL SATELLITES
Some of Pluto's surface is free of visible craters, meaning that the surface of the dwarf planet is quite active.
DON'T FORGET ABOUT PLUTO!
These bugs have been blasted with radiation to make them stronger.
Uh-oh. There's one missing.
RADIOACTIVE BUGS
by Babcock

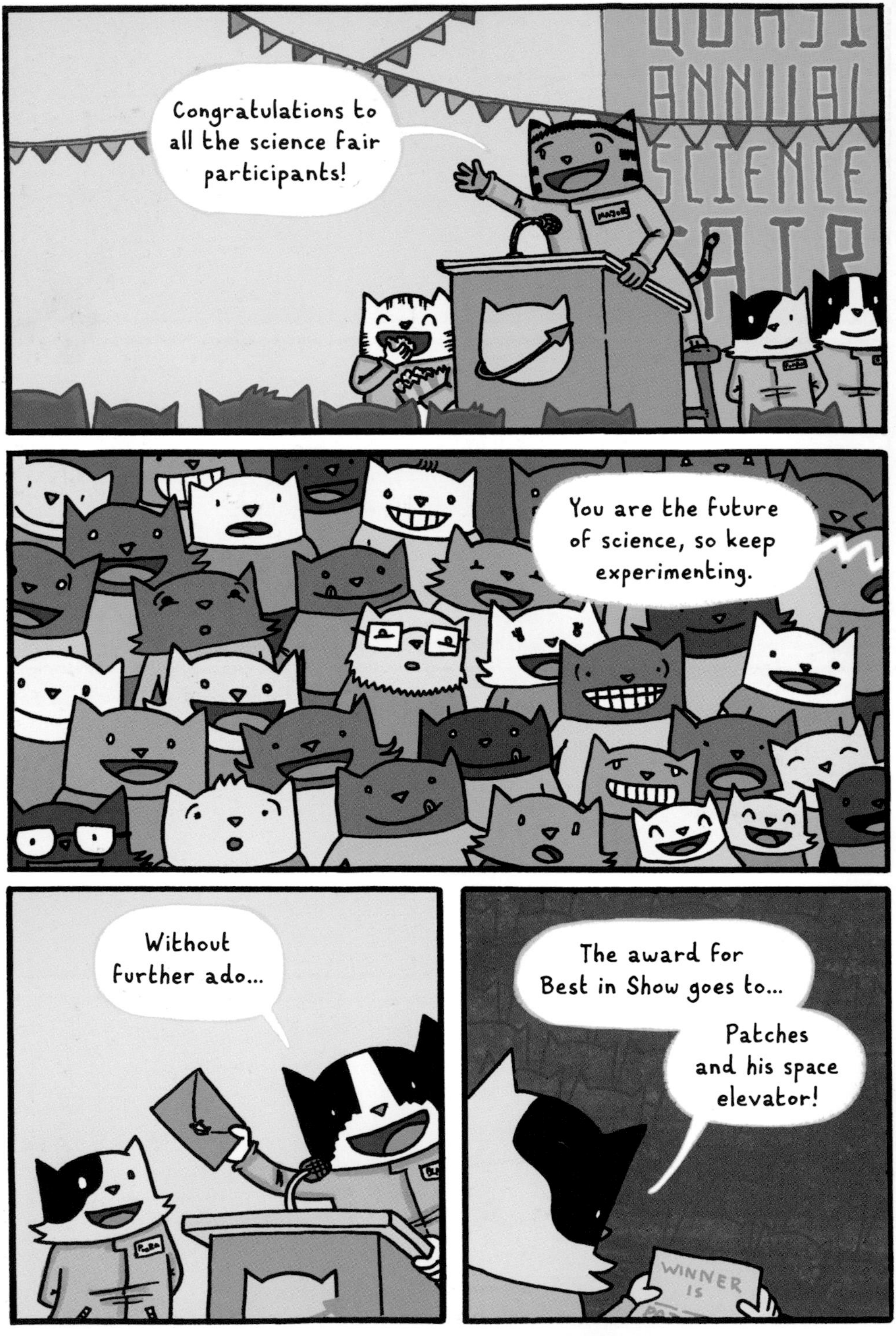
ANNUAL
SCIENCE
Congratulations to all the science fair participants!
You are the future of science, so keep experimenting.
Without further ado...
The award for Best in Show goes to...
Patches and his space elevator!
WINNER IS

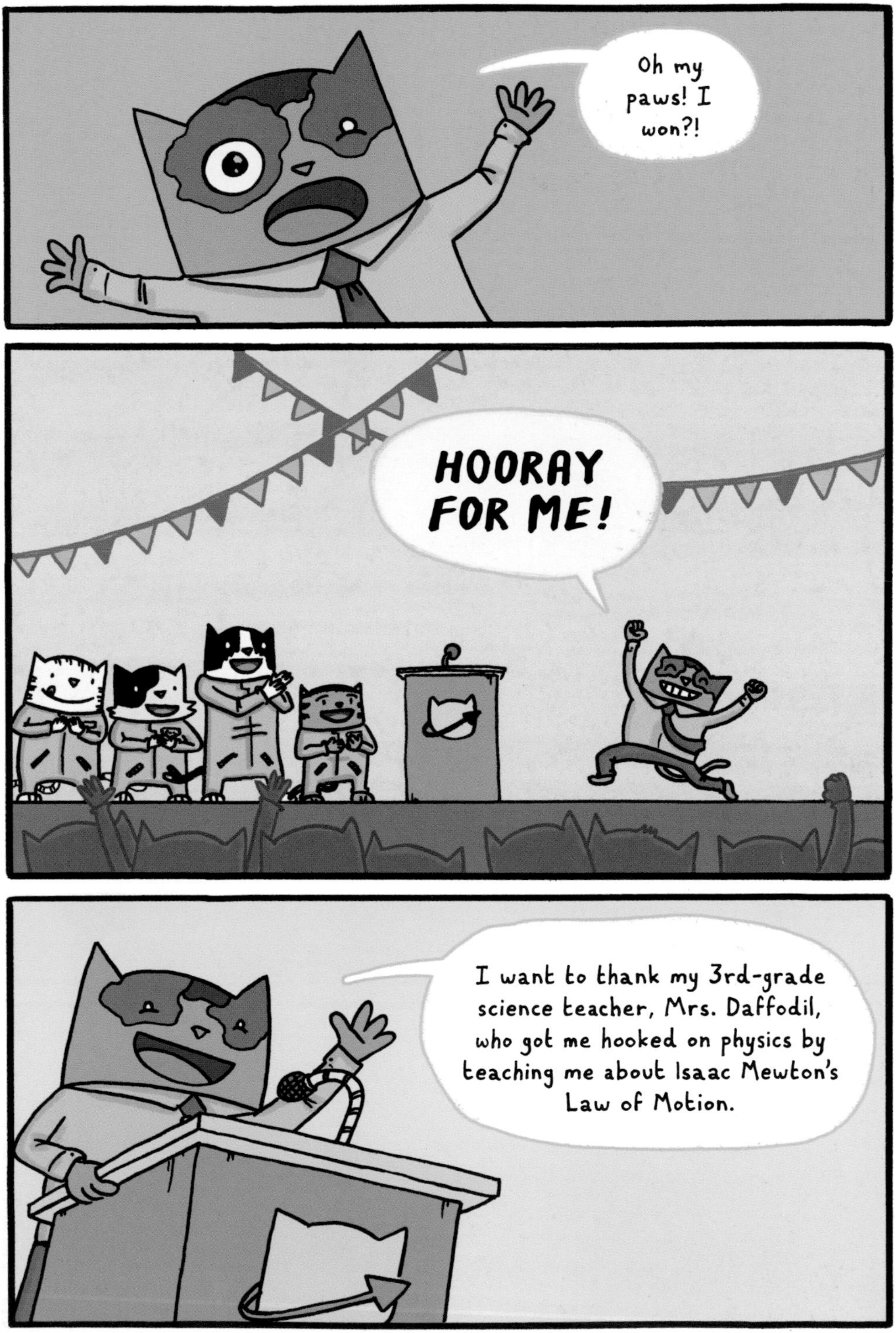
Oh my paws! I won?!
HOORAY FOR ME!
I want to thank my 3rd-grade science teacher, Mrs. Daffodil, who got me hooked on physics by teaching me about Isaac Mewton's Law of Motion.

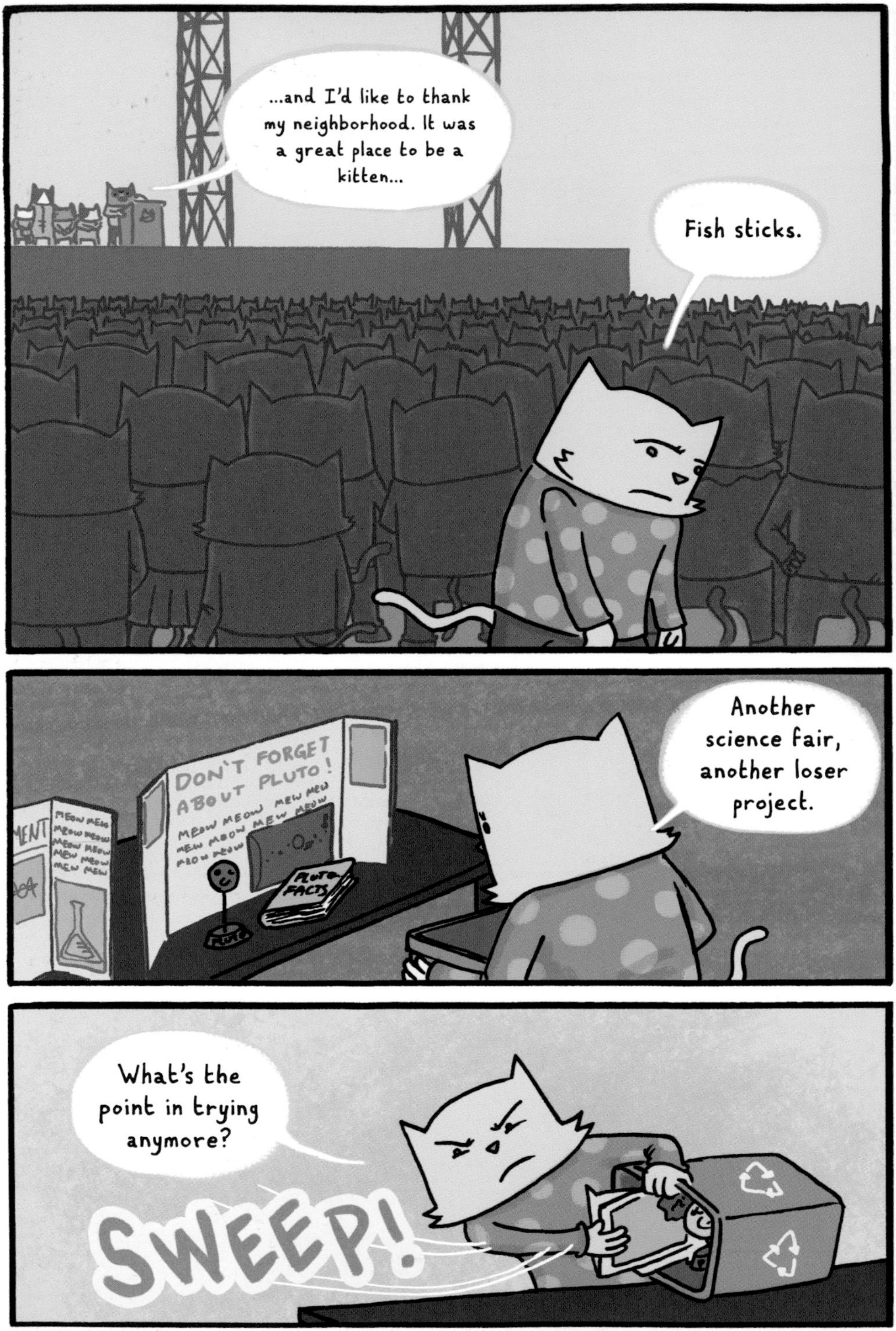

...and I'd like to thank my neighborhood. It was a great place to be a kitten...
Fish sticks.
DON'T FORGET ABOUT PLUTO!
PLUTO FACTS
Another science fair, another loser project.
What's the point in trying anymore?
SWEEP!

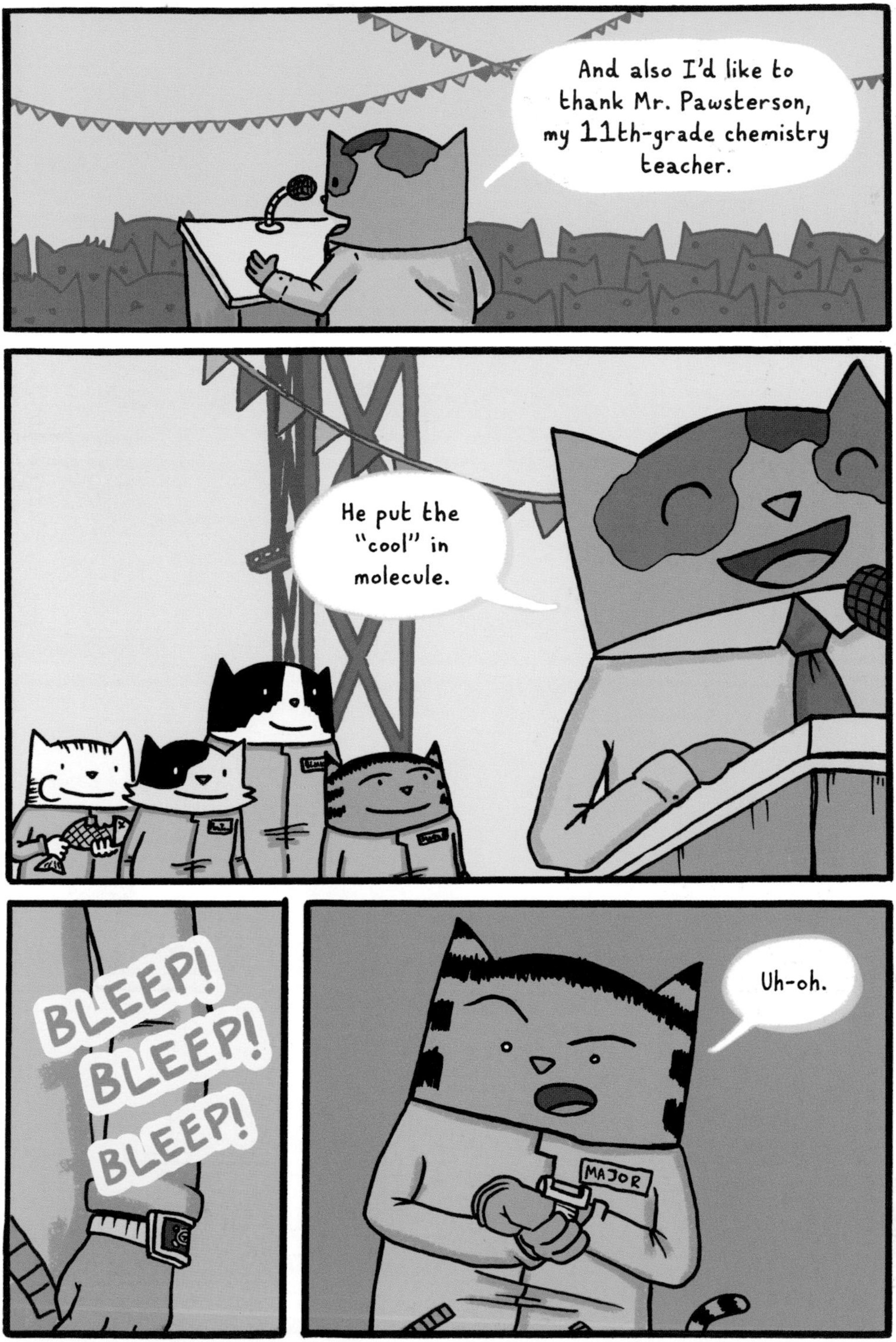
And also I'd like to thank Mr. Pawsterson, my 11th-grade chemistry teacher.
He put the "cool" in molecule.
BLEEP! BLEEP! BLEEP!
Uh-oh.
MAJOR

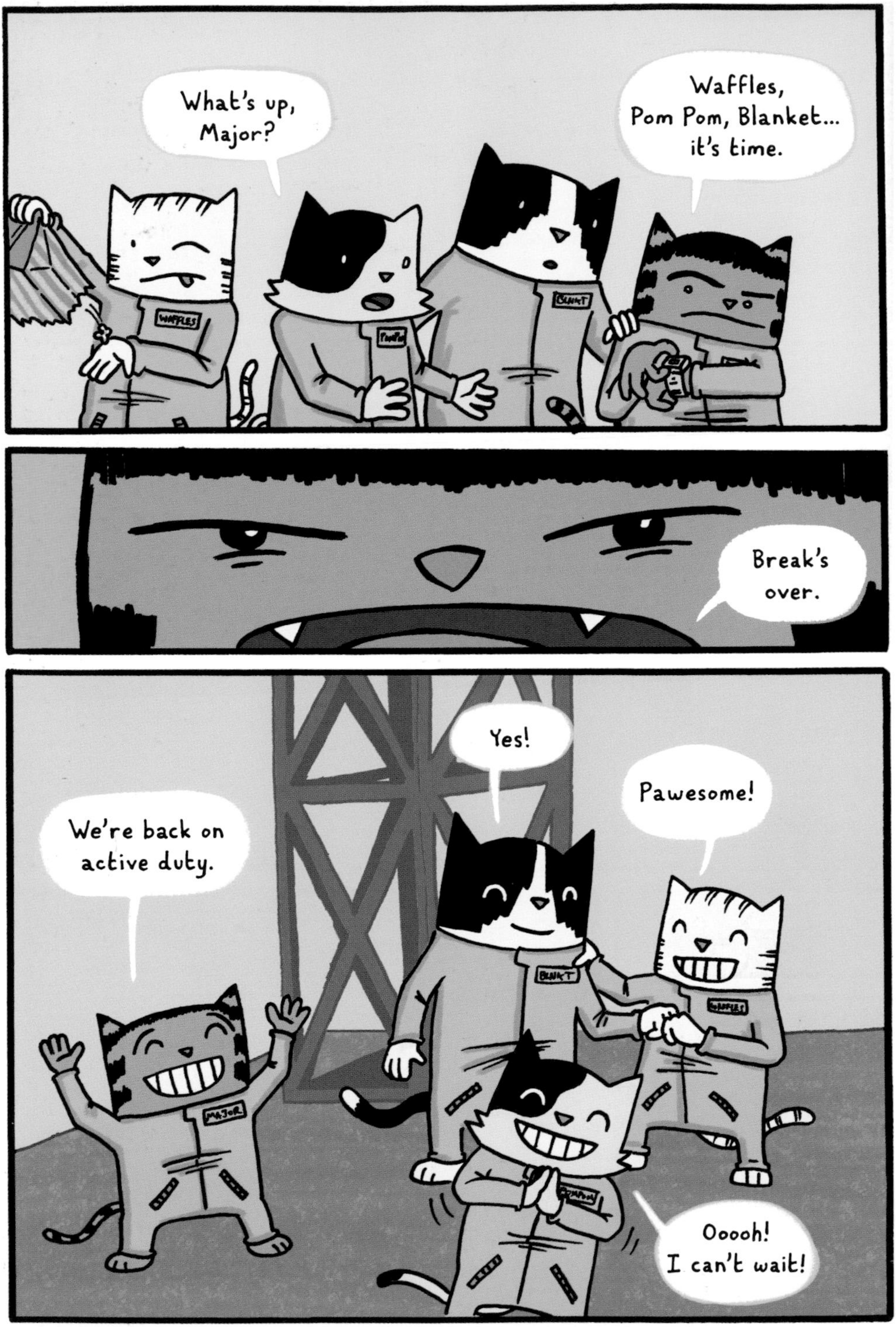
What's up, Major?
Waffles, Pom Pom, Blanket... it's time.
WAFFLES
POMPOM
BLNKT
Break's over.
Yes!
Pawesome!
We're back on active duty.
BLNKT
WAFFLES
MAJOR
POMPOM
Ooooh! I can't wait!

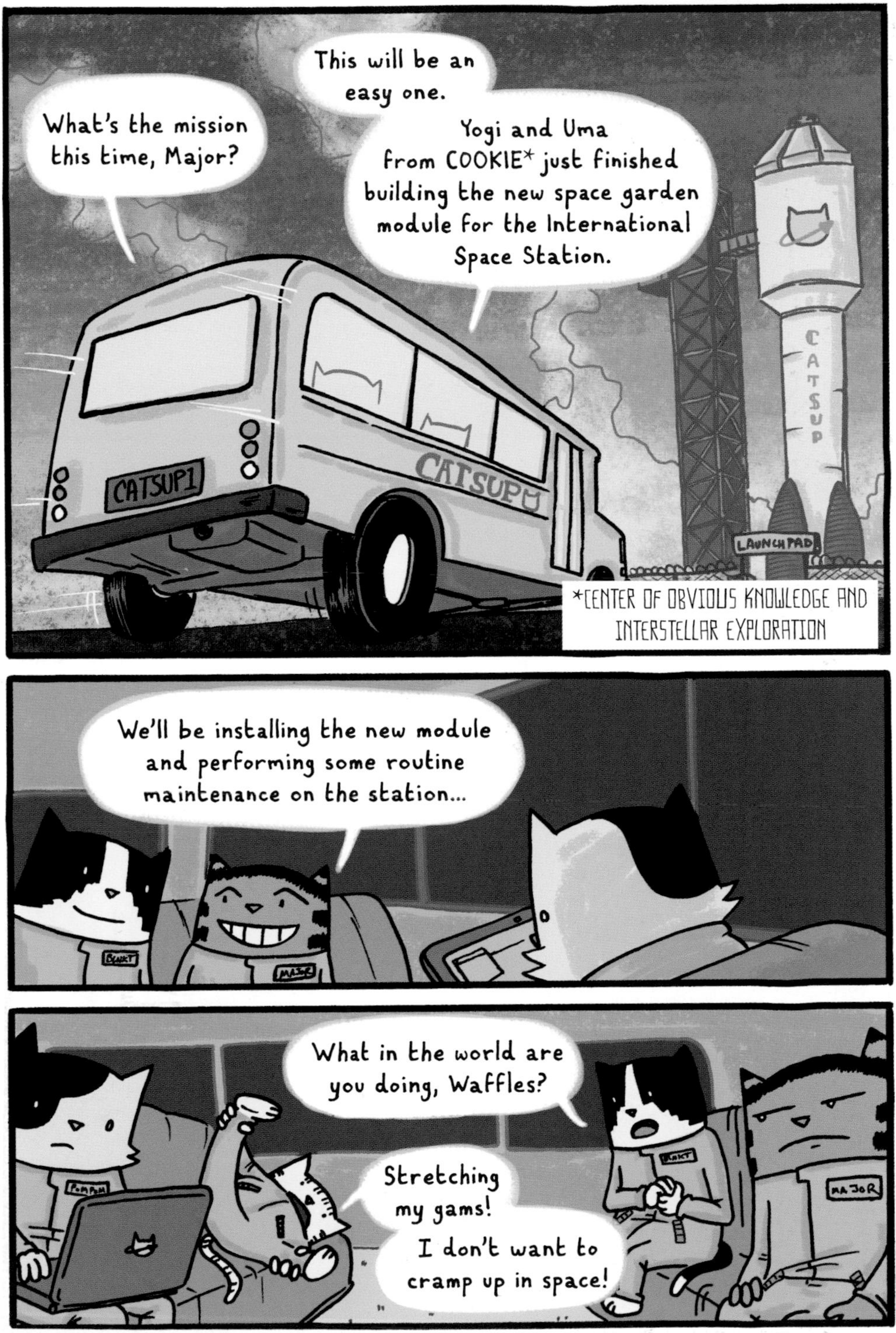
What's the mission this time, Major?
This will be an easy one.
Yogi and Uma from COOKIE* just finished building the new space garden module for the International Space Station.
CATSUP1
CATSUP
CATSUP
LAUNCH PAD
*CENTER OF OBVIOUS KNOWLEDGE AND INTERSTELLAR EXPLORATION
We'll be installing the new module and performing some routine maintenance on the station...
MAJOR
What in the world are you doing, Waffles?
Stretching my gams!
I don't want to cramp up in space!
MAJOR

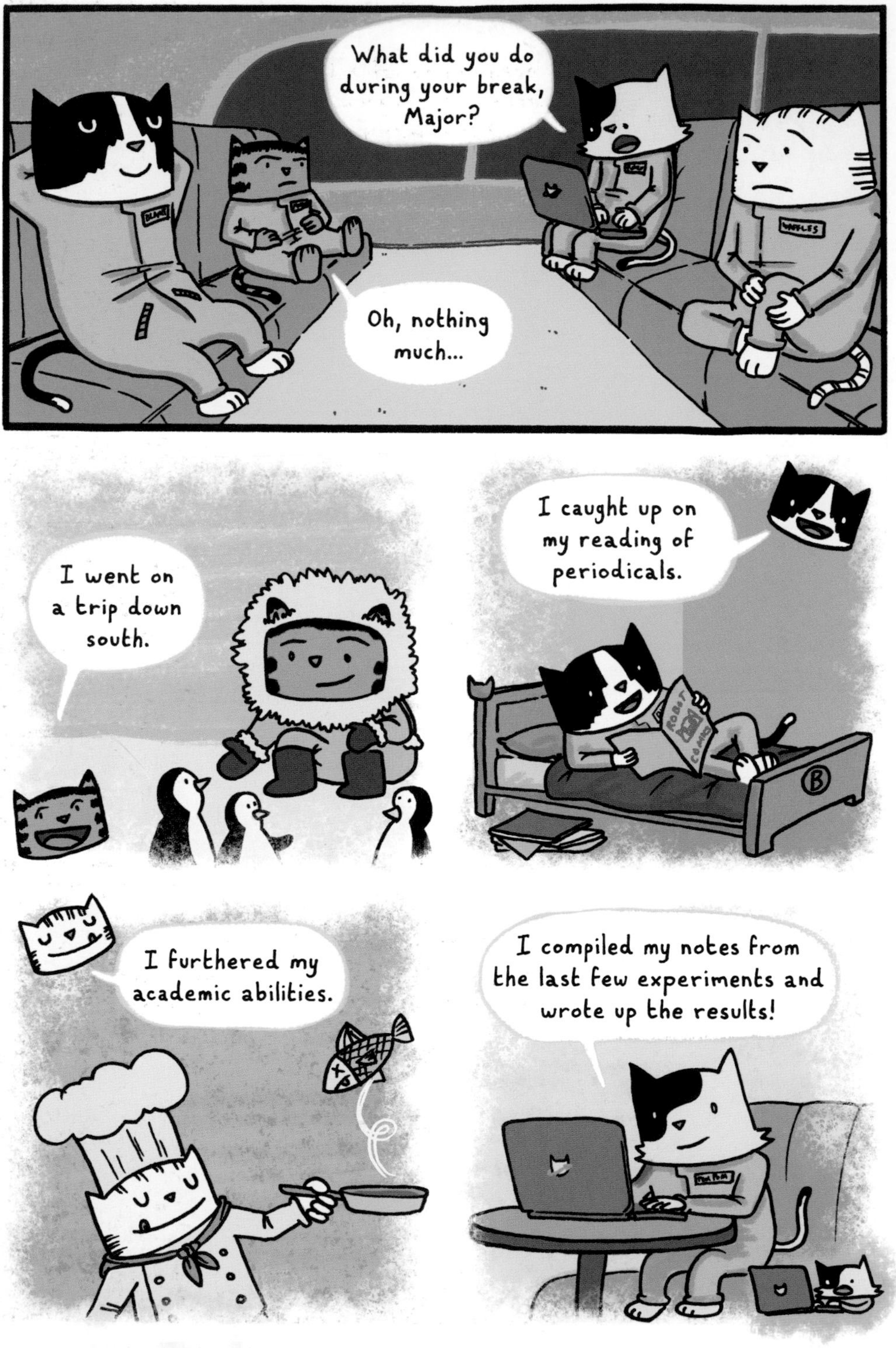
What did you do during your break, Major?
Oh, nothing much...
I went on a trip down south.
I caught up on my reading of periodicals.
I furthered my academic abilities.
I compiled my notes from the last few experiments and wrote up the results!

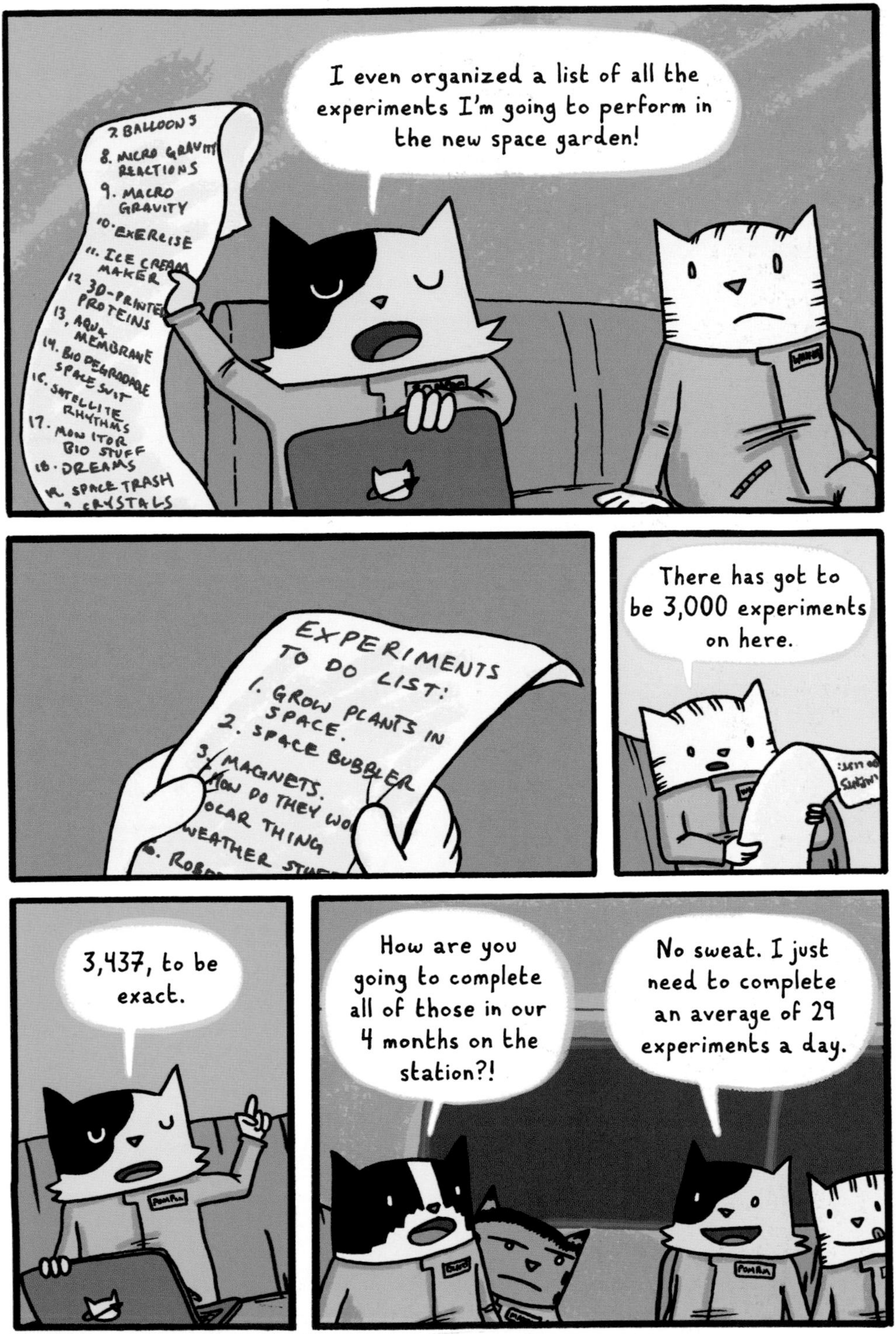

I even organized a list of all the experiments I'm going to perform in the new space garden!
7. BALLOONS
9. MACRO GRAVITY
10. EXERCISE
11. ICE CREAM MAKER
13. AQUA MEMBRANE
17. MONITOR BIO STUFF
18. DREAMS
EXPERIMENTS TO DO LIST:
1. GROW PLANTS IN SPACE.
2. SPACE BUBBLER
3. MAGNETS. HOW DO THEY WO
There has got to be 3,000 experiments on here.
3,437, to be exact.
How are you going to complete all of those in our 4 months on the station?!
No sweat. I just need to complete an average of 29 experiments a day.

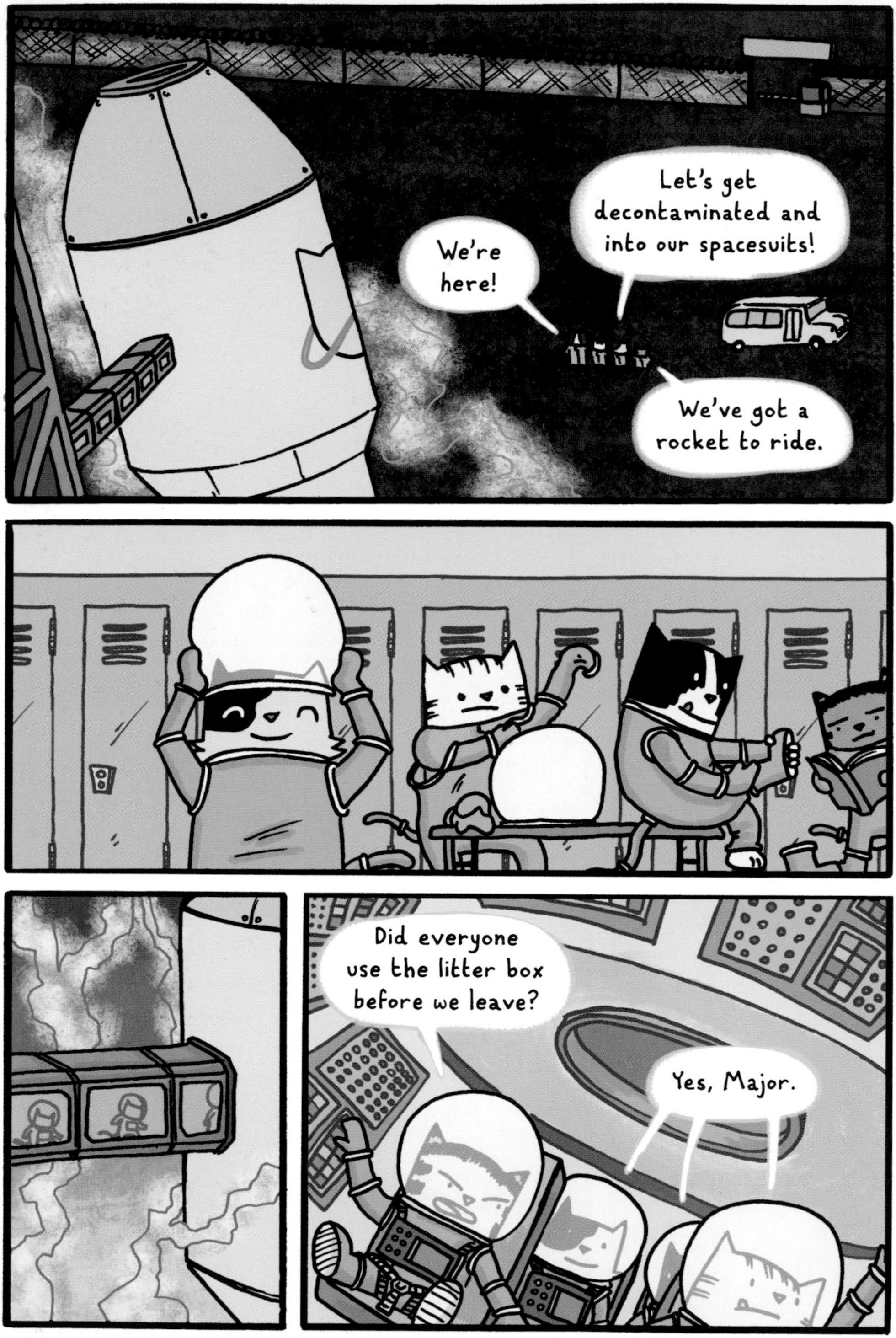
We're here!
Let's get decontaminated and into our spacesuits!
We've got a rocket to ride.
Did everyone use the litter box before we leave?
Yes, Major.

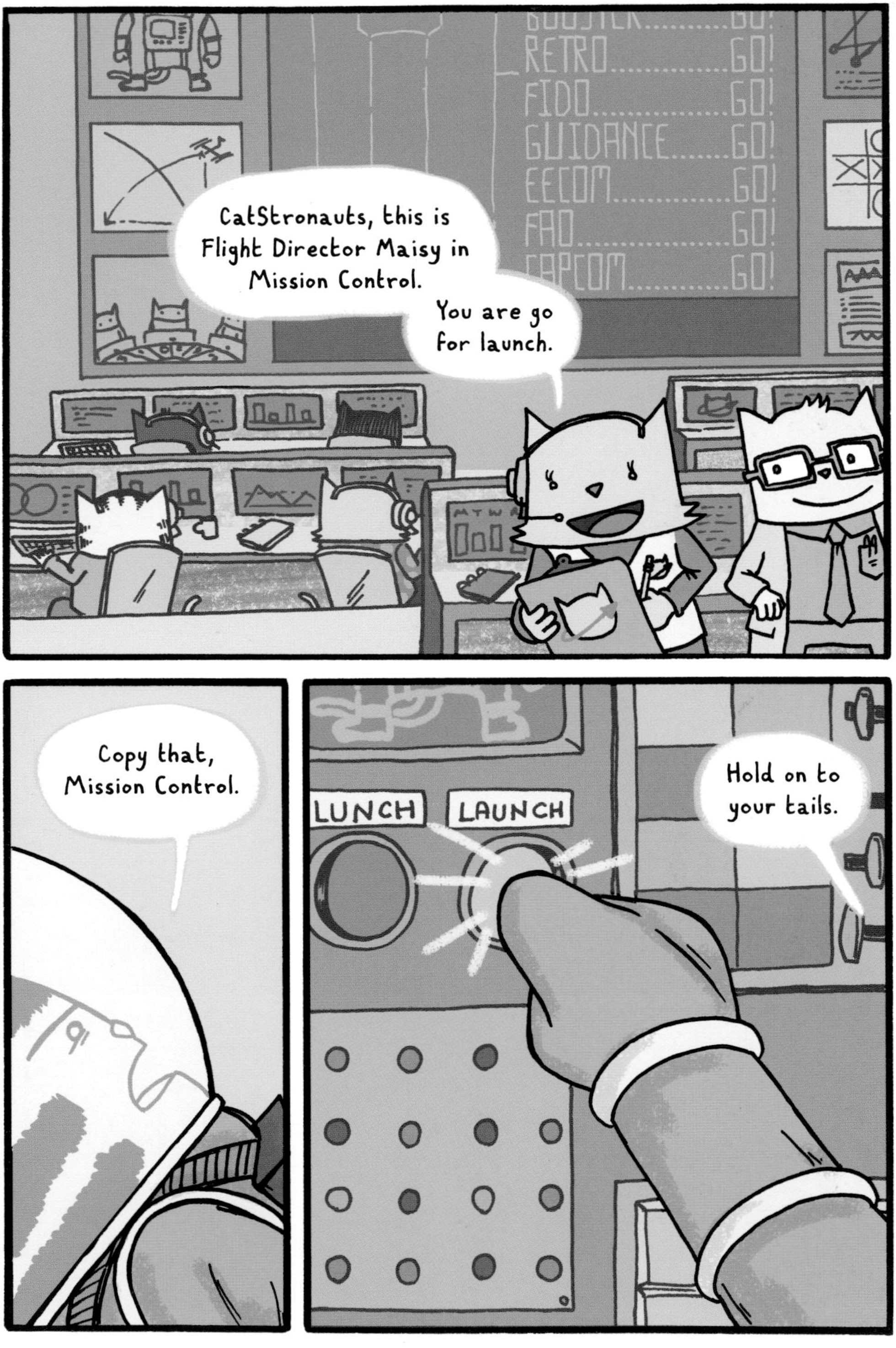
RETRO..........GO!
FIDO..........GO!
GUIDANCE.......GO!
EECOM..........GO!
FAO..........GO!
CAPCOM..........GO!
CatStronauts, this is Flight Director Maisy in Mission Control.
You are go for launch.
Copy that, Mission Control.
LUNCH
LAUNCH
Hold on to your tails.

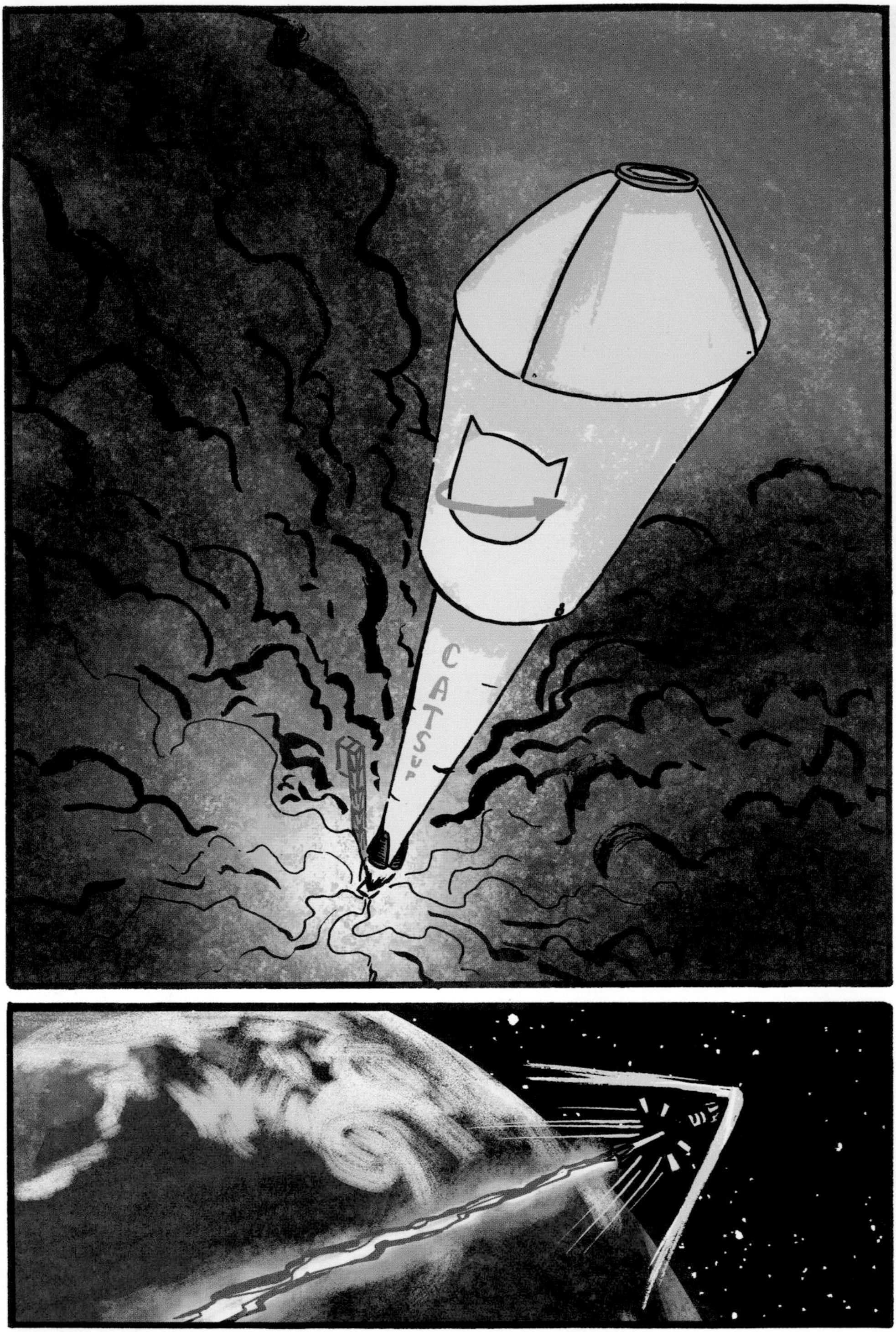
CATSUP

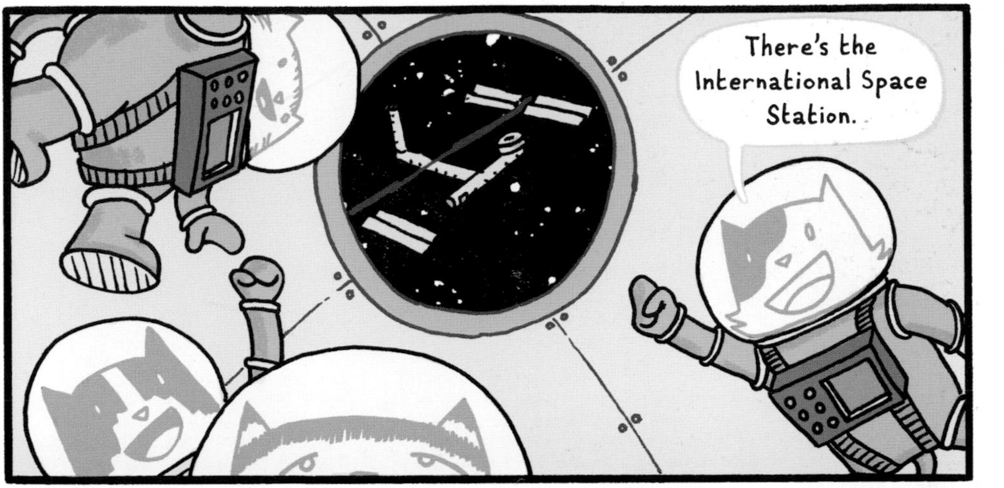
There's the International Space Station.

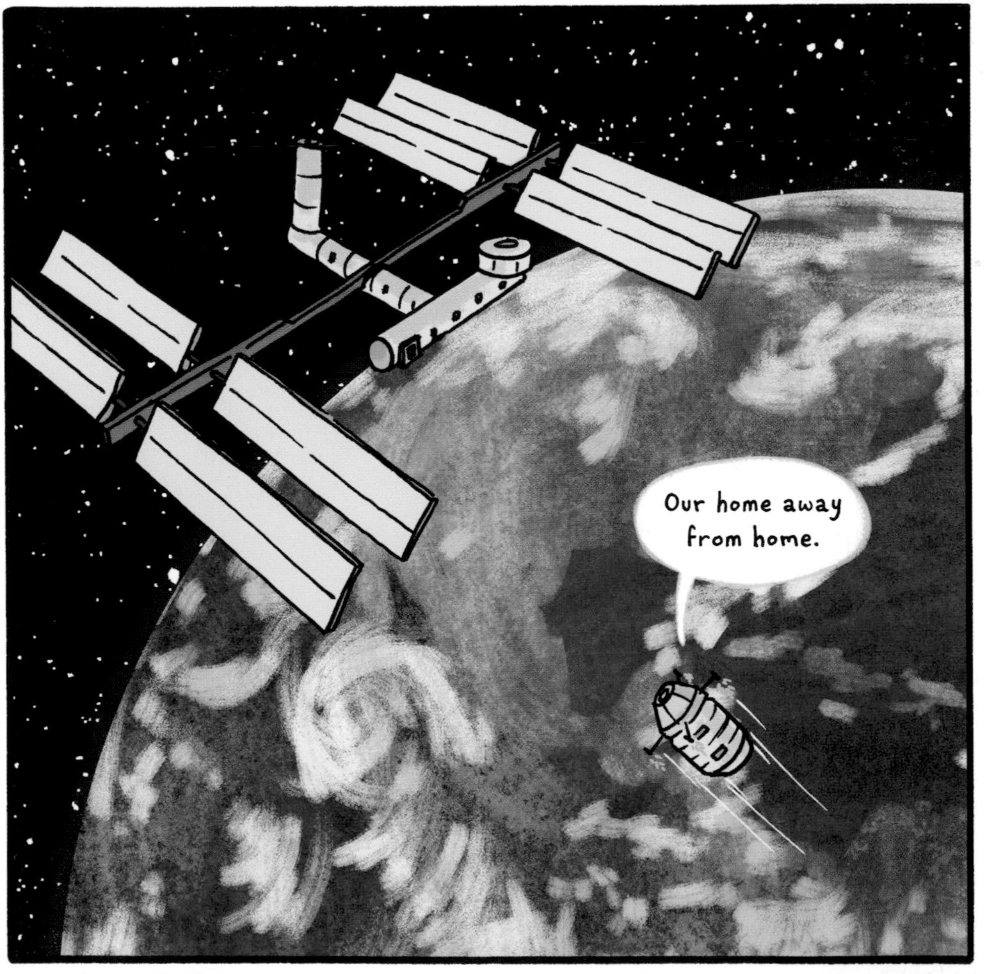
Our home away from home.

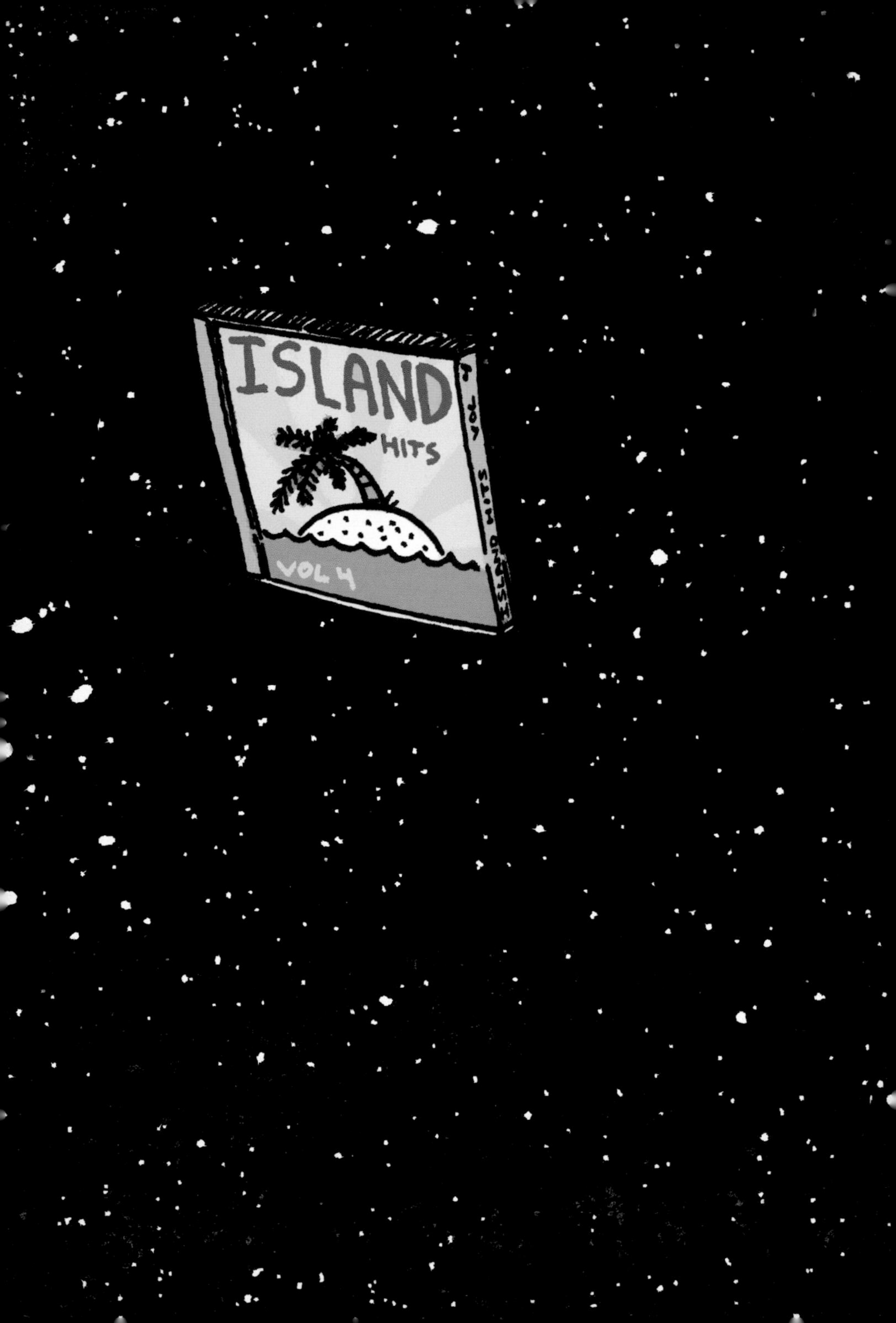
ISLAND
HITS
VOL 4

CHAPTER 2

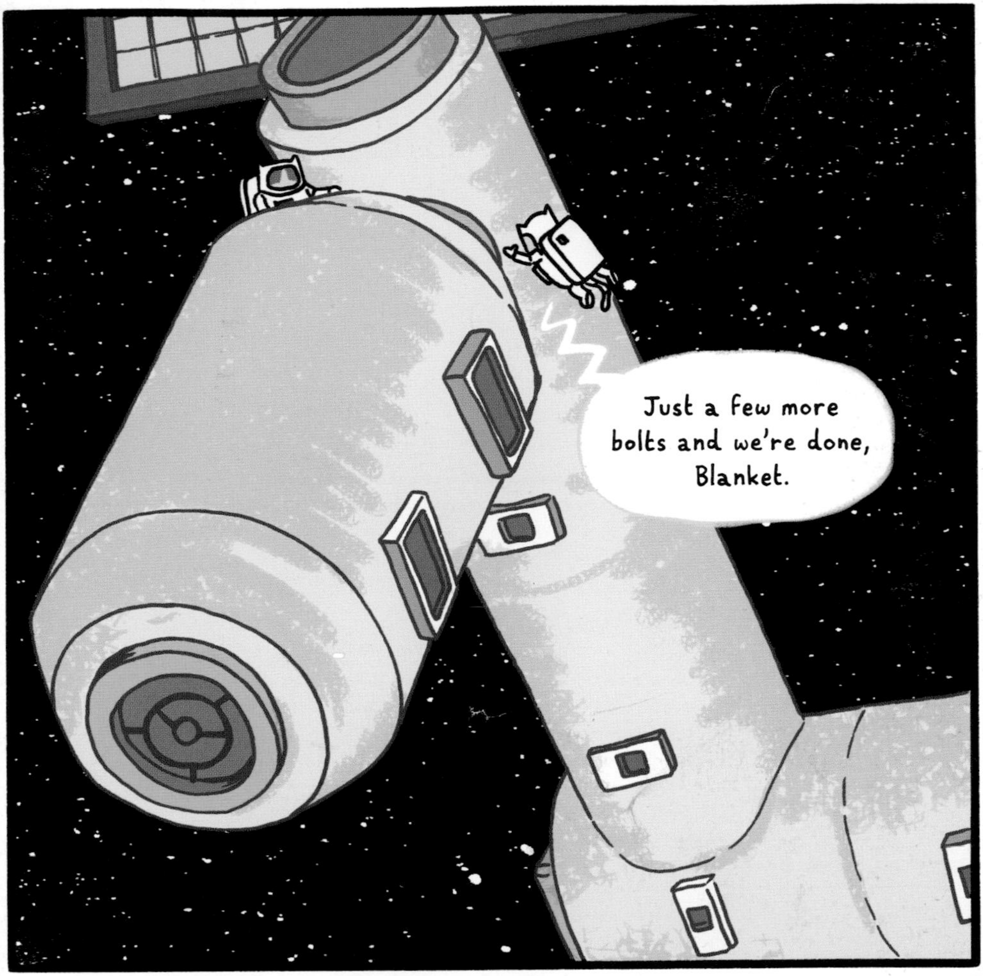
Just a few more bolts and we're done, Blanket.

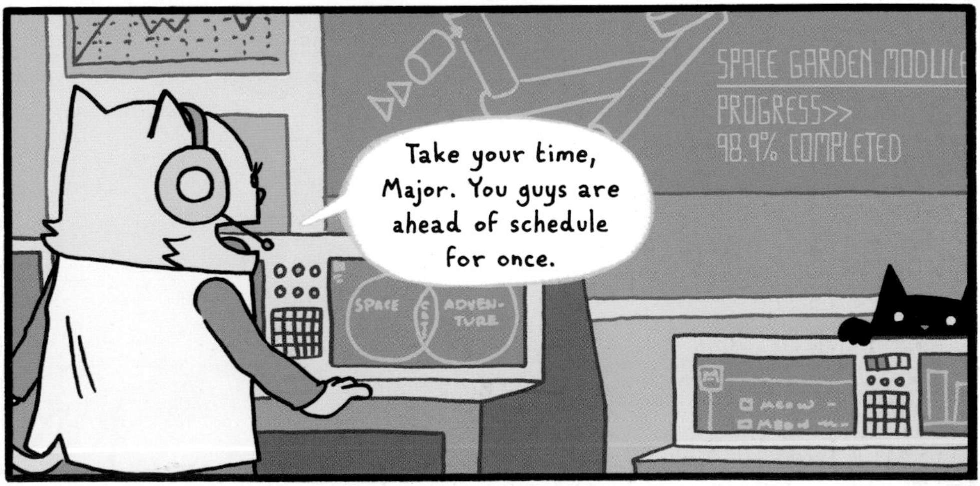
SPACE GARDEN MODUL
PROGRESS>>
98.9% COMPLETED
Take your time, Major. You guys are ahead of schedule for once.
SPACE
ADVEN-TURE

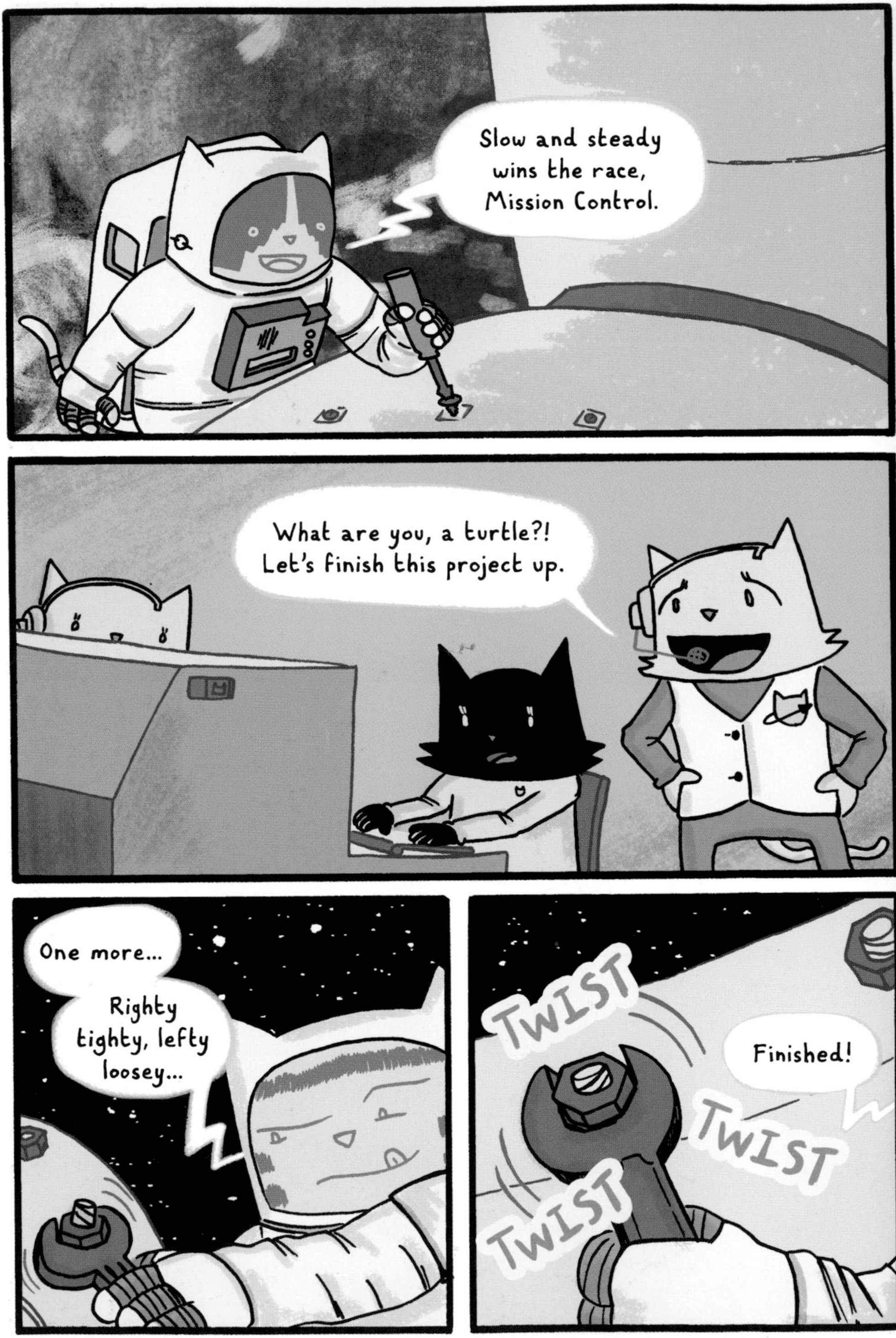
Slow and steady wins the race, Mission Control.
What are you, a turtle?! Let's finish this project up.
One more...
Righty tighty, lefty loosey...
TWIST
Finished!
TWIST
TWIST

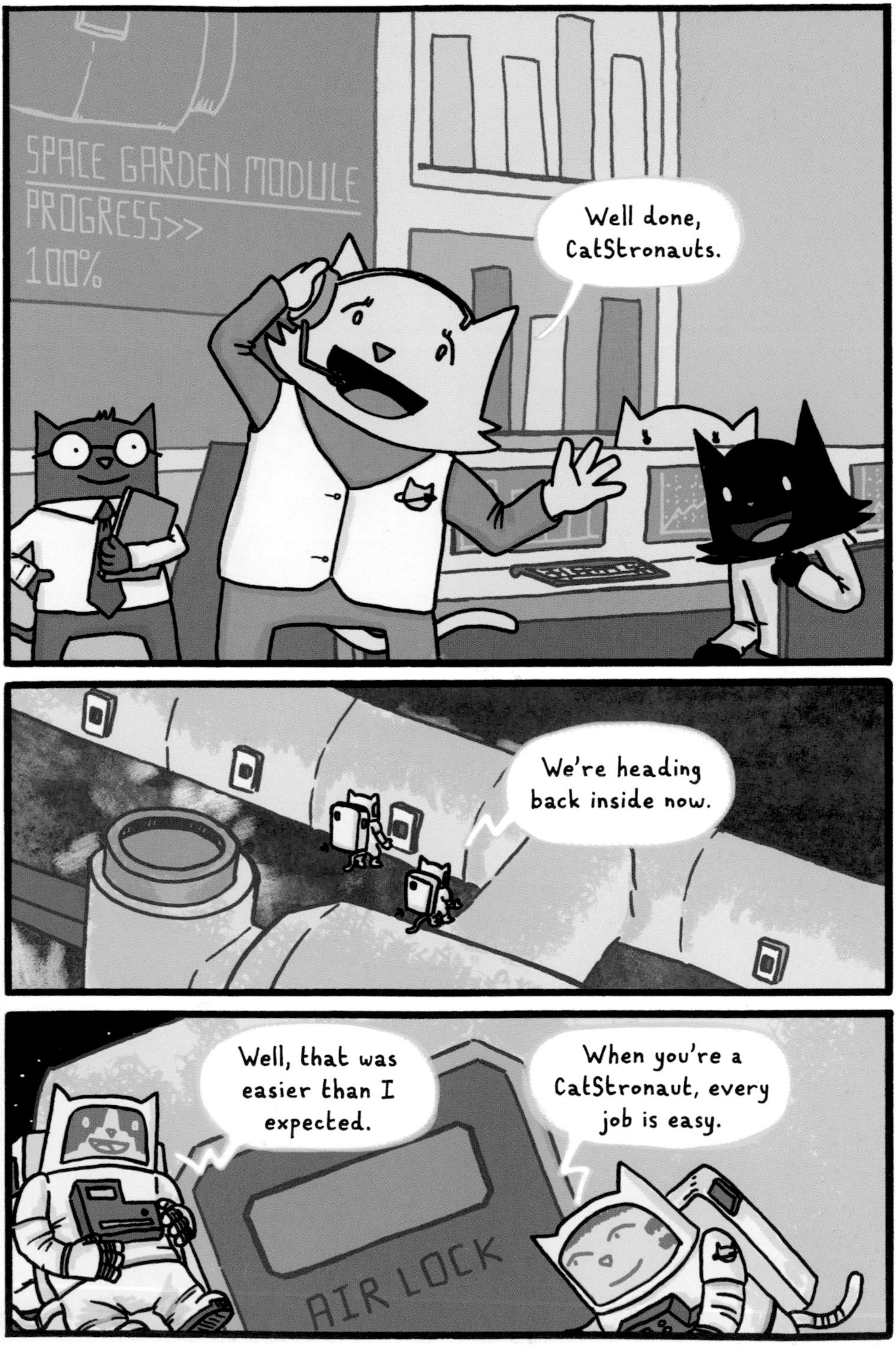
SPACE GARDEN MODULE
PROGRESS>>
100%
Well done, CatStronauts.
We're heading back inside now.
Well, that was easier than I expected.
When you're a CatStronaut, every job is easy.
AIR LOCK

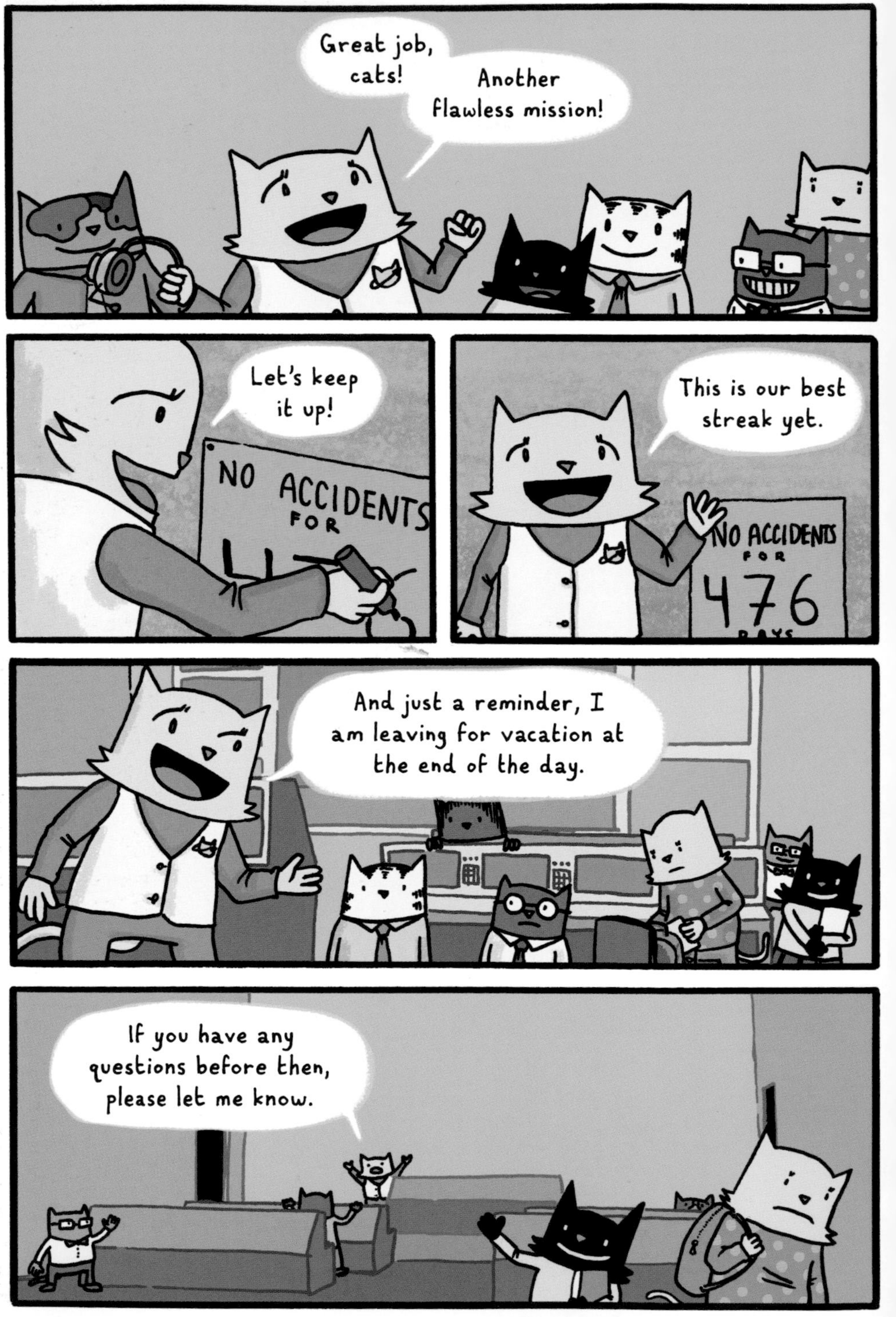
Great job, cats!
Another flawless mission!
Let's keep it up!
NO ACCIDENTS FOR
This is our best streak yet.
NO ACCIDENTS FOR 476
And just a reminder, I am leaving for vacation at the end of the day.
If you have any questions before then, please let me know.

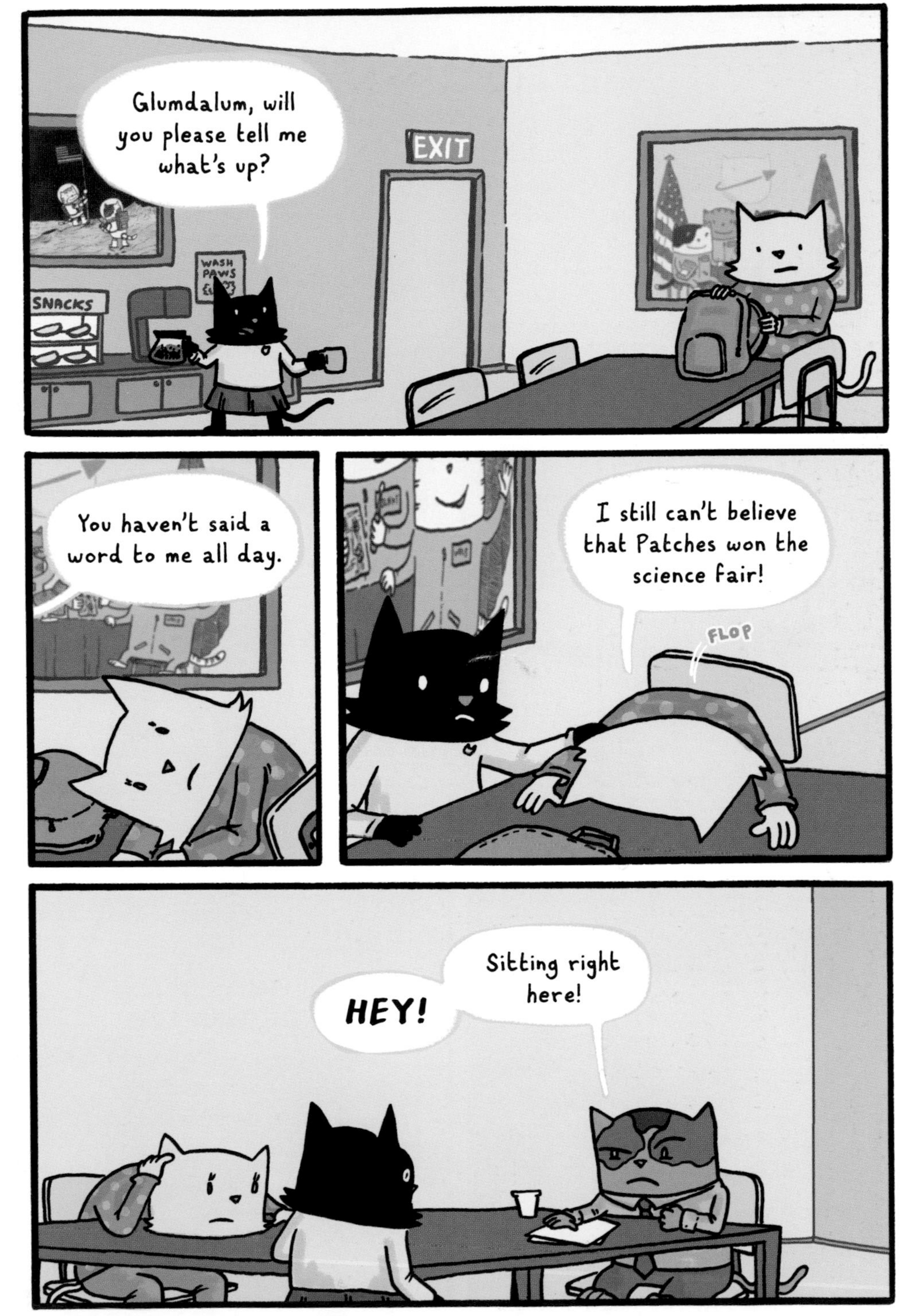
Glumdalum, will you please tell me what's up?
EXIT
WASH PAWS
SNACKS
You haven't said a word to me all day.
I still can't believe that Patches won the science fair!
FLOP
HEY!
Sitting right here!

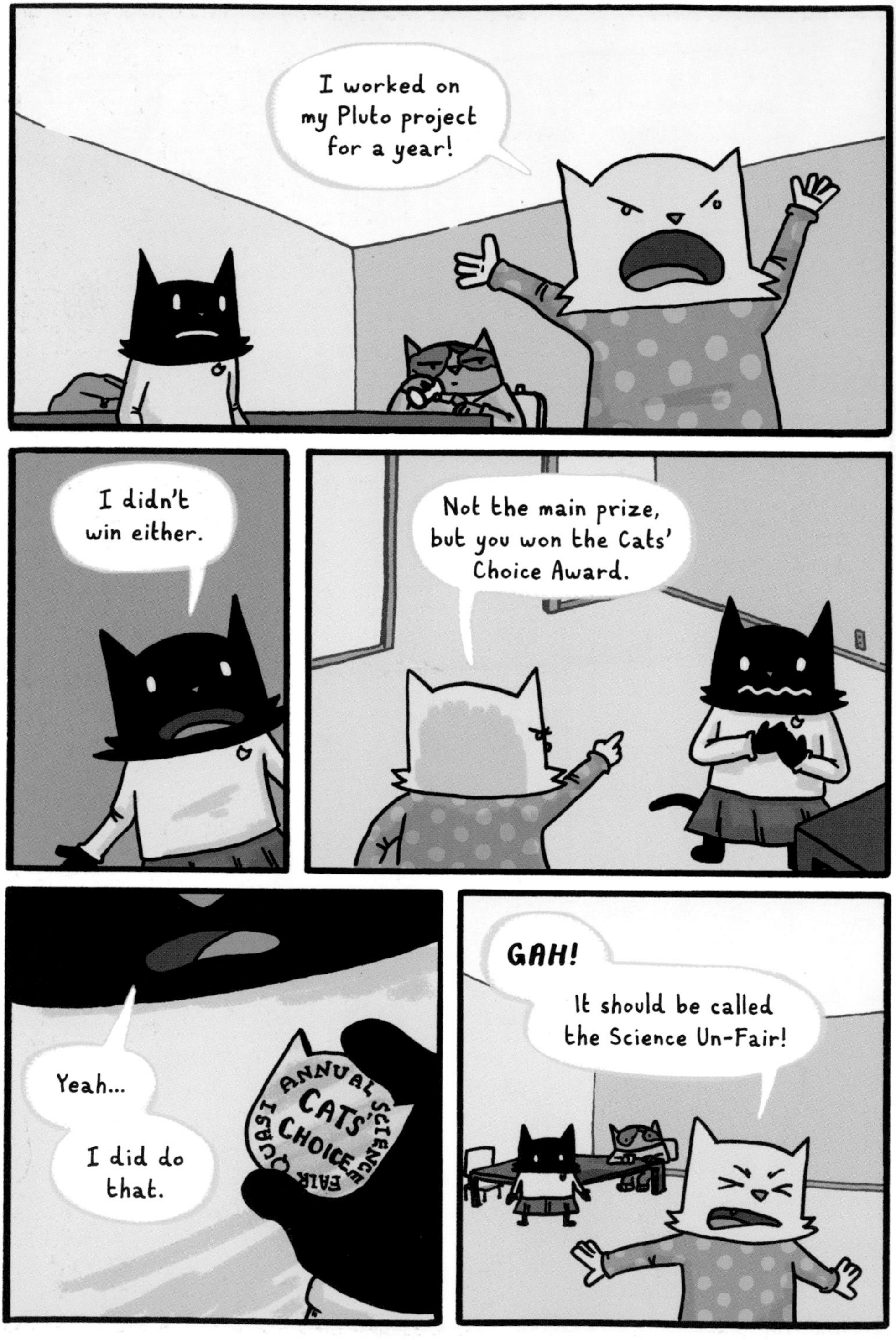
I worked on my Pluto project for a year!
I didn't win either.
Not the main prize, but you won the Cats' Choice Award.
Yeah...
I did do that.
ANNUAL QUASI SCIENCE FAIR CATS' CHOICE
GAH!
It should be called the Science Un-Fair!

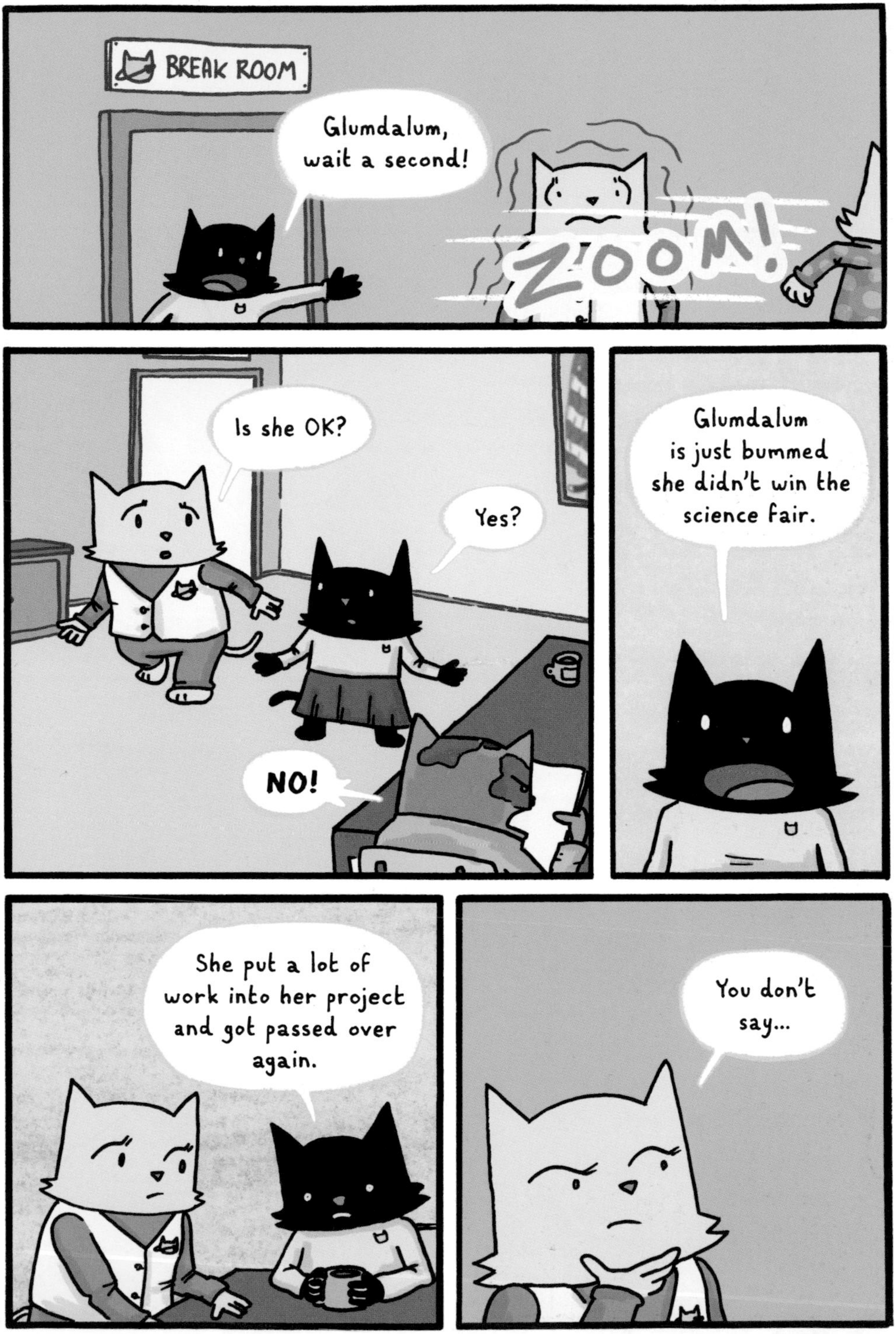
BREAK ROOM
Glumdalum, wait a second!
ZOOM!
Is she OK?
Yes?
NO!
Glumdalum is just bummed she didn't win the science fair.
She put a lot of work into her project and got passed over again.
You don't say...

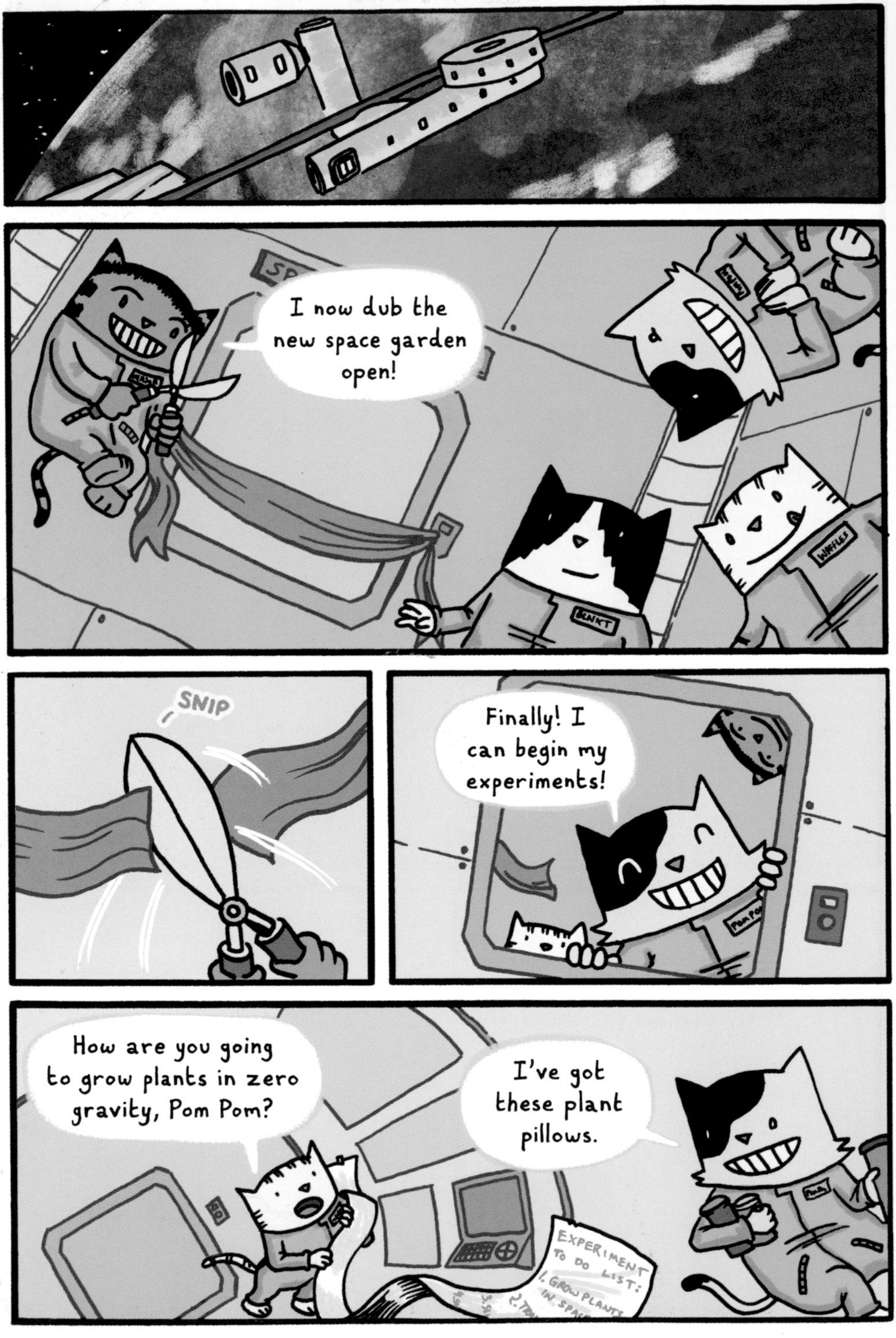
I now dub the new space garden open!
SNIP
Finally! I can begin my experiments!
How are you going to grow plants in zero gravity, Pom Pom?
I've got these plant pillows.
EXPERIMENT TO DO LIST:
1. GROW PLANTS IN SPACE

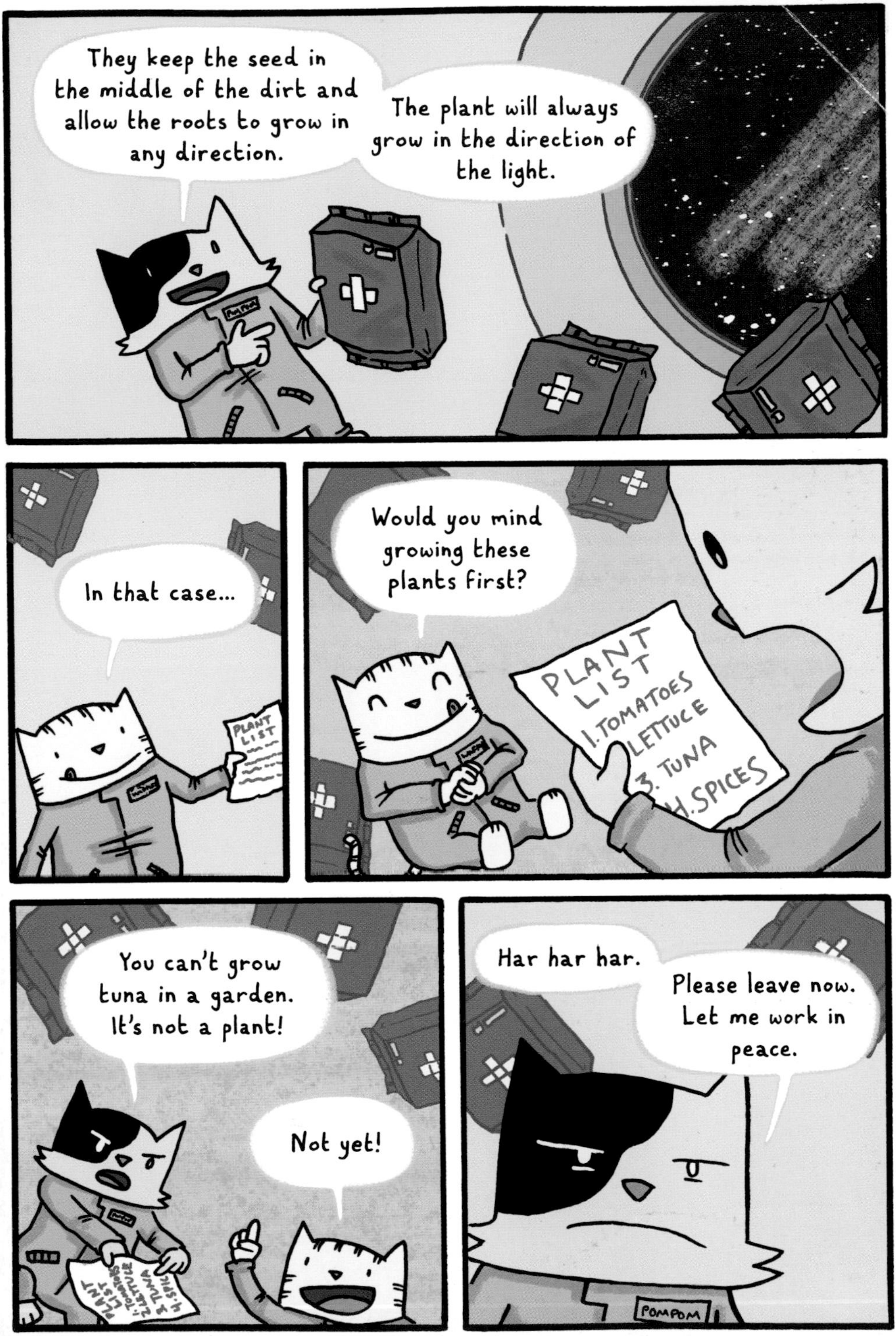
They keep the seed in the middle of the dirt and allow the roots to grow in any direction.
The plant will always grow in the direction of the light.
In that case...
Would you mind growing these plants first?
PLANT LIST
1. TOMATOES
LETTUCE
3. TUNA
4. SPICES
You can't grow tuna in a garden. It's not a plant!
Not yet!
Har har har.
Please leave now. Let me work in peace.
POMPOM

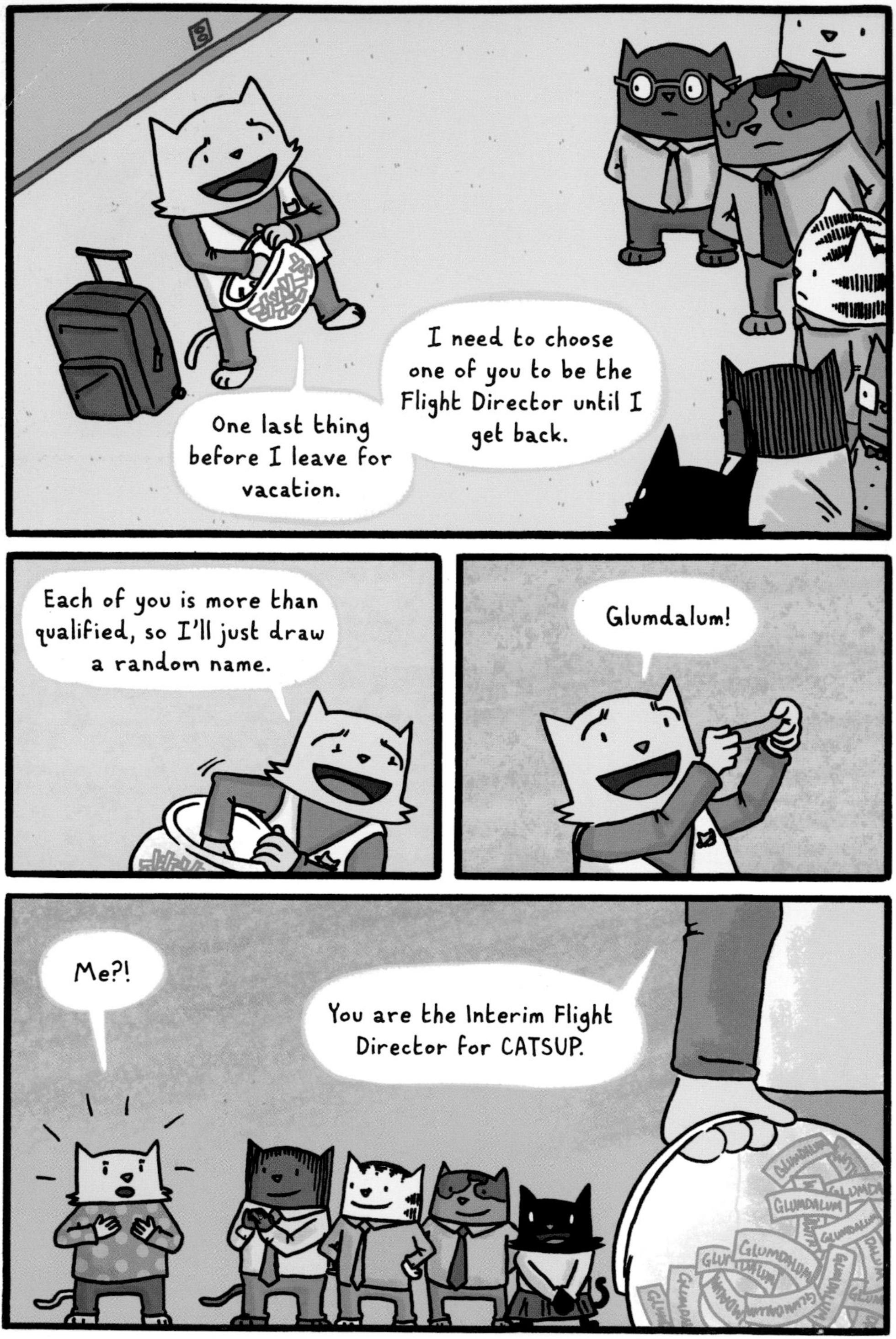
One last thing before I leave for vacation.
I need to choose one of you to be the Flight Director until I get back.
Each of you is more than qualified, so I'll just draw a random name.
Glumdalum!
Me?!
You are the Interim Flight Director for CATSUP.

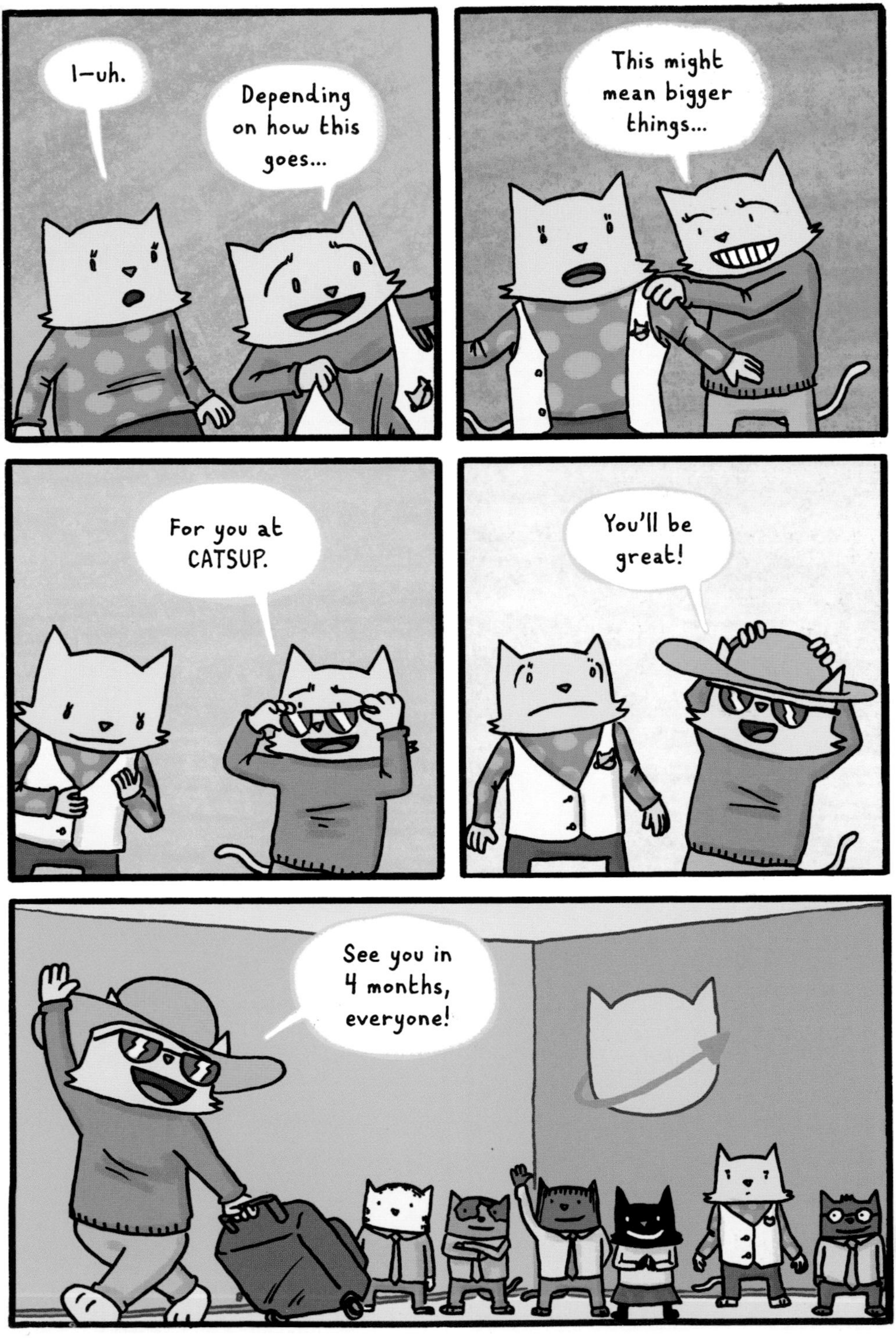
I—uh.
Depending on how this goes...
This might mean bigger things...
For you at CATSUP.
You'll be great!
See you in 4 months, everyone!

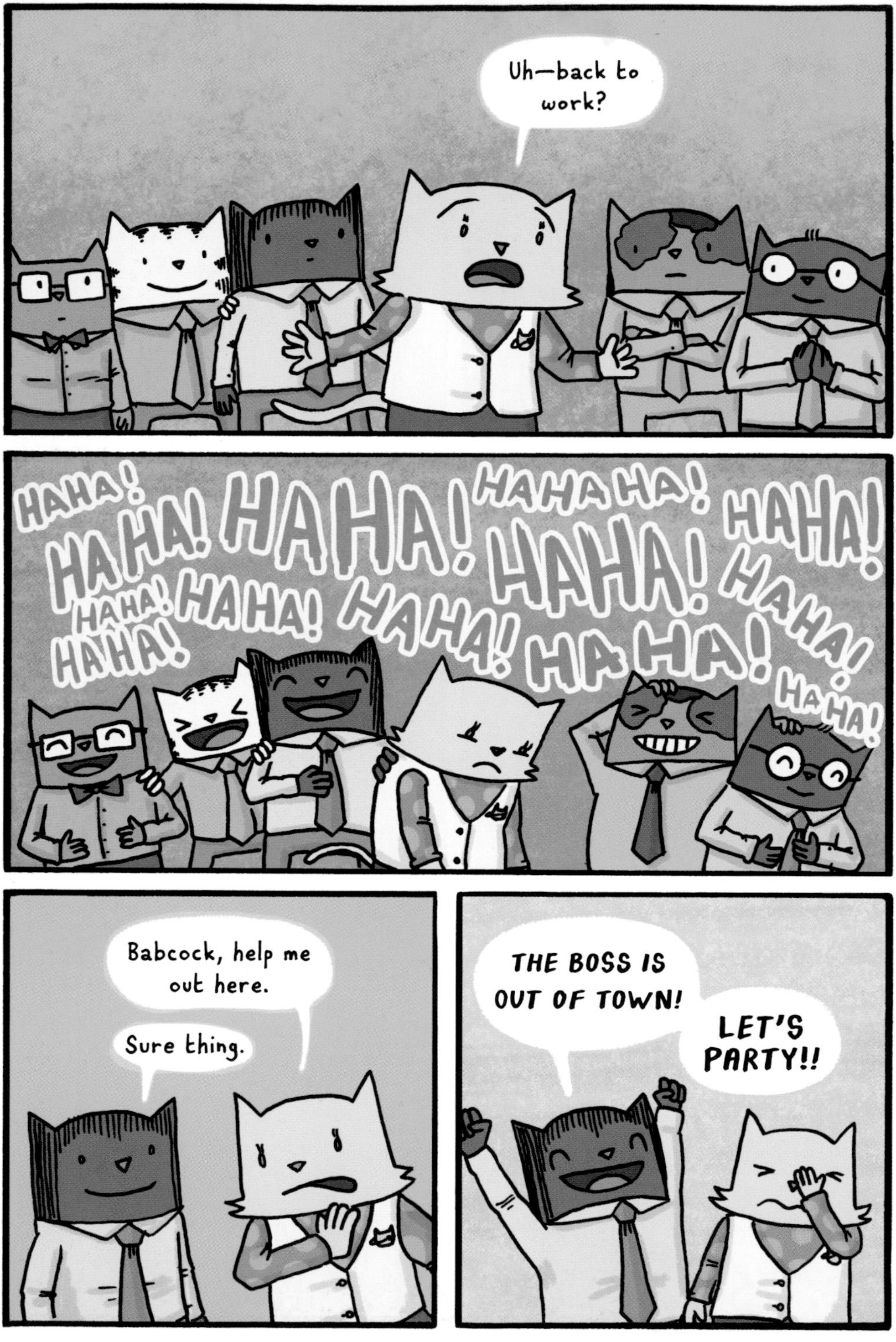
Uh—back to work?
HAHA! HAHA! HAHA! HAHAHA! HAHA! HAHA! HAHA! HAHA! HAHA! HAHA! HAHA! HAHA! HAHA! HAHA!
Babcock, help me out here.
Sure thing.
THE BOSS IS OUT OF TOWN!
LET'S PARTY!!

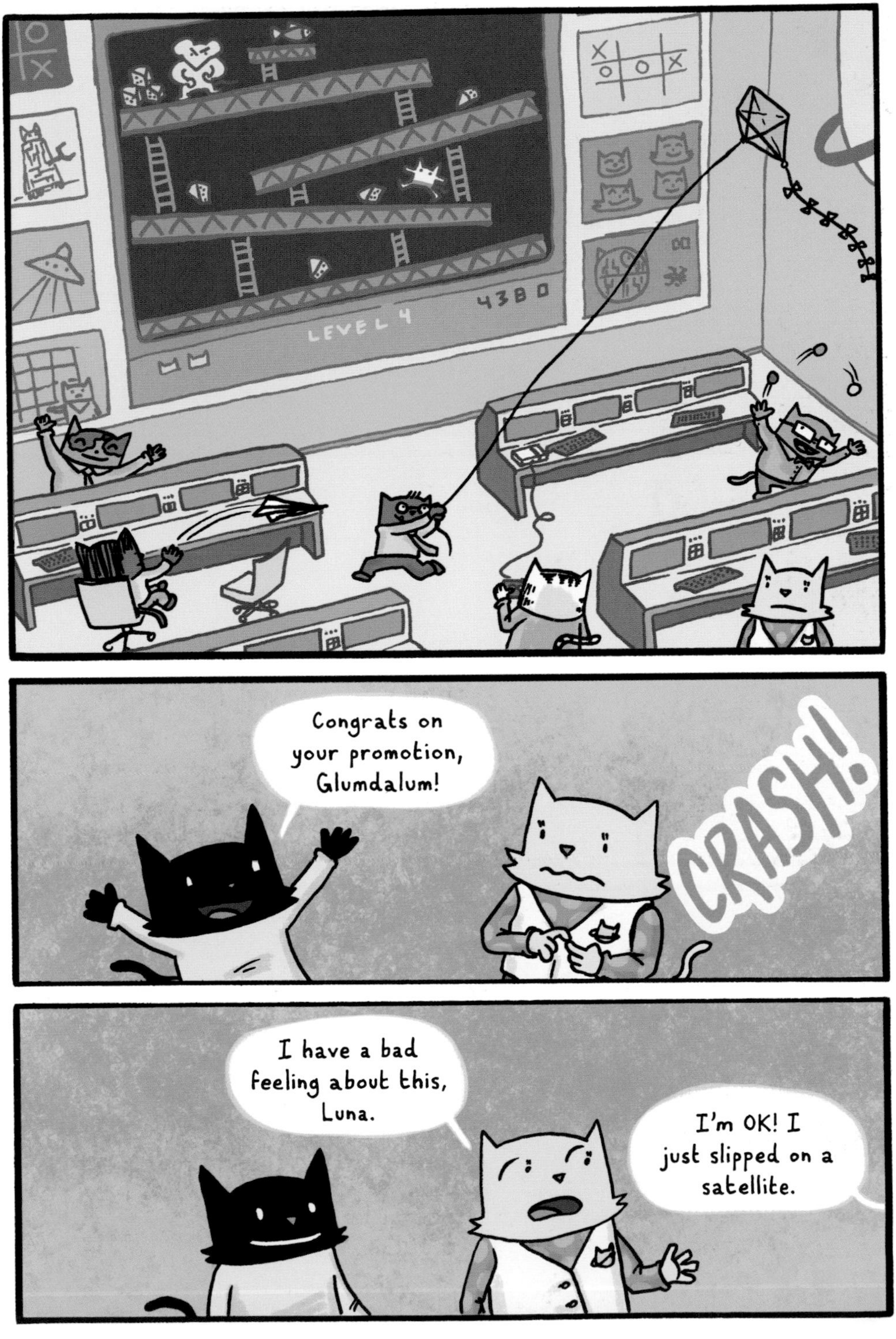
4380
LEVEL 4
Congrats on your promotion, Glumdalum!
CRASH!
I have a bad feeling about this, Luna.
I'm OK! I just slipped on a satellite.

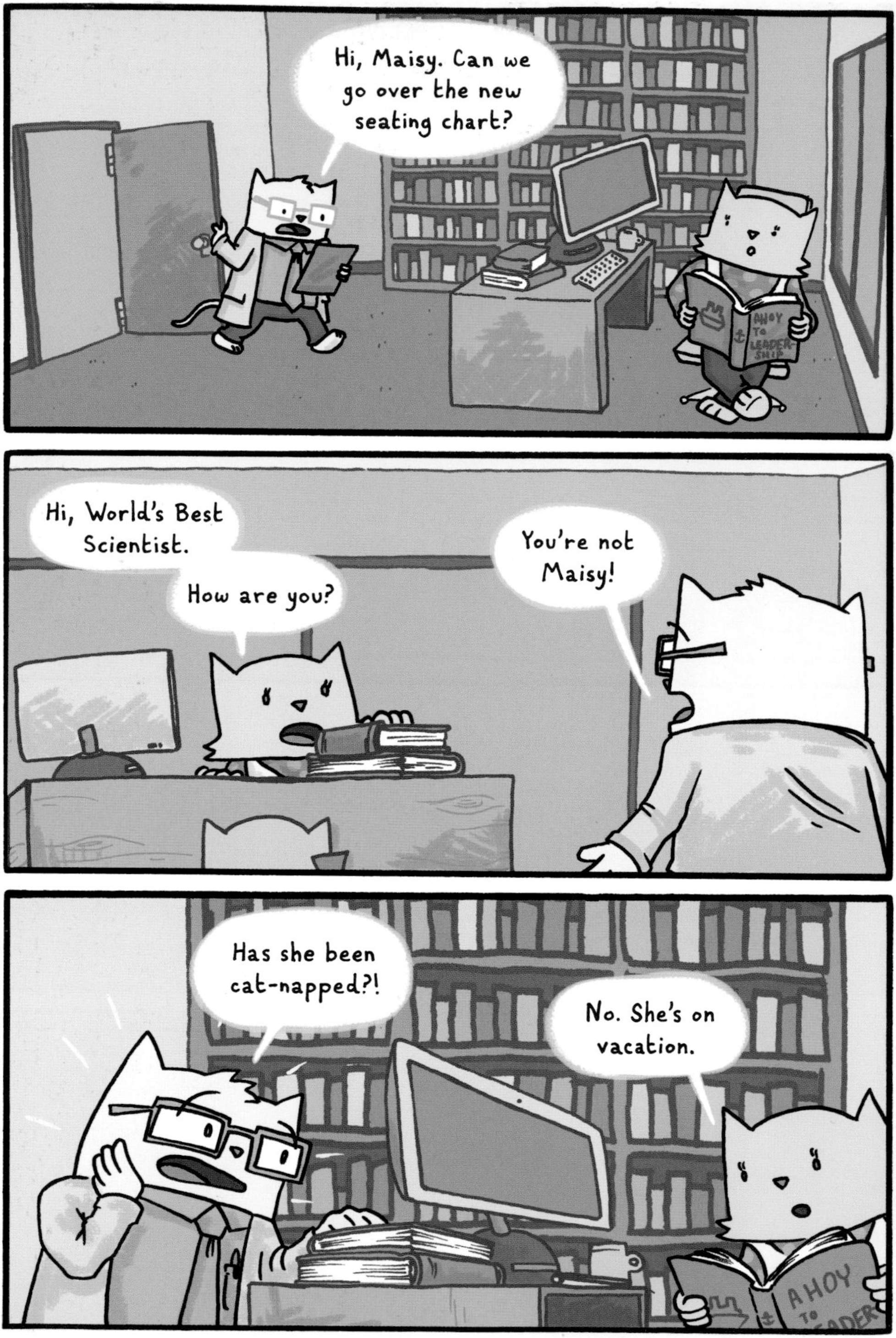
Hi, Maisy. Can we go over the new seating chart?
AHOY TO LEADER-SHIP
Hi, World's Best Scientist.
How are you?
You're not Maisy!
Has she been cat-napped?!
No. She's on vacation.

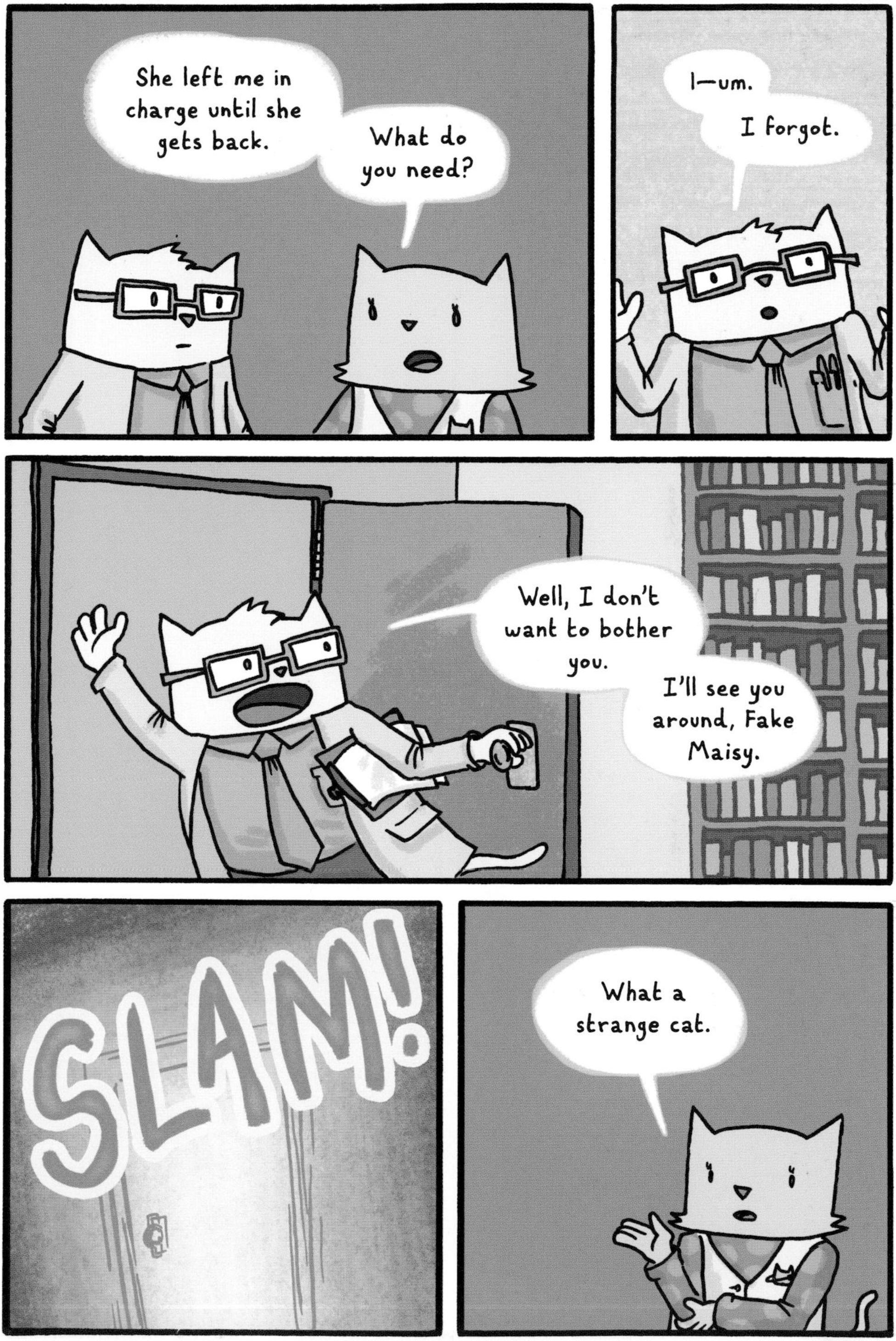
She left me in charge until she gets back.
What do you need?
I—um.
I forgot.
Well, I don't want to bother you.
I'll see you around, Fake Maisy.
SLAM!
What a strange cat.

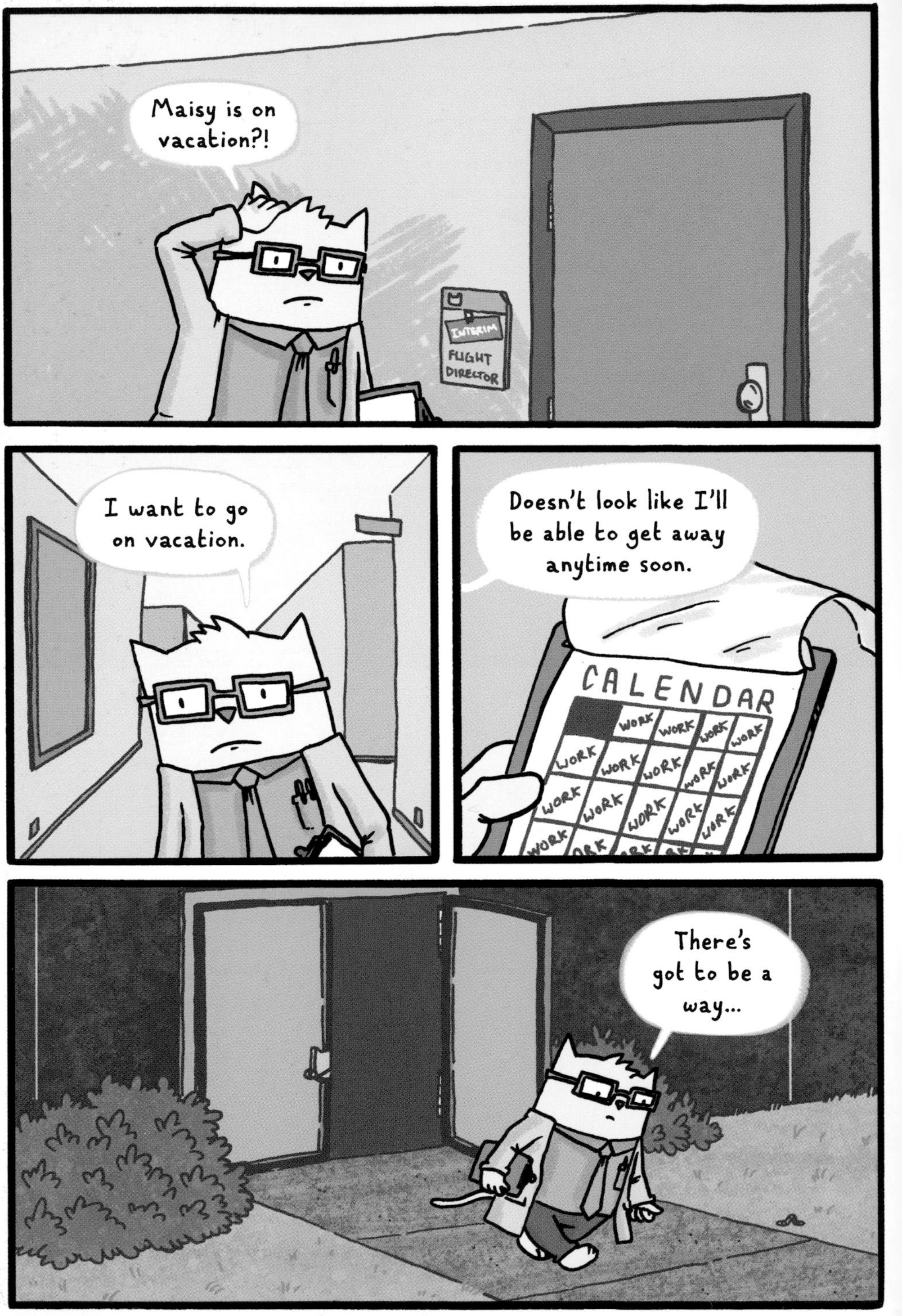
Maisy is on vacation?!
INTERIM
FLIGHT DIRECTOR
I want to go on vacation.
Doesn't look like I'll be able to get away anytime soon.
CALENDAR
WORK WORK WORK WORK
WORK WORK WORK WORK WORK
WORK WORK WORK WORK WORK
WORK
There's got to be a way...

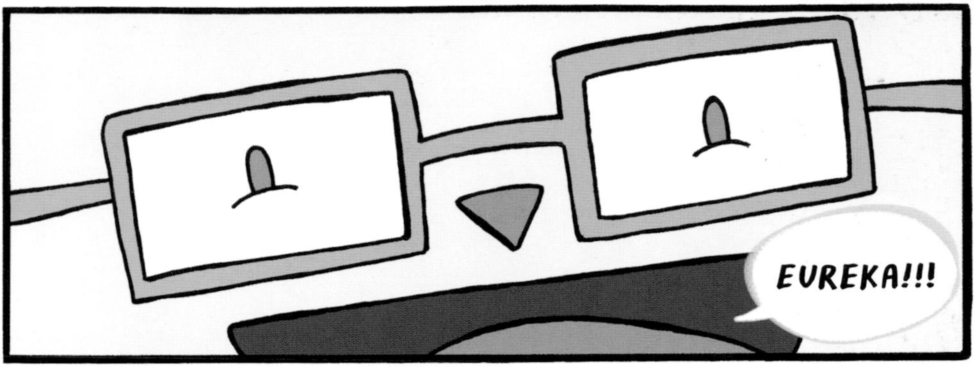
EUREKA!!!

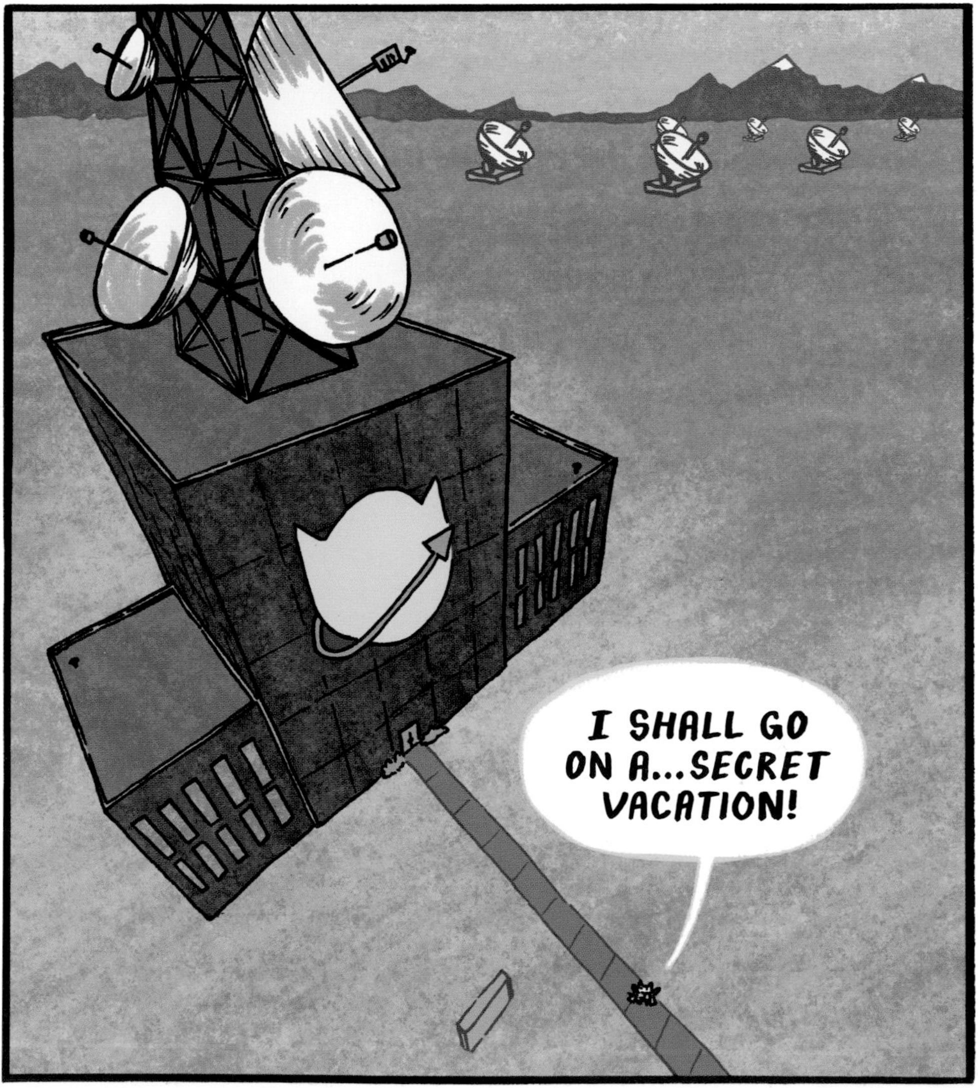
I SHALL GO ON A...SECRET VACATION!

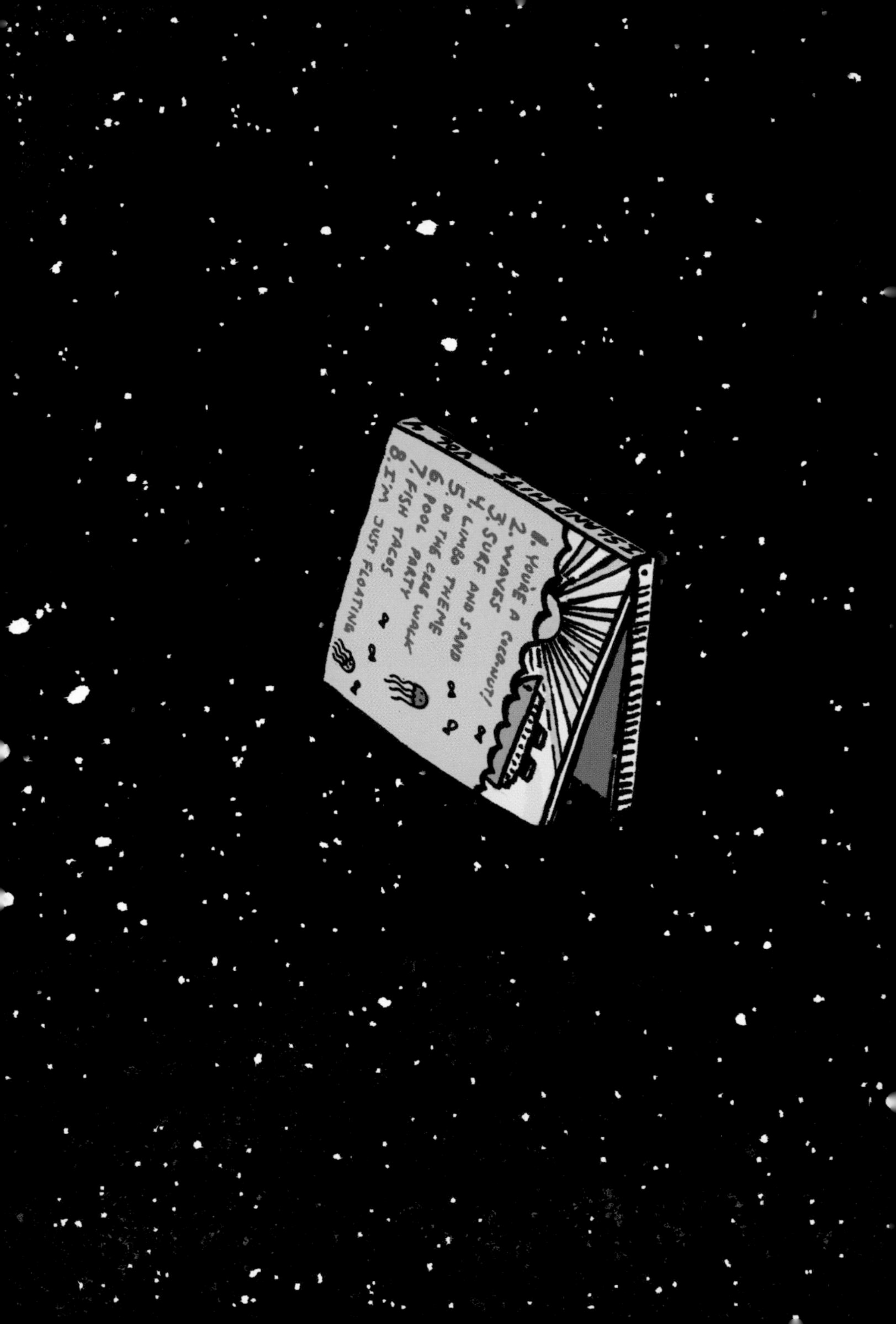
1. YOU'RE A COCONUT!
2. WAVES
3. SURF AND SAND
4. LIMBO THEME
5. DO THE CRAB WALK
6. POOL PARTY
7. FISH TACOS
8. I'M JUST FLOATING

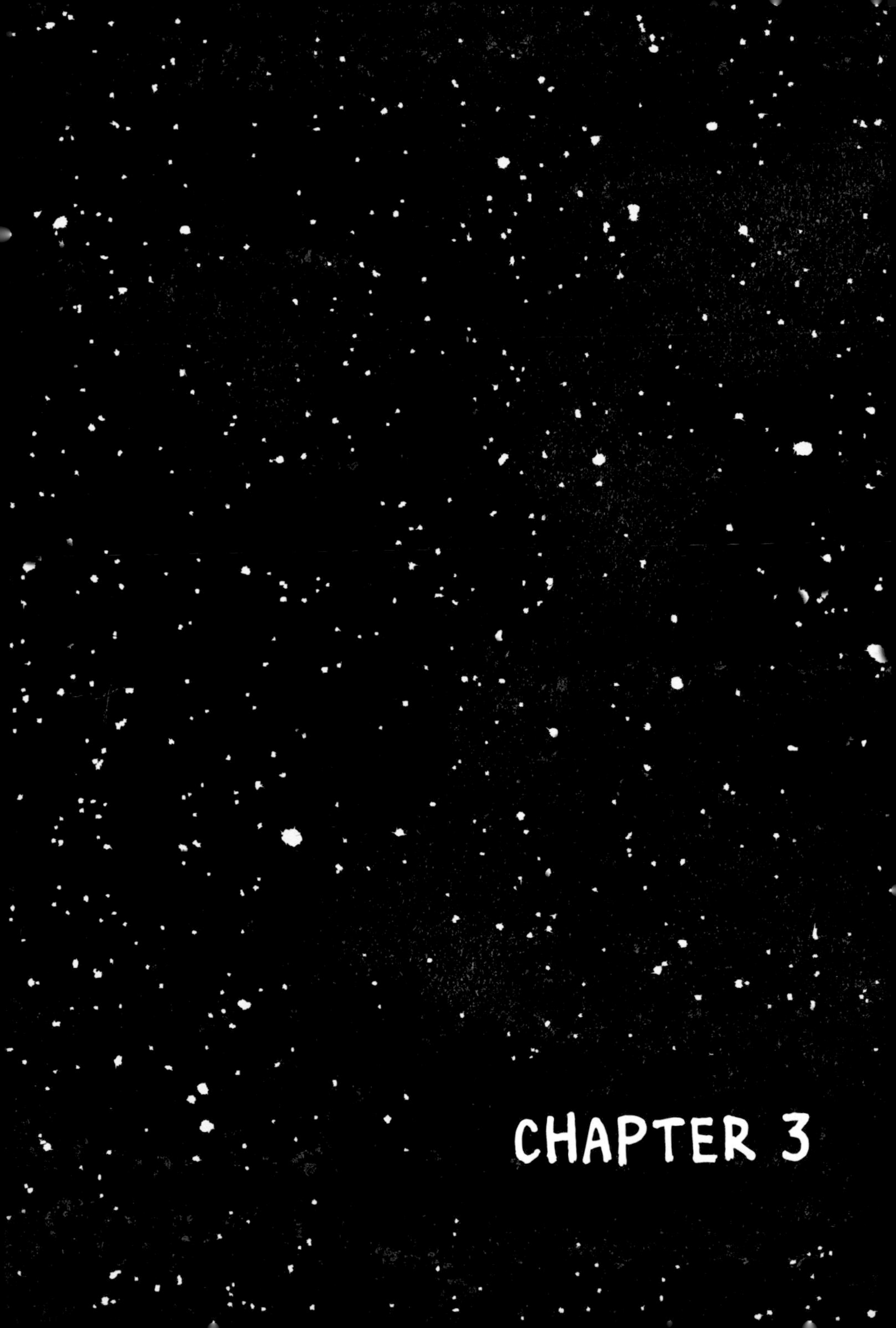

CHAPTER 3

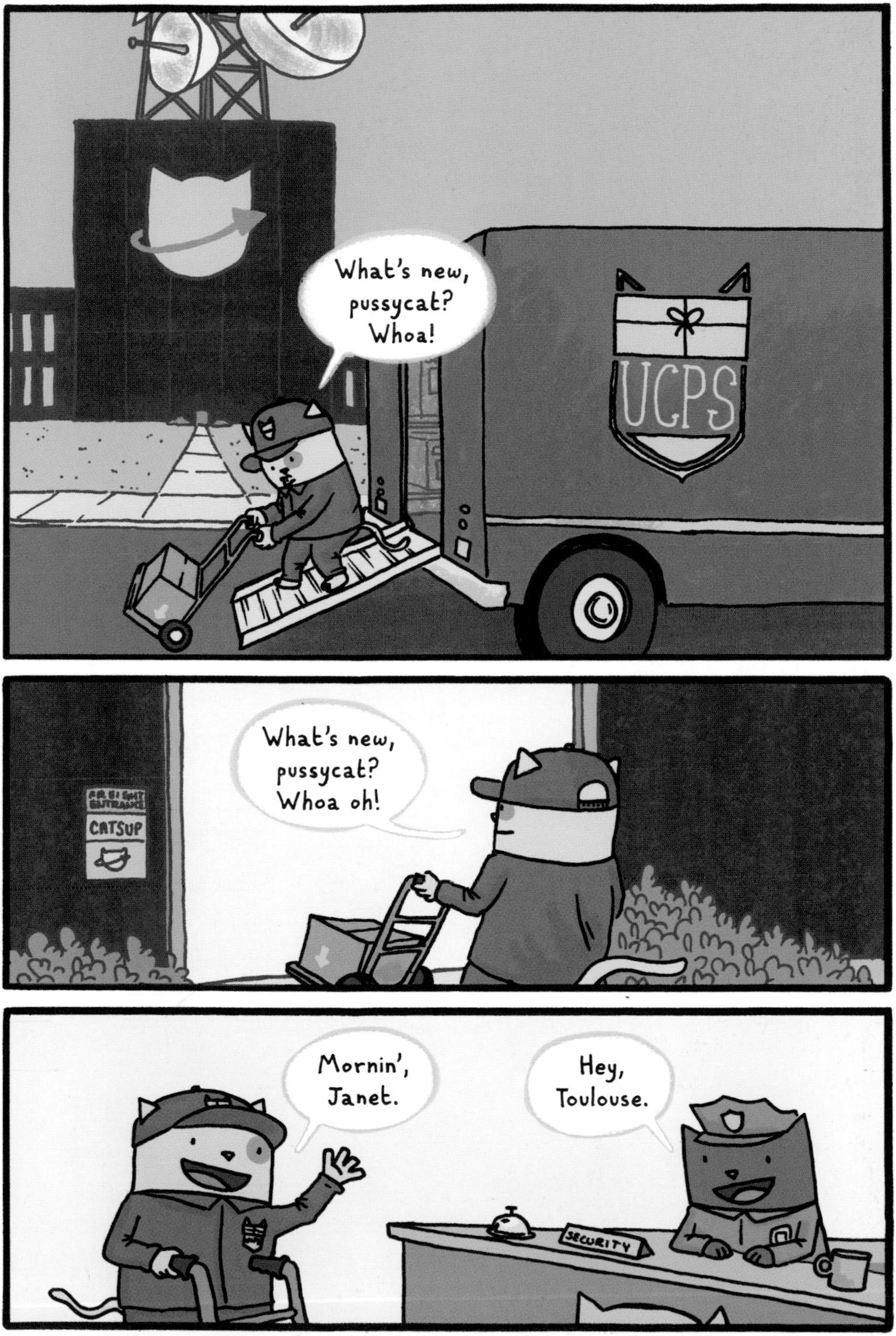
What's new, pussycat? Whoa!
UCPS
What's new, pussycat? Whoa oh!
CATSUP
Mornin', Janet.
Hey, Toulouse.
SECURITY

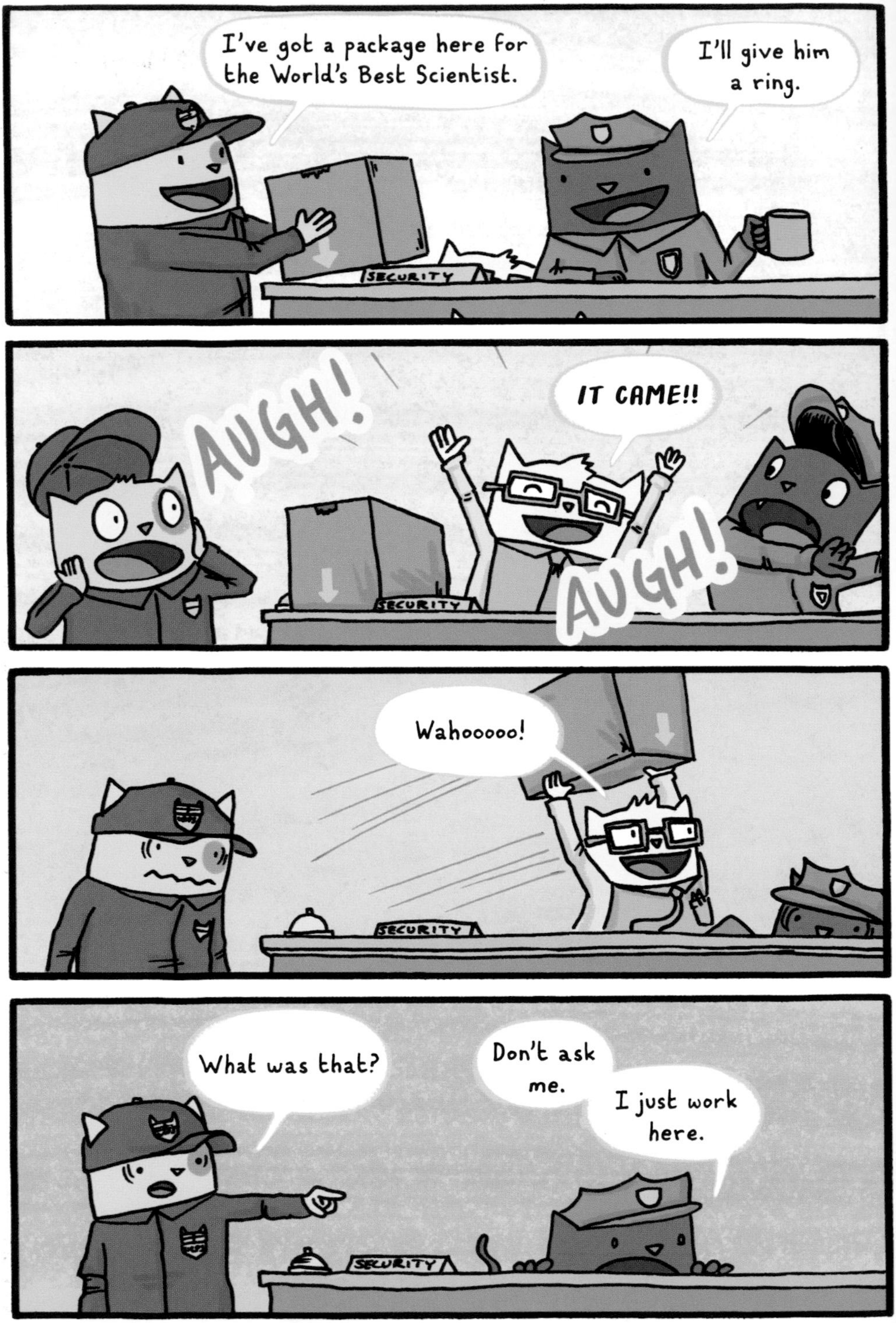
I've got a package here for the World's Best Scientist.
I'll give him a ring.
SECURITY
AUGH!
IT CAME!!
AUGH!
SECURITY
Wahooooo!
SECURITY
What was that?
Don't ask me.
I just work here.
SECURITY

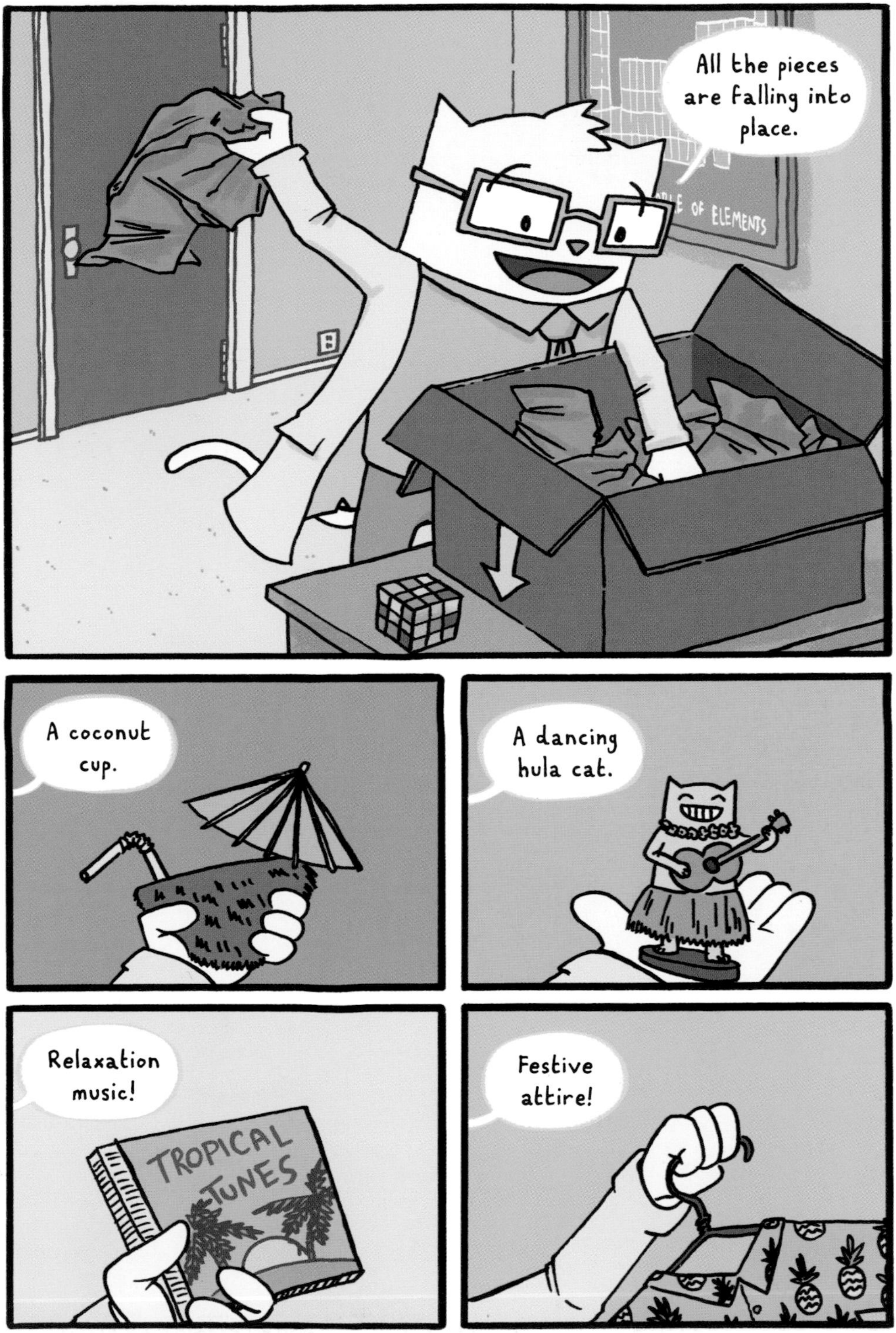

All the pieces are falling into place.
OF ELEMENTS
A coconut cup.
A dancing hula cat.
Relaxation music!
TROPICAL TUNES
Festive attire!

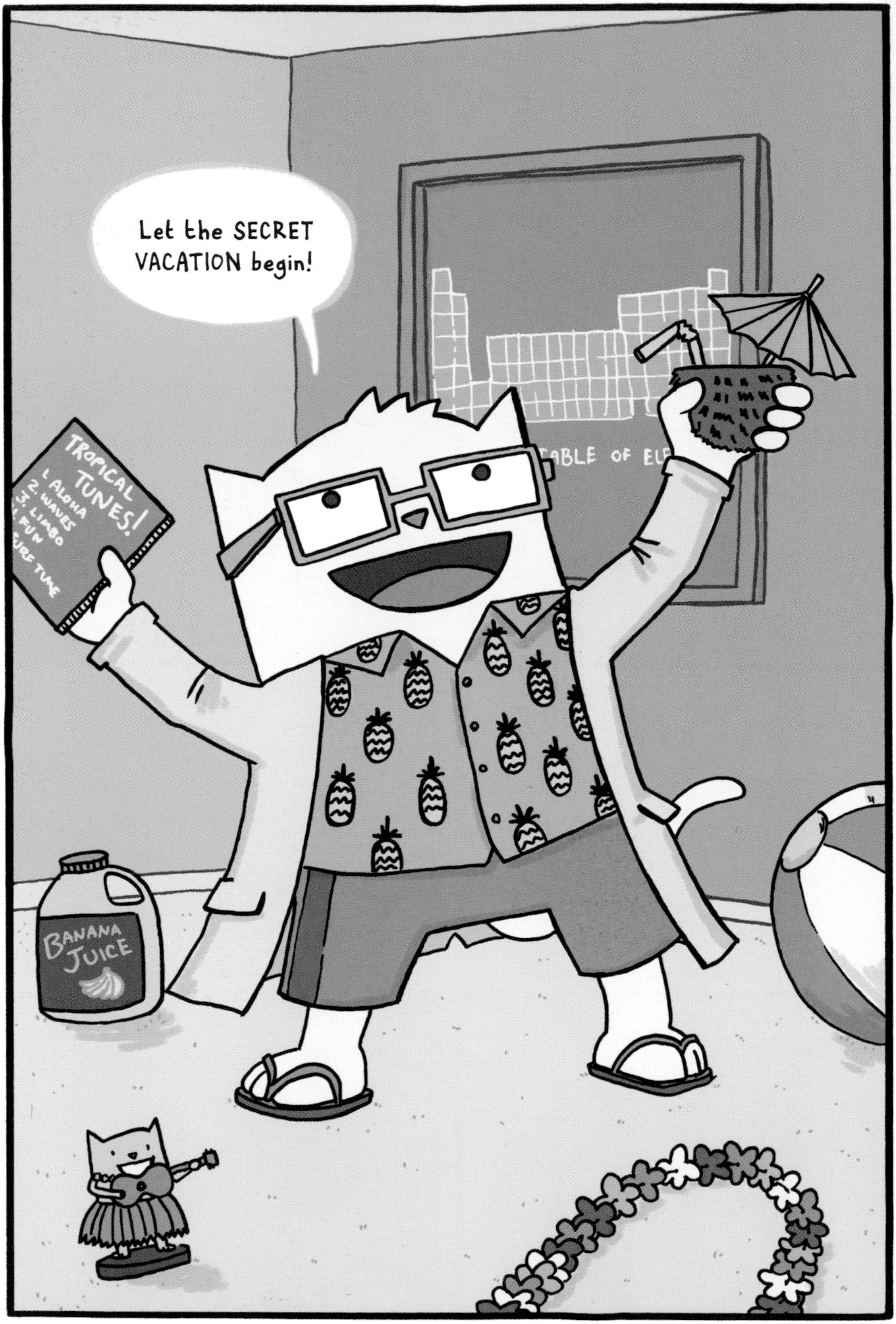
Let the SECRET VACATION begin!
TROPICAL TUNES!
1. ALOHA
2. WAVES
3. LIMBO
FUN
SURF TUNE
BANANA JUICE

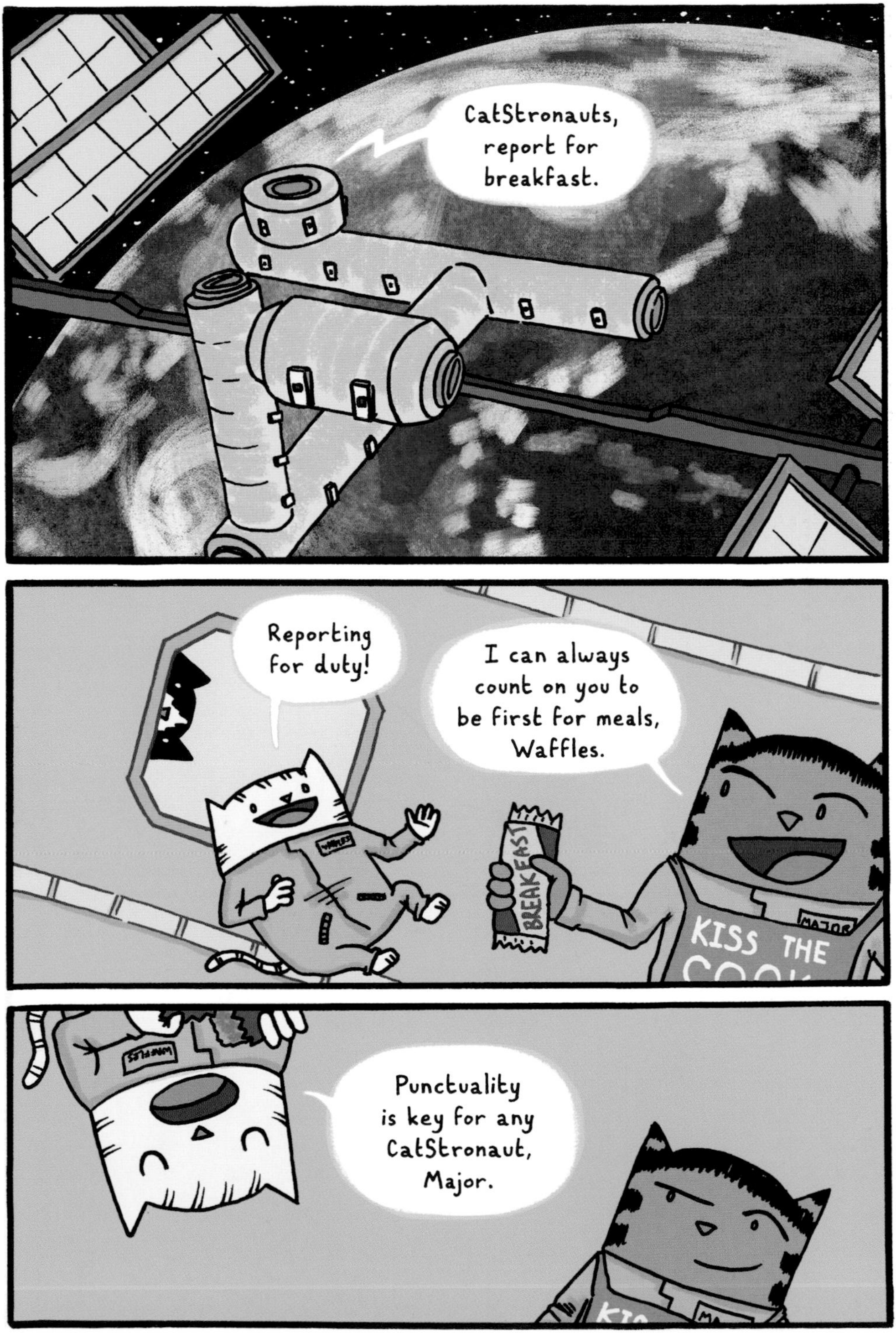
CatStronauts, report for breakfast.
Reporting for duty!
I can always count on you to be first for meals, Waffles.
BREAKFAST
KISS THE
MAJOR
WAFFLES
Punctuality is key for any CatStronaut, Major.

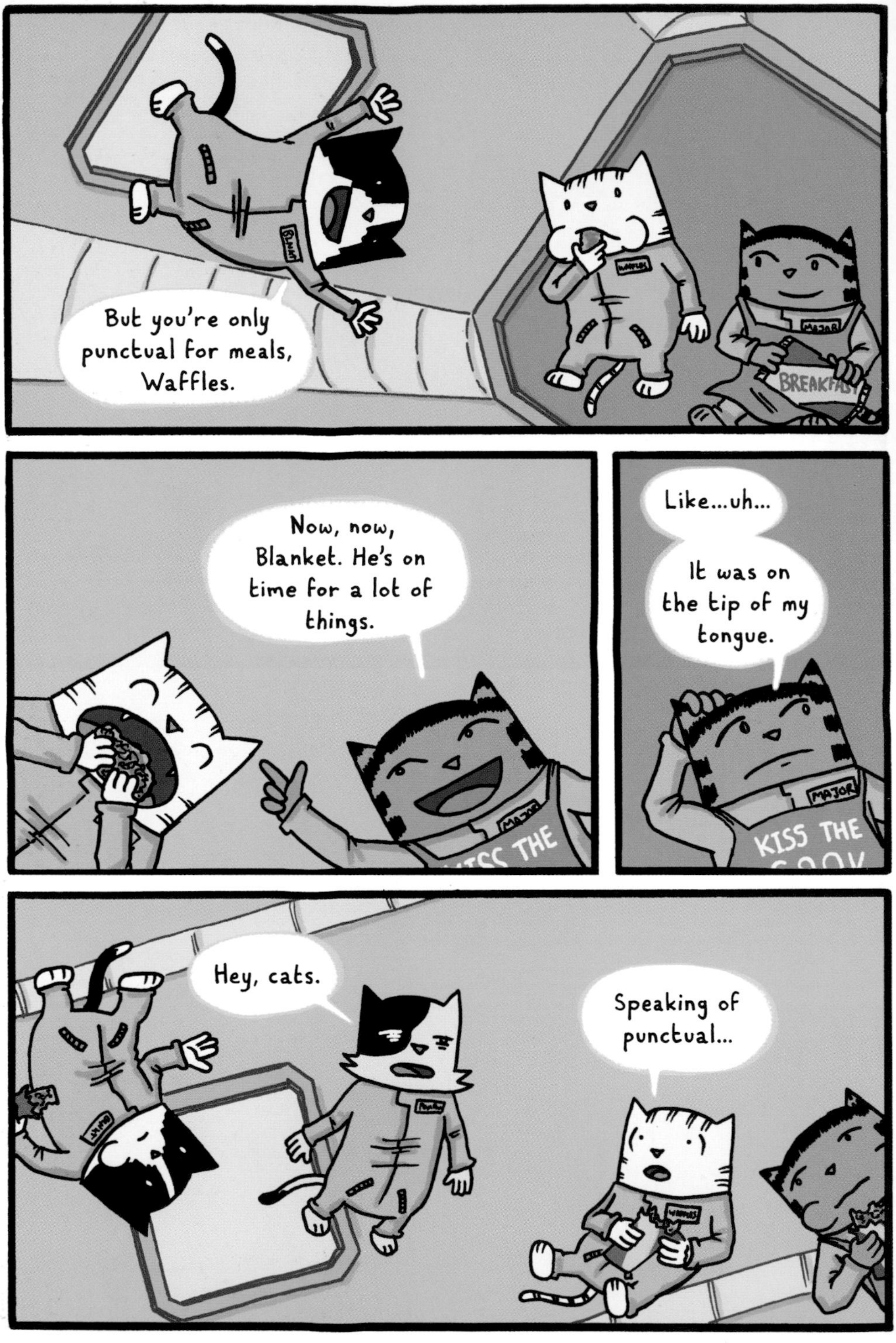

BLANKET
But you're only punctual for meals, Waffles.
WAFFLES
MAJOR
BREAKFAST
Now, now, Blanket. He's on time for a lot of things.
MAJOR
KISS THE
Like...uh...
It was on the tip of my tongue.
MAJOR
KISS THE
Hey, cats.
Speaking of punctual...

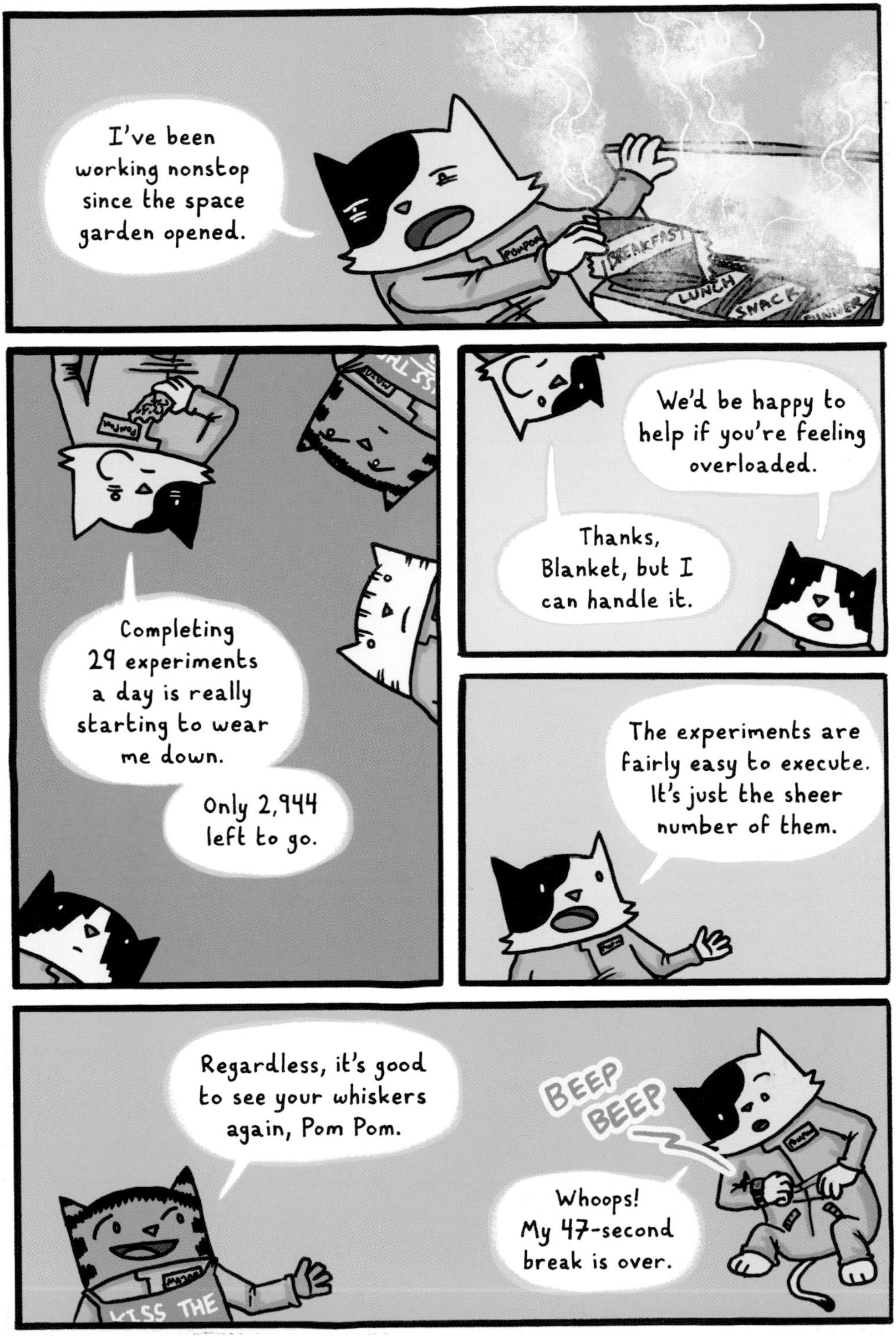
I've been working nonstop since the space garden opened.
POMPOM
BREAKFAST
LUNCH
SNACK
DINNER
Completing 29 experiments a day is really starting to wear me down.
Only 2,944 left to go.
We'd be happy to help if you're feeling overloaded.
Thanks, Blanket, but I can handle it.
The experiments are fairly easy to execute. It's just the sheer number of them.
Regardless, it's good to see your whiskers again, Pom Pom.
KISS THE
BEEP
BEEP
Whoops! My 47-second break is over.

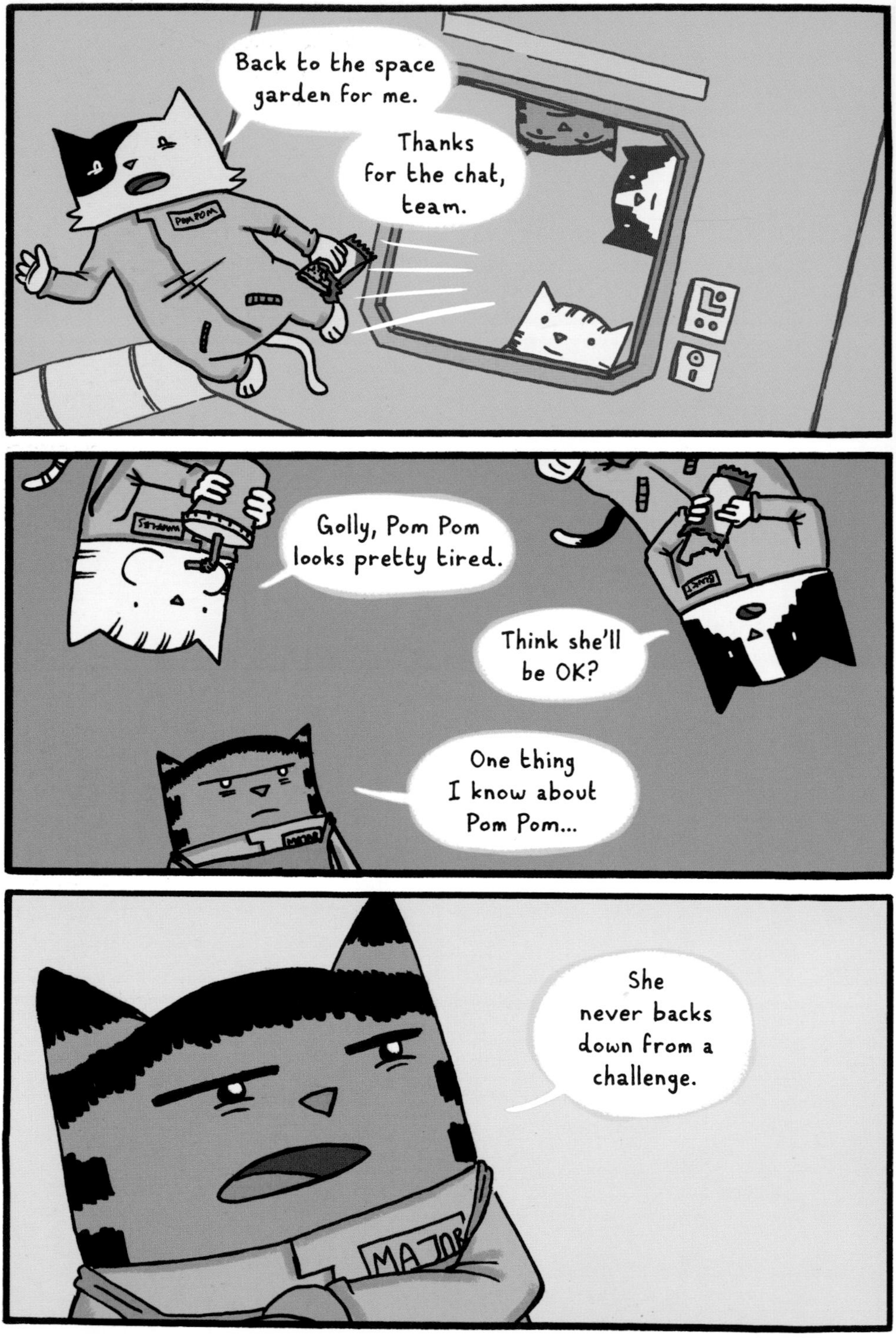
Back to the space garden for me.
Thanks for the chat, team.
Golly, Pom Pom looks pretty tired.
Think she'll be OK?
One thing I know about Pom Pom...
She never backs down from a challenge.

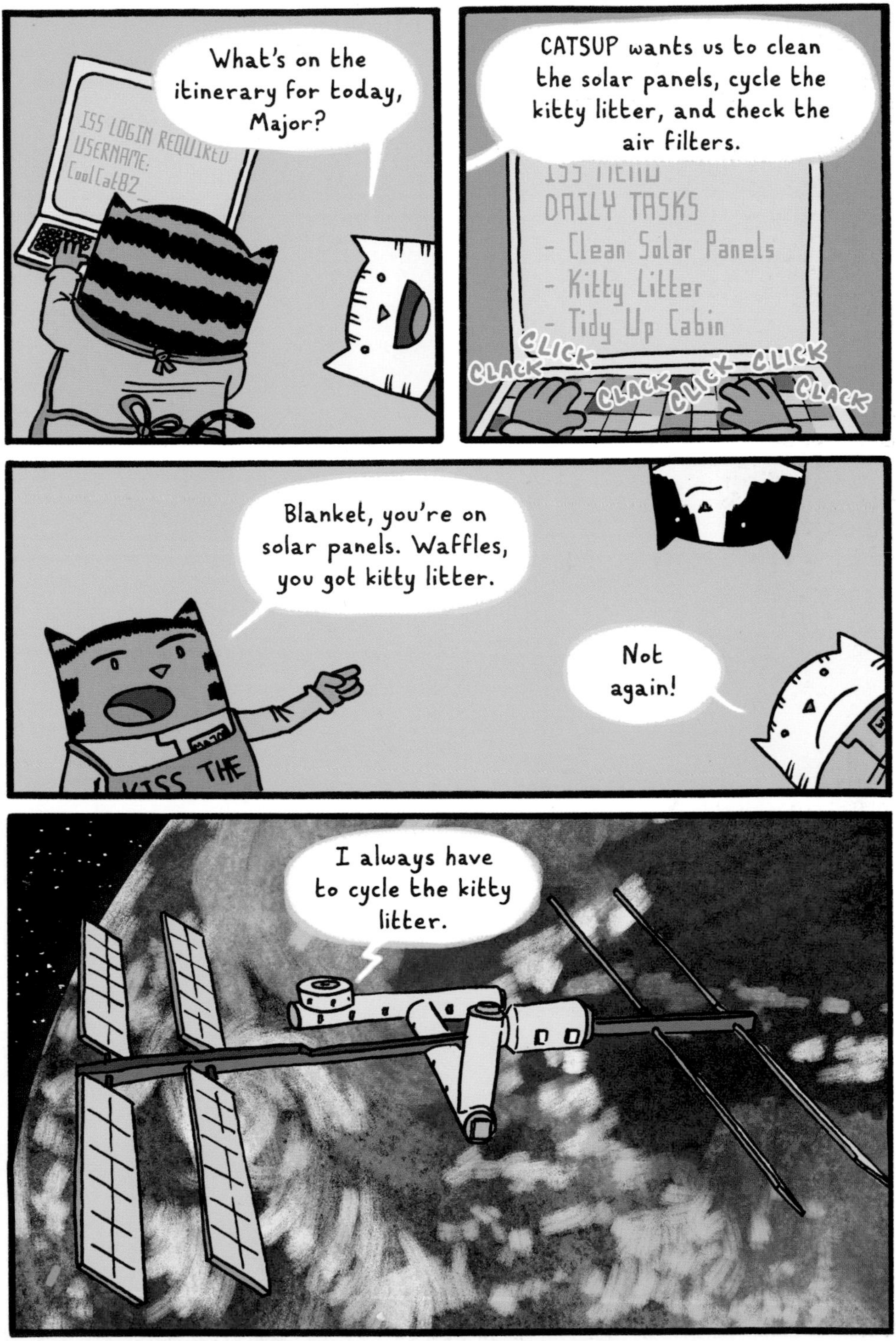
ISS LOGIN REQUIRED
USERNAME:
CoolCat82_
What's on the itinerary for today, Major?
CATSUP wants us to clean the solar panels, cycle the kitty litter, and check the air filters.
DAILY TASKS
- Clean Solar Panels
- Kitty Litter
- Tidy Up Cabin
CLICK CLACK CLACK CLICK CLICK CLACK
Blanket, you're on solar panels. Waffles, you got kitty litter.
Not again!
I always have to cycle the kitty litter.

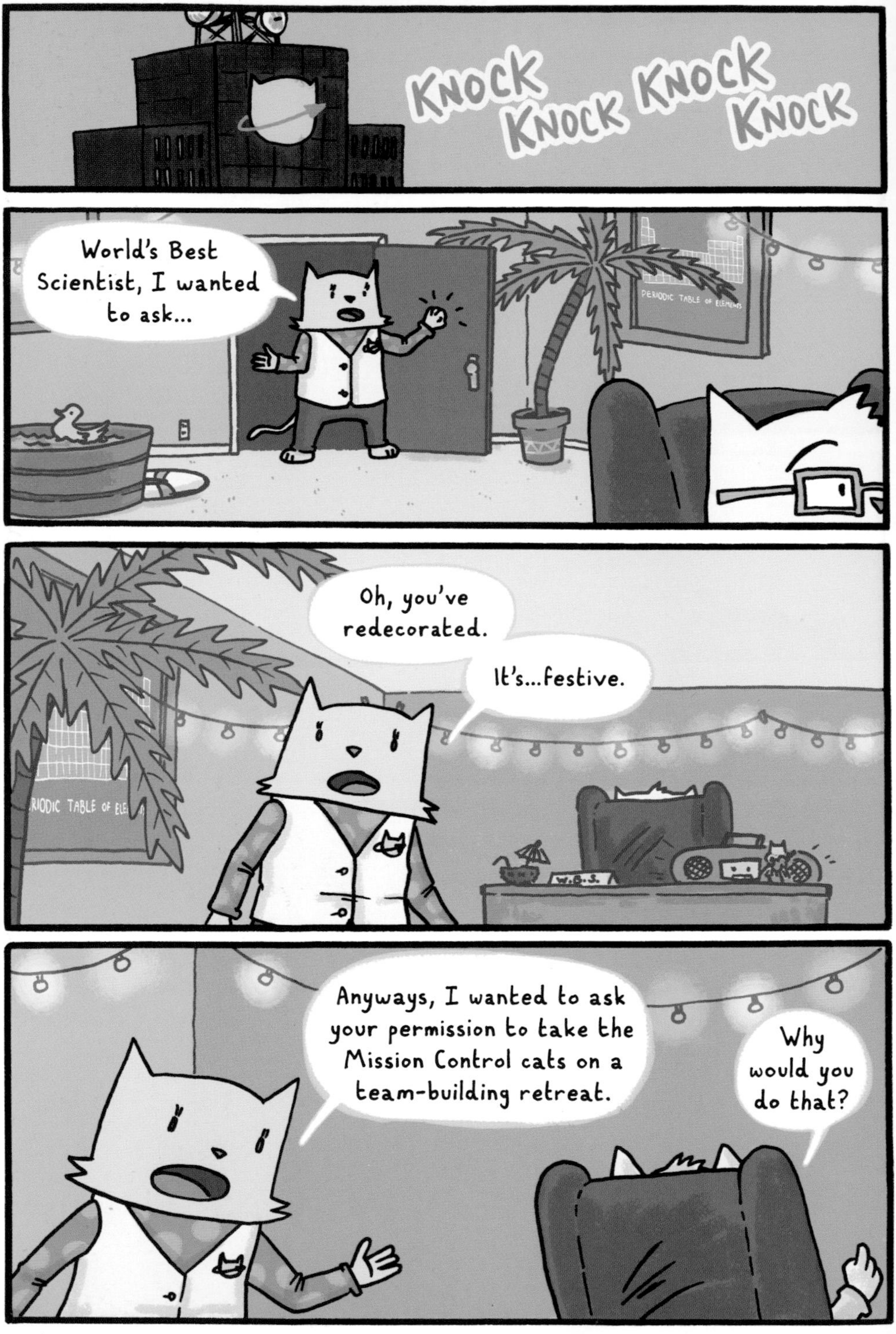
KNOCK KNOCK KNOCK KNOCK KNOCK
World's Best Scientist, I wanted to ask...
PERIODIC TABLE OF ELEMENTS
Oh, you've redecorated.
It's...festive.
W.B.S.
Anyways, I wanted to ask your permission to take the Mission Control cats on a team-building retreat.
Why would you do that?

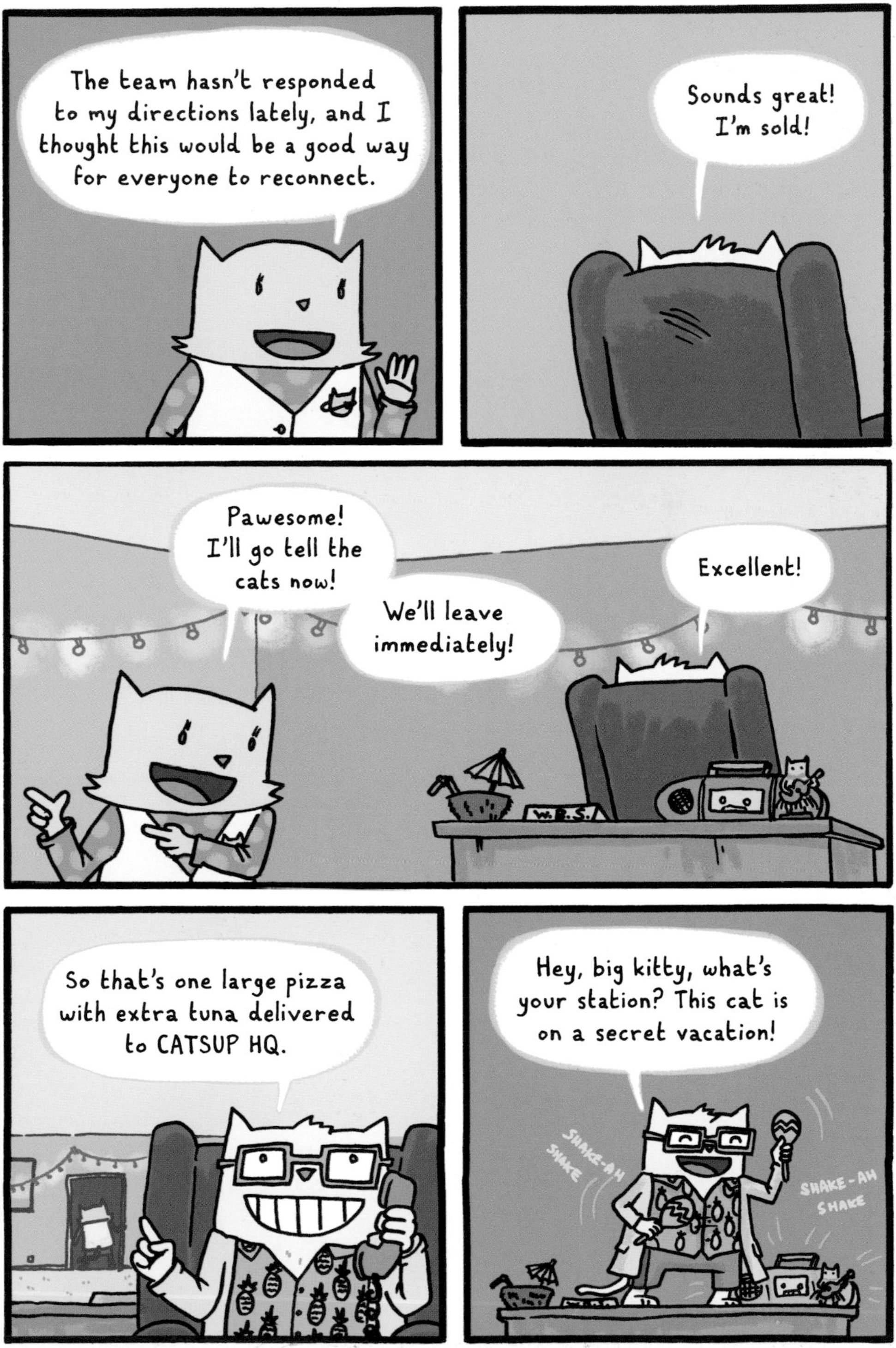
The team hasn't responded to my directions lately, and I thought this would be a good way for everyone to reconnect.
Sounds great! I'm sold!
Pawesome! I'll go tell the cats now!
We'll leave immediately!
Excellent!
W.B.S.
So that's one large pizza with extra tuna delivered to CATSUP HQ.
Hey, big kitty, what's your station? This cat is on a secret vacation!
SHAKE-AH SHAKE
SHAKE-AH SHAKE

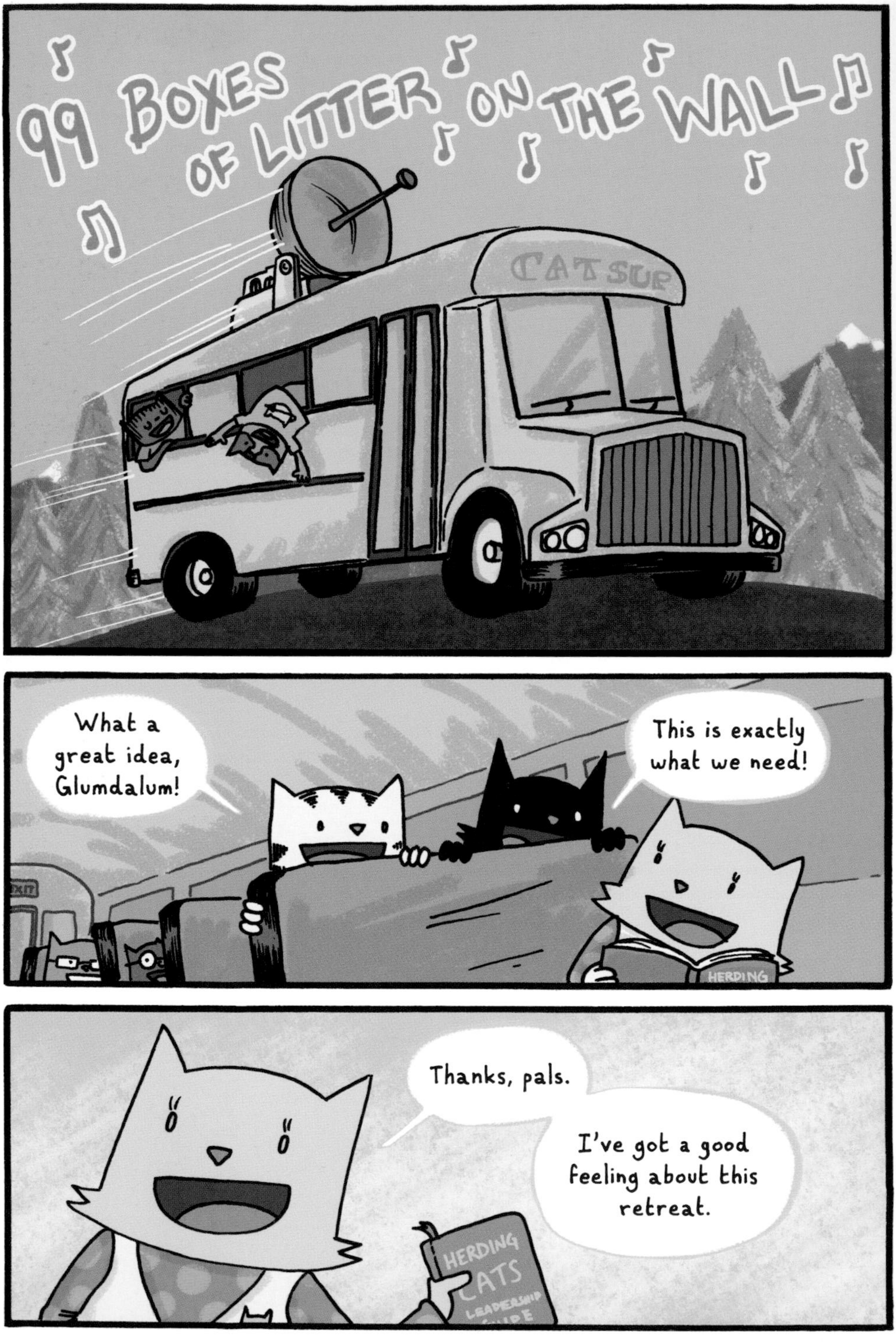

99 BOXES OF LITTER ON THE WALL
CATSUP
What a great idea, Glumdalum!
This is exactly what we need!
EXIT
HERDING
Thanks, pals.
I've got a good feeling about this retreat.
HERDING CATS LEADERSHIP

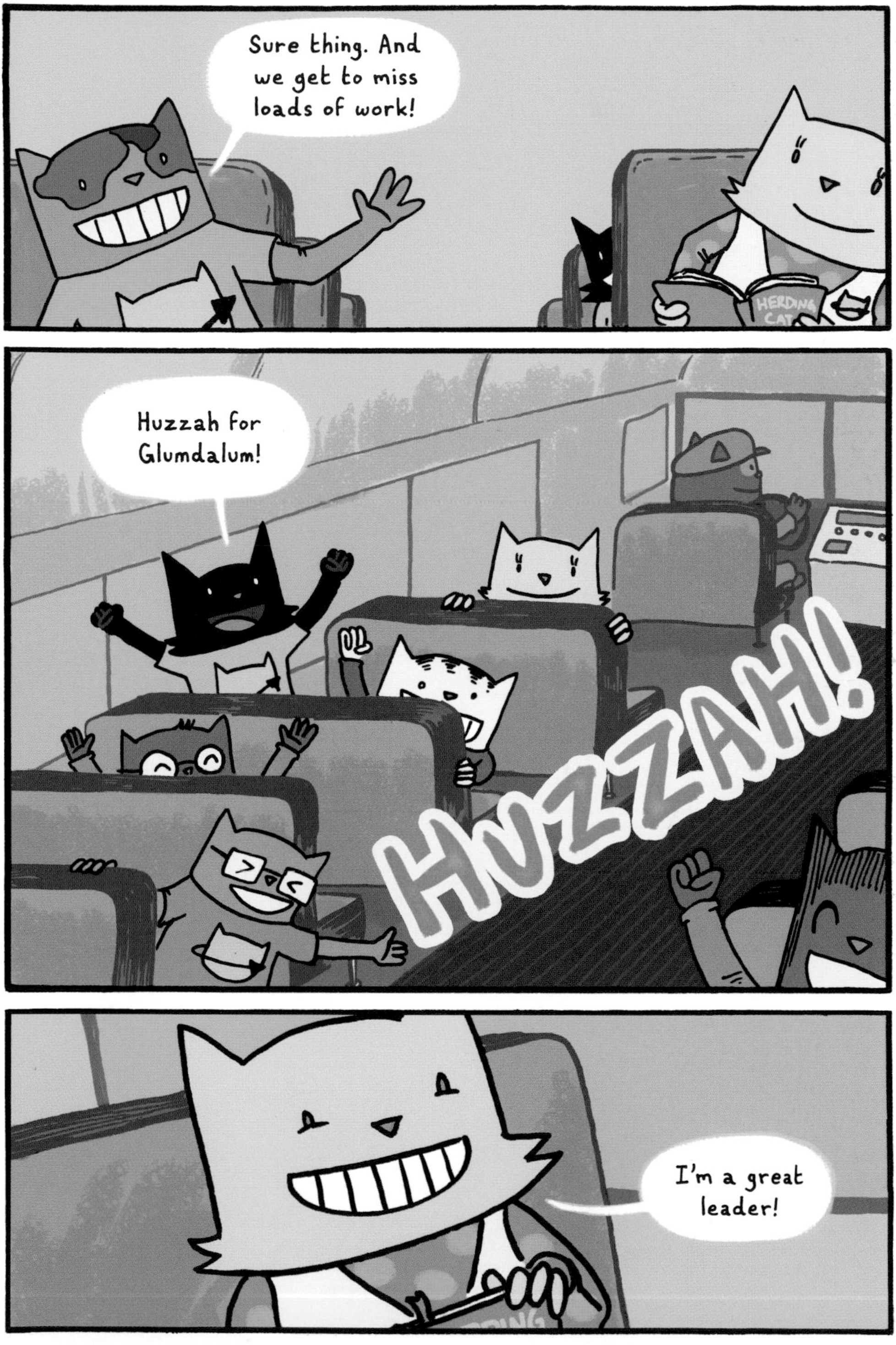
Sure thing. And we get to miss loads of work!
HERDING CAT
Huzzah for Glumdalum!
HUZZAH!
I'm a great leader!

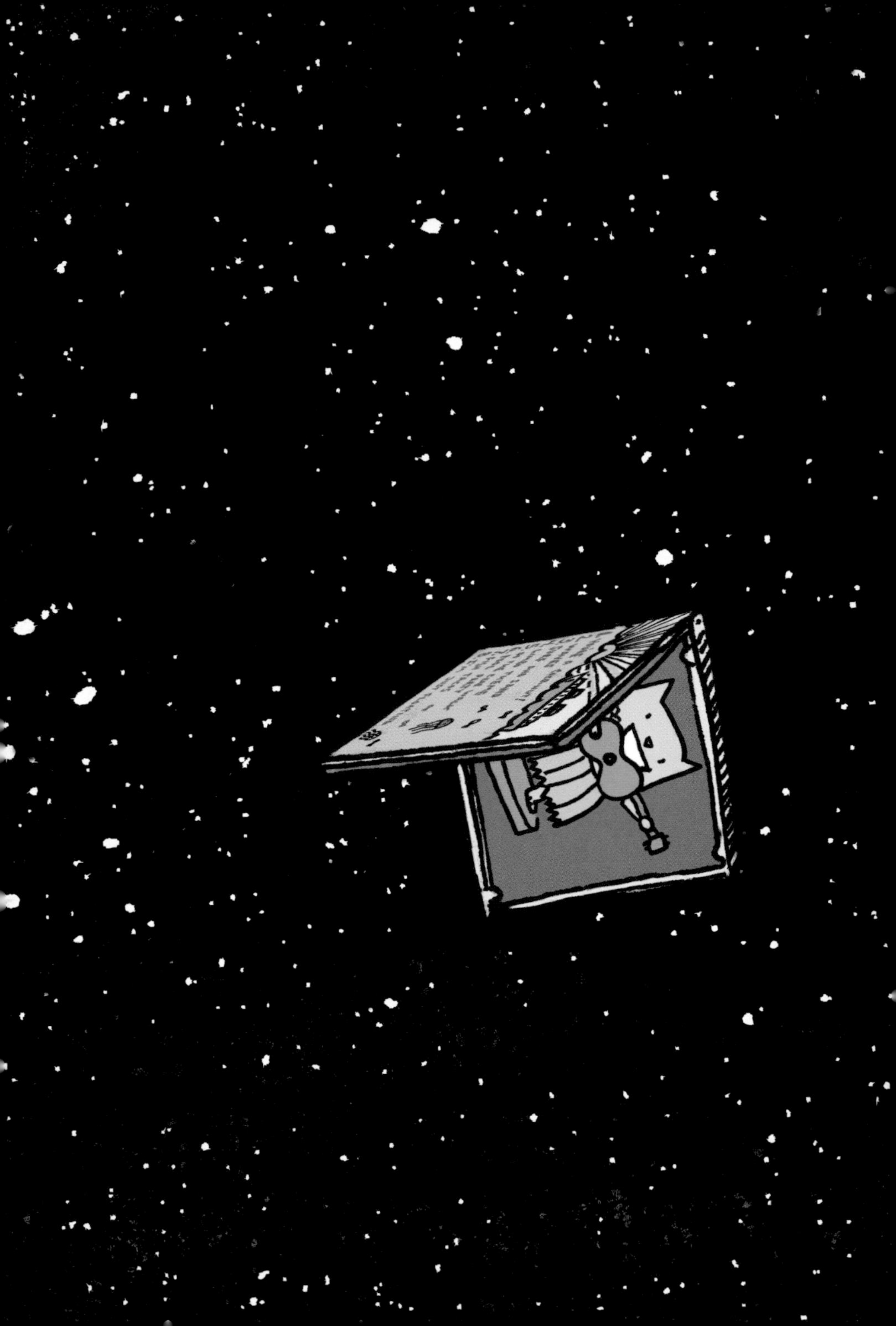

CHAPTER 4

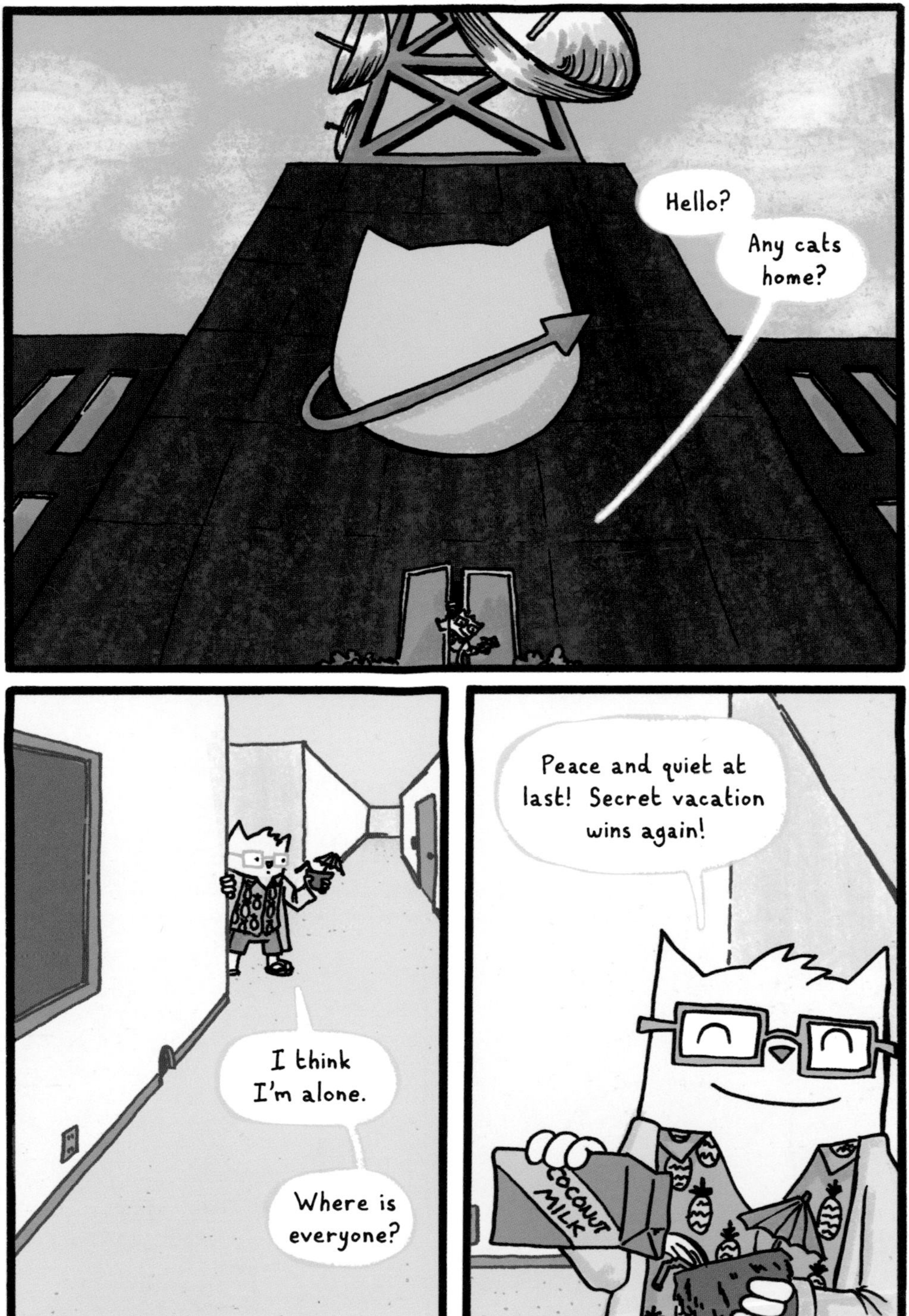
Hello?
Any cats home?
I think I'm alone.
Where is everyone?
Peace and quiet at last! Secret vacation wins again!
COCONUT MILK

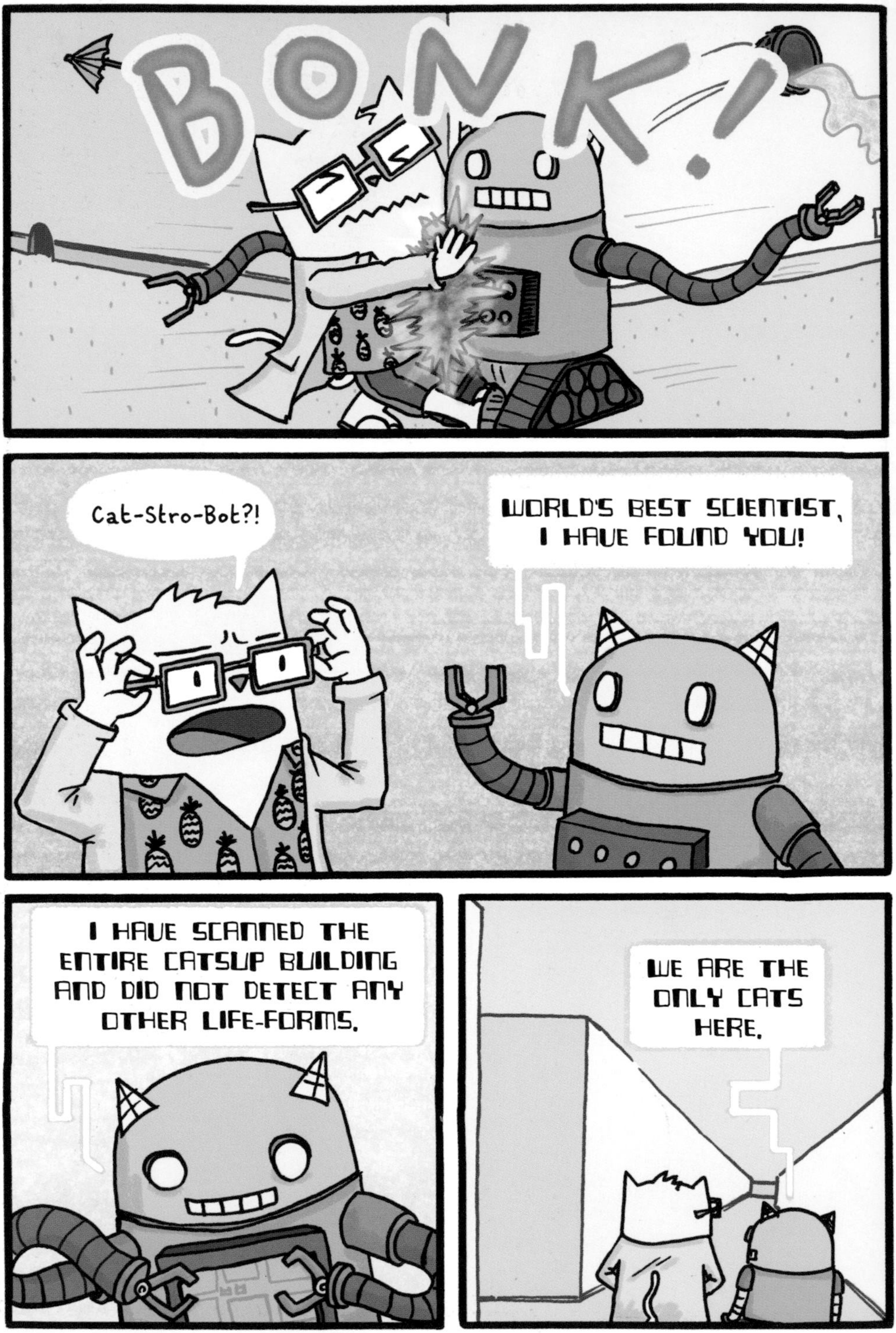
BONK!
Cat-Stro-Bot?!
WORLD'S BEST SCIENTIST, I HAVE FOUND YOU!
I HAVE SCANNED THE ENTIRE CATSUP BUILDING AND DID NOT DETECT ANY OTHER LIFE-FORMS.
WE ARE THE ONLY CATS HERE.

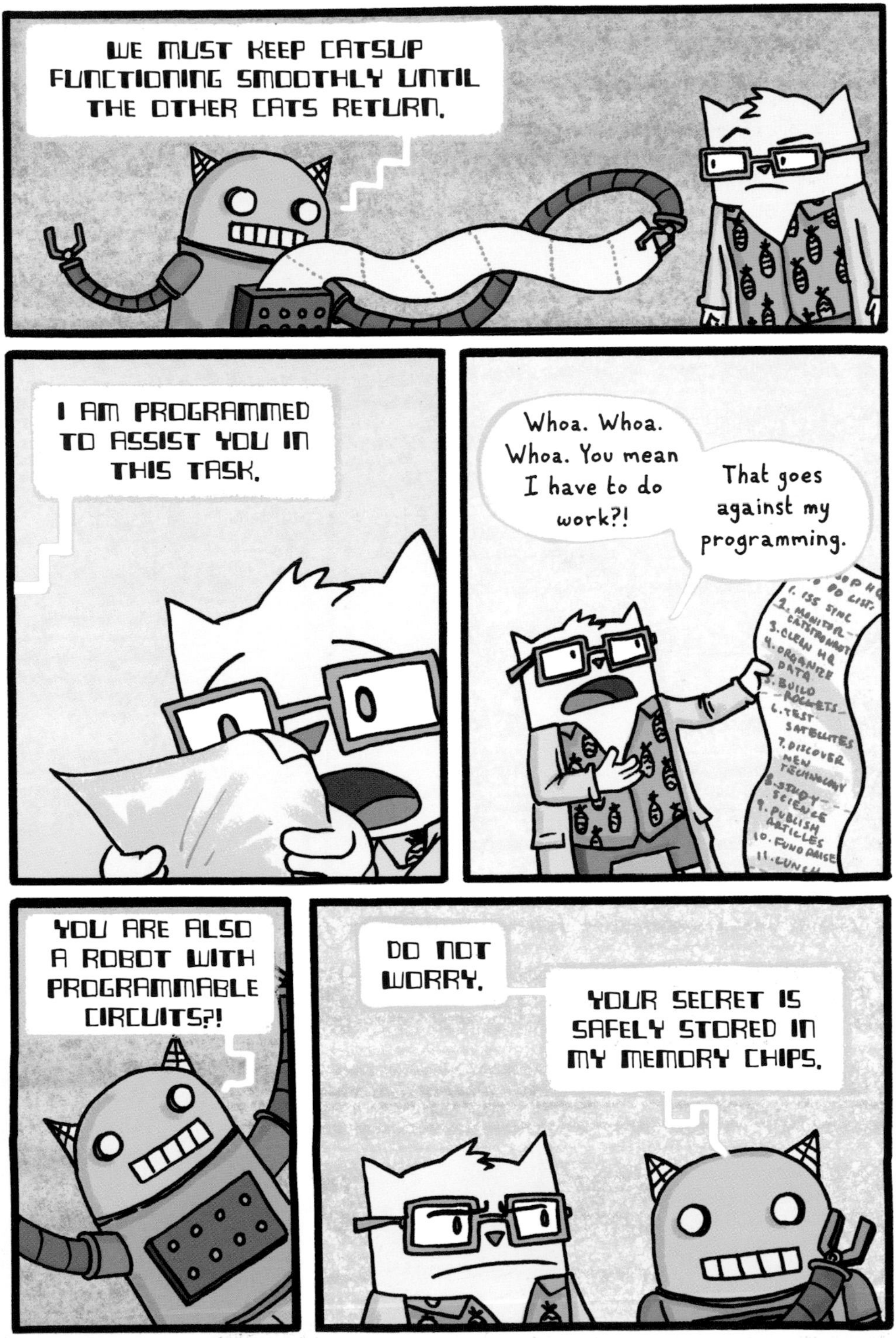
WE MUST KEEP CATSUP FUNCTIONING SMOOTHLY UNTIL THE OTHER CATS RETURN.
I AM PROGRAMMED TO ASSIST YOU IN THIS TASK.
Whoa. Whoa. Whoa. You mean I have to do work?!
That goes against my programming.
1. ISS SYNC
2. MONITOR CATSTRONAUTS
3. CLEAN HQ
4. ORGANIZE DATA
5. BUILD ROCKETS
6. TEST SATELLITES
7. DISCOVER NEW TECHNOLOGY
8. STUDY SCIENCE
9. PUBLISH ARTICLES
10. FUNDRAISE
YOU ARE ALSO A ROBOT WITH PROGRAMMABLE CIRCUITS?!
DO NOT WORRY.
YOUR SECRET IS SAFELY STORED IN MY MEMORY CHIPS.

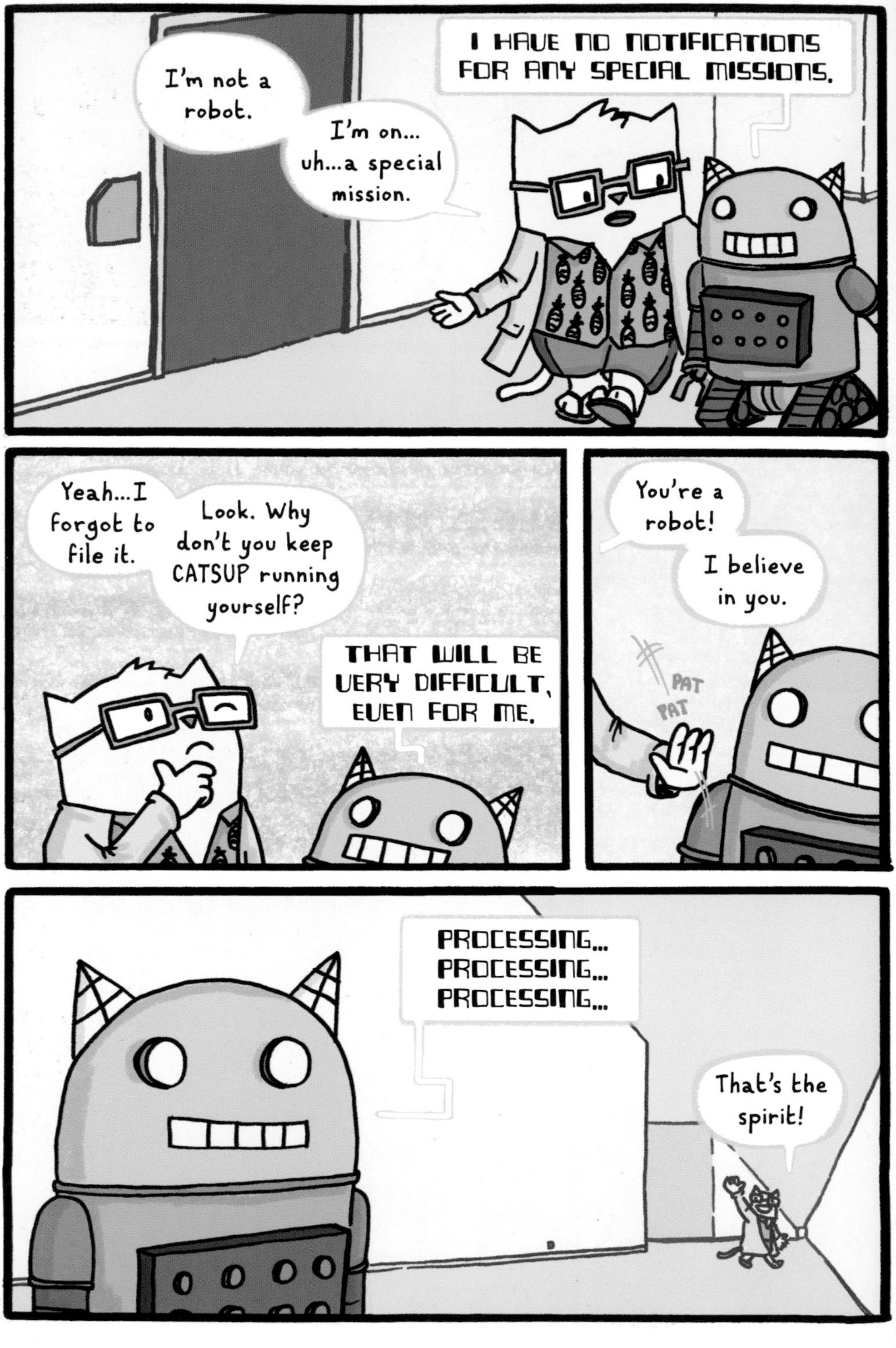
I'm not a robot.
I'm on... uh...a special mission.
I HAVE NO NOTIFICATIONS FOR ANY SPECIAL MISSIONS.
Yeah...I forgot to file it.
Look. Why don't you keep CATSUP running yourself?
THAT WILL BE VERY DIFFICULT, EVEN FOR ME.
You're a robot!
I believe in you.
PAT
PAT
PROCESSING...
PROCESSING...
PROCESSING...
That's the spirit!

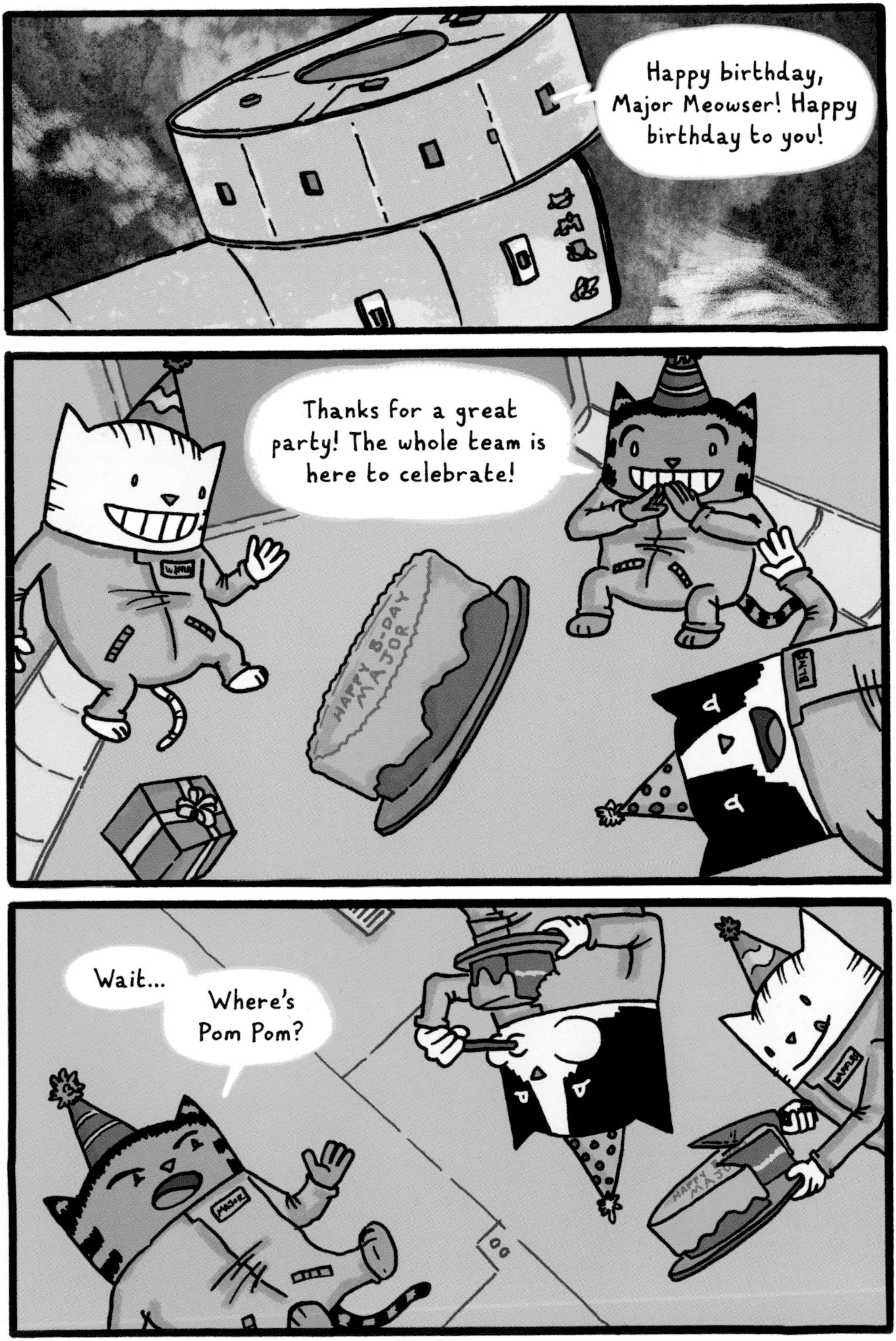
Happy birthday, Major Meowser! Happy birthday to you!
Thanks for a great party! The whole team is here to celebrate!
HAPPY B-DAY MAJOR
Wait...
Where's Pom Pom?

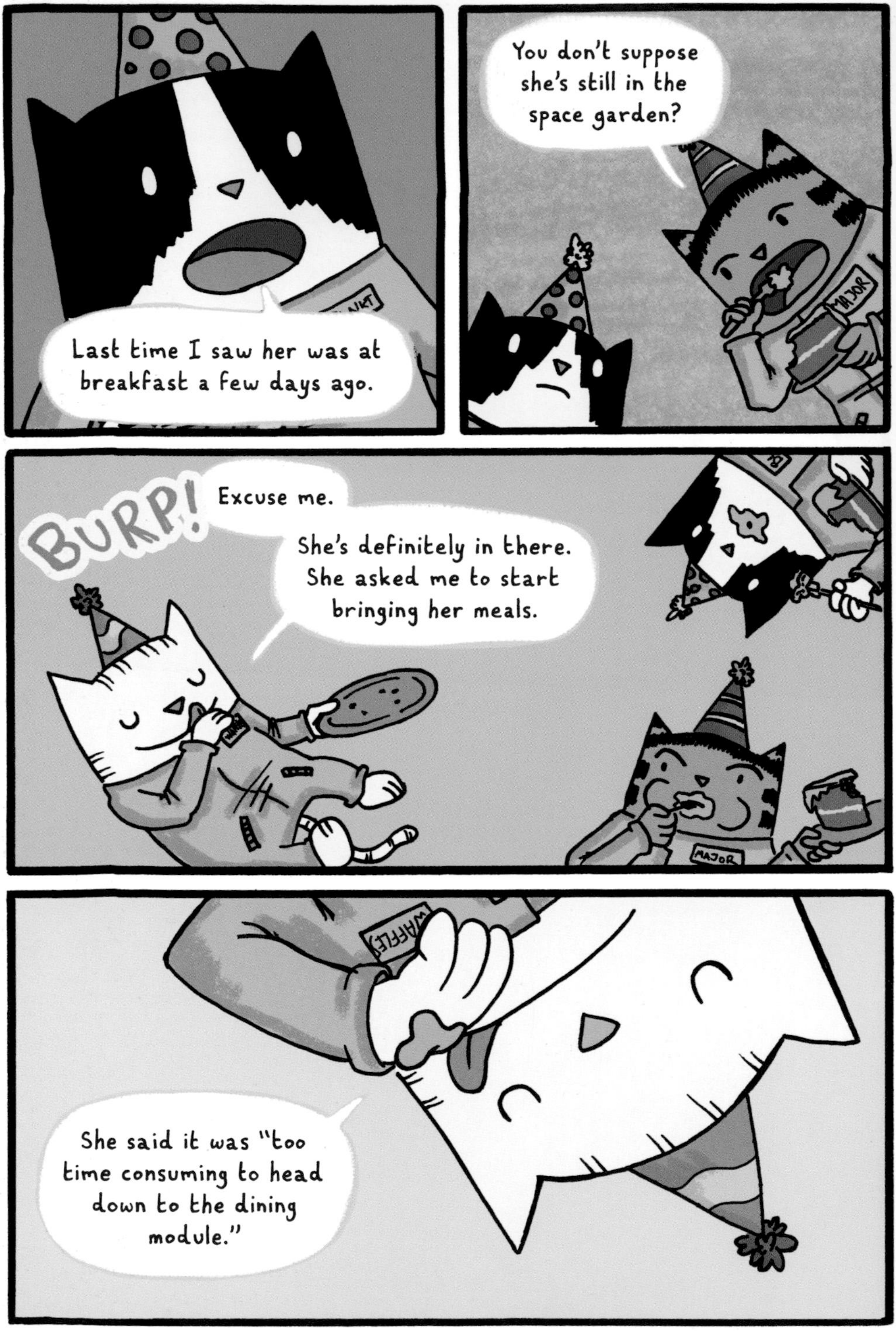
Last time I saw her was at breakfast a few days ago.
You don't suppose she's still in the space garden?
BURP!
Excuse me.
She's definitely in there. She asked me to start bringing her meals.
MAJOR
She said it was "too time consuming to head down to the dining module."

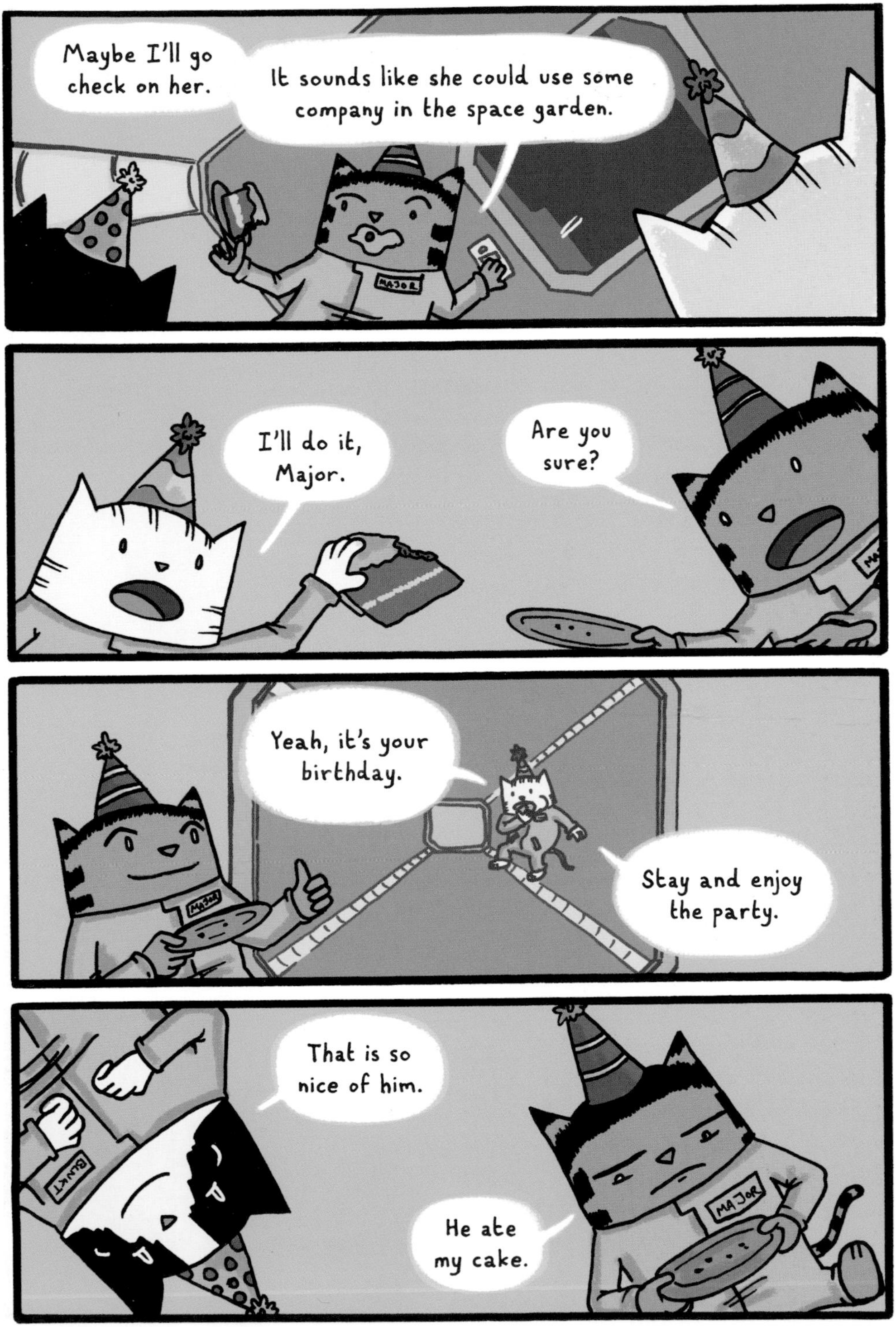
Maybe I'll go check on her.
It sounds like she could use some company in the space garden.
MAJOR
I'll do it, Major.
Are you sure?
Yeah, it's your birthday.
Stay and enjoy the party.
MAJOR
That is so nice of him.
He ate my cake.
MAJOR

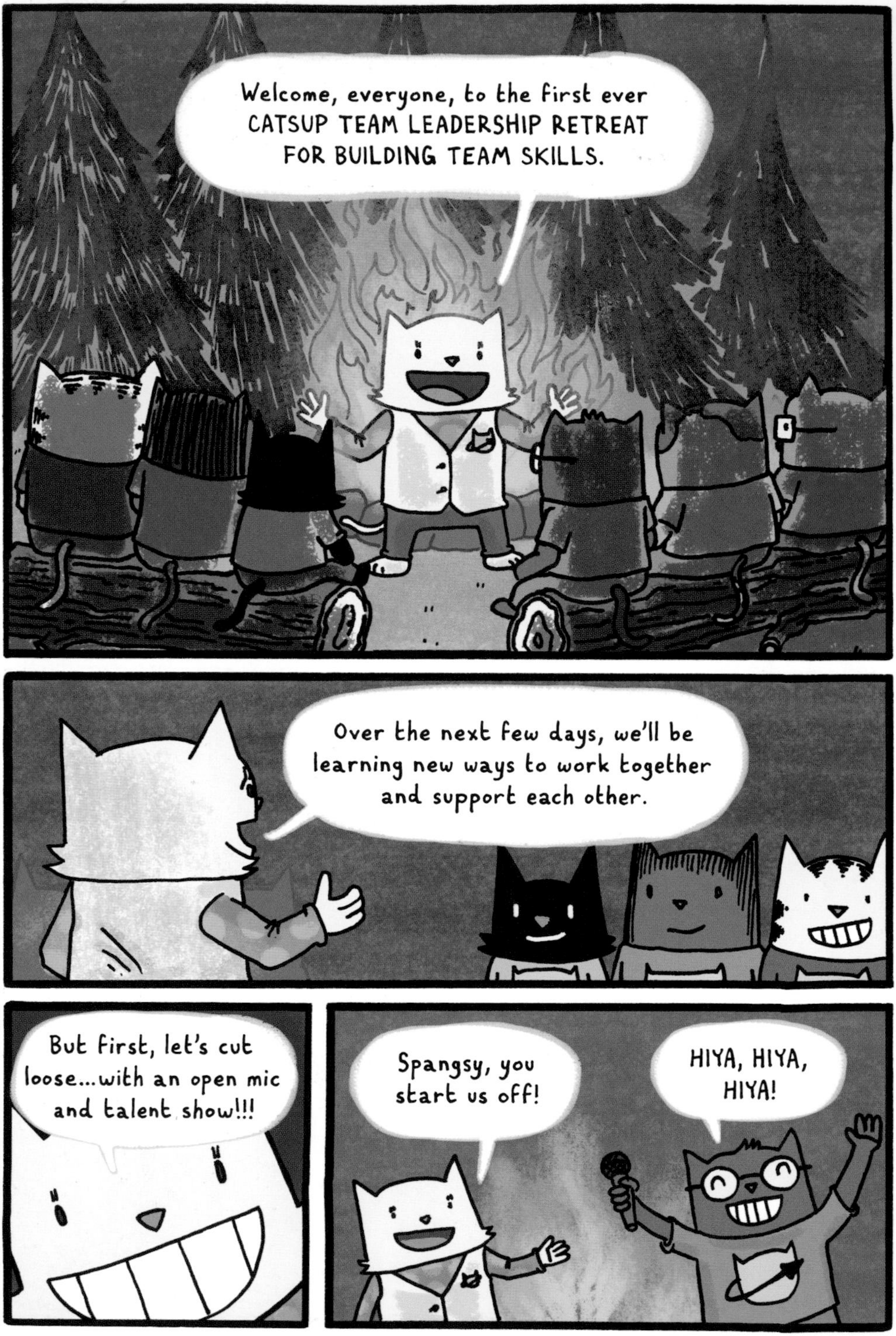
Welcome, everyone, to the first ever CATSUP TEAM LEADERSHIP RETREAT FOR BUILDING TEAM SKILLS.
Over the next few days, we'll be learning new ways to work together and support each other.
But first, let's cut loose...with an open mic and talent show!!!
Spangsy, you start us off!
HIYA, HIYA, HIYA!

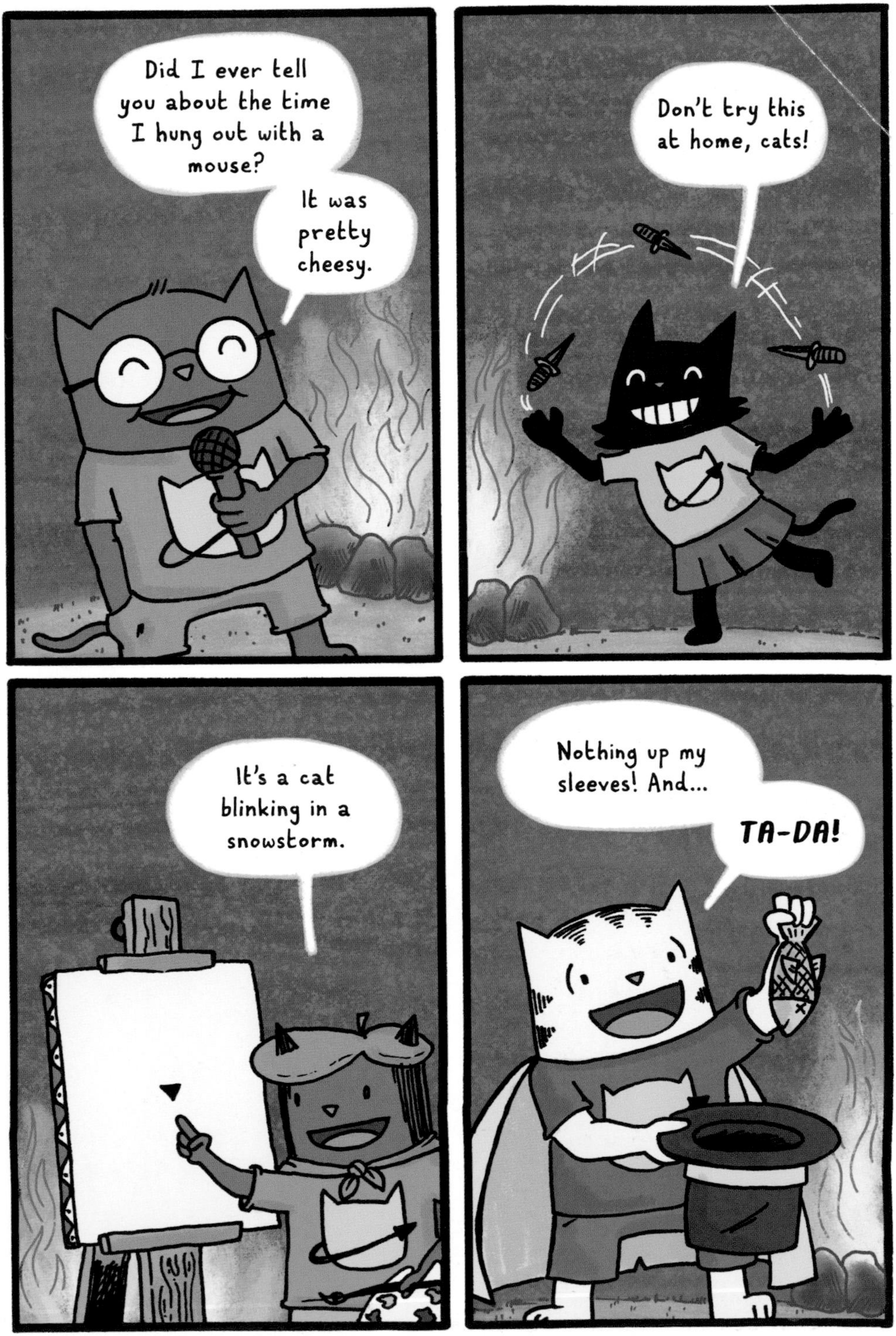
Did I ever tell you about the time I hung out with a mouse?
It was pretty cheesy.
Don't try this at home, cats!
It's a cat blinking in a snowstorm.
Nothing up my sleeves! And...
TA-DA!

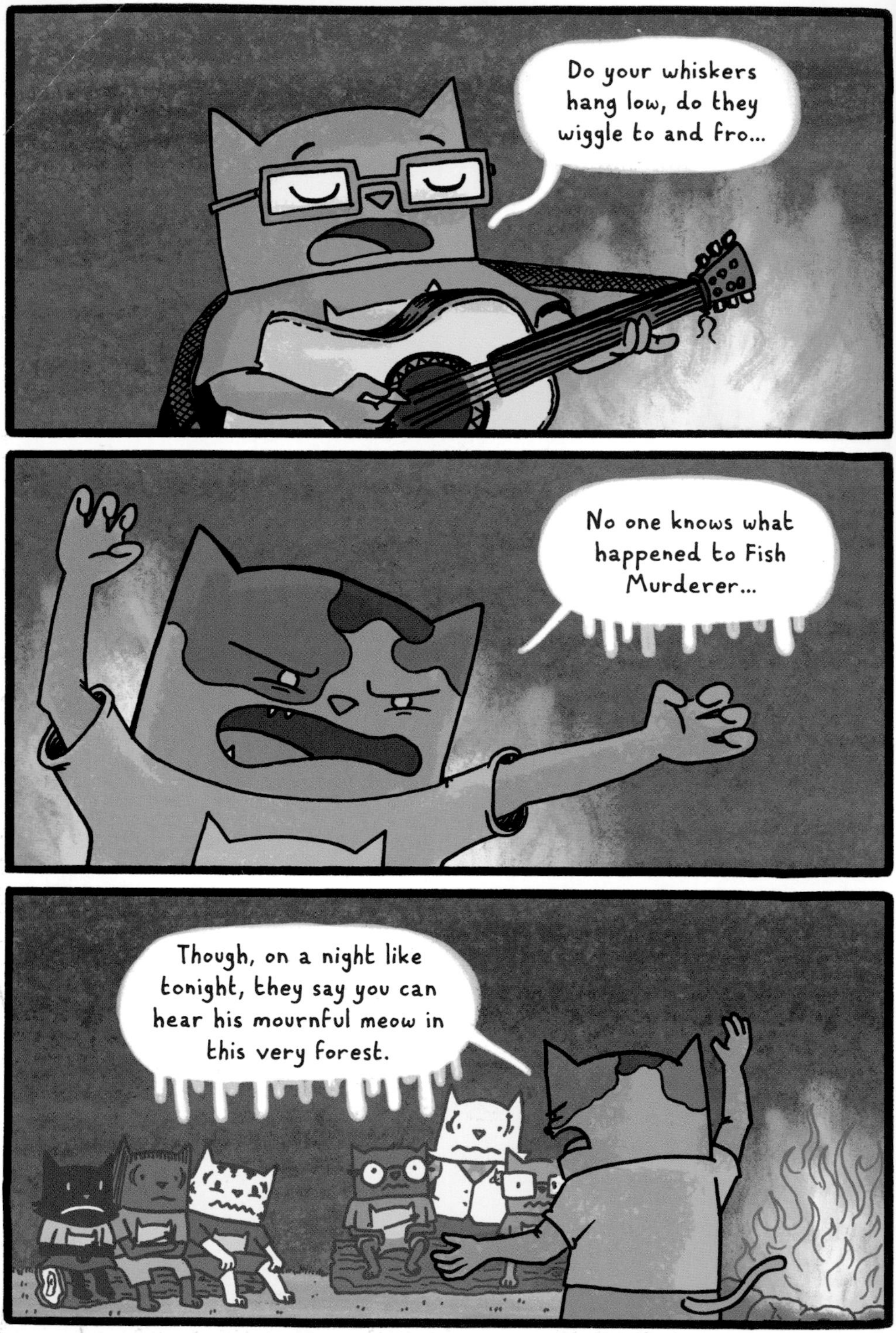
Do your whiskers hang low, do they wiggle to and fro...
No one knows what happened to Fish Murderer...
Though, on a night like tonight, they say you can hear his mournful meow in this very forest.

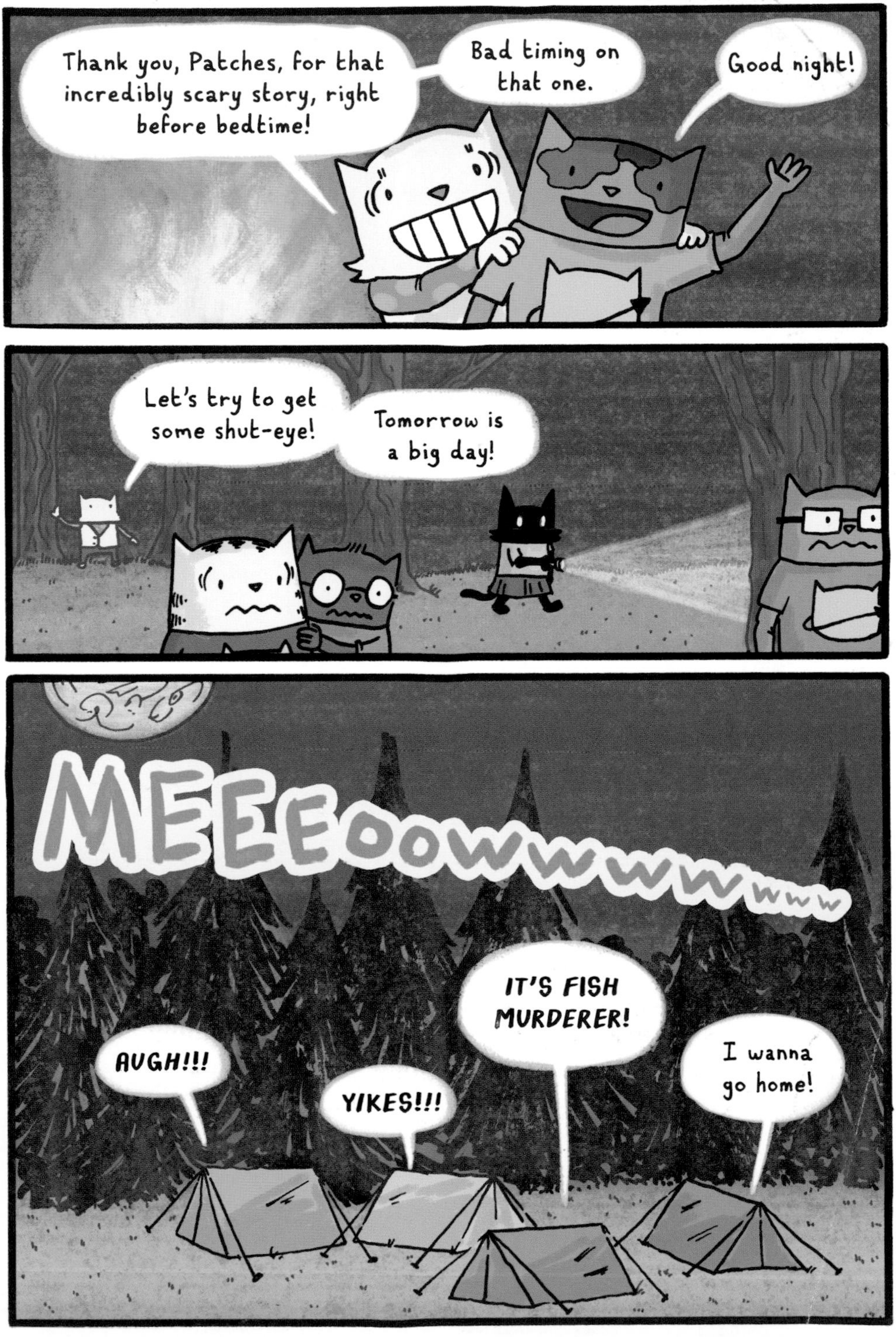
Thank you, Patches, for that incredibly scary story, right before bedtime!
Bad timing on that one.
Good night!
Let's try to get some shut-eye!
Tomorrow is a big day!
MEEEOOWWWWWwww
AUGH!!!
YIKES!!!
IT'S FISH MURDERER!
I wanna go home!

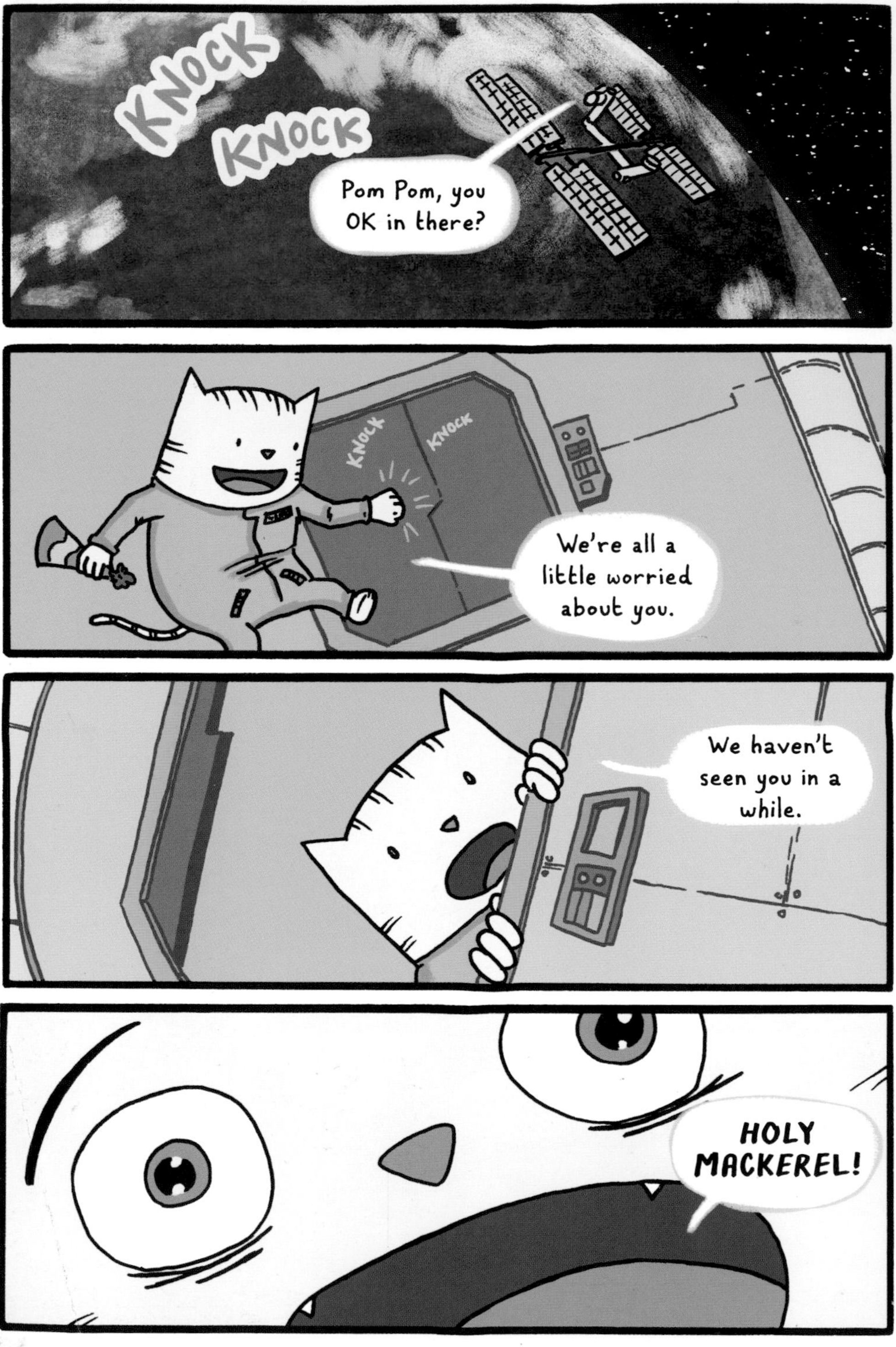
KNOCK
KNOCK
Pom Pom, you OK in there?
KNOCK
KNOCK
We're all a little worried about you.
We haven't seen you in a while.
HOLY MACKEREL!

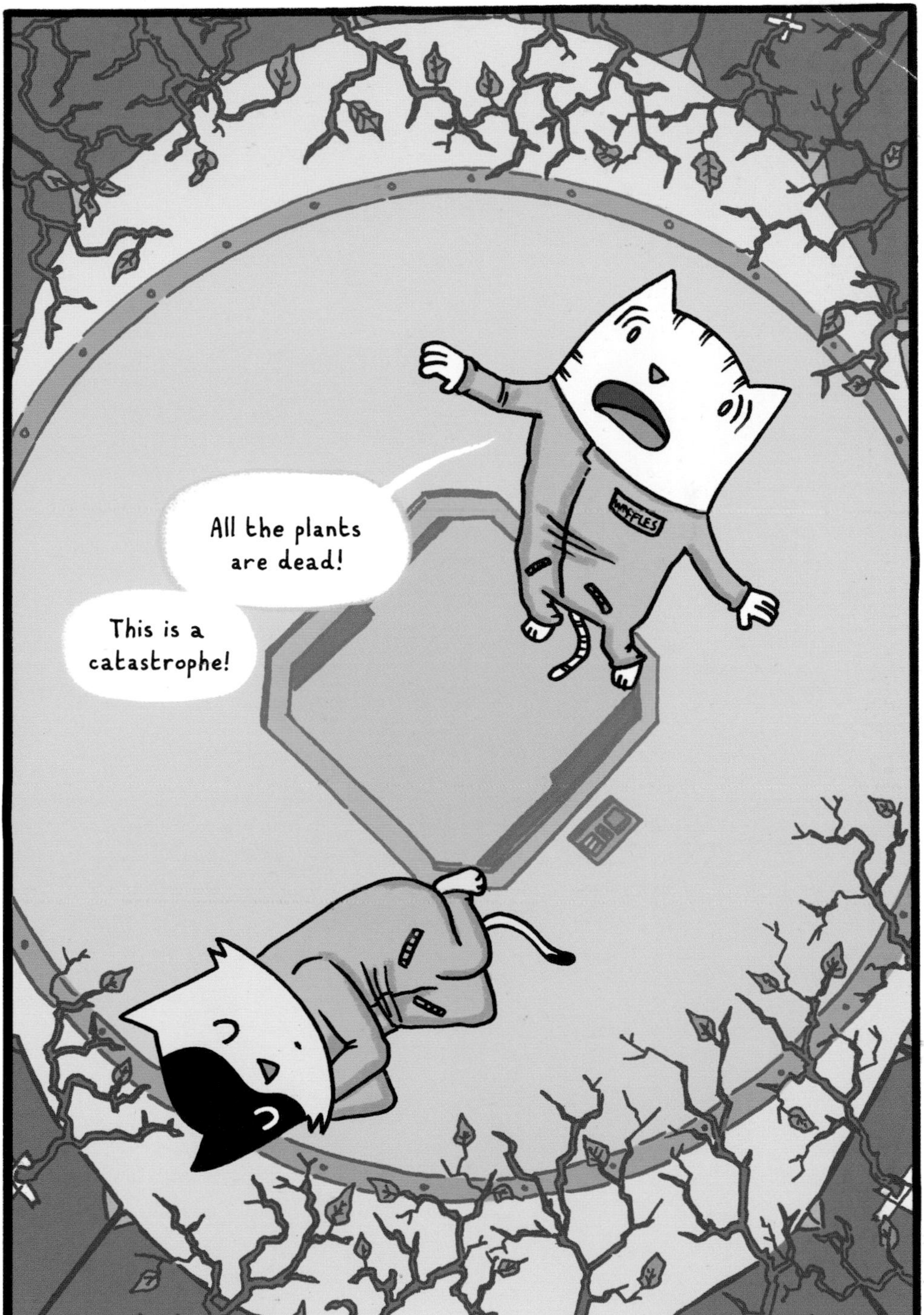
WAFFLES
All the plants are dead!
This is a catastrophe!

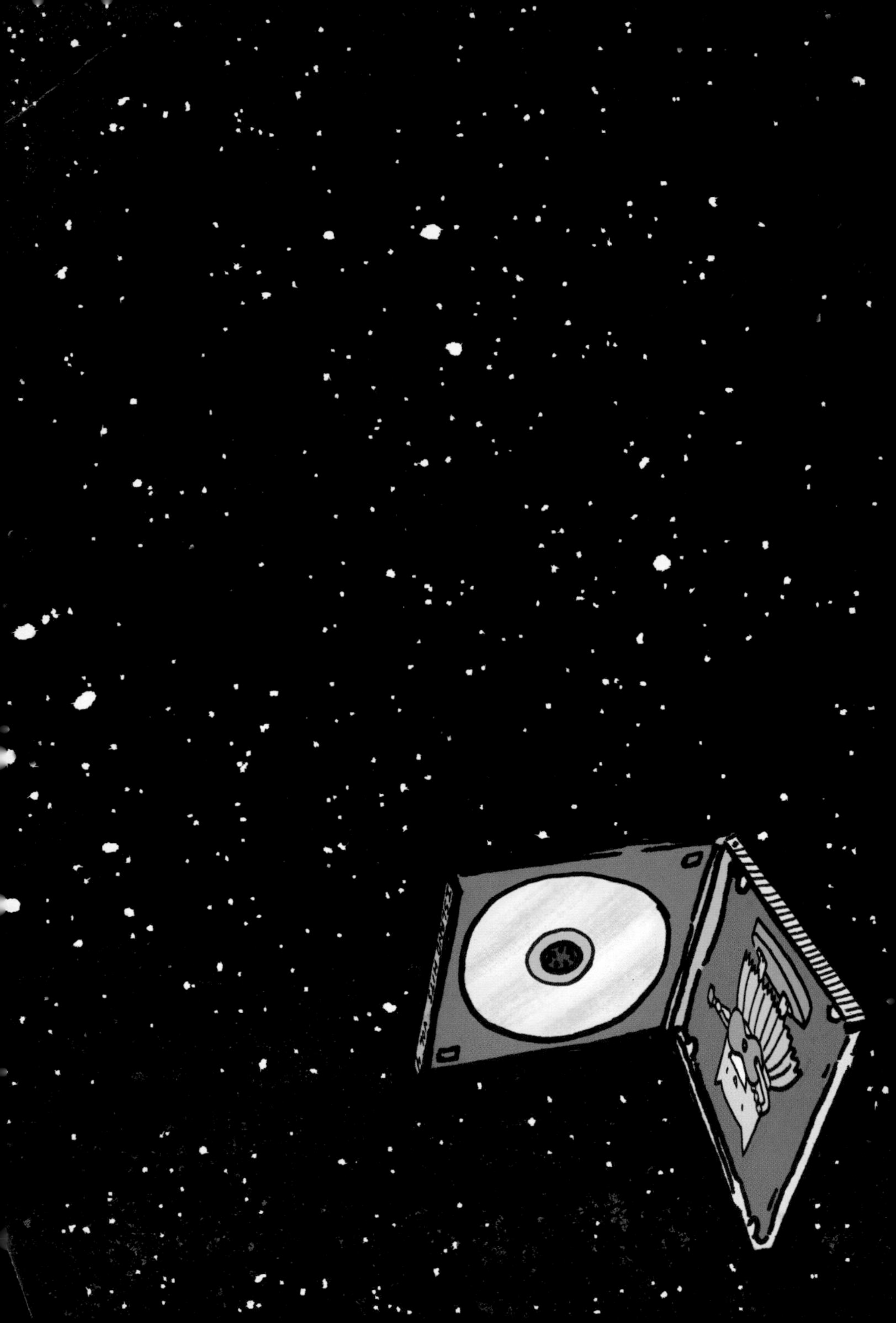

CHAPTER 5

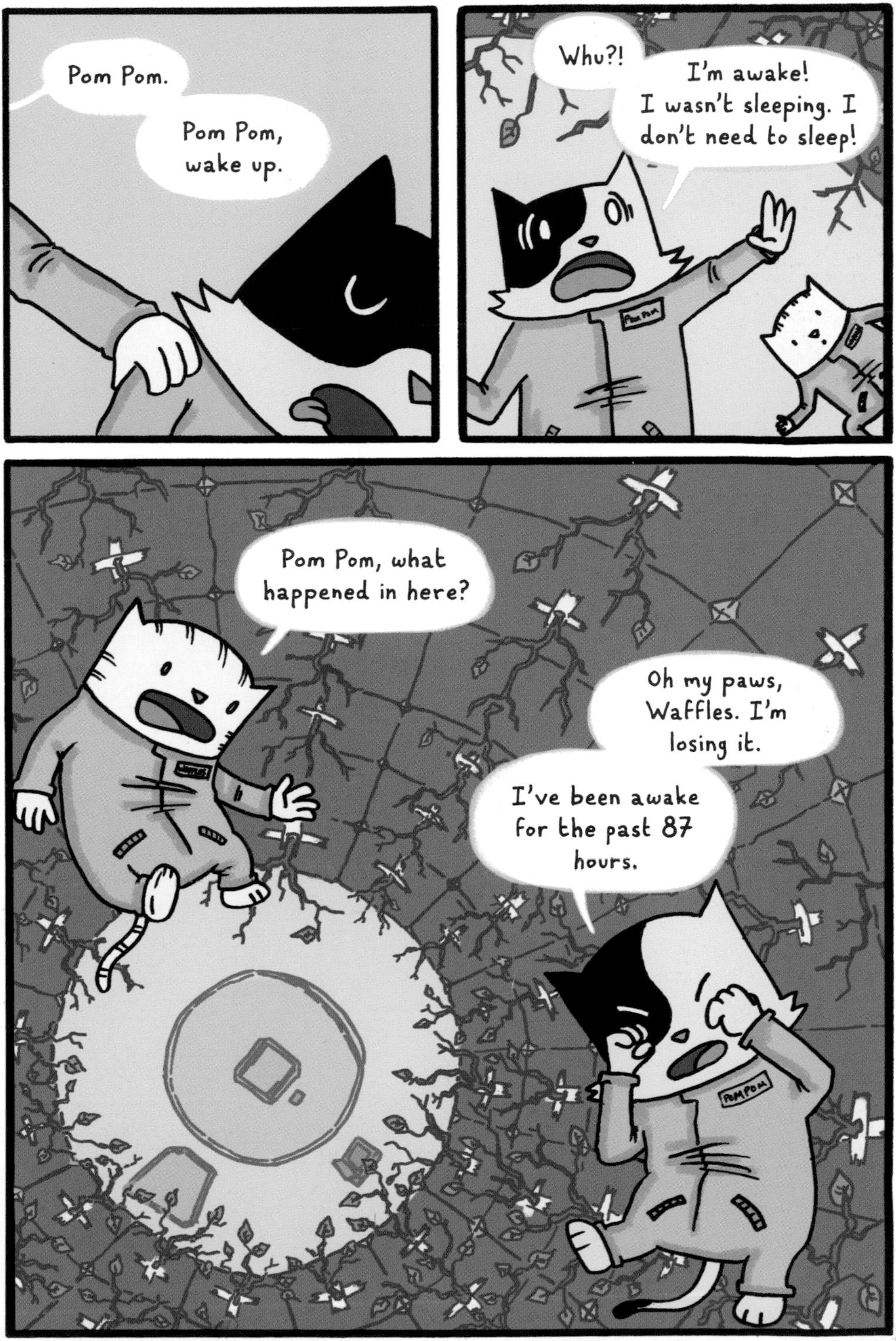
Pom Pom.
Pom Pom, wake up.
Whu?!
I'm awake! I wasn't sleeping. I don't need to sleep!
Pom Pom, what happened in here?
Oh my paws, Waffles. I'm losing it.
I've been awake for the past 87 hours.

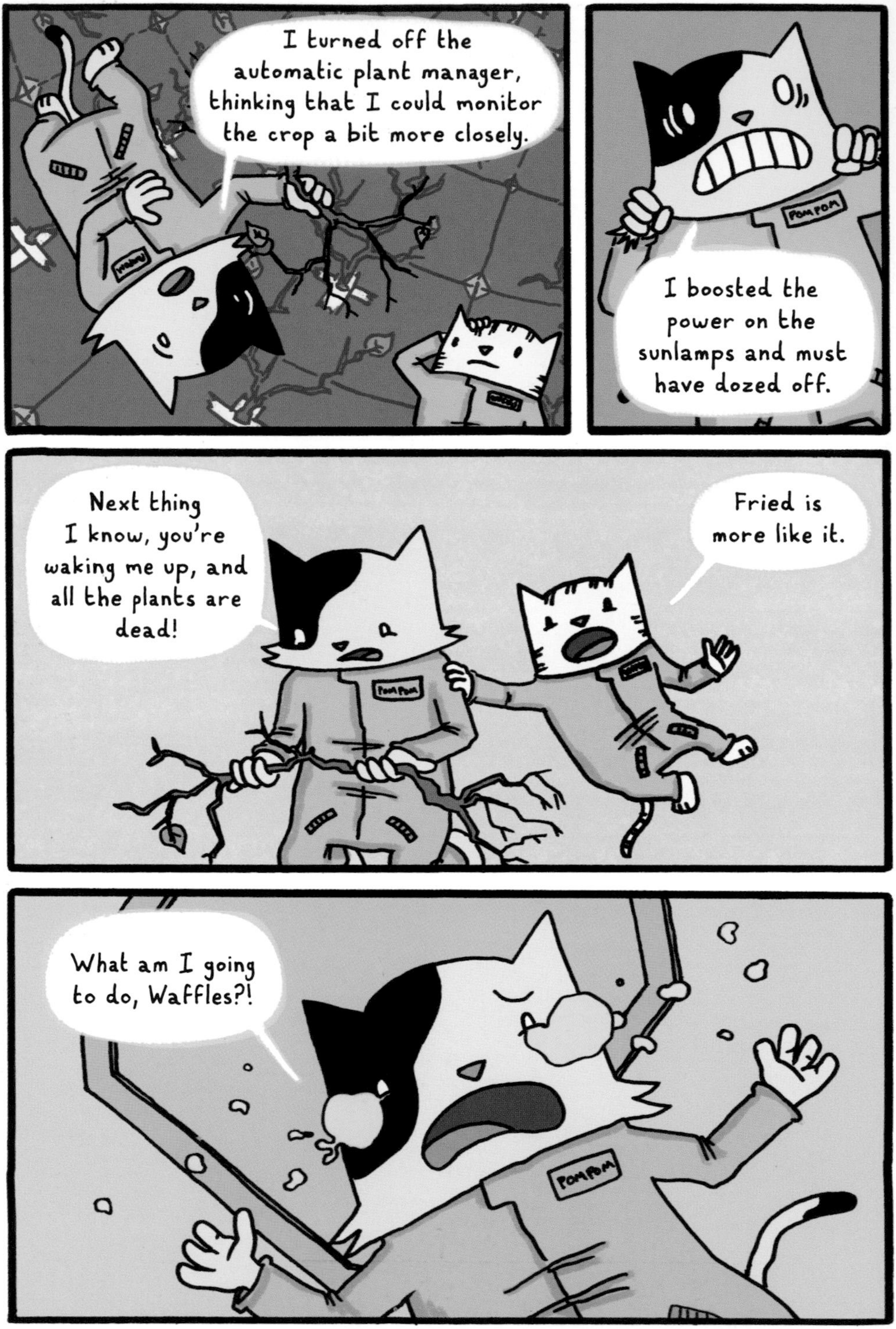
I turned off the automatic plant manager, thinking that I could monitor the crop a bit more closely.
I boosted the power on the sunlamps and must have dozed off.
Next thing I know, you're waking me up, and all the plants are dead!
Fried is more like it.
What am I going to do, Waffles?!

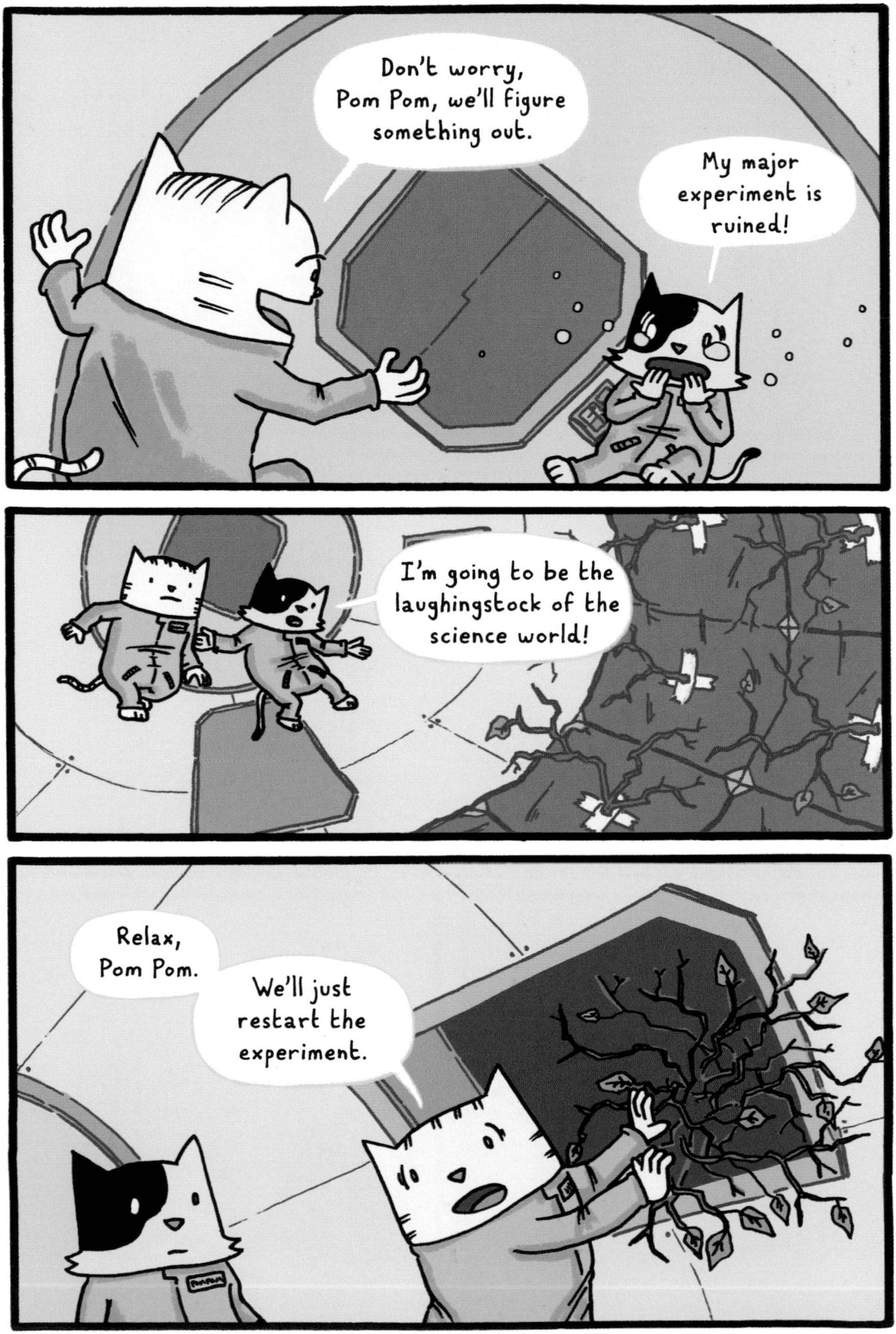
Don't worry, Pom Pom, we'll figure something out.
My major experiment is ruined!
I'm going to be the laughingstock of the science world!
Relax, Pom Pom.
We'll just restart the experiment.

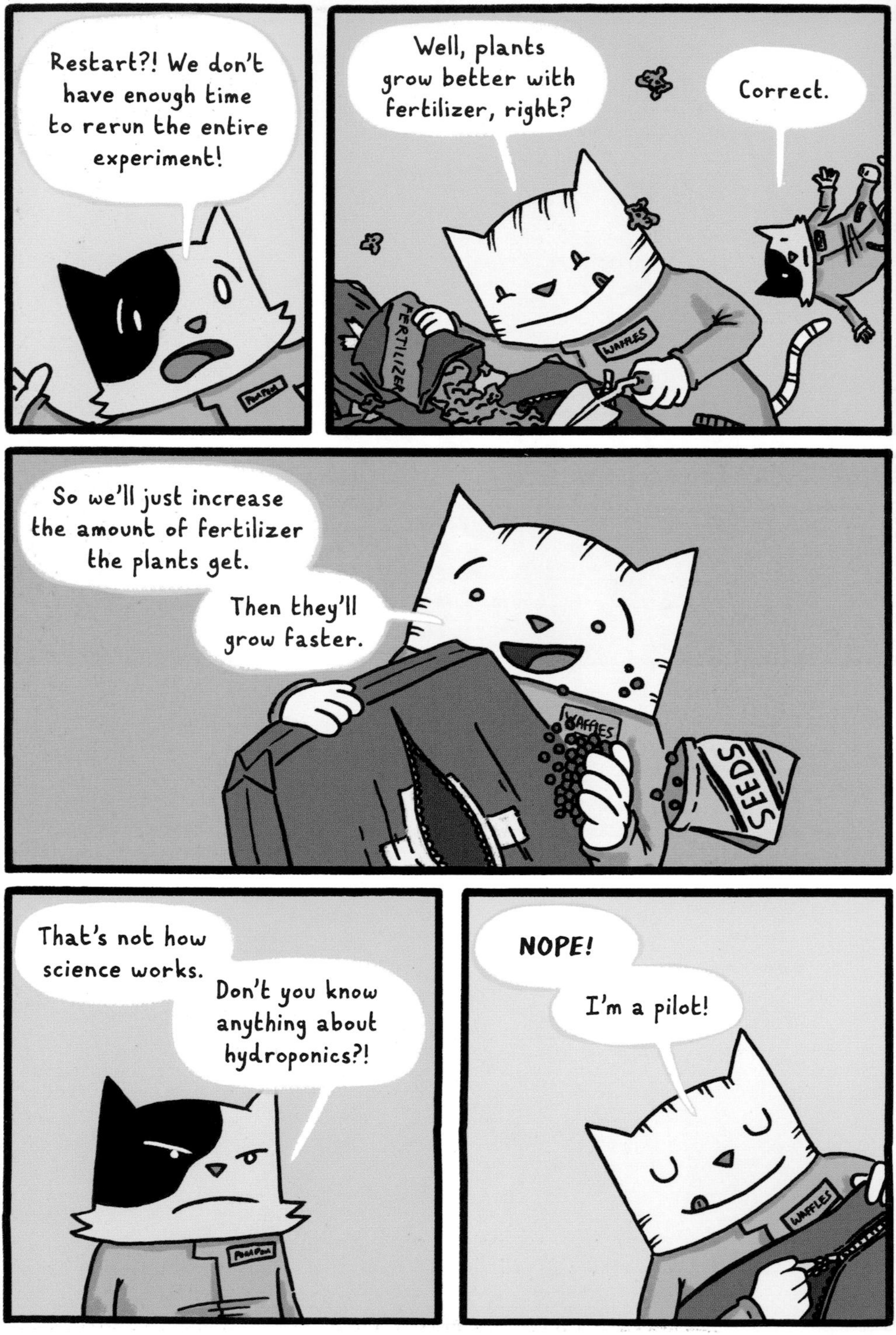
Restart?! We don't have enough time to rerun the entire experiment!
Well, plants grow better with fertilizer, right?
Correct.
FERTILIZER
WAFFLES
So we'll just increase the amount of fertilizer the plants get.
Then they'll grow faster.
WAFFLES
SEEDS
That's not how science works.
Don't you know anything about hydroponics?!
NOPE!
I'm a pilot!
WAFFLES

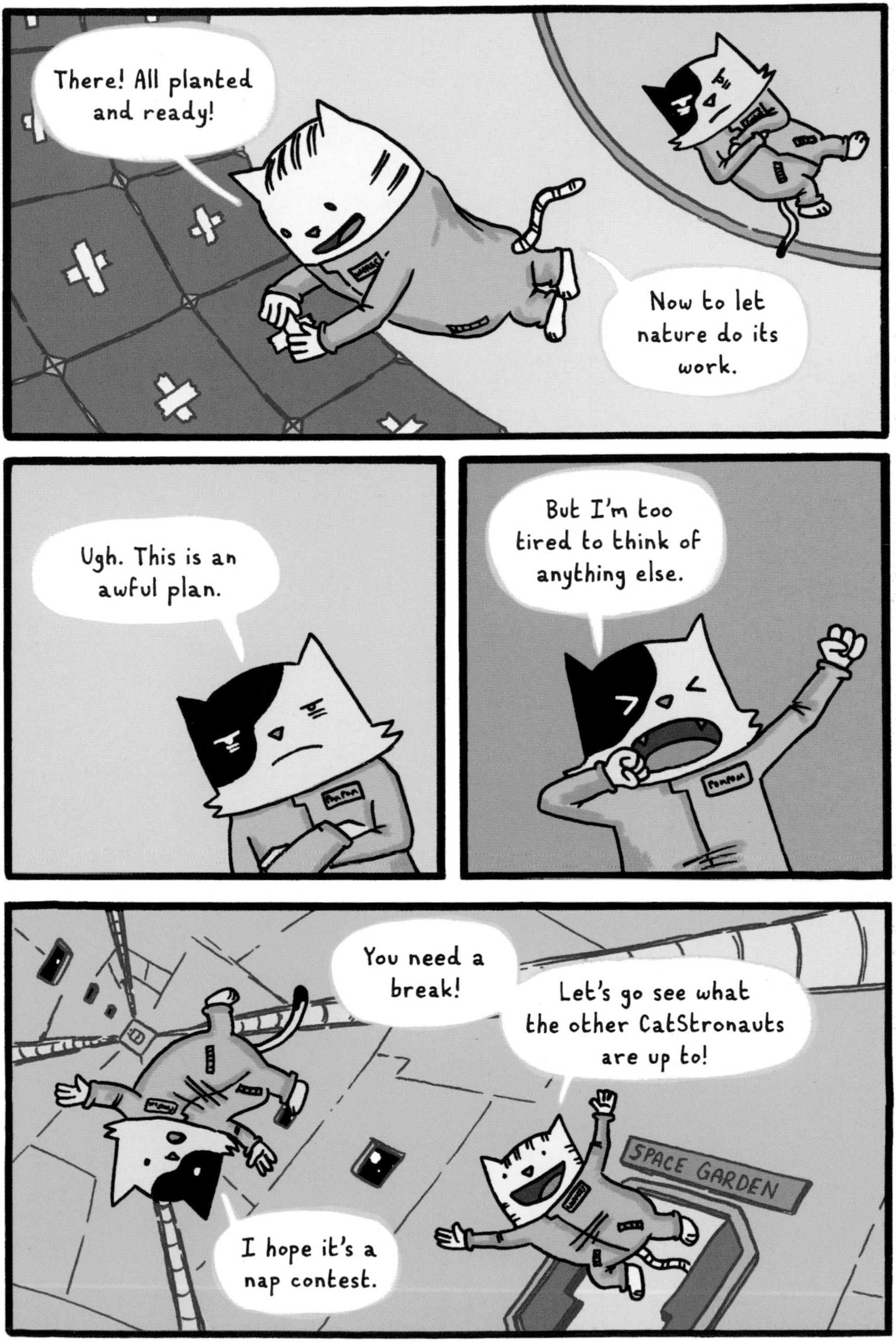
There! All planted and ready!
Now to let nature do its work.
Ugh. This is an awful plan.
But I'm too tired to think of anything else.
You need a break!
Let's go see what the other CatStronauts are up to!
SPACE GARDEN
I hope it's a nap contest.

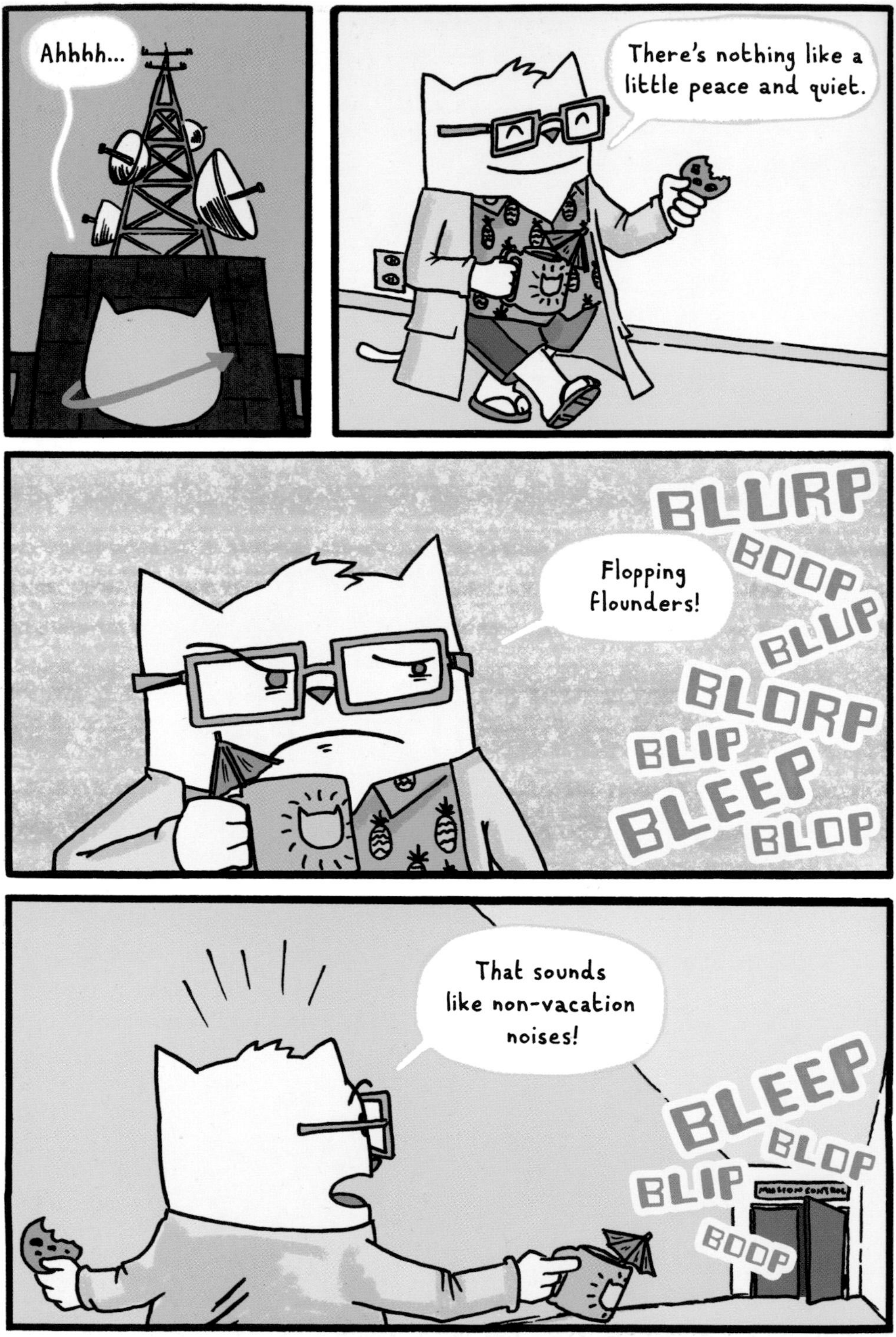
Ahhhh...
There's nothing like a little peace and quiet.
BLURP
BOOP
BLUP
BLORP
BLIP
BLEEP
BLOP
Flopping flounders!
That sounds like non-vacation noises!
BLEEP
BLOP
BLIP
BOOP

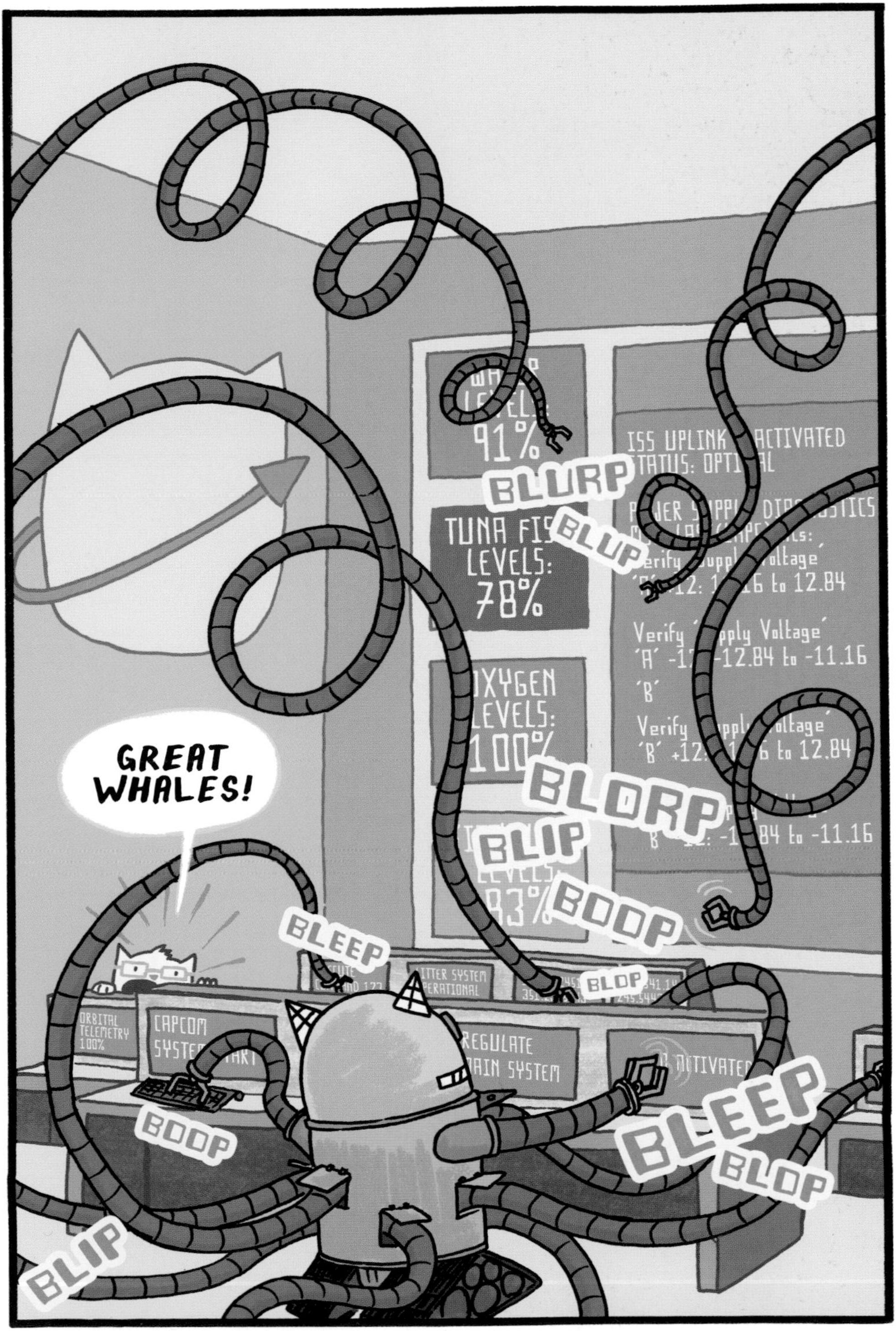

91%
BLURP
ISS UPLINK
ACTIVATED
TUNA FIS
BLUP
LEVELS:
78%
Verify
Verify
OXYGEN
LEVELS:
GREAT WHALES!
BLORP
BLIP
BOOP
BLEEP
BLOP
ORBITAL TELEMETRY 100%
CAPCOM
REGULATE
BOOP
BLEEP
BLOP
BLIP

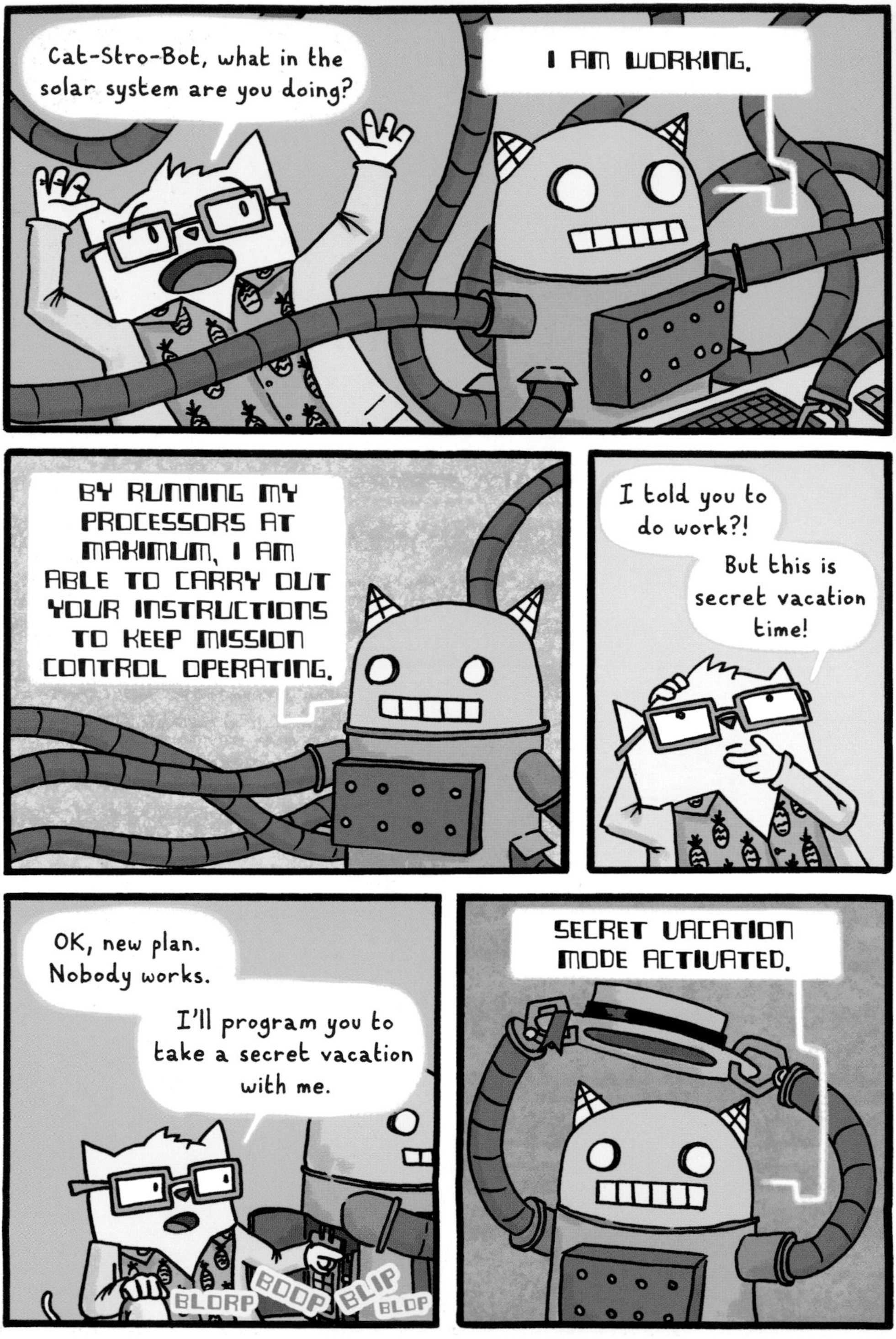
Cat-Stro-Bot, what in the solar system are you doing?
I AM WORKING.
BY RUNNING MY PROCESSORS AT MAXIMUM, I AM ABLE TO CARRY OUT YOUR INSTRUCTIONS TO KEEP MISSION CONTROL OPERATING.
I told you to do work?!
But this is secret vacation time!
OK, new plan. Nobody works.
I'll program you to take a secret vacation with me.
BLORP
BOOP
BLIP
BLOP
SECRET VACATION MODE ACTIVATED.

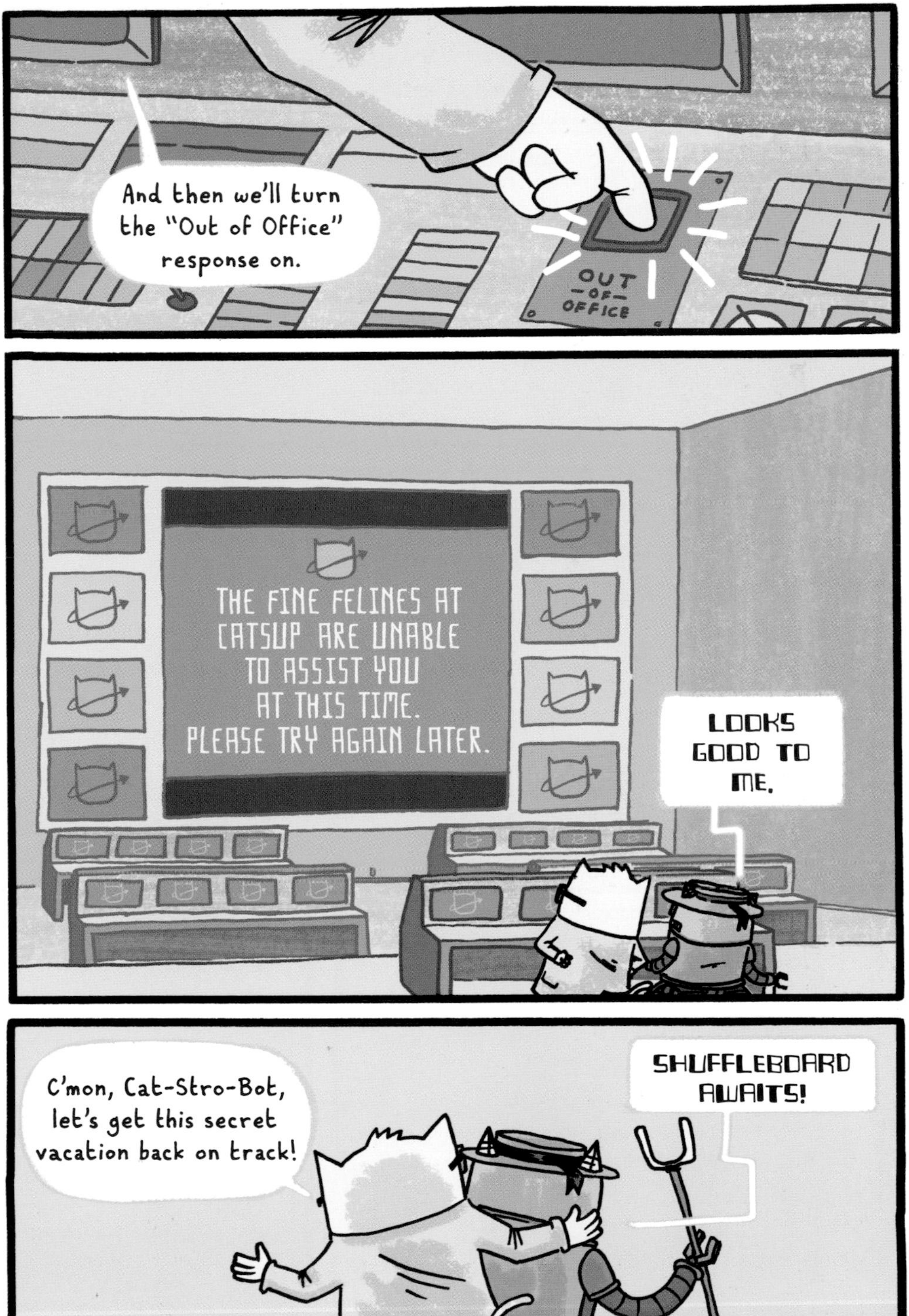
And then we'll turn the "Out of Office" response on.
OUT -OF- OFFICE
THE FINE FELINES AT CATSUP ARE UNABLE TO ASSIST YOU AT THIS TIME. PLEASE TRY AGAIN LATER.
LOOKS GOOD TO ME.
C'mon, Cat-Stro-Bot, let's get this secret vacation back on track!
SHUFFLEBOARD AWAITS!

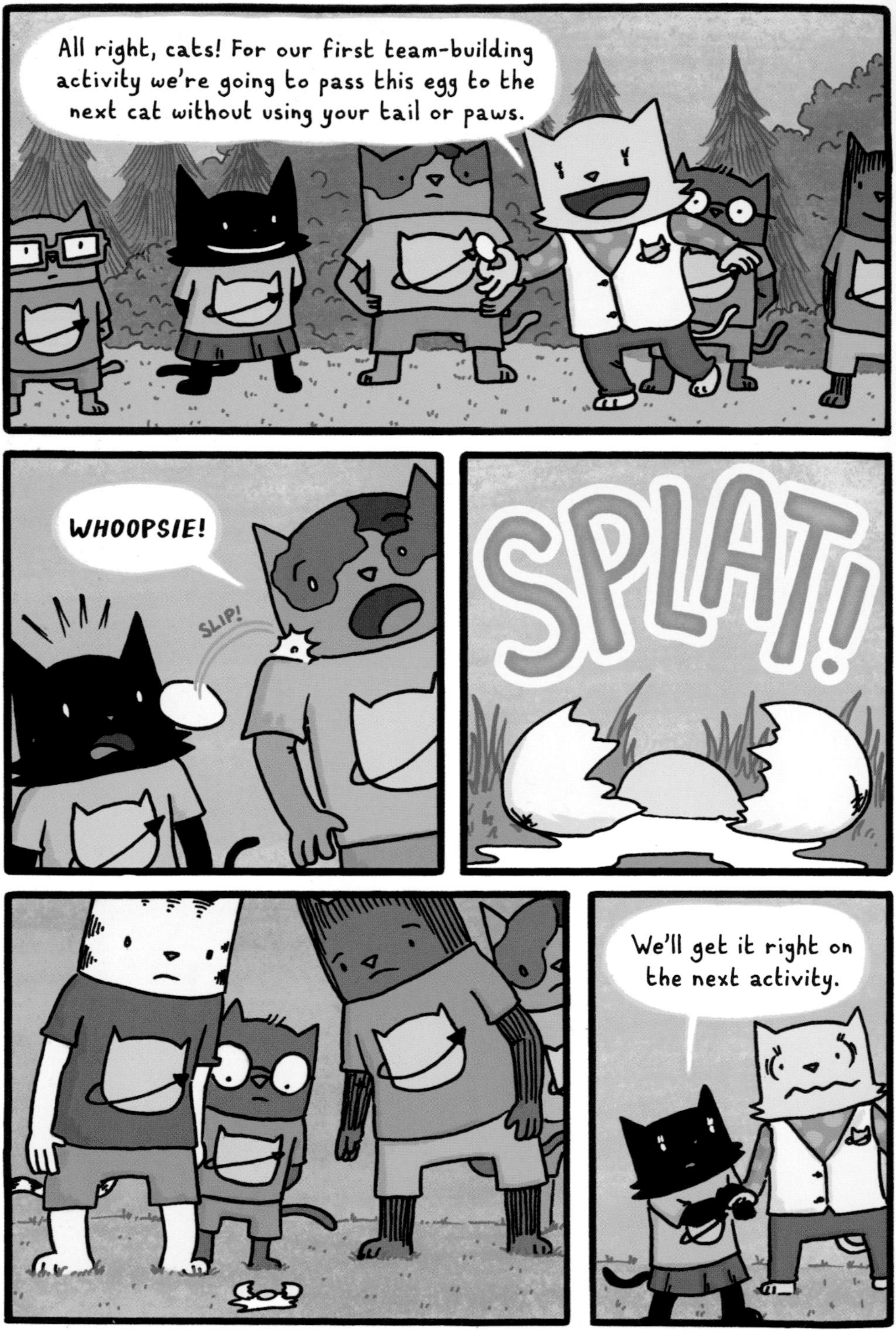
All right, cats! For our first team-building activity we're going to pass this egg to the next cat without using your tail or paws.
WHOOPSIE!
SLIP!
SPLAT!
We'll get it right on the next activity.

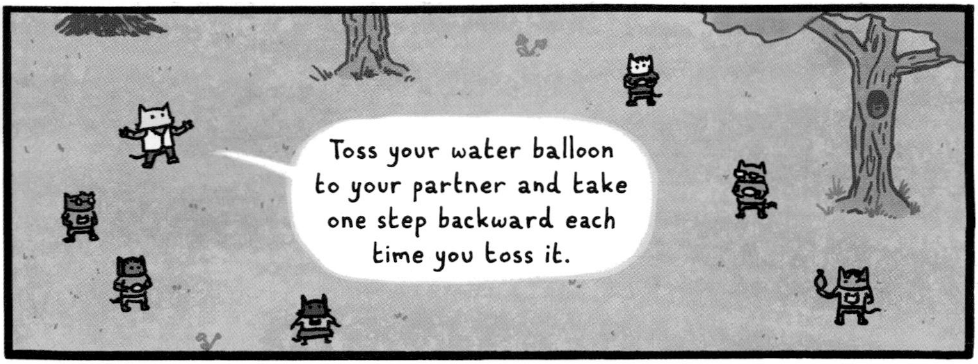
Toss your water balloon to your partner and take one step backward each time you toss it.

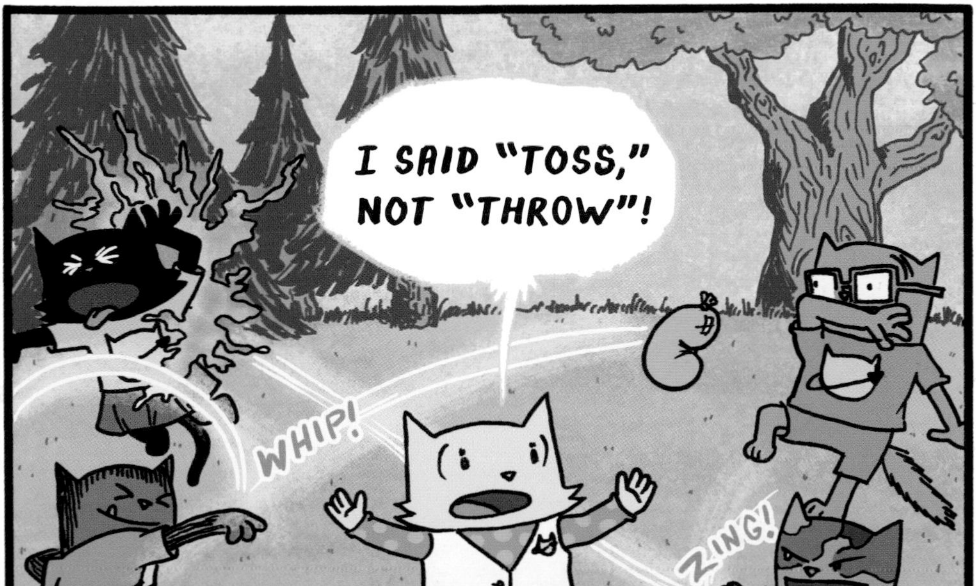
I SAID "TOSS," NOT "THROW"!
WHIP!
ZING!

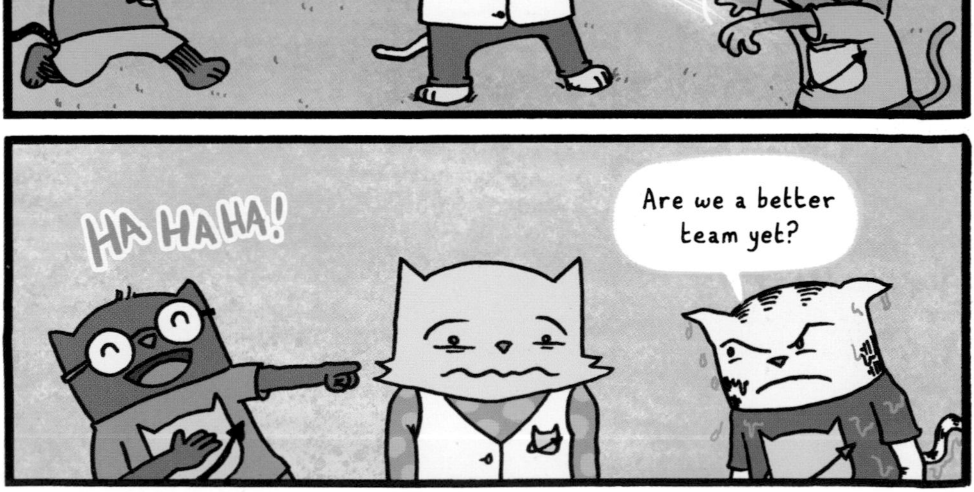
HA HA HA!
Are we a better team yet?

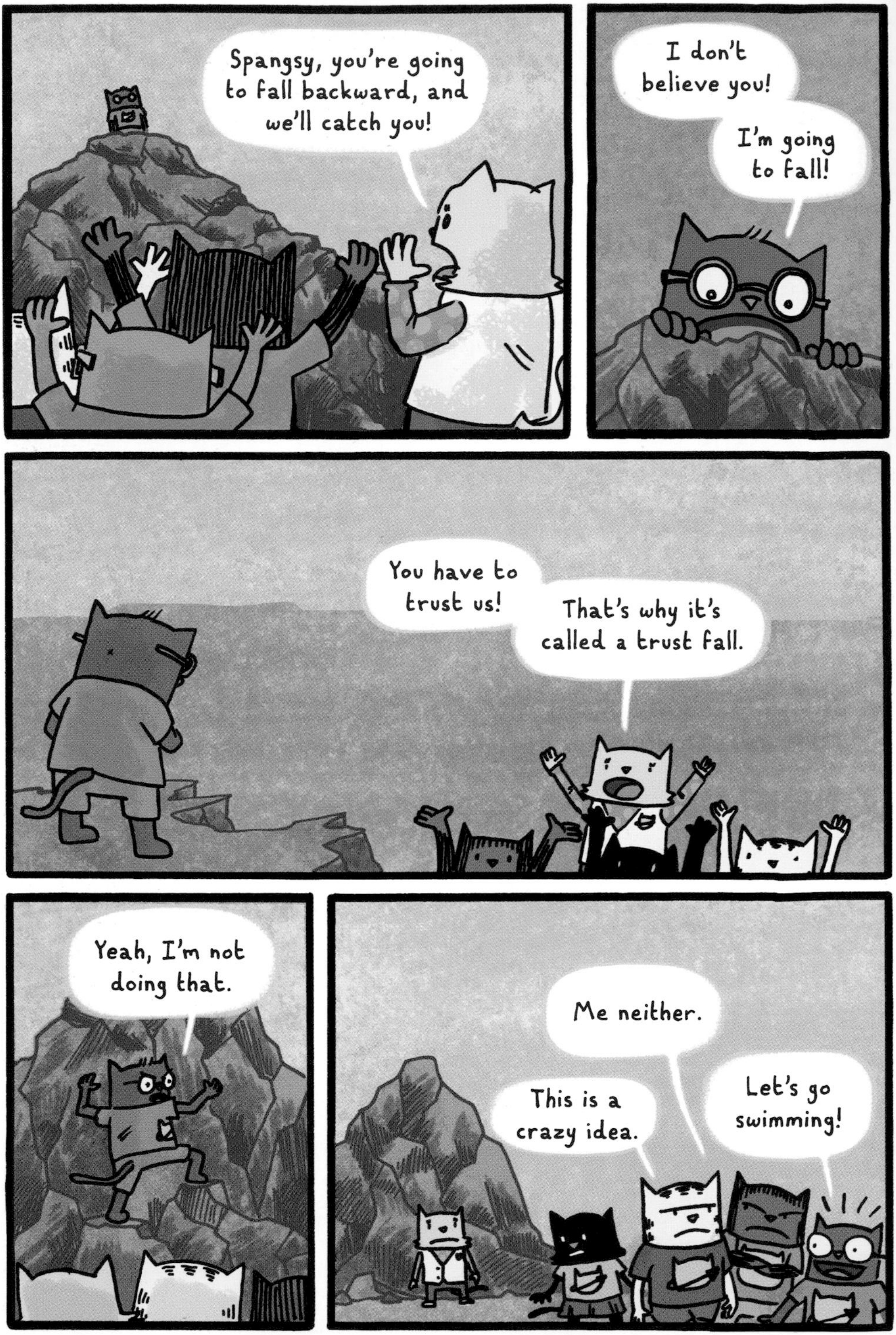
Spangsy, you're going to fall backward, and we'll catch you!
I don't believe you!
I'm going to fall!
You have to trust us!
That's why it's called a trust fall.
Yeah, I'm not doing that.
Me neither.
This is a crazy idea.
Let's go swimming!

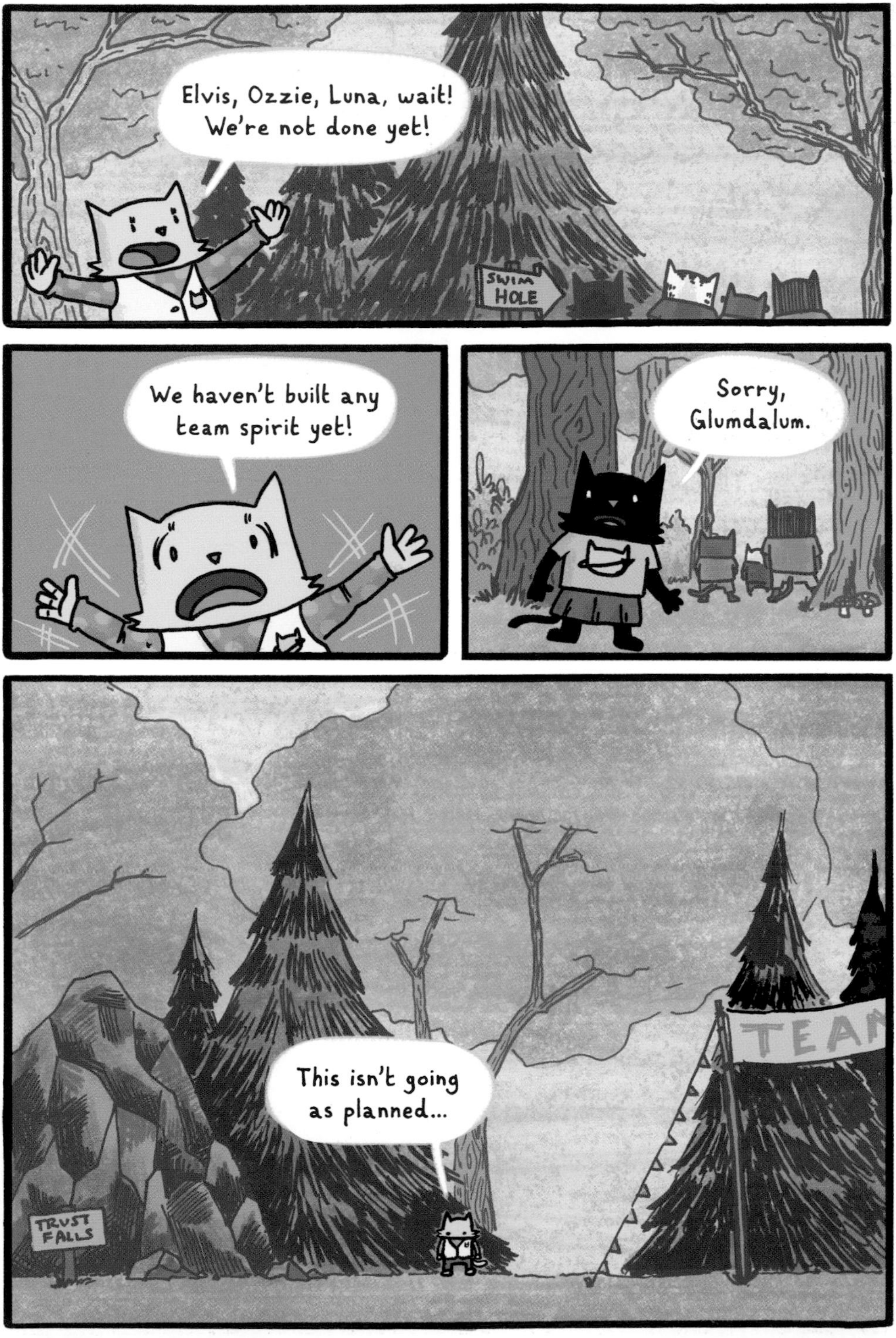
Elvis, Ozzie, Luna, wait! We're not done yet!
SWIM HOLE
We haven't built any team spirit yet!
Sorry, Glumdalum.
TRUST FALLS
TEAM
This isn't going as planned...

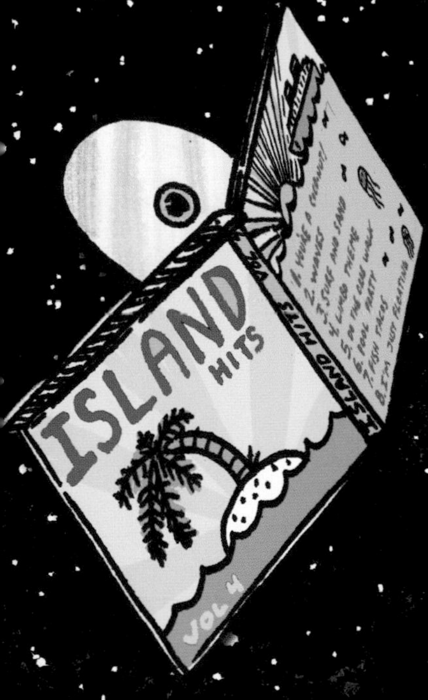
ISLAND
HITS
VOL 4

CHAPTER 6

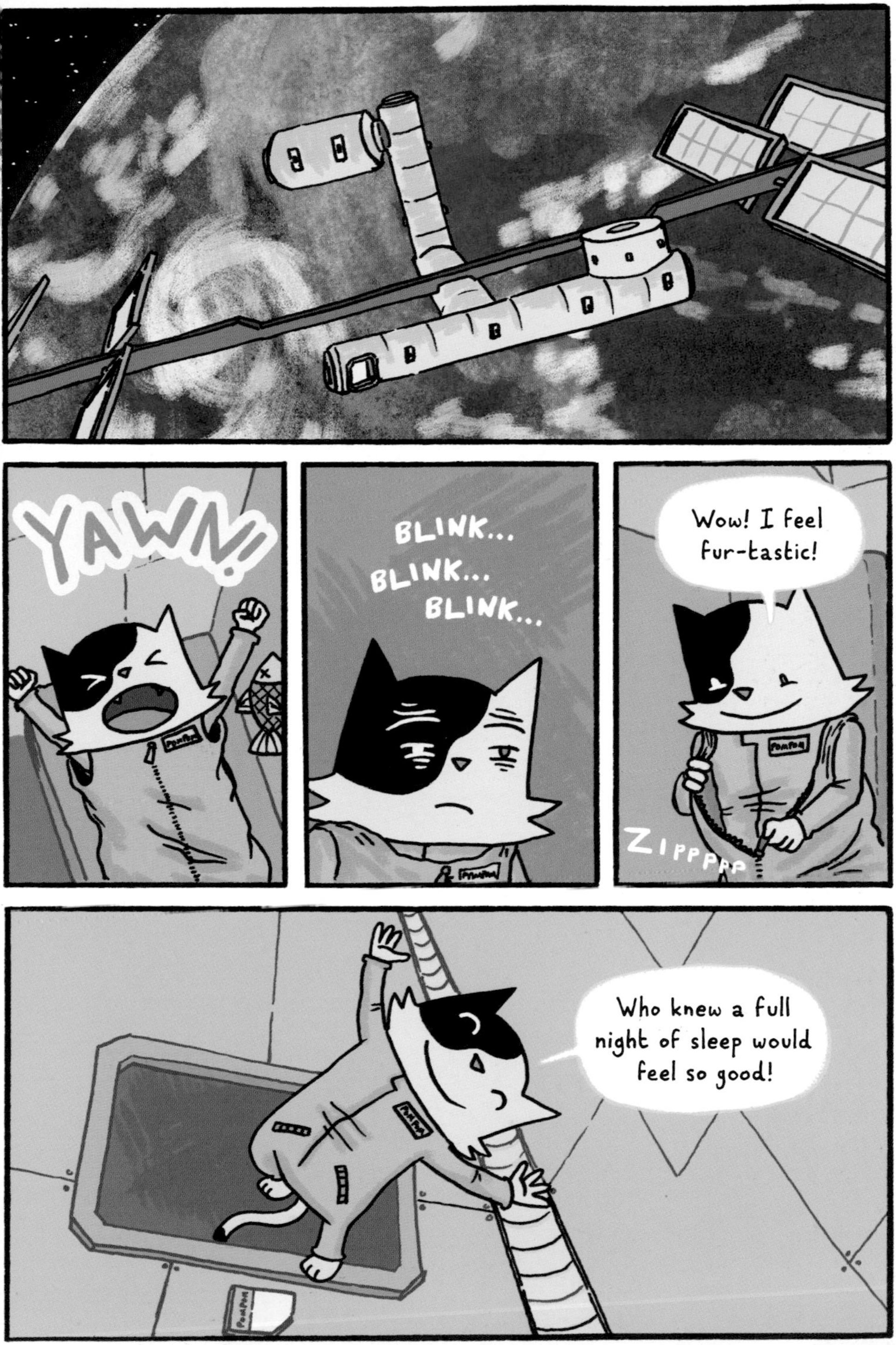
YAWN!
BLINK...
BLINK...
BLINK...
Wow! I feel fur-tastic!
ZIPPPPP
Who knew a full night of sleep would feel so good!

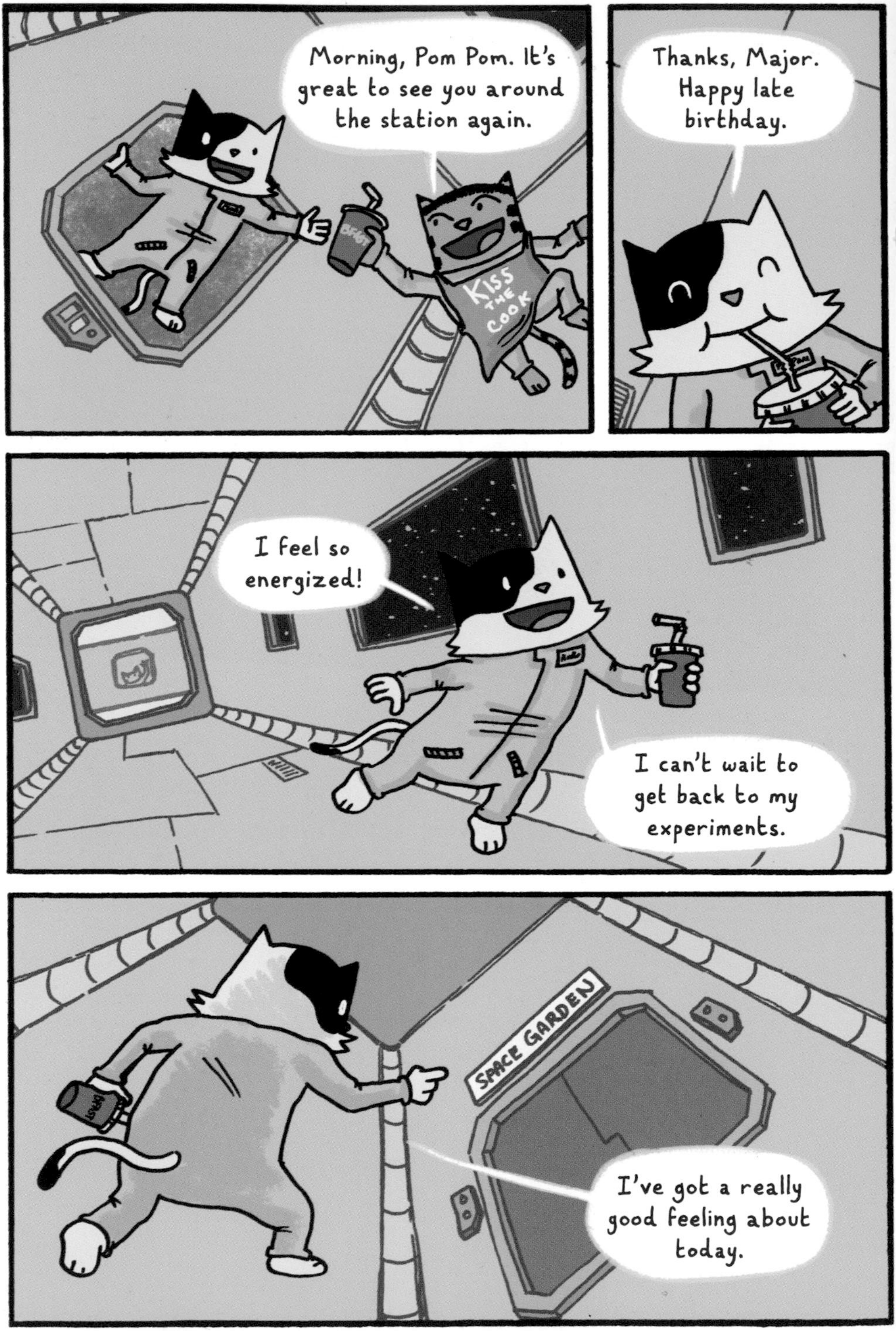
Morning, Pom Pom. It's great to see you around the station again.
KISS THE COOK
Thanks, Major. Happy late birthday.
I feel so energized!
I can't wait to get back to my experiments.
SPACE GARDEN
I've got a really good feeling about today.

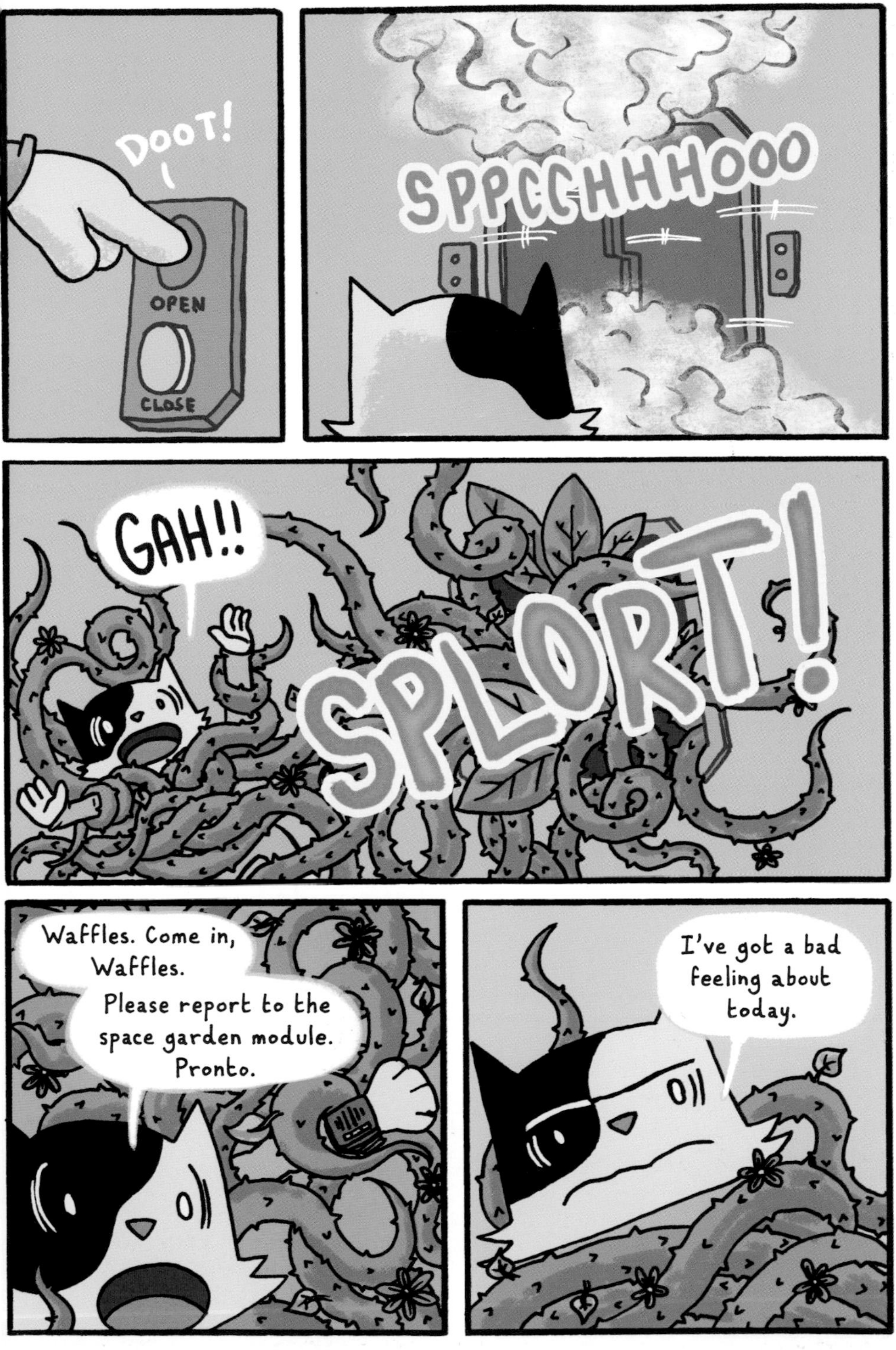
DOOT!
OPEN
CLOSE
SPPCCHHHOOO
GAH!!
SPLORT!
Waffles. Come in, Waffles.
Please report to the space garden module. Pronto.
I've got a bad feeling about today.

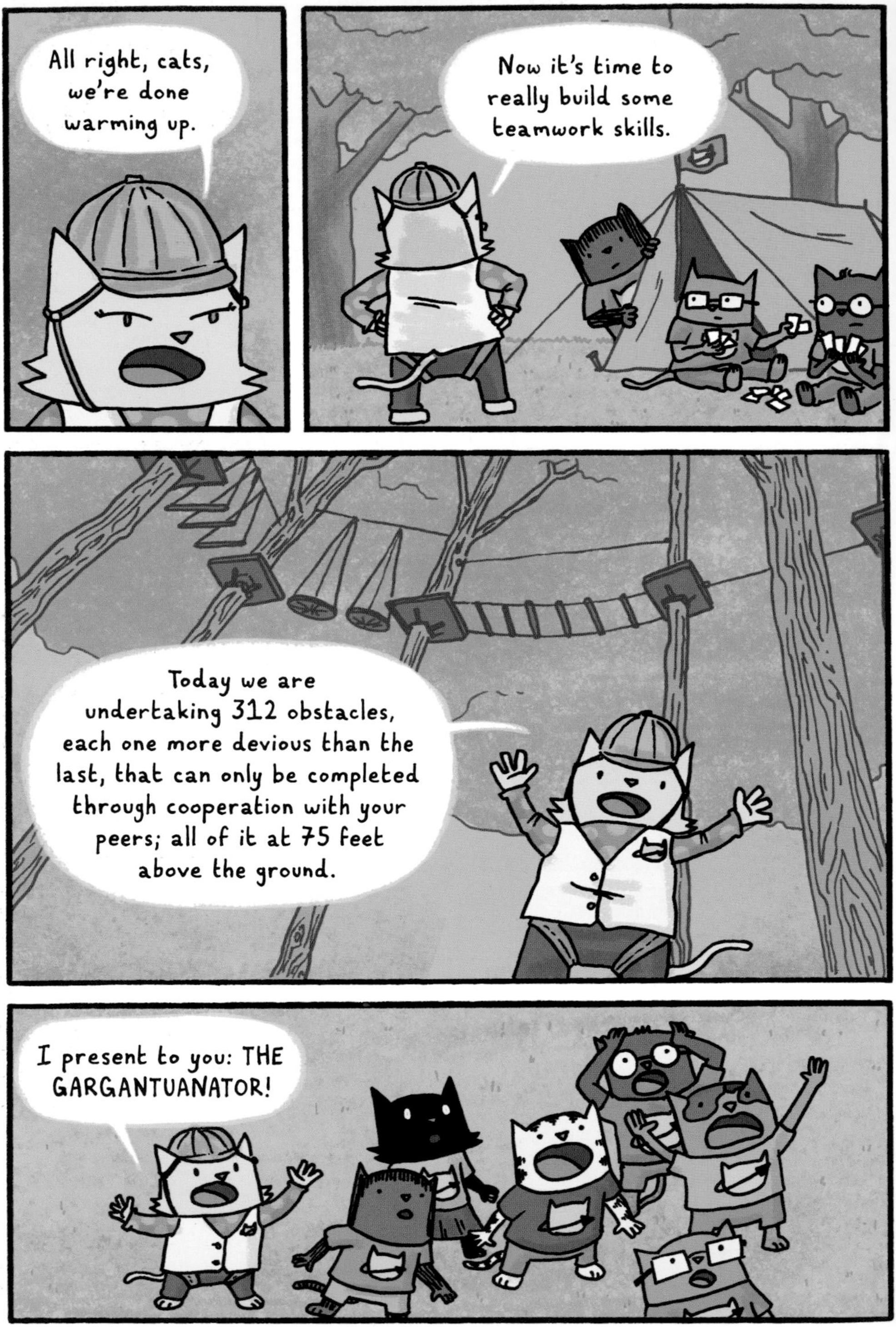
All right, cats, we're done warming up.
Now it's time to really build some teamwork skills.
Today we are undertaking 312 obstacles, each one more devious than the last, that can only be completed through cooperation with your peers; all of it at 75 feet above the ground.
I present to you: THE GARGANTUANATOR!

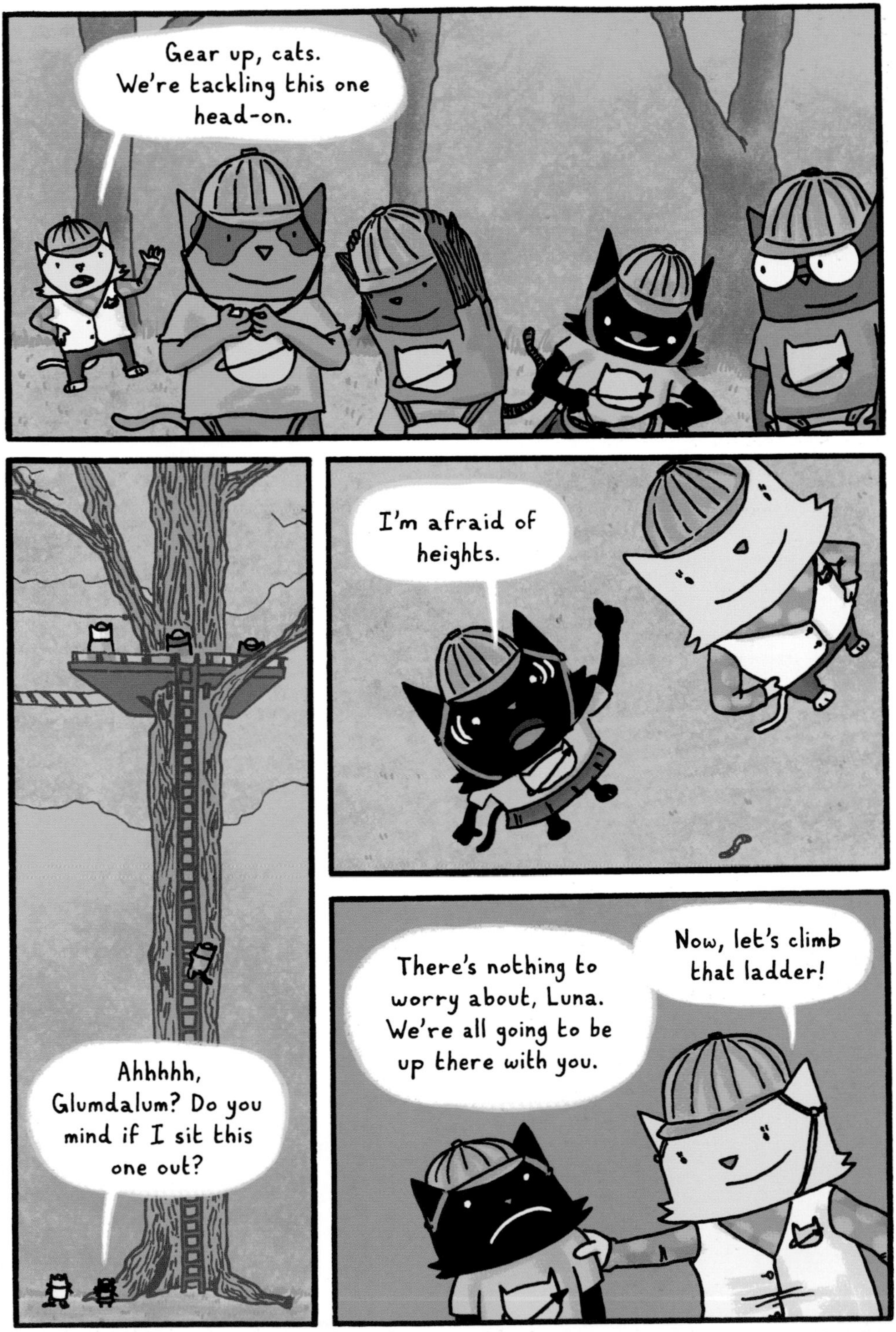
Gear up, cats. We're tackling this one head-on.
Ahhhhh, Glumdalum? Do you mind if I sit this one out?
I'm afraid of heights.
There's nothing to worry about, Luna. We're all going to be up there with you.
Now, let's climb that ladder!

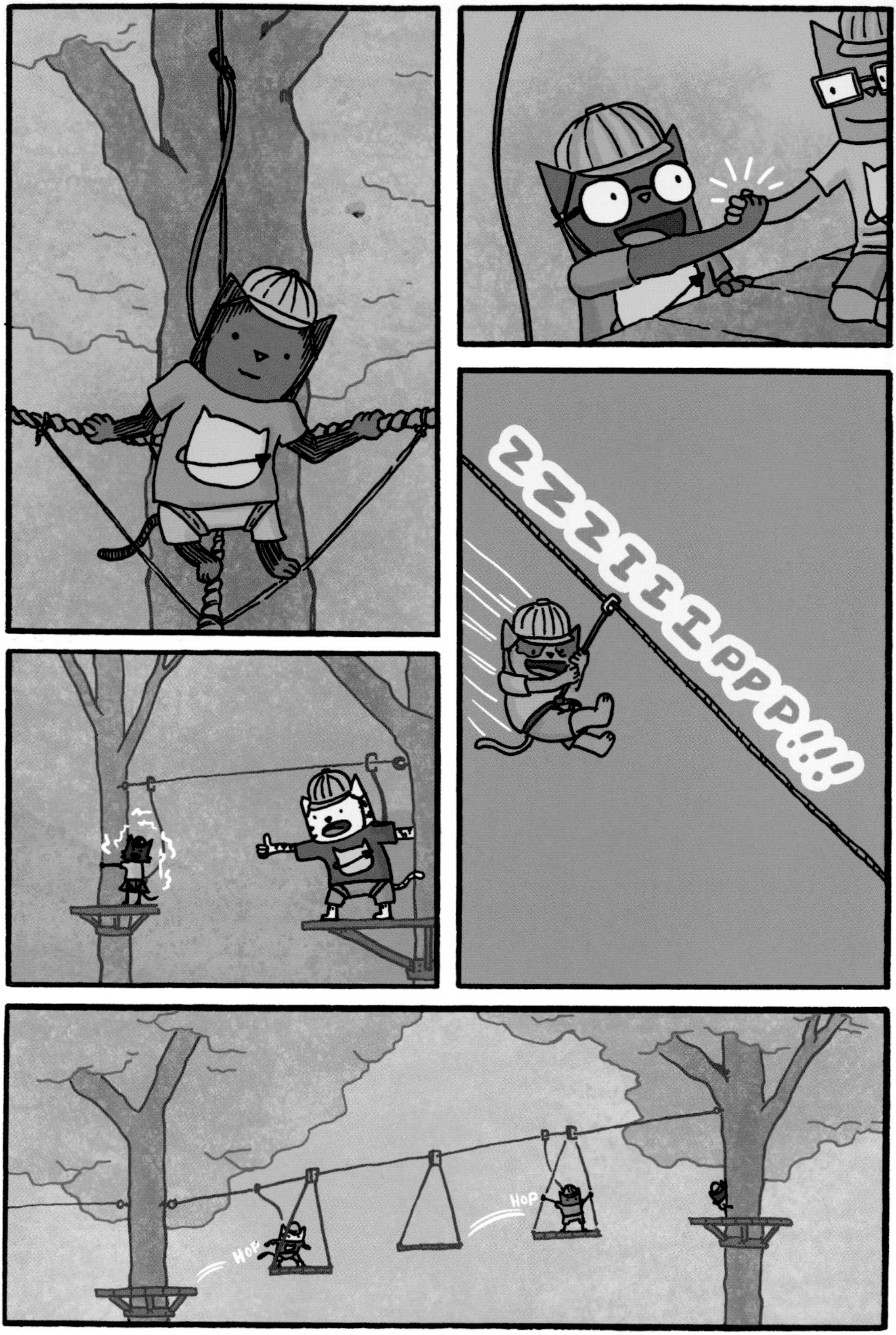
ZZZIIIPPP!!!
HOP
HOP

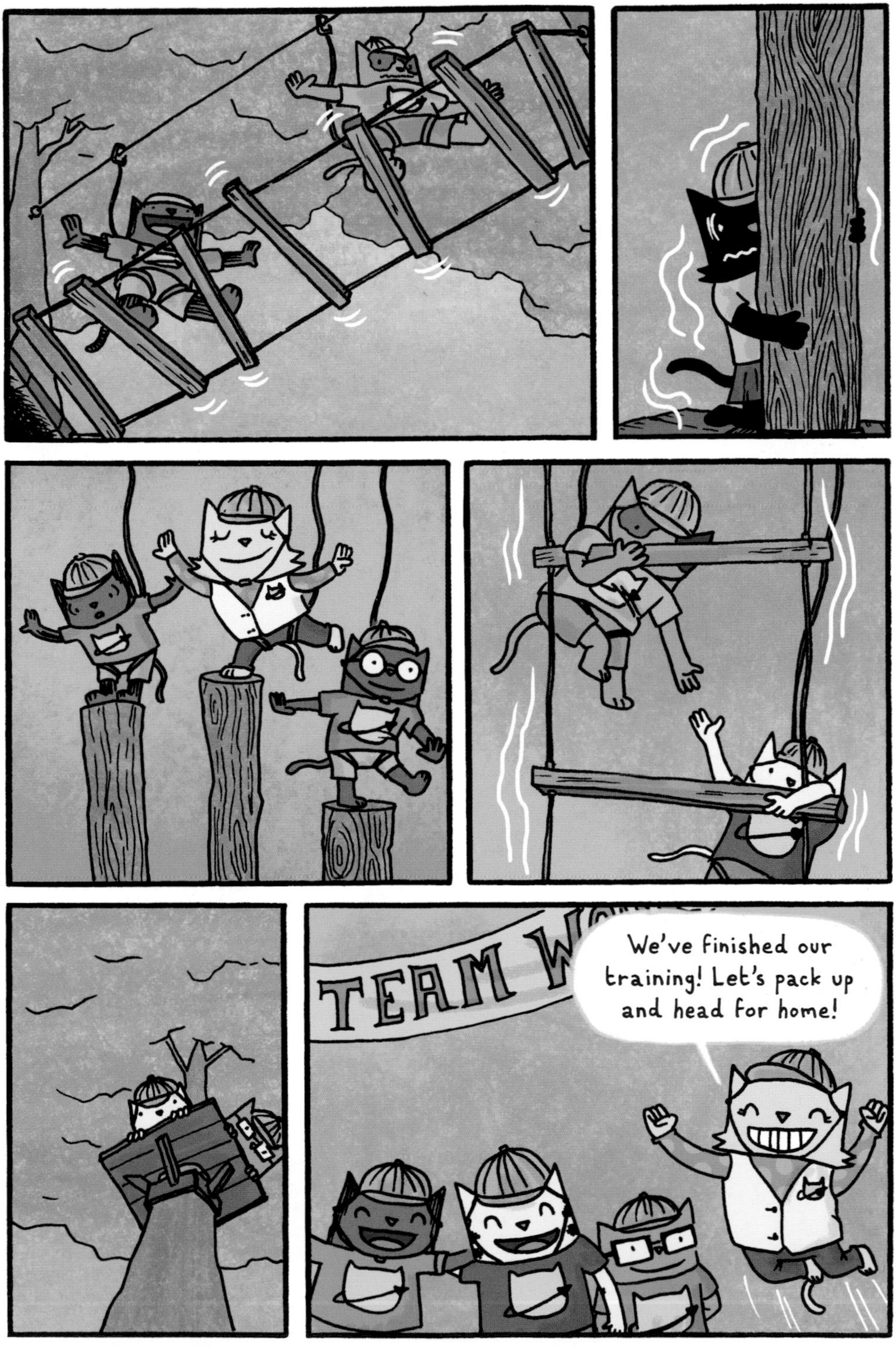
TEAM W
We've finished our training! Let's pack up and head for home!

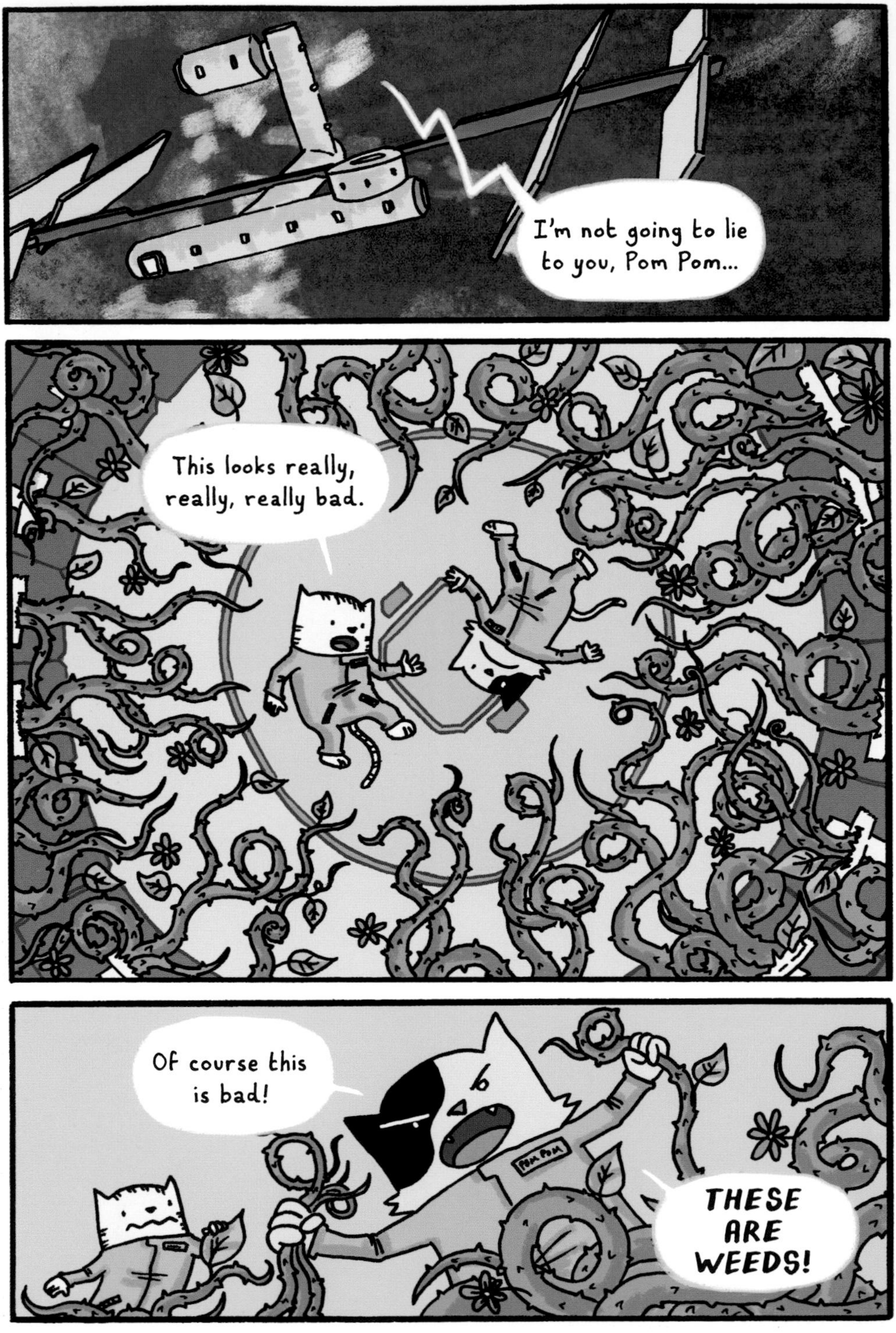
I'm not going to lie to you, Pom Pom...
This looks really, really, really bad.
Of course this is bad!
THESE ARE WEEDS!
POM POM

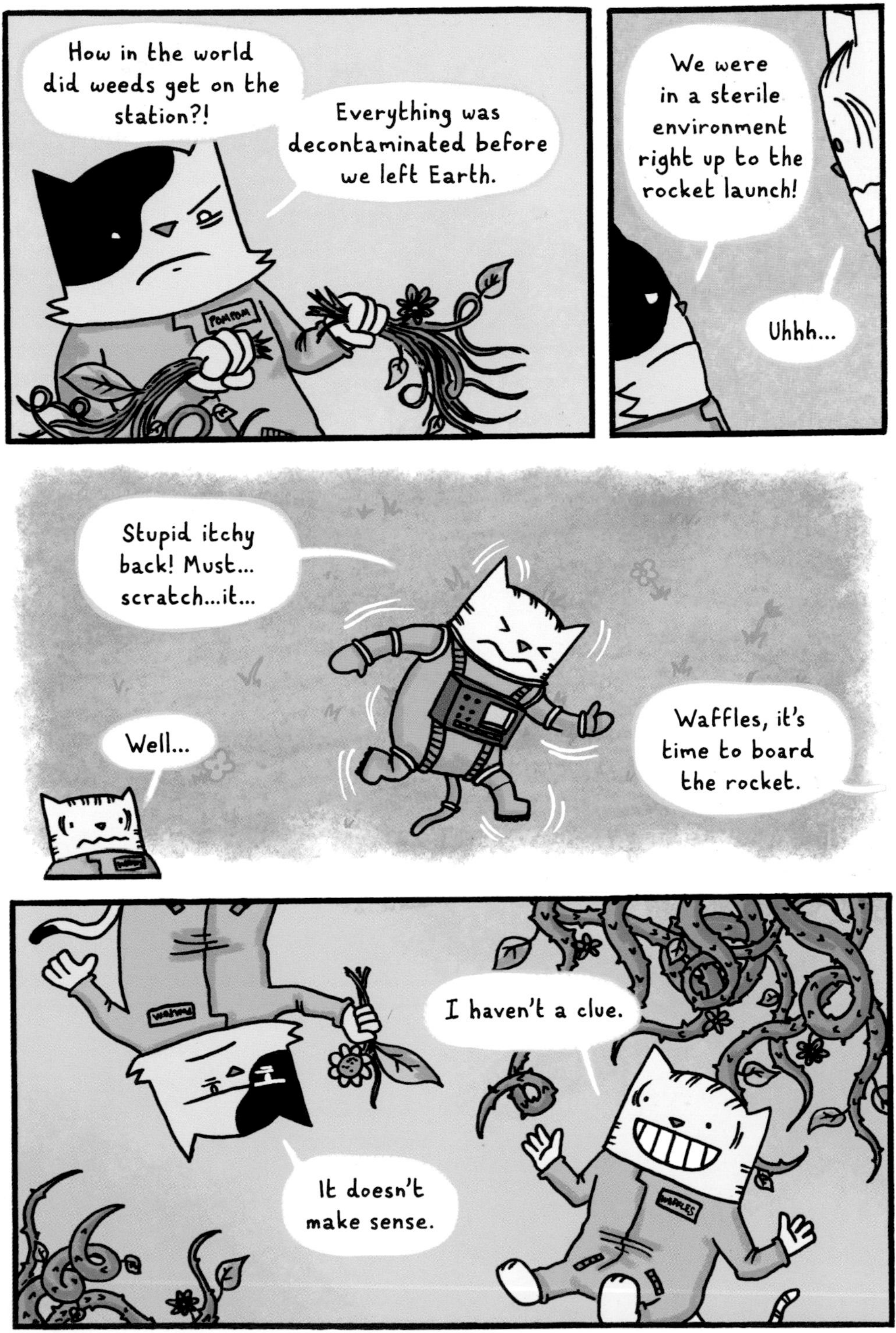
How in the world did weeds get on the station?!
Everything was decontaminated before we left Earth.
POMPOM
We were in a sterile environment right up to the rocket launch!
Uhhh...
Stupid itchy back! Must... scratch...it...
Well...
Waffles, it's time to board the rocket.
I haven't a clue.
It doesn't make sense.
WAFFLES

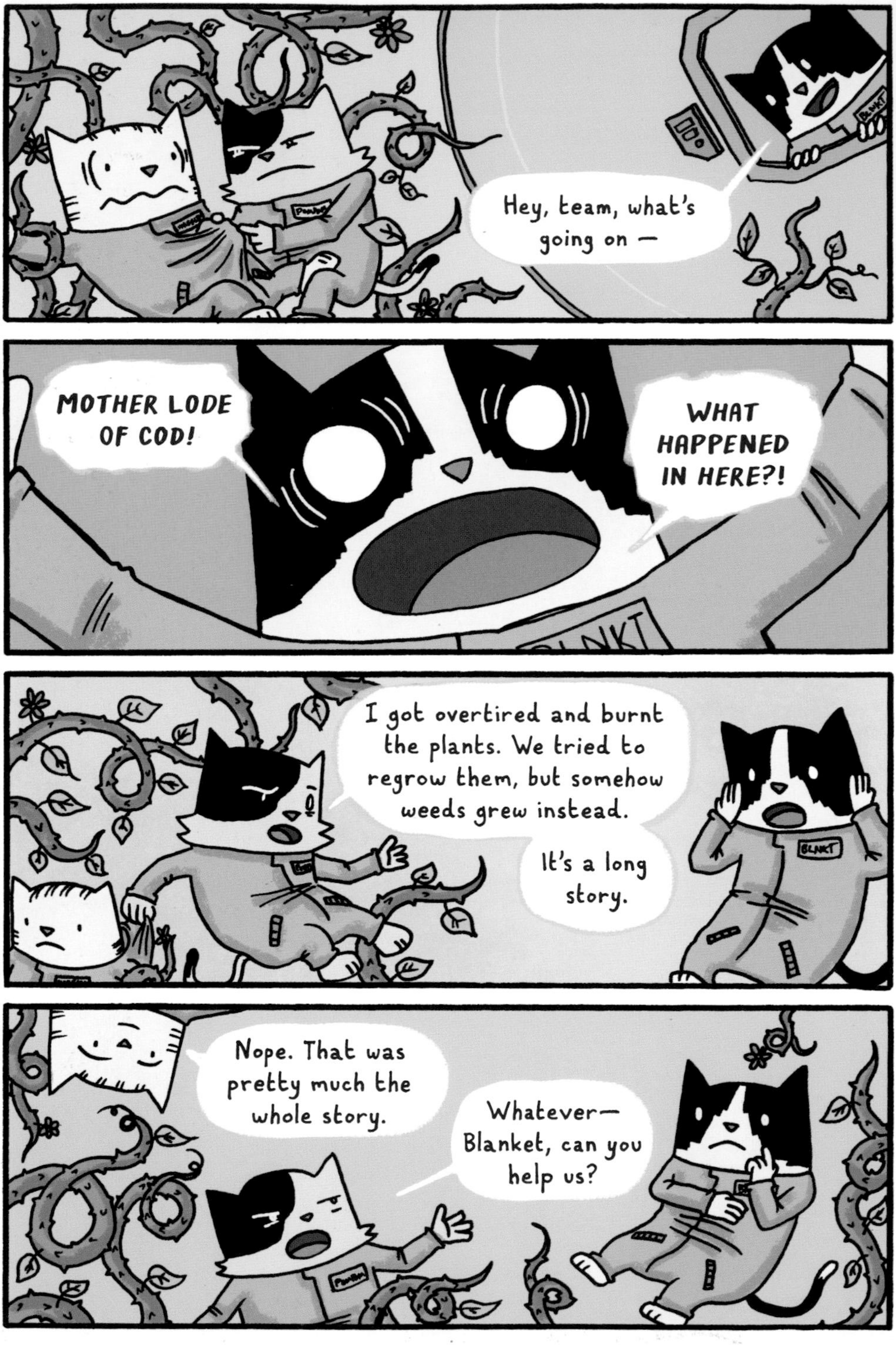
Hey, team, what's going on —
MOTHER LODE OF COD!
WHAT HAPPENED IN HERE?!
I got overtired and burnt the plants. We tried to regrow them, but somehow weeds grew instead.
It's a long story.
BLNKT
Nope. That was pretty much the whole story.
Whatever— Blanket, can you help us?

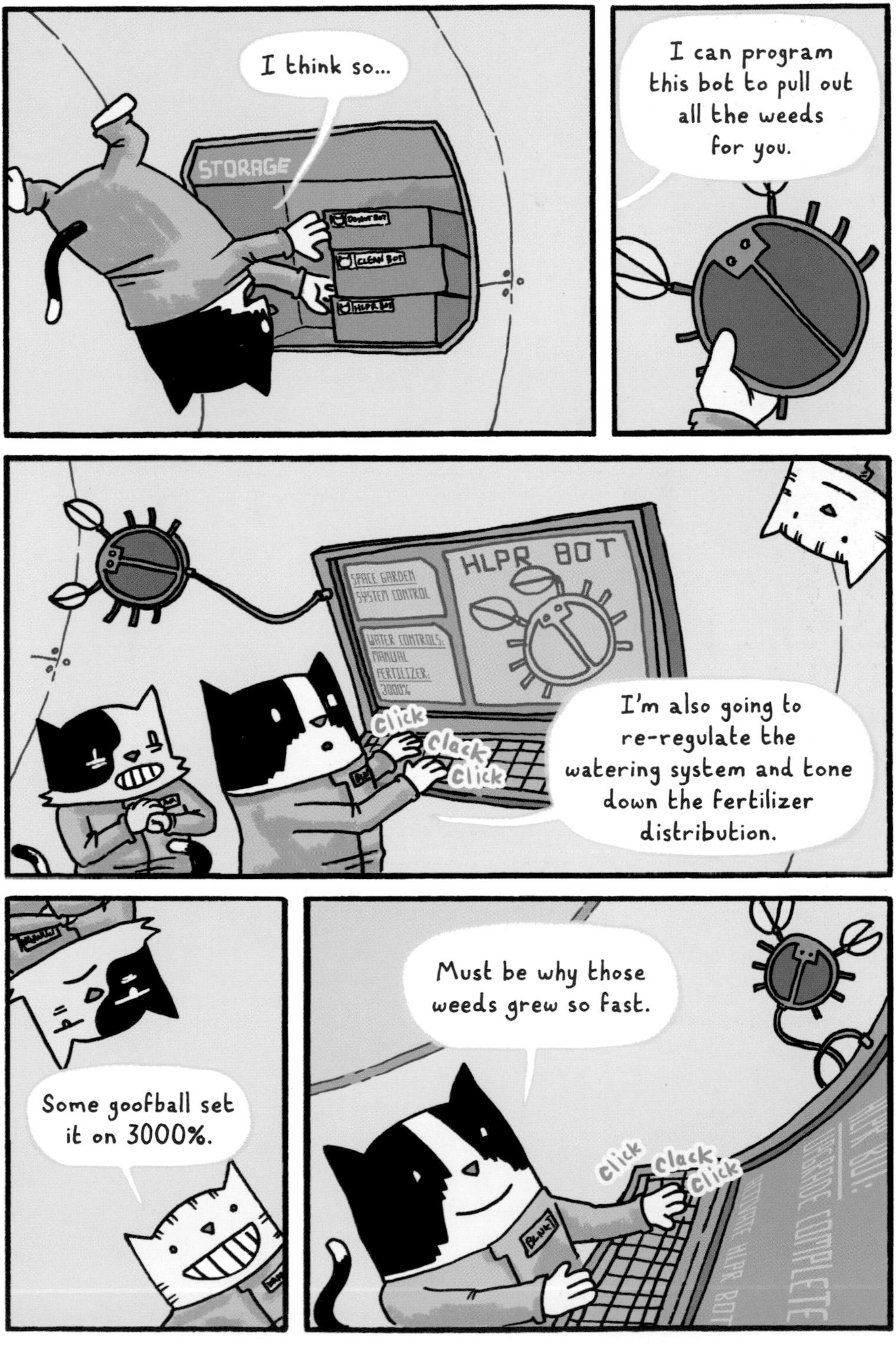
I think so...
STORAGE
CLEAN BOT
I can program this bot to pull out all the weeds for you.
HLPR BOT
SPACE GARDEN SYSTEM CONTROL
WATER CONTROLS: MANUAL
FERTILIZER: 3000%
Click
Clack
Click
I'm also going to re-regulate the watering system and tone down the fertilizer distribution.
Some goofball set it on 3000%.
Must be why those weeds grew so fast.
Click
Clack
Click
HLPR BOT:
UPGRADE COMPLETE
ACTIVATE HLPR BOT

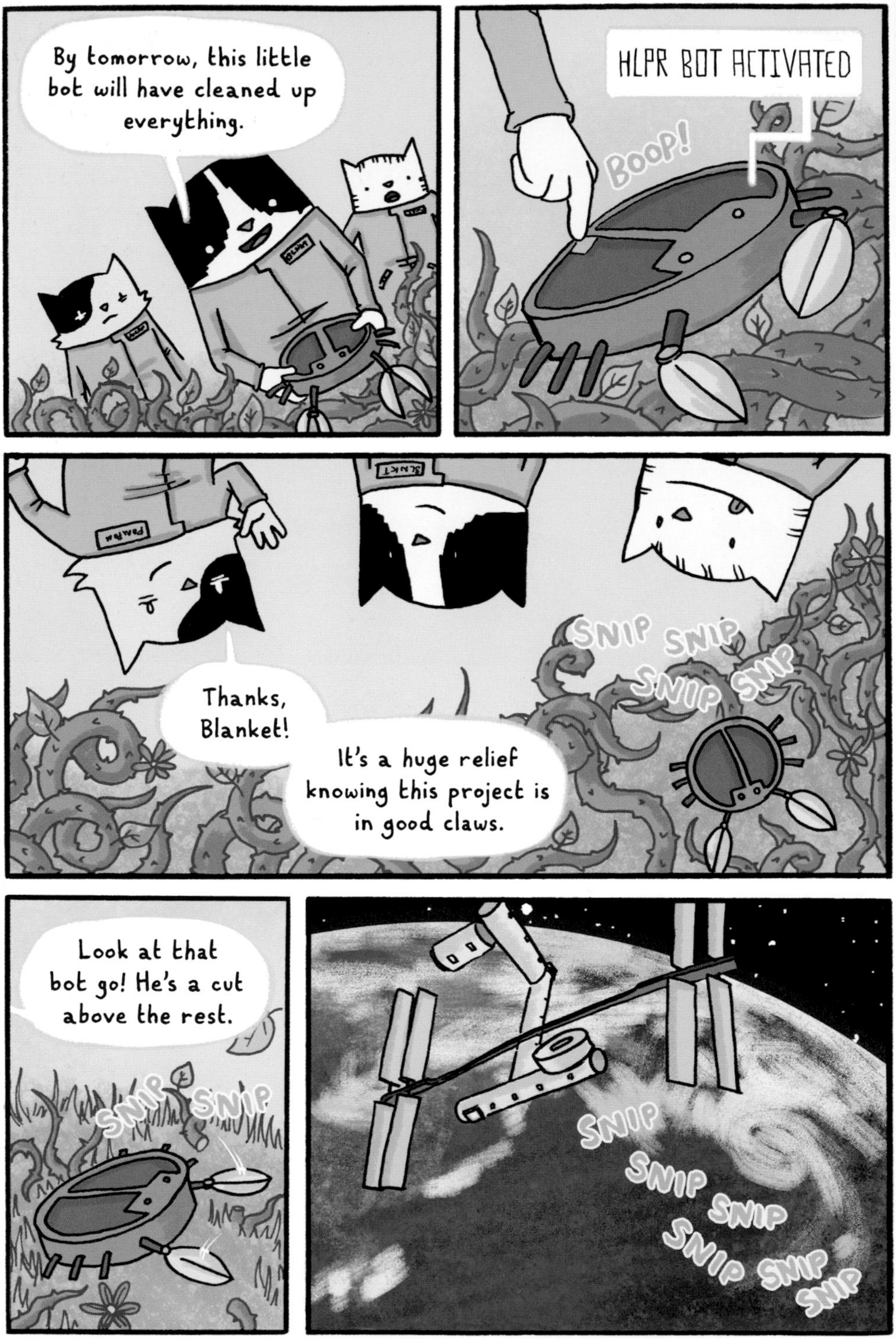
By tomorrow, this little bot will have cleaned up everything.
HLPR BOT ACTIVATED
BOOP!
SNIP SNIP SNIP SNIP
Thanks, Blanket!
It's a huge relief knowing this project is in good claws.
Look at that bot go! He's a cut above the rest.
SNIP SNIP
SNIP SNIP SNIP SNIP SNIP SNIP

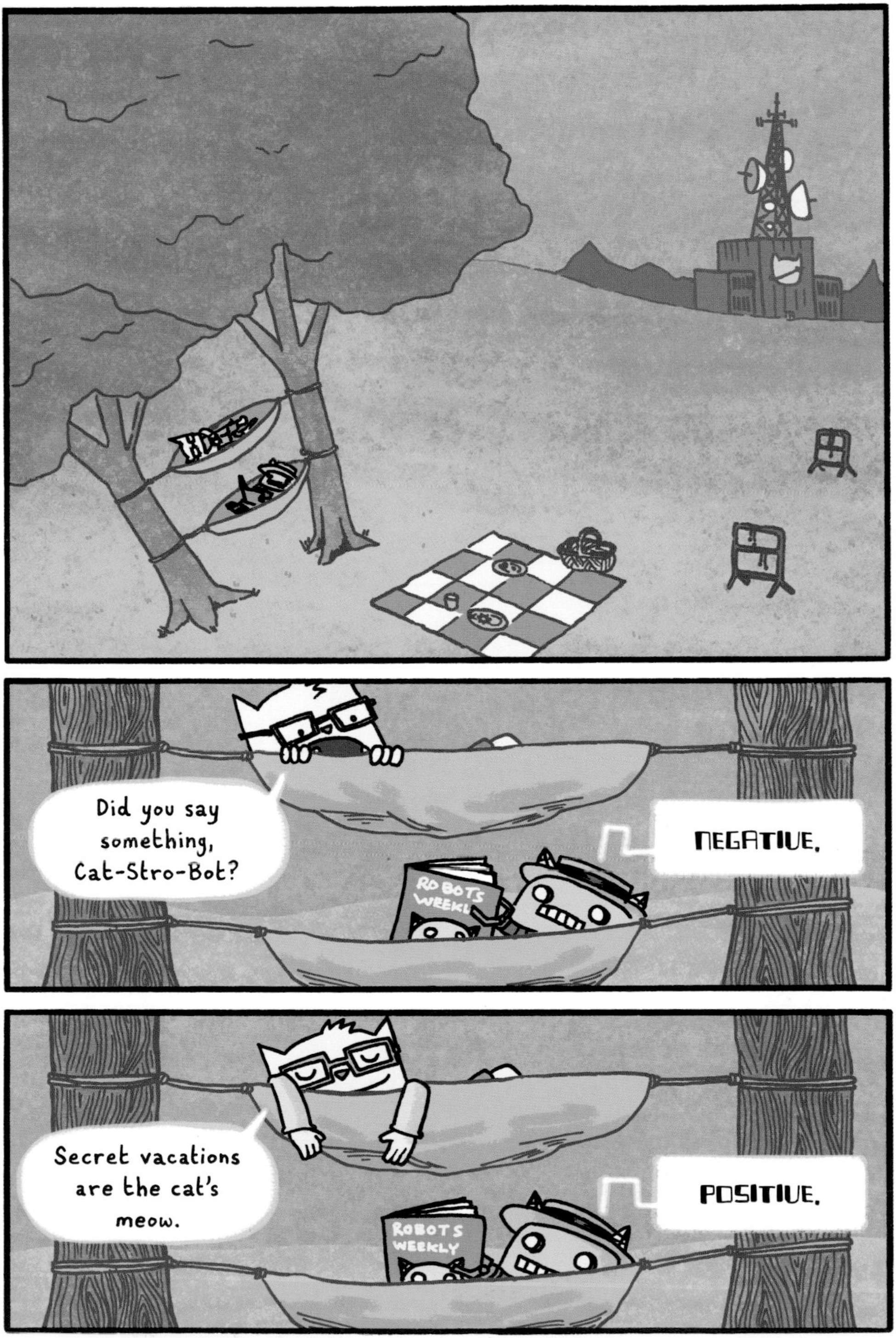
Did you say something, Cat-Stro-Bot?
NEGATIVE.
Secret vacations are the cat's meow.
POSITIVE.
ROBOTS WEEKLY

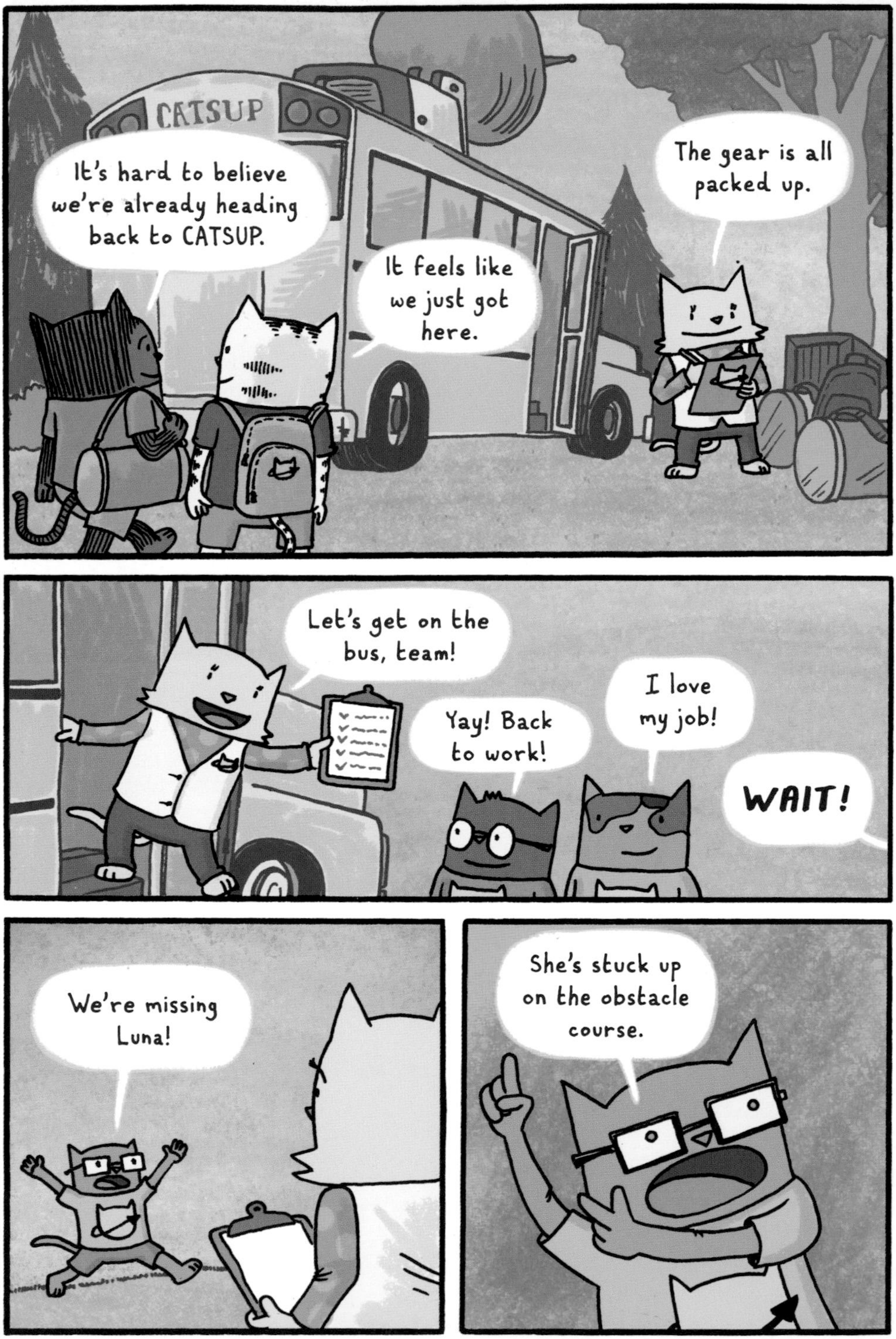
CATSUP
It's hard to believe we're already heading back to CATSUP.
It feels like we just got here.
The gear is all packed up.
Let's get on the bus, team!
Yay! Back to work!
I love my job!
WAIT!
We're missing Luna!
She's stuck up on the obstacle course.

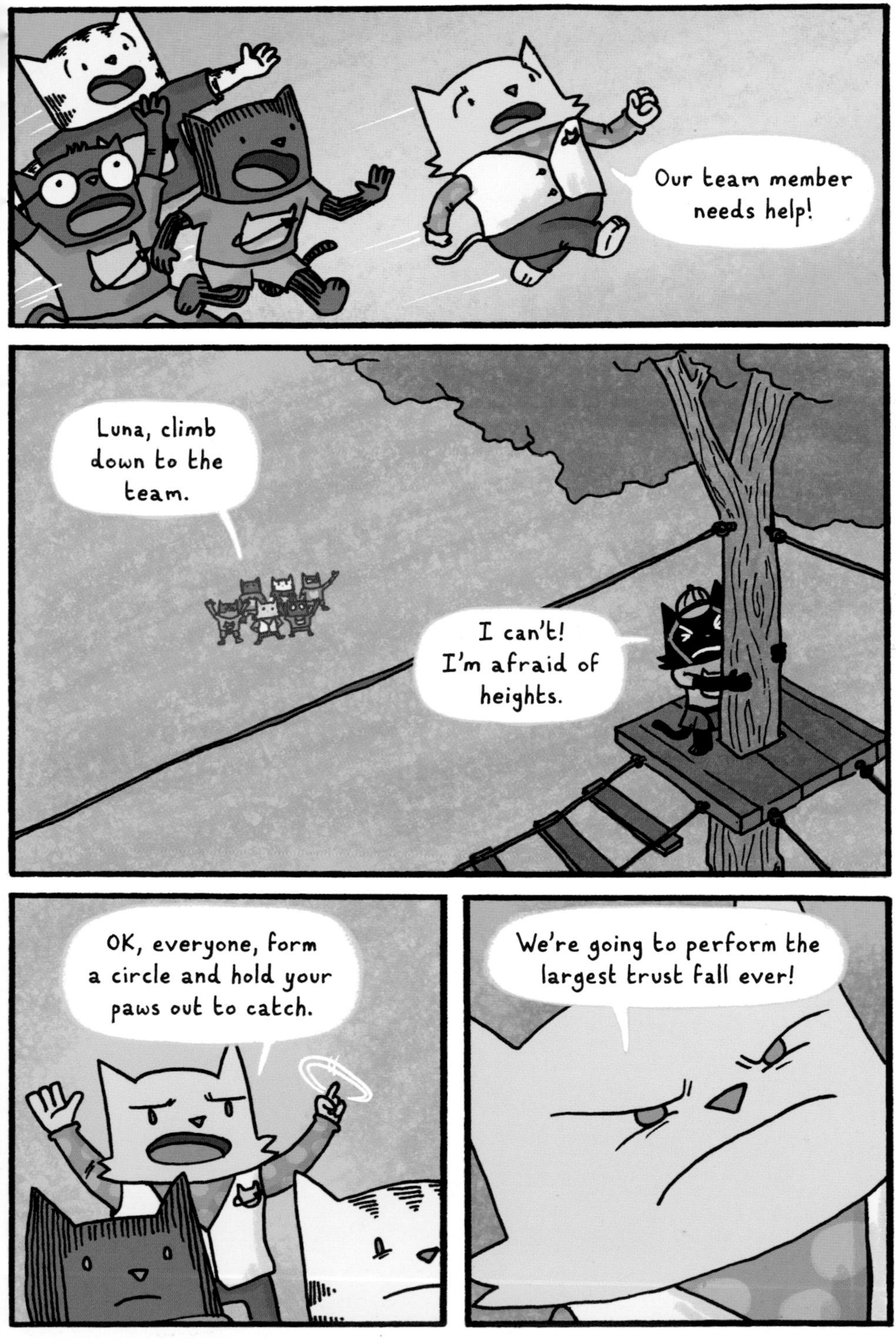

Our team member needs help!
Luna, climb down to the team.
I can't! I'm afraid of heights.
OK, everyone, form a circle and hold your paws out to catch.
We're going to perform the largest trust fall ever!

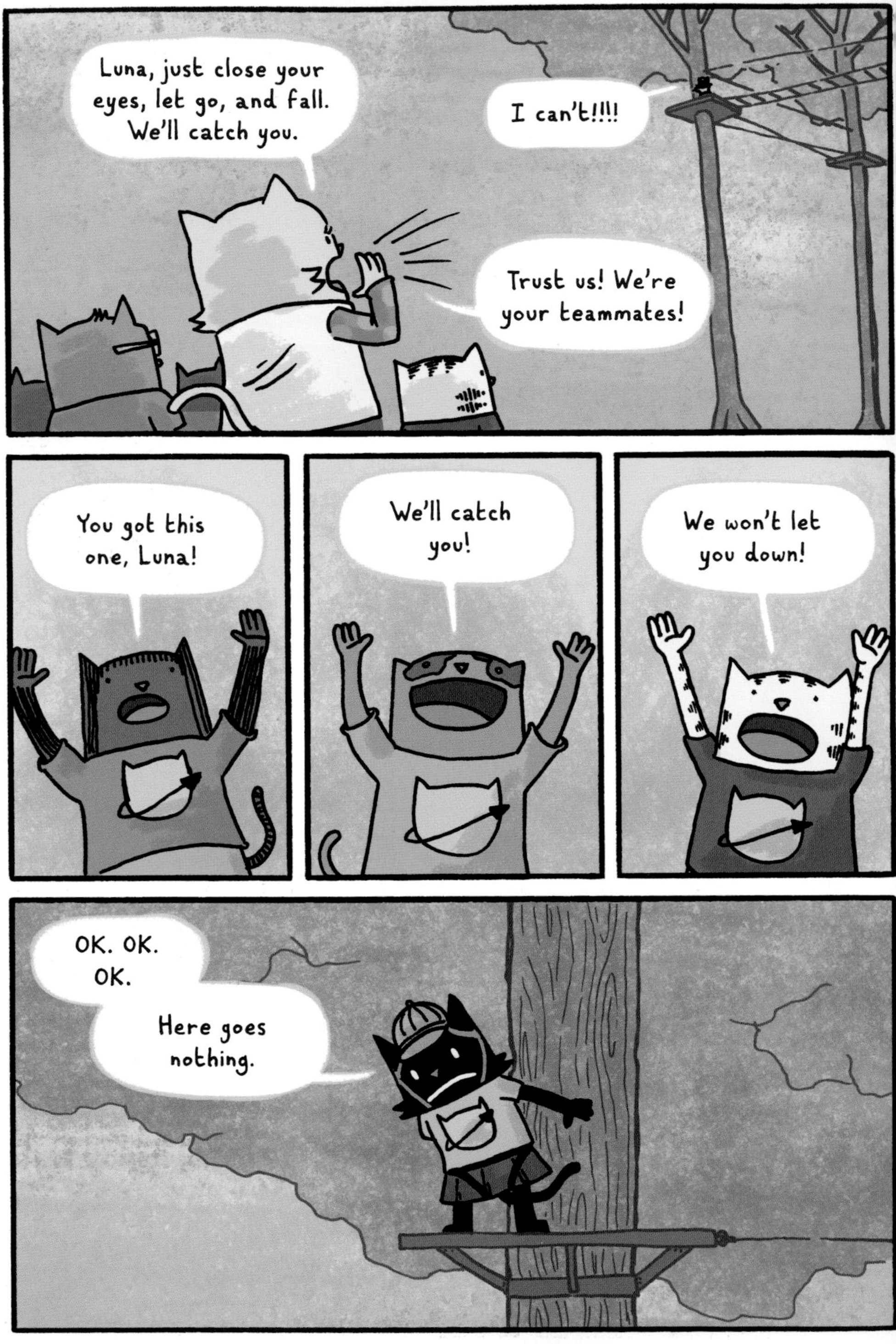
Luna, just close your eyes, let go, and fall. We'll catch you.
I can't!!!!
Trust us! We're your teammates!
You got this one, Luna!
We'll catch you!
We won't let you down!
OK. OK. OK.
Here goes nothing.

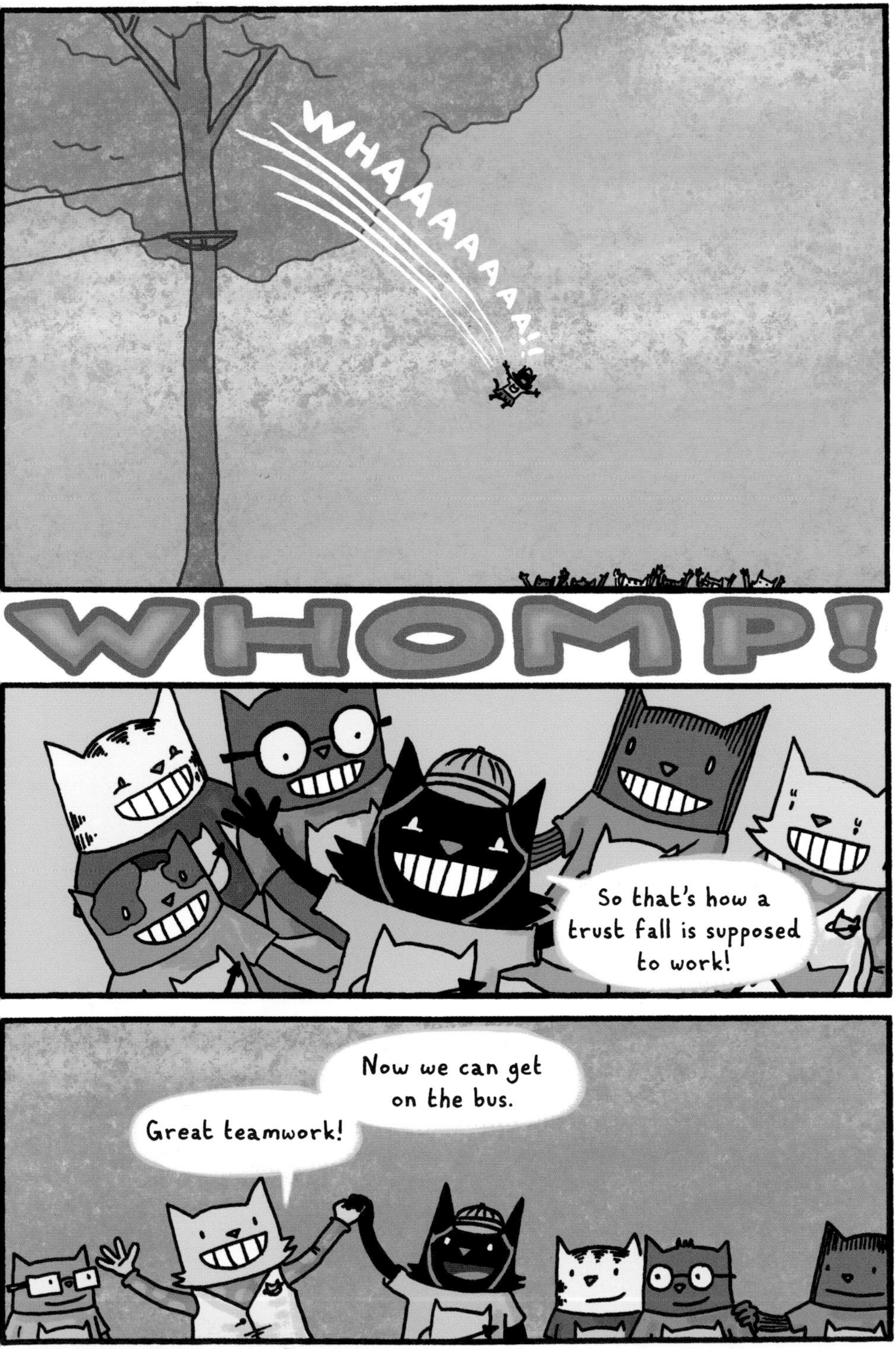
WHAAAAAAAA!!
WHOMP!
So that's how a trust fall is supposed to work!
Great teamwork!
Now we can get on the bus.

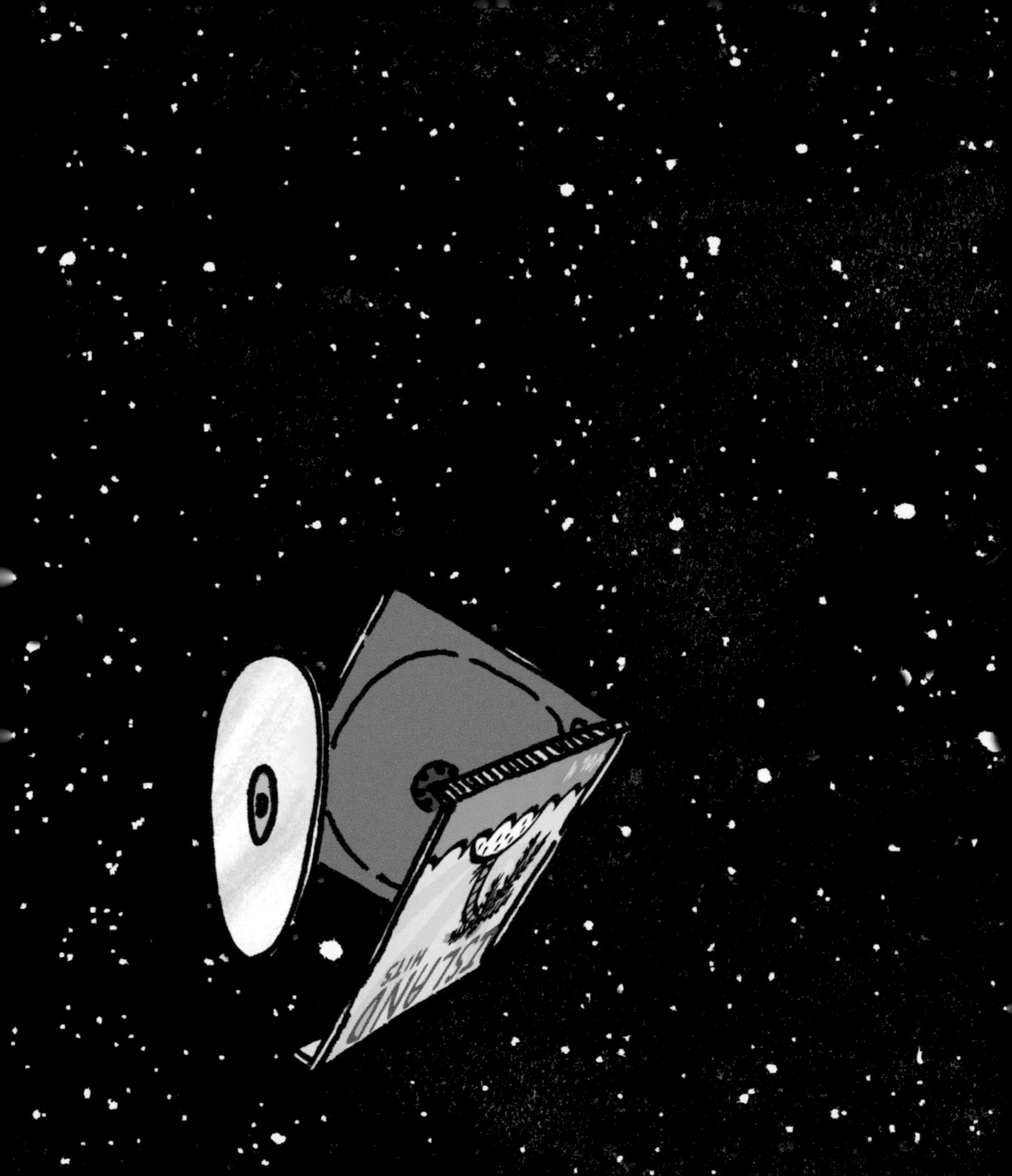

CHAPTER 7

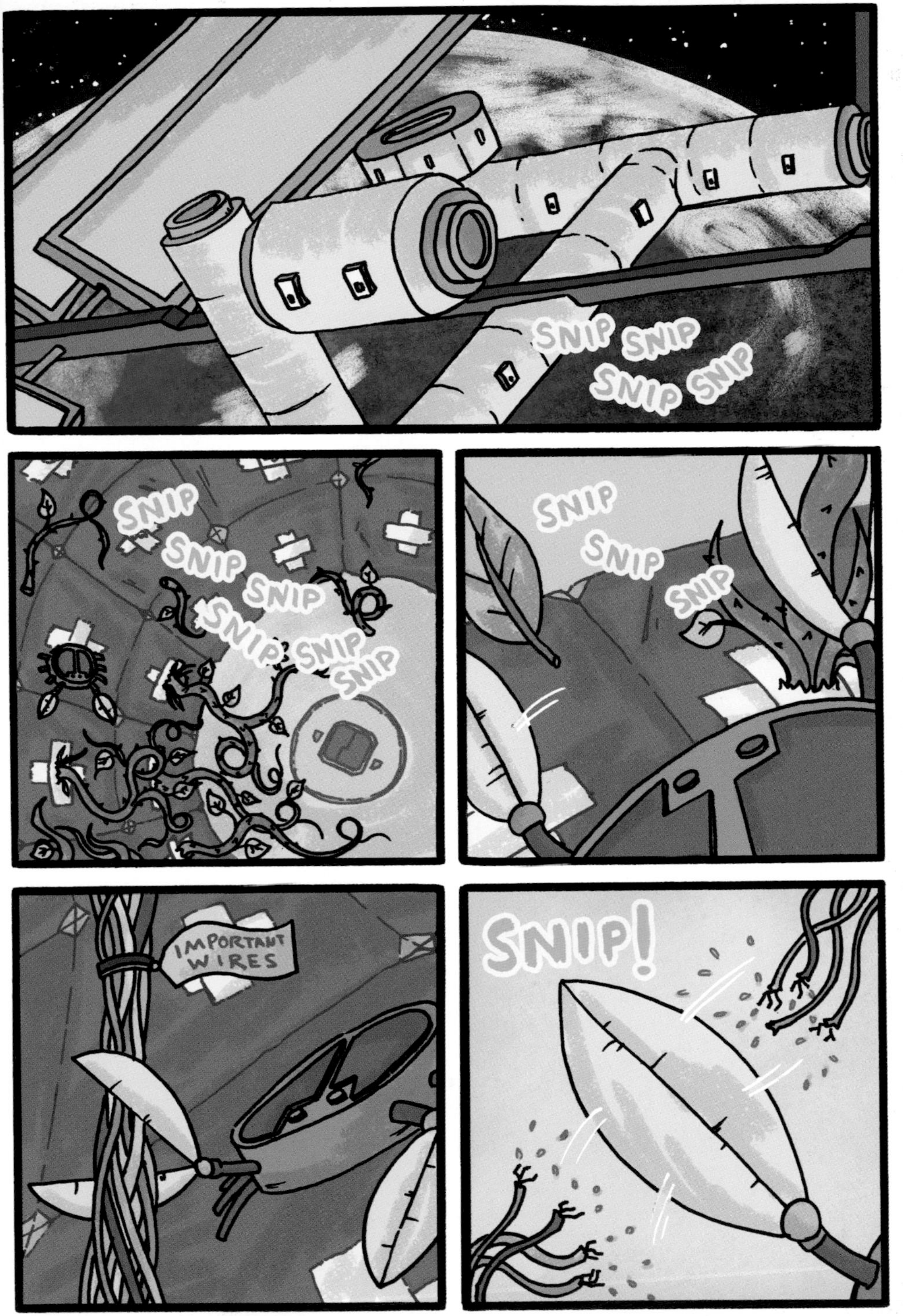
SNIP SNIP
SNIP SNIP
SNIP
SNIP
SNIP
SNIP
SNIP
SNIP
SNIP
SNIP
SNIP
IMPORTANT WIRES
SNIP!

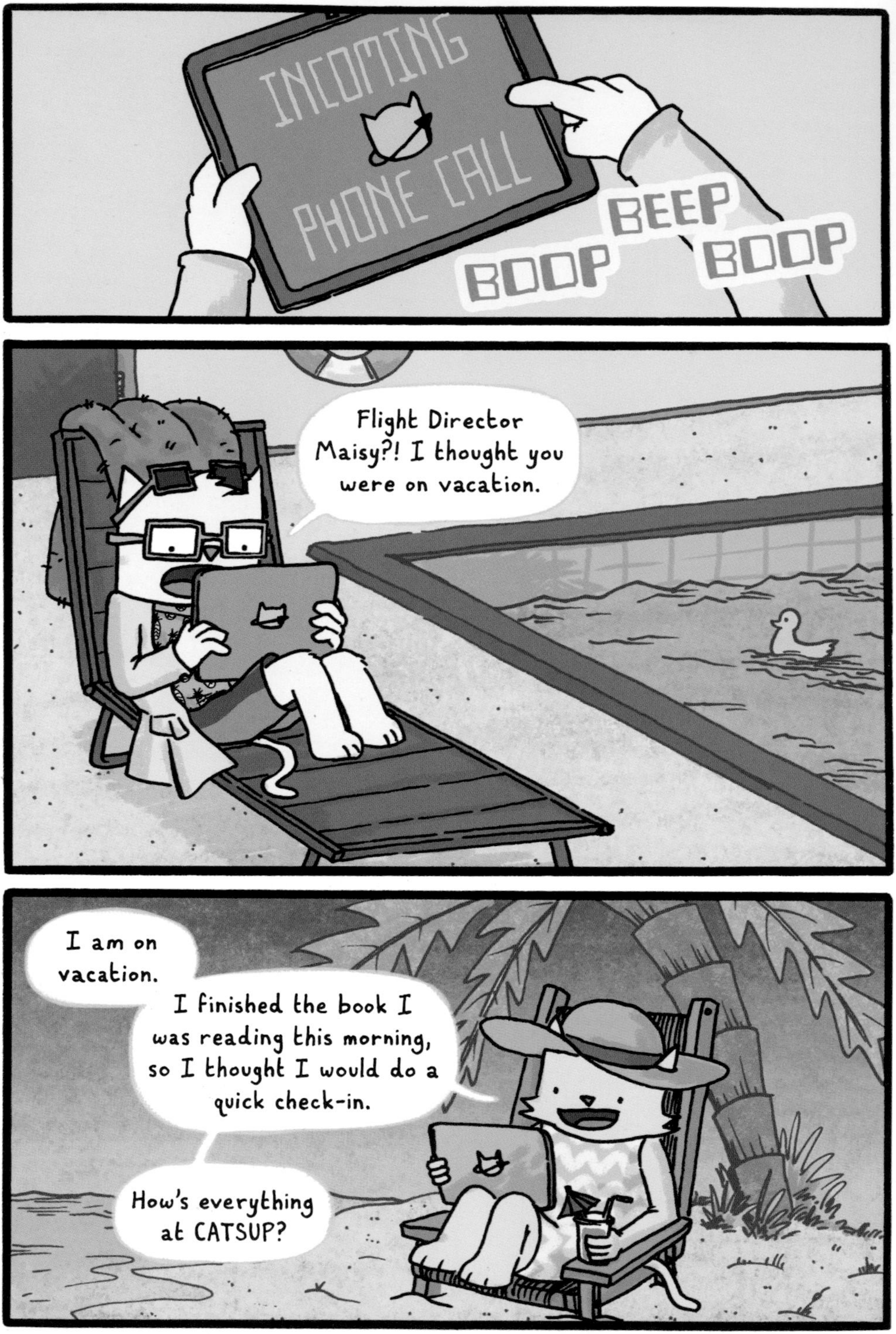
INCOMING
PHONE CALL
BOOP BEEP BOOP
Flight Director Maisy?! I thought you were on vacation.
I am on vacation.
I finished the book I was reading this morning, so I thought I would do a quick check-in.
How's everything at CATSUP?

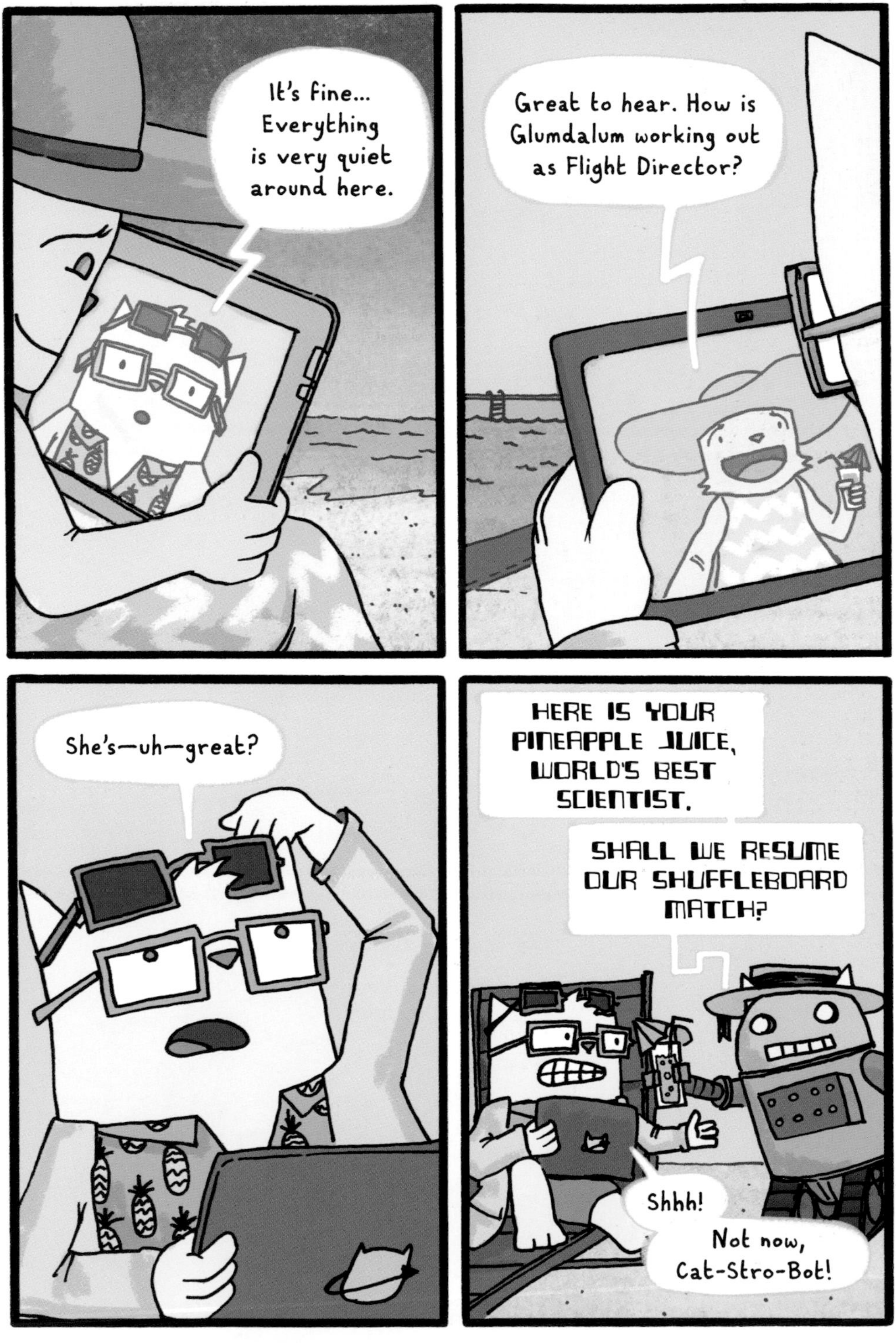
It's fine... Everything is very quiet around here.
Great to hear. How is Glumdalum working out as Flight Director?
She's—uh—great?
HERE IS YOUR PINEAPPLE JUICE, WORLD'S BEST SCIENTIST.
SHALL WE RESUME OUR SHUFFLEBOARD MATCH?
Shhh!
Not now, Cat-Stro-Bot!

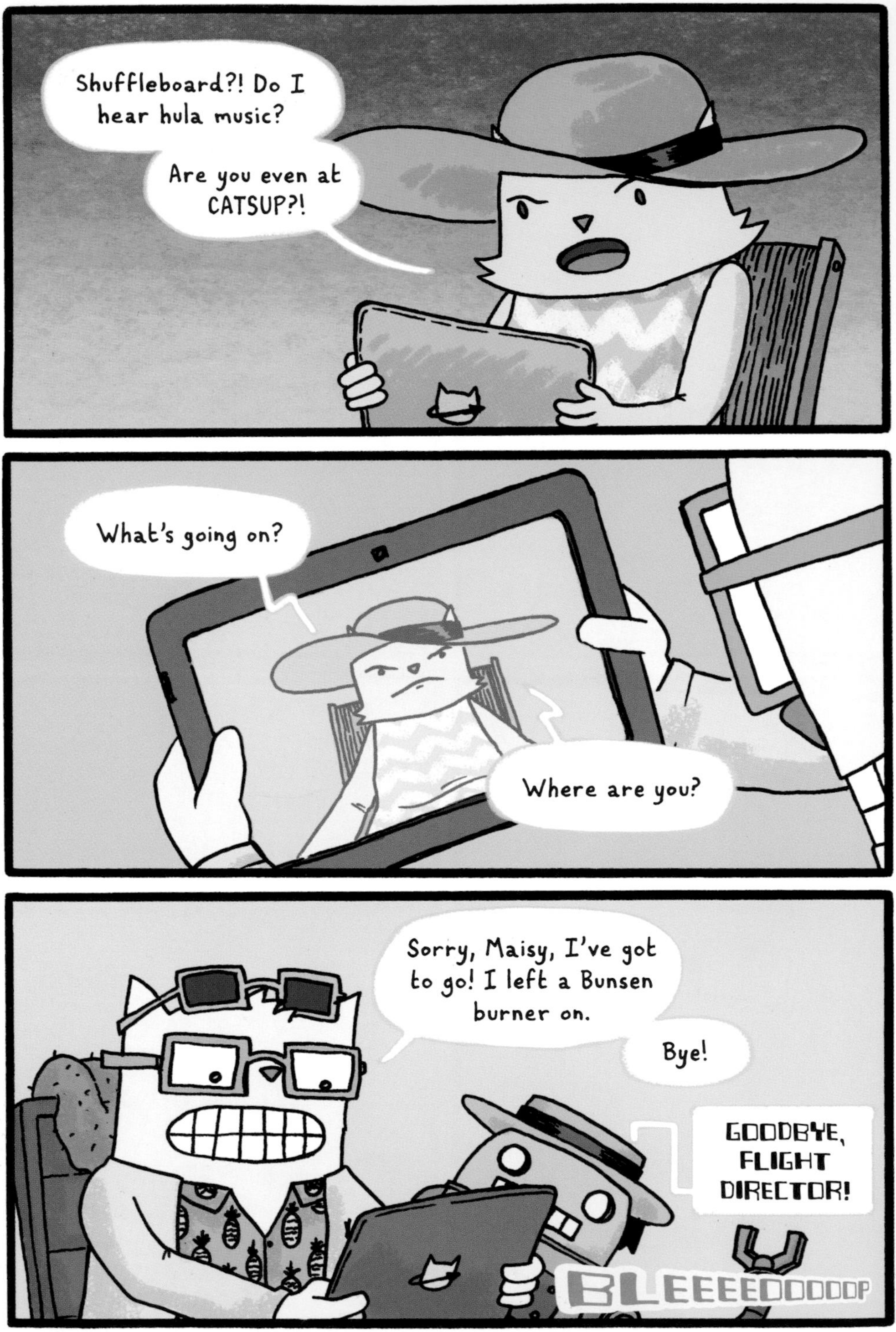
Shuffleboard?! Do I hear hula music?
Are you even at CATSUP?!
What's going on?
Where are you?
Sorry, Maisy, I've got to go! I left a Bunsen burner on.
Bye!
GOODBYE, FLIGHT DIRECTOR!
BLEEEEDDDDDP

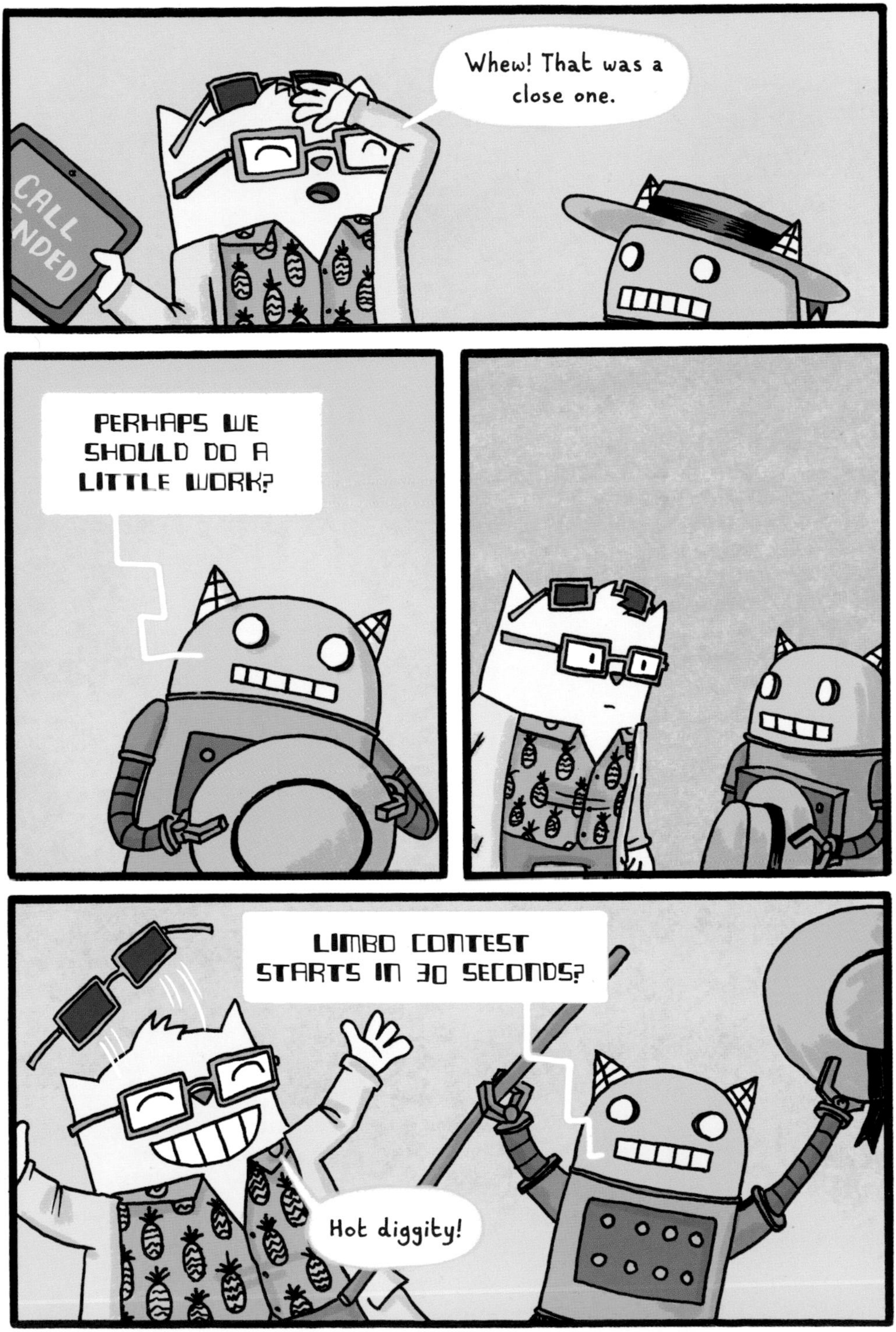
CALL ENDED
Whew! That was a close one.
PERHAPS WE SHOULD DO A LITTLE WORK?
LIMBO CONTEST STARTS IN 30 SECONDS?
Hot diggity!

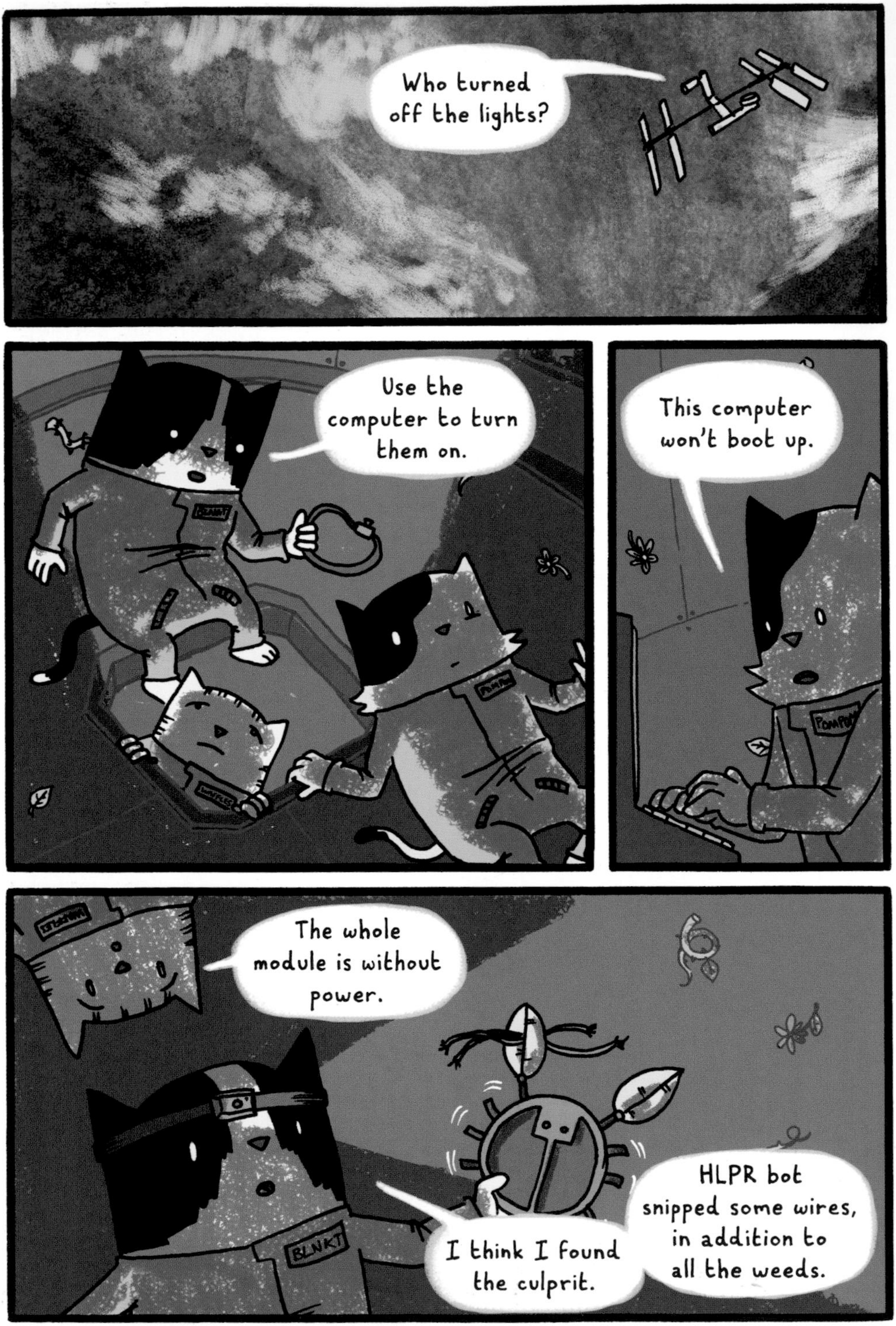
Who turned off the lights?
Use the computer to turn them on.
This computer won't boot up.
The whole module is without power.
I think I found the culprit.
HLPR bot snipped some wires, in addition to all the weeds.
BLNKT
POMPOM

Can you fix it?

I need to get these experiments back up and running.

EXPERIMENT
TO DO LIST
1. GROW PLANTS
2. SPACE BUBBL
3. M
4. S
LOONS
O GRAV
O GRAVITY
ERCISE!!

I should be able to...just give me a minute.

That should do it.

BERWWP

Try it now.

Cross your tails that this works, everyone!

BOOOOOOWP!

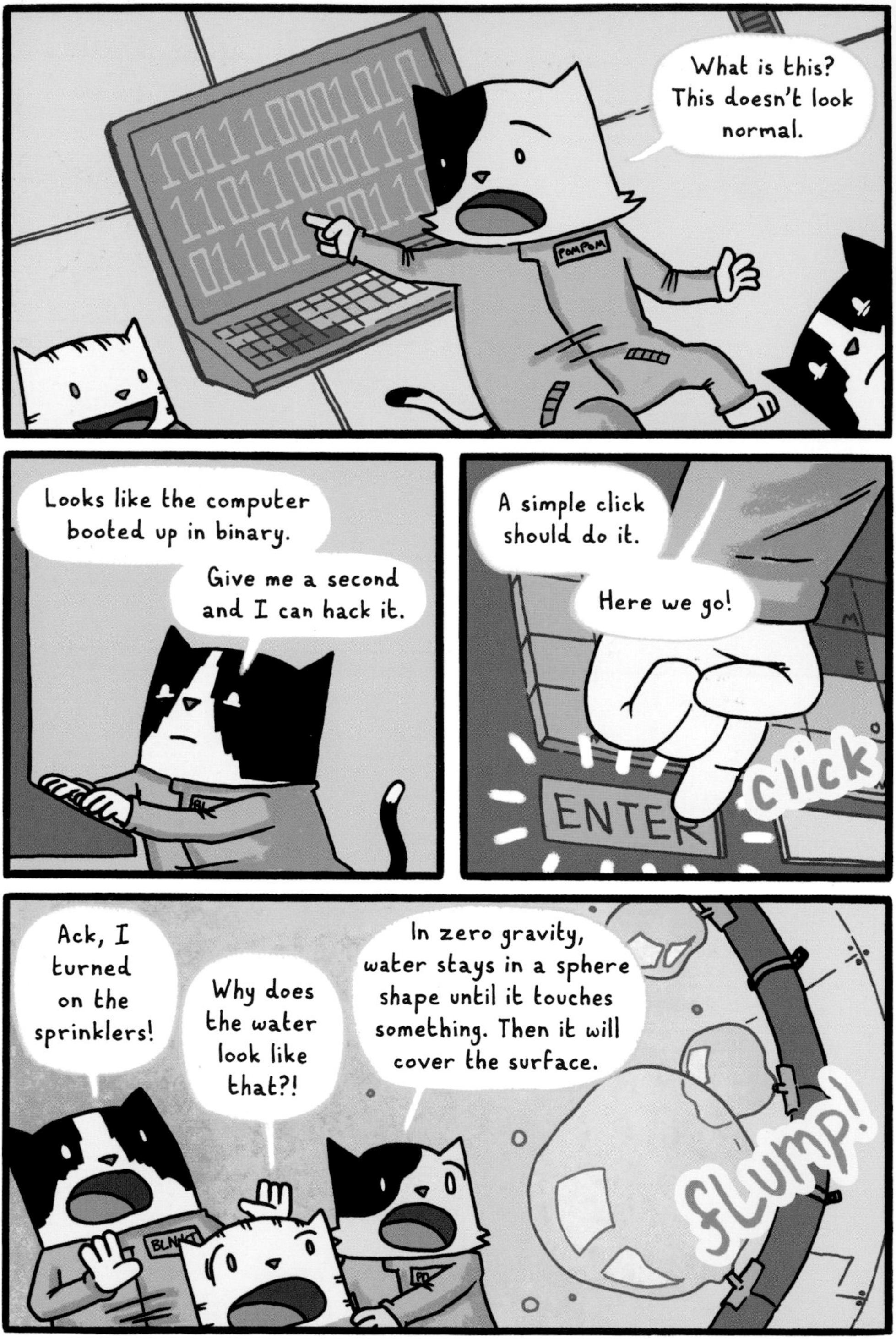
What is this? This doesn't look normal.
POMPOM
Looks like the computer booted up in binary.
Give me a second and I can hack it.
A simple click should do it.
Here we go!
ENTER
click
Ack, I turned on the sprinklers!
Why does the water look like that?!
In zero gravity, water stays in a sphere shape until it touches something. Then it will cover the surface.
BLNKT
flump!

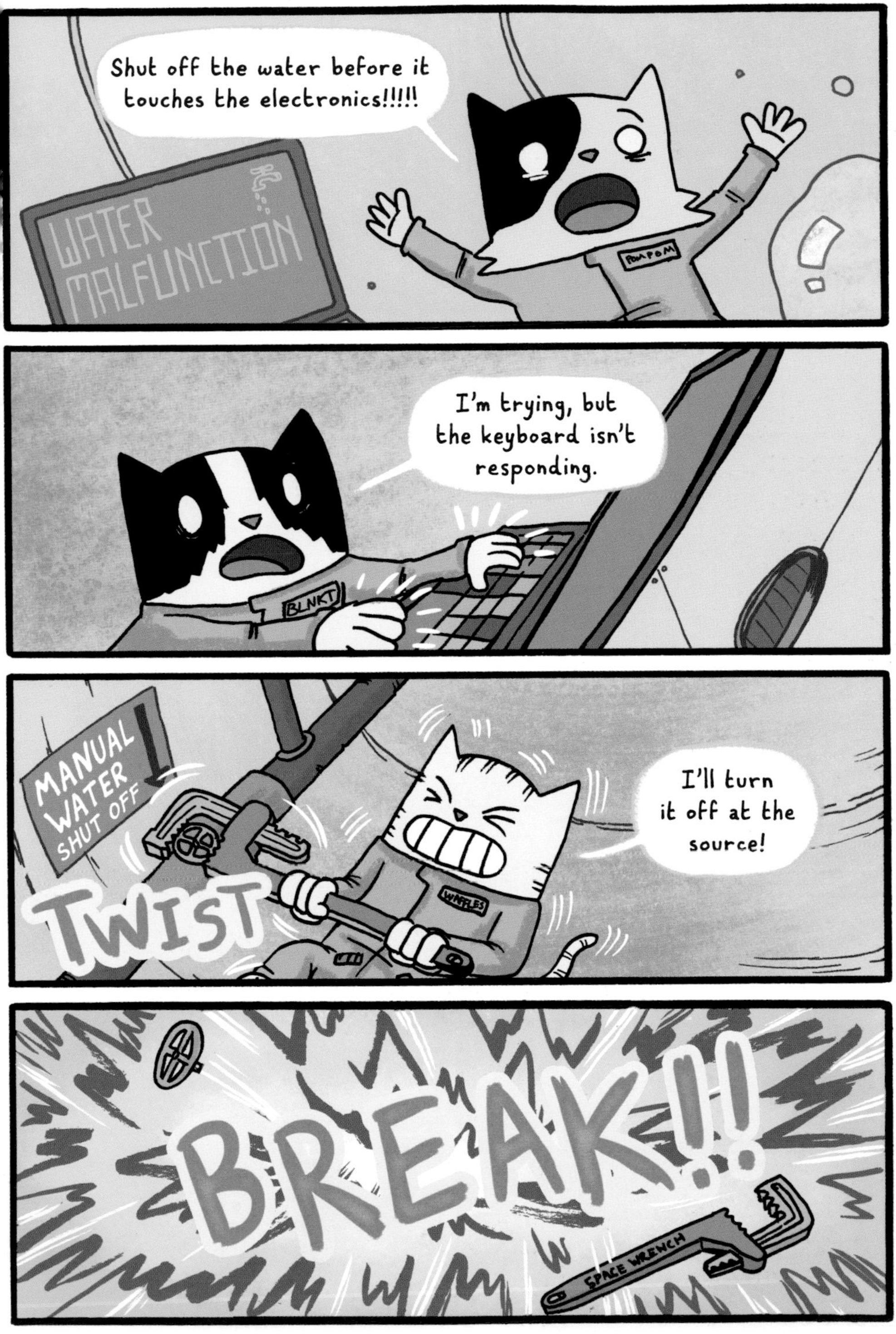
Shut off the water before it touches the electronics!!!!!
WATER MALFUNCTION
POMPOM
I'm trying, but the keyboard isn't responding.
BLNKT
MANUAL WATER SHUT OFF
I'll turn it off at the source!
WAFFLES
TWIST
BREAK!!
SPACE WRENCH

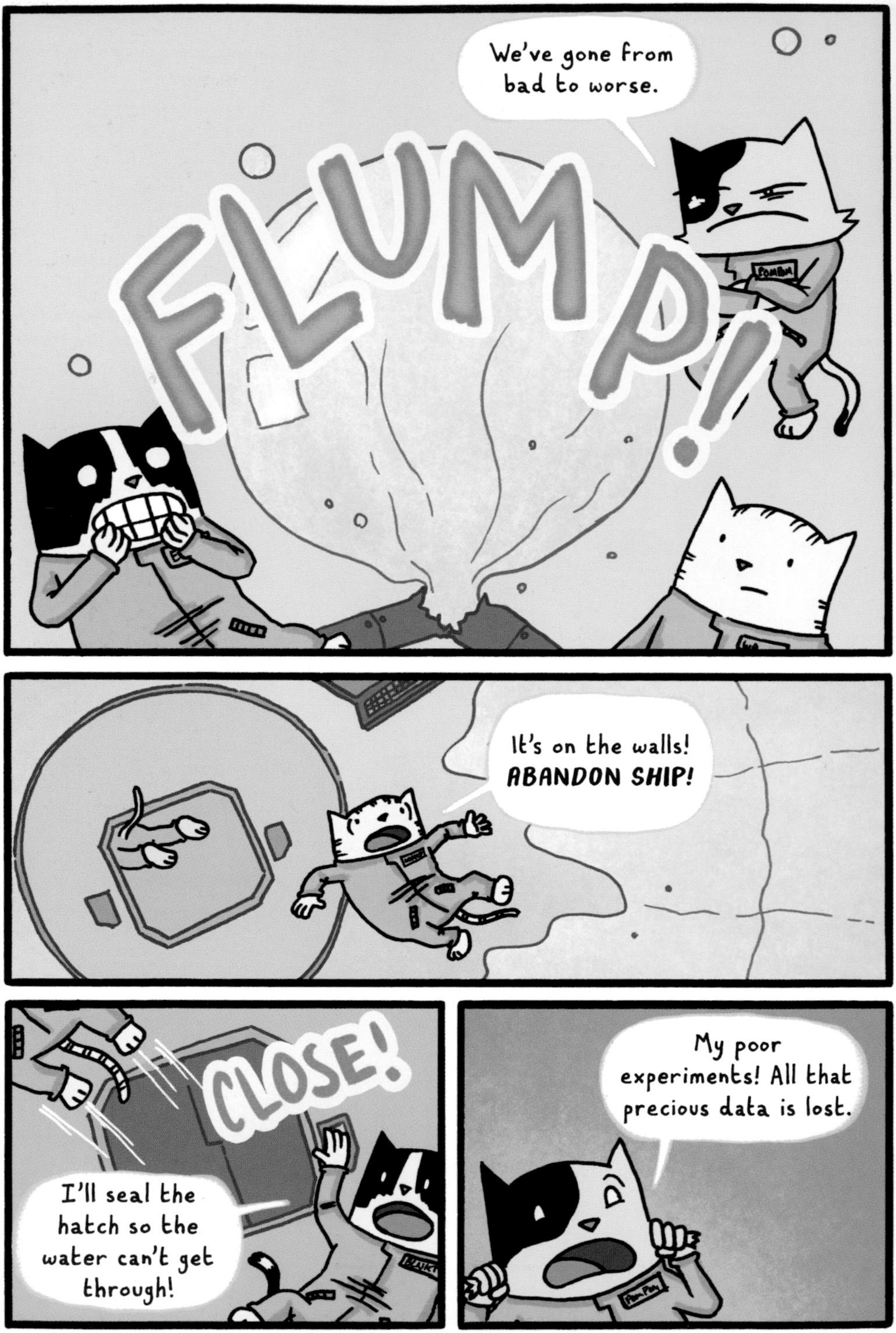
We've gone from bad to worse.
FLUMP!
It's on the walls! **ABANDON SHIP!**
CLOSE!
I'll seal the hatch so the water can't get through!
My poor experiments! All that precious data is lost.

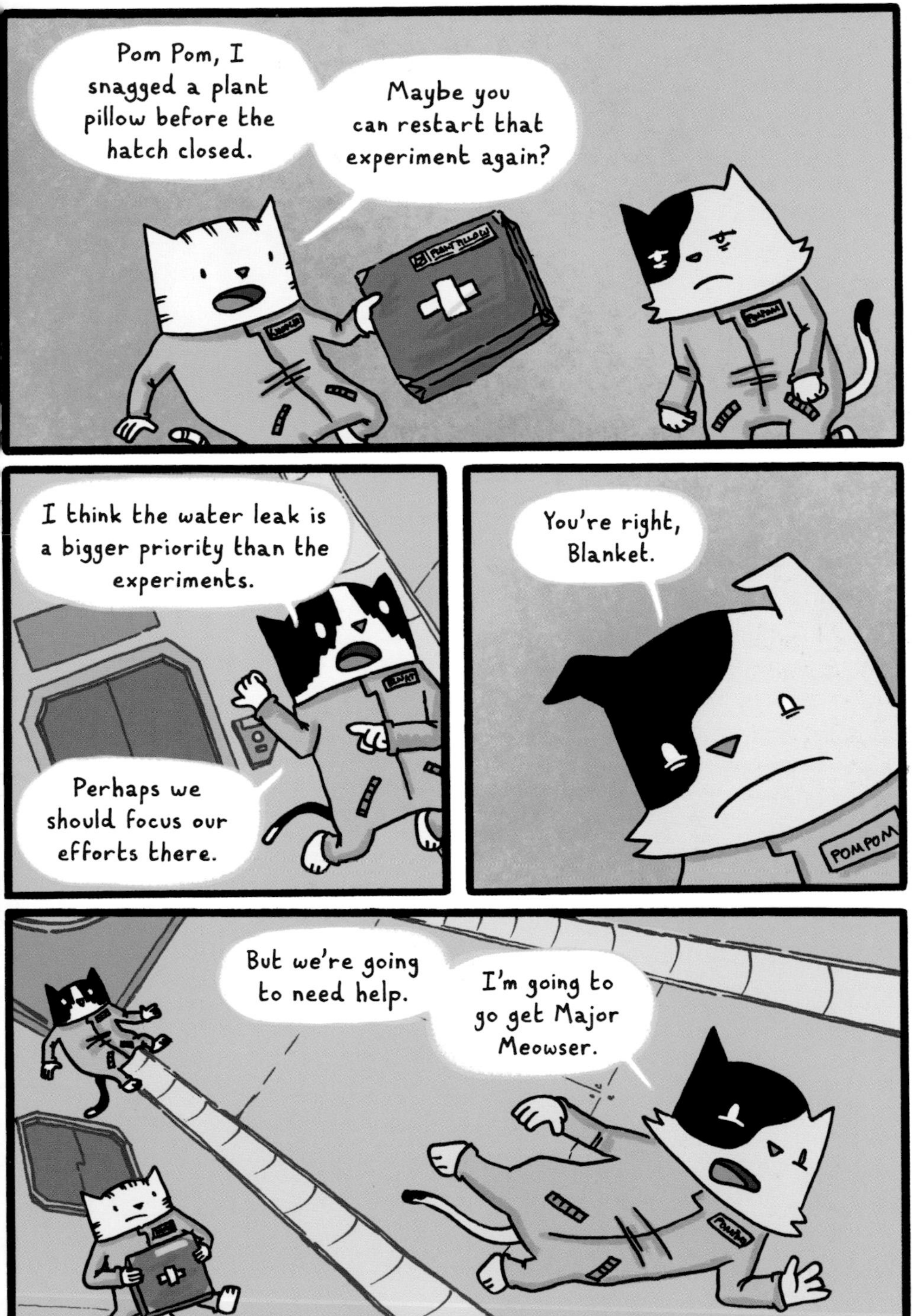
Pom Pom, I snagged a plant pillow before the hatch closed.
Maybe you can restart that experiment again?
I think the water leak is a bigger priority than the experiments.
Perhaps we should focus our efforts there.
You're right, Blanket.
POMPOM
But we're going to need help.
I'm going to go get Major Meowser.

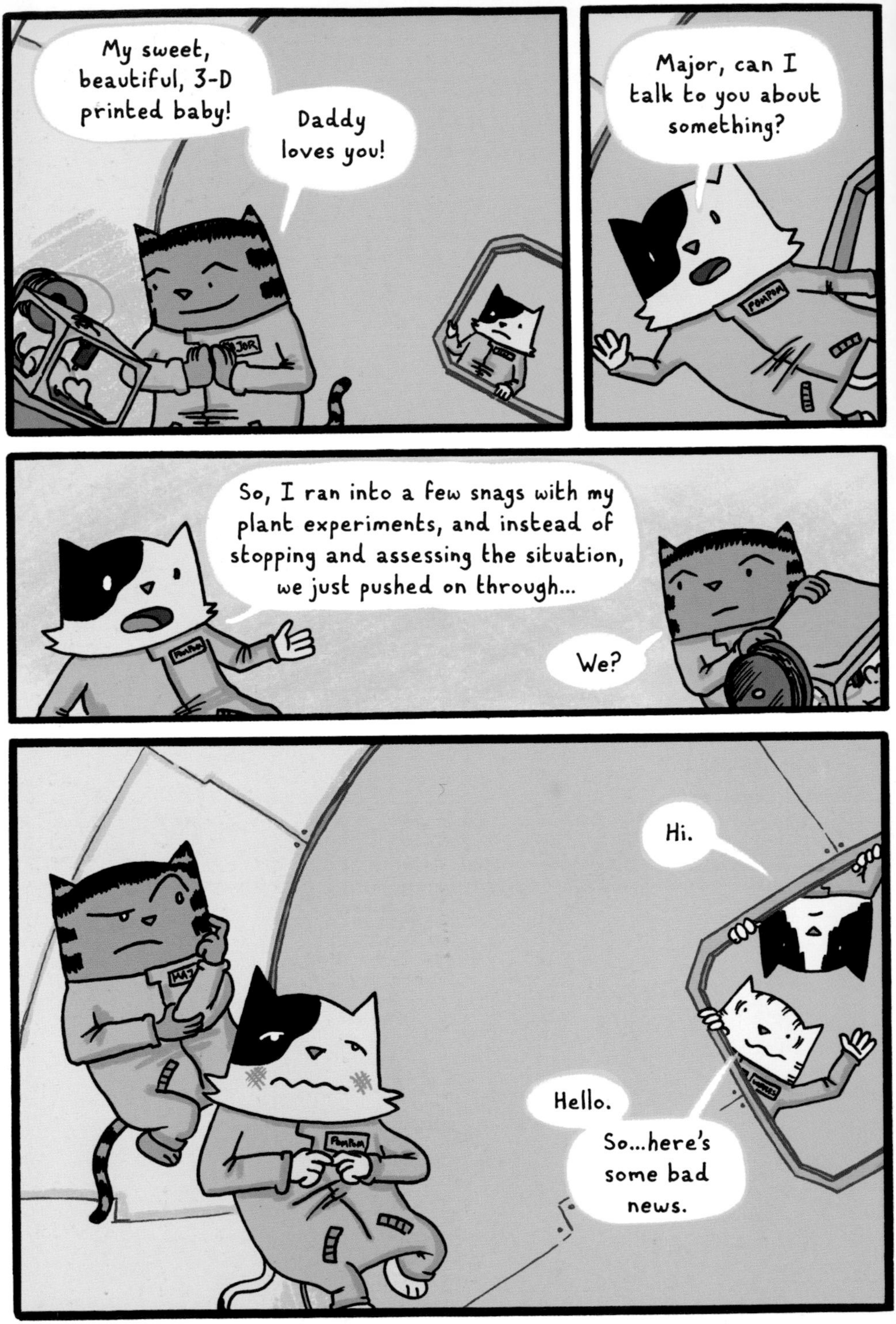
My sweet, beautiful, 3-D printed baby!
Daddy loves you!
Major, can I talk to you about something?
So, I ran into a few snags with my plant experiments, and instead of stopping and assessing the situation, we just pushed on through...
We?
Hi.
Hello.
So...here's some bad news.

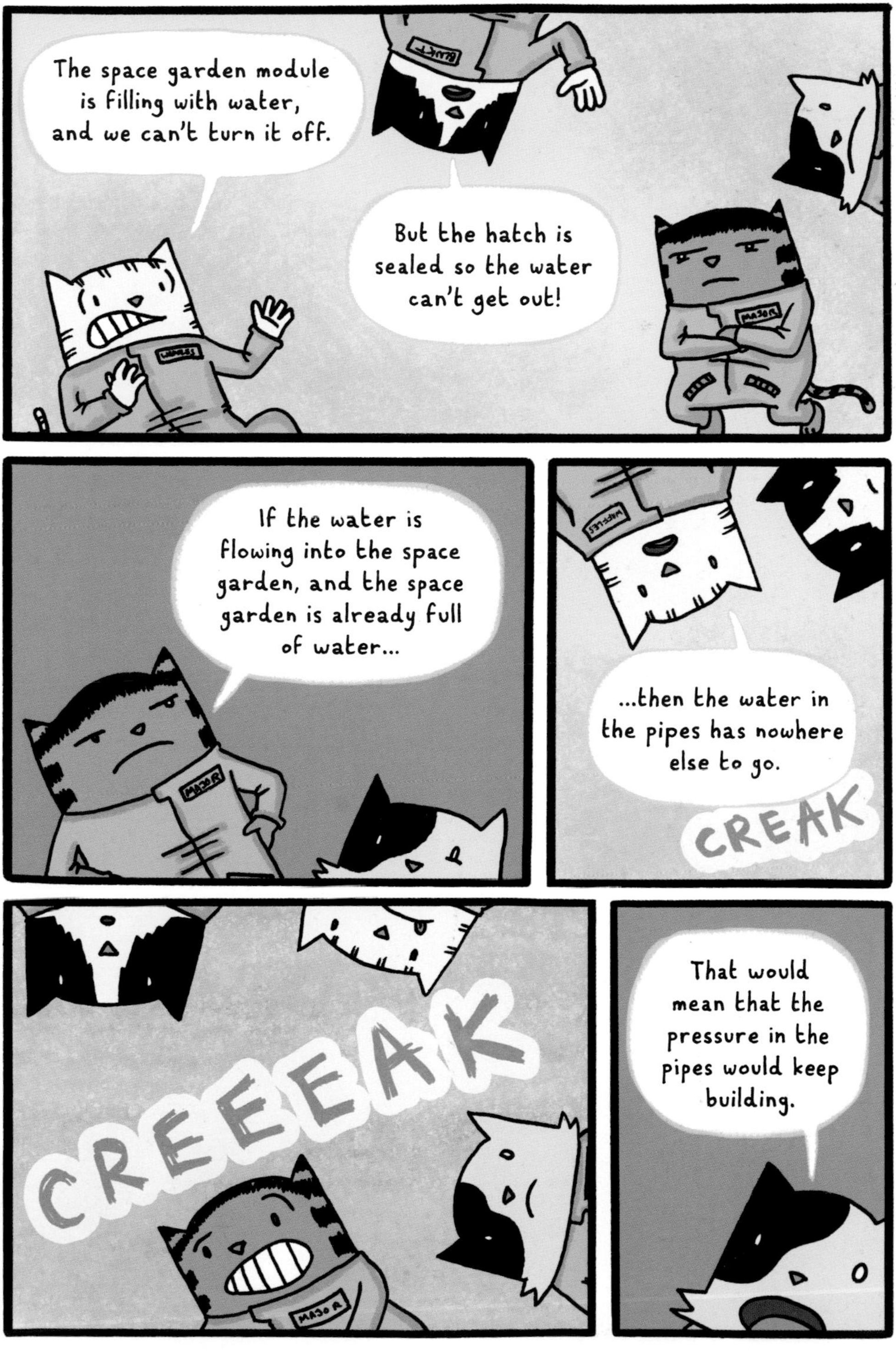

The space garden module is filling with water, and we can't turn it off.
But the hatch is sealed so the water can't get out!
If the water is flowing into the space garden, and the space garden is already full of water...
...then the water in the pipes has nowhere else to go.
CREAK
CREEEAK
That would mean that the pressure in the pipes would keep building.

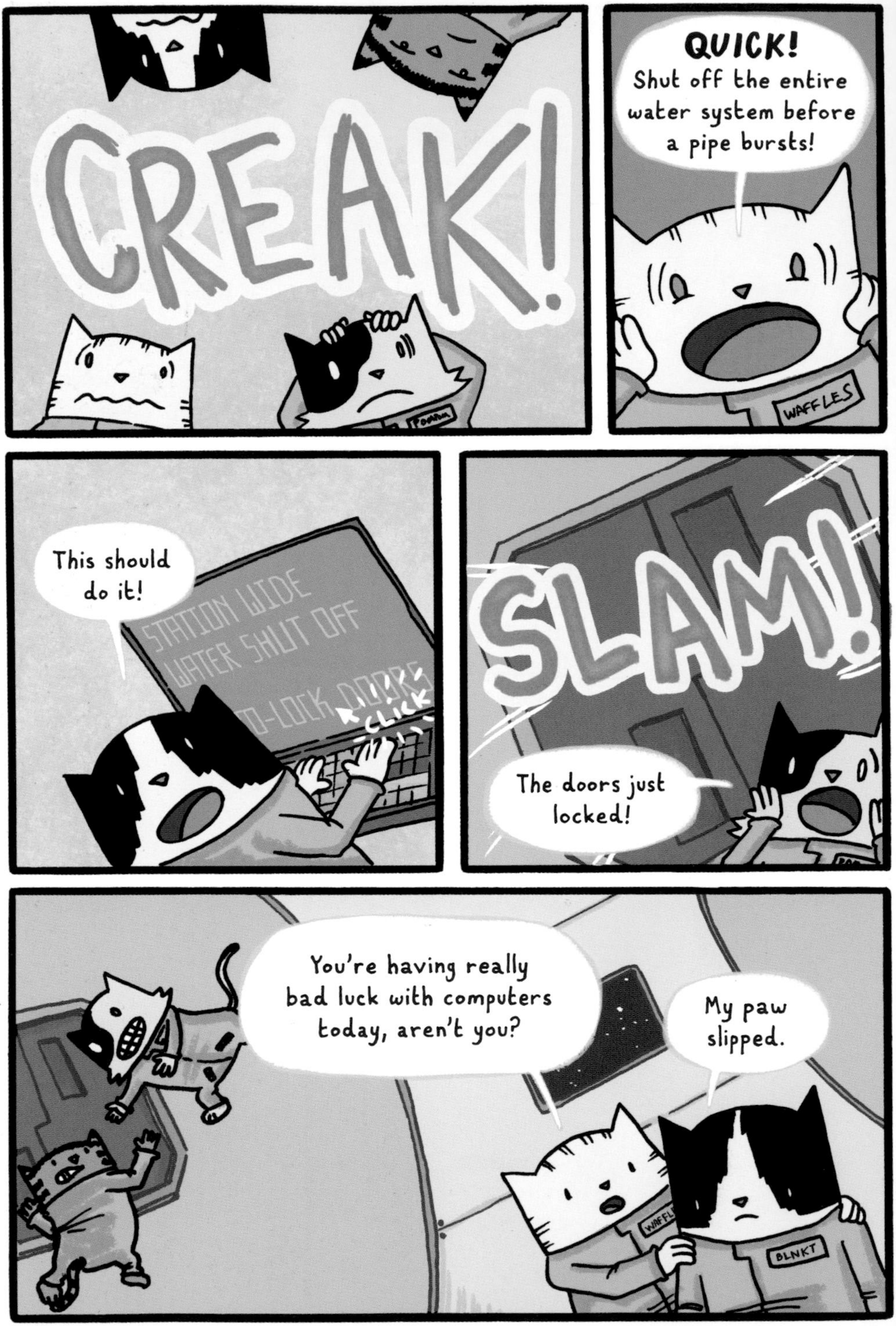
CREAK!
QUICK! Shut off the entire water system before a pipe bursts!
WAFFLES
This should do it!
STATION WIDE
WATER SHUT OFF
CLICK
SLAM!
The doors just locked!
You're having really bad luck with computers today, aren't you?
My paw slipped.
BLNKT

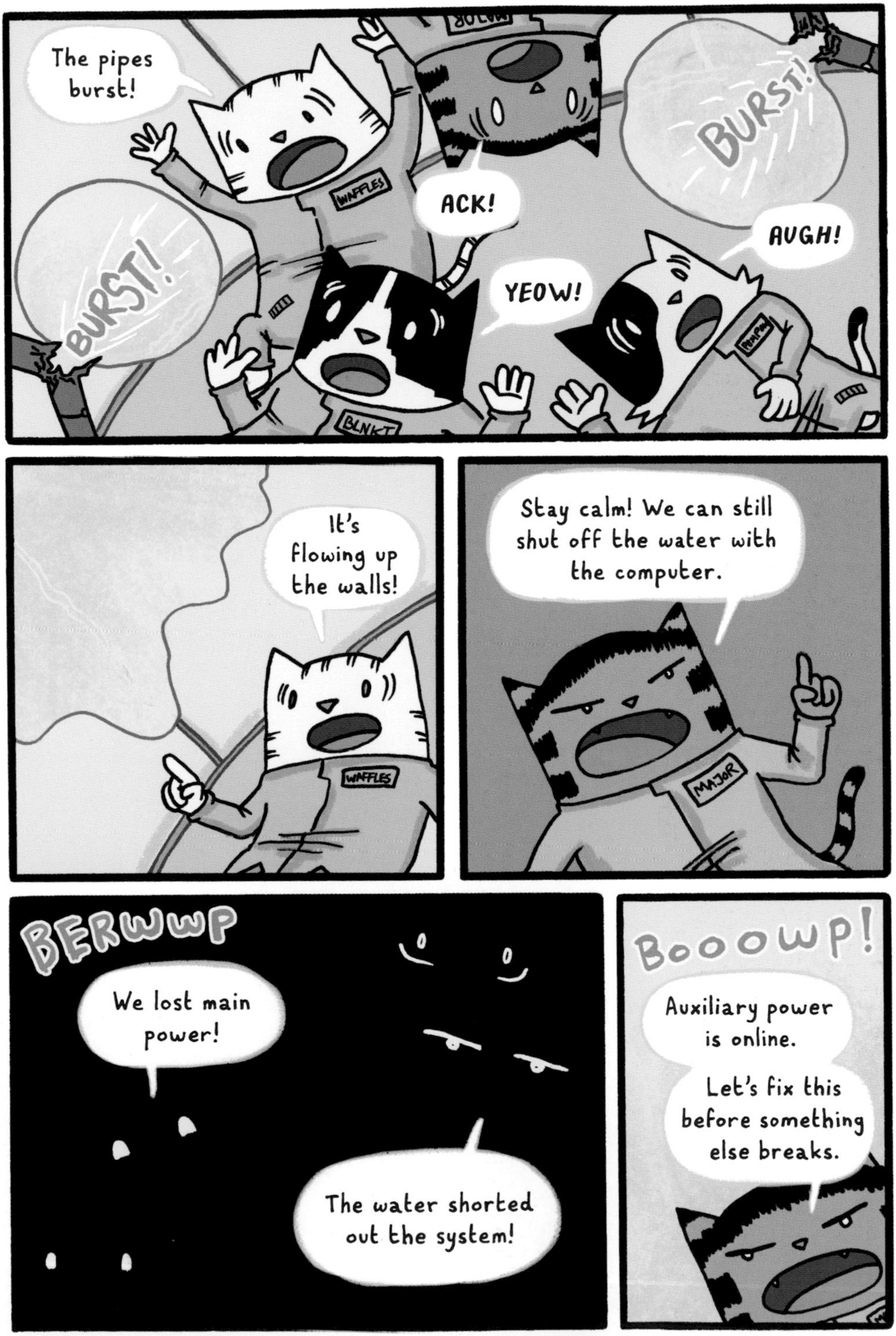
The pipes burst!
BURST!
ACK!
BURST!
YEOW!
AUGH!
WAFFLES
BLNKT
MAJOR
It's flowing up the walls!
Stay calm! We can still shut off the water with the computer.
BERWWP
We lost main power!
The water shorted out the system!
Booowp!
Auxiliary power is online.
Let's fix this before something else breaks.

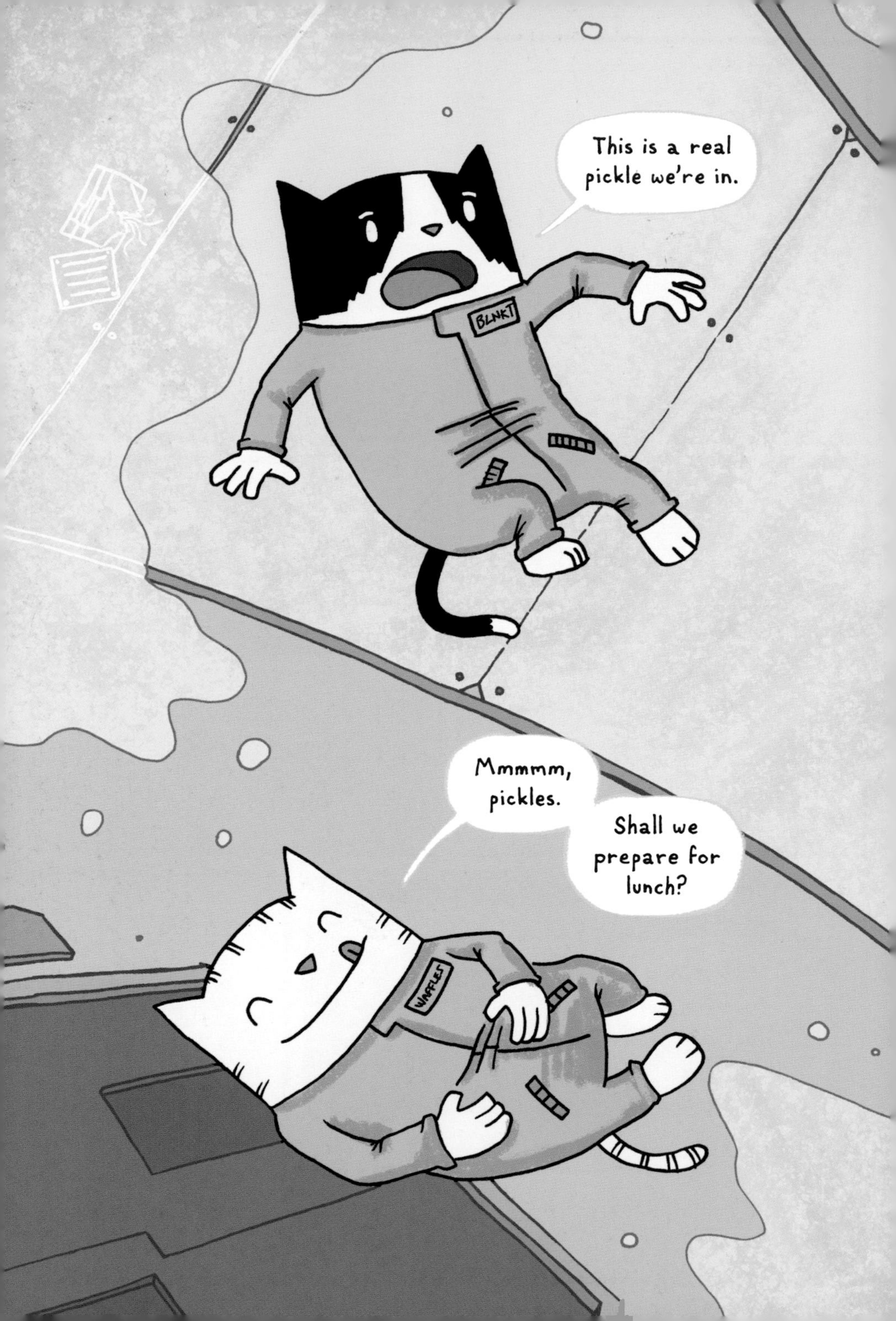
This is a real pickle we're in.
BLNKT
Mmmmm, pickles.
Shall we prepare for lunch?
WAFFLES

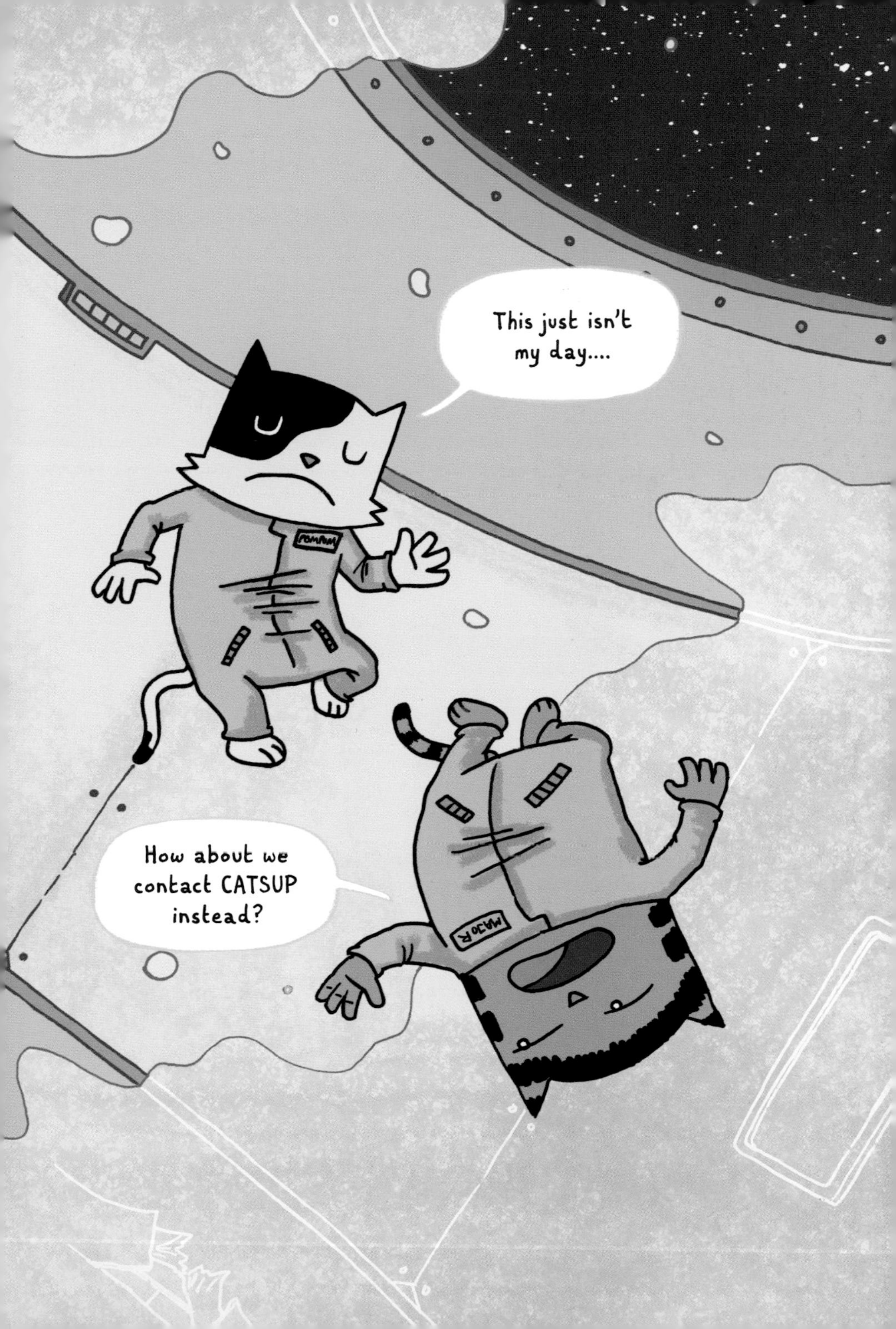
This just isn't my day....
How about we contact CATSUP instead?

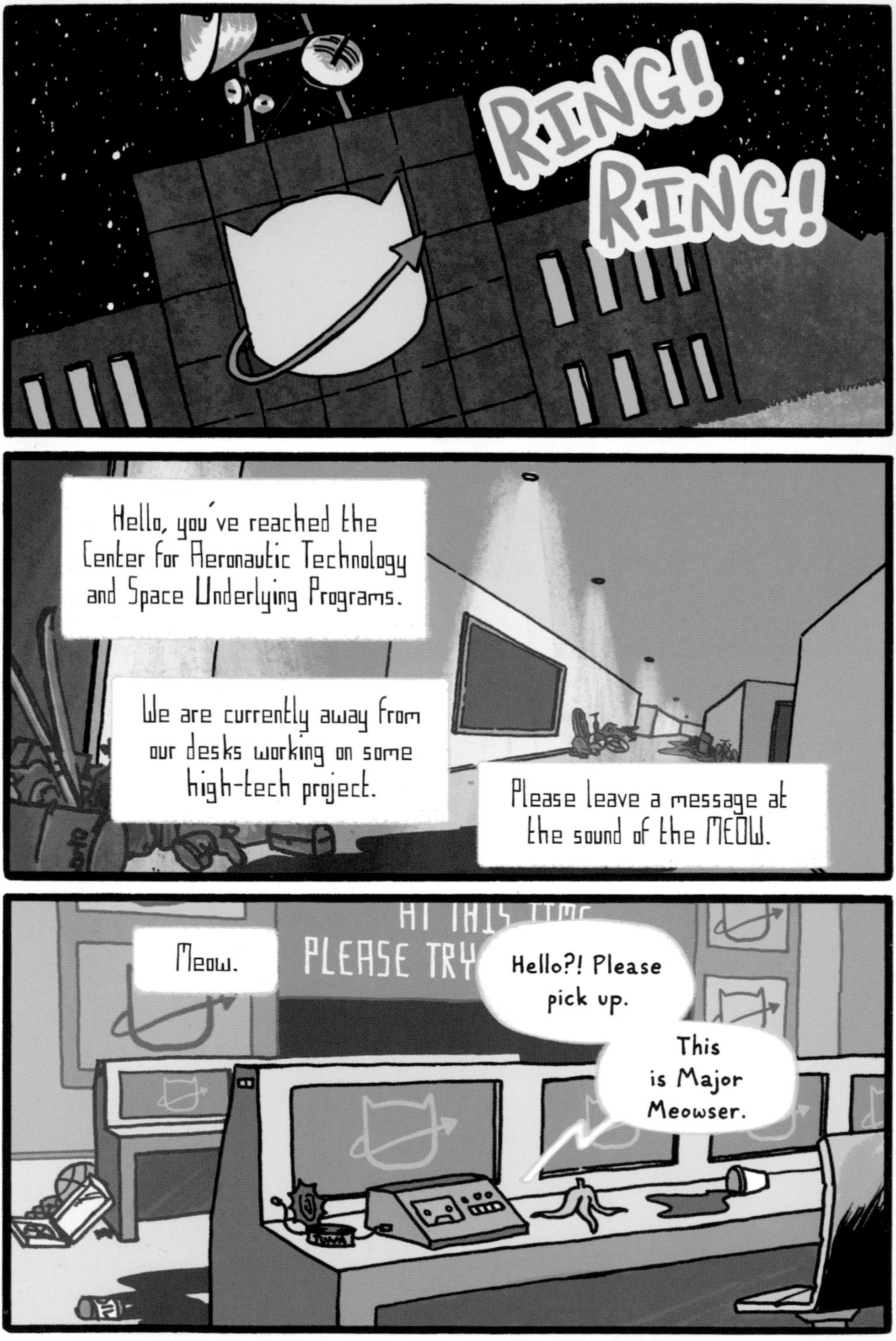
RING!
RING!
Hello, you've reached the Center for Aeronautic Technology and Space Underlying Programs.
We are currently away from our desks working on some high-tech project.
Please leave a message at the sound of the MEOW.
Meow.
PLEASE TRY
Hello?! Please pick up.
This is Major Meowser.

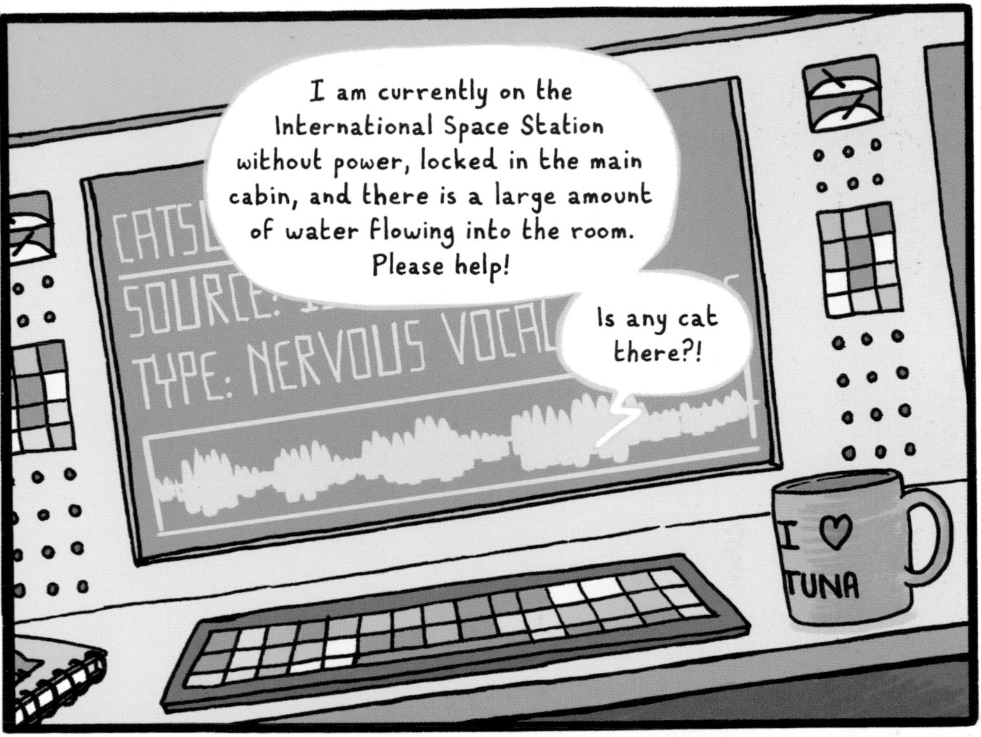
I am currently on the International Space Station without power, locked in the main cabin, and there is a large amount of water flowing into the room. Please help!
Is any cat there?!
I ♥ TUNA

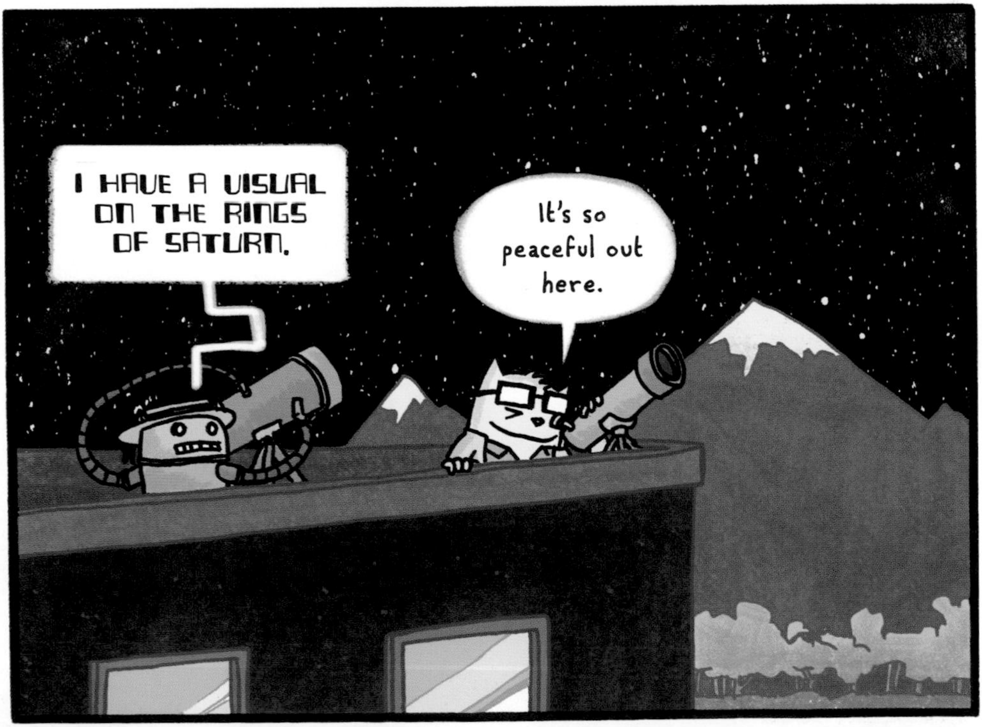
I HAVE A VISUAL ON THE RINGS OF SATURN.
It's so peaceful out here.

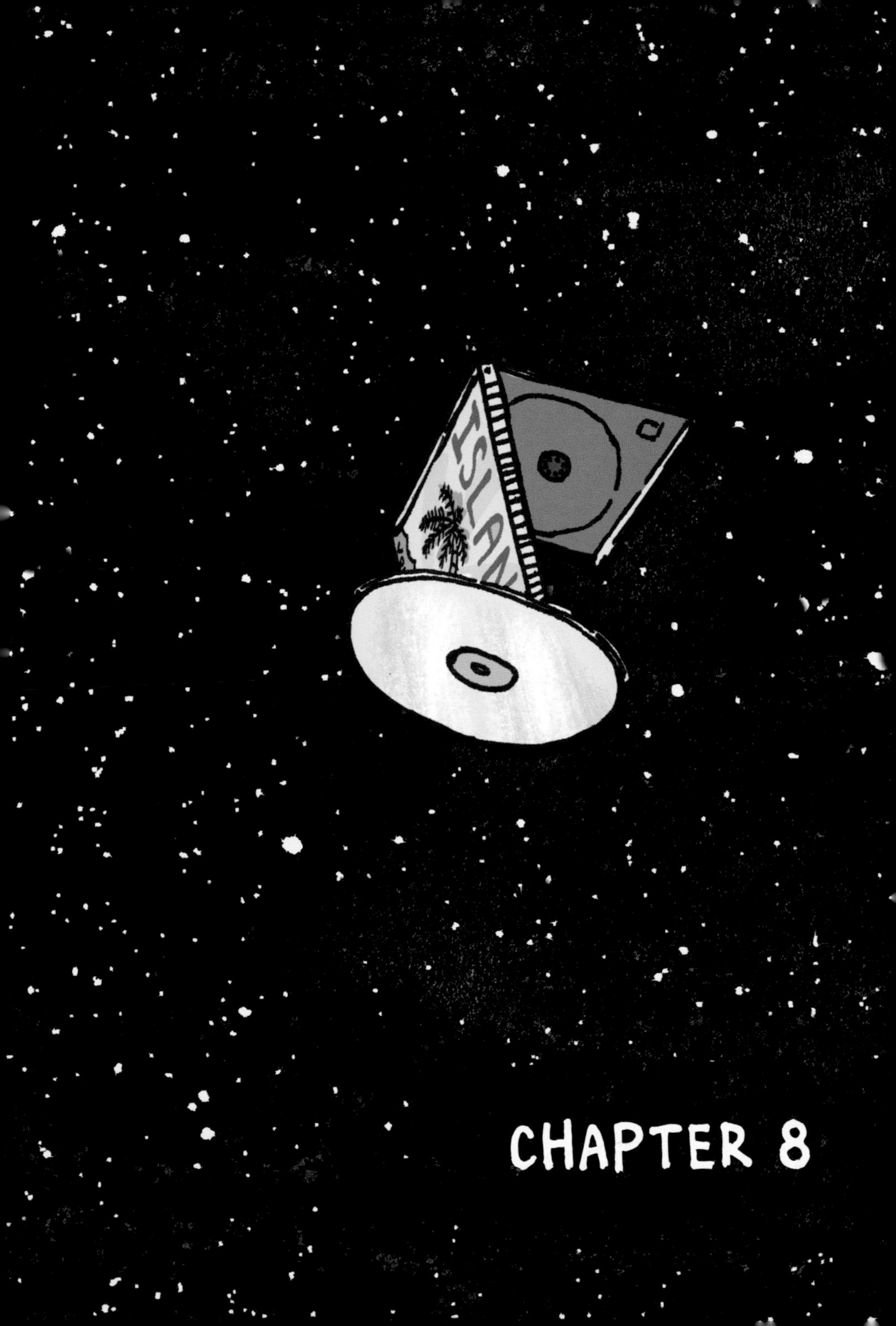
ISLAN

CHAPTER 8

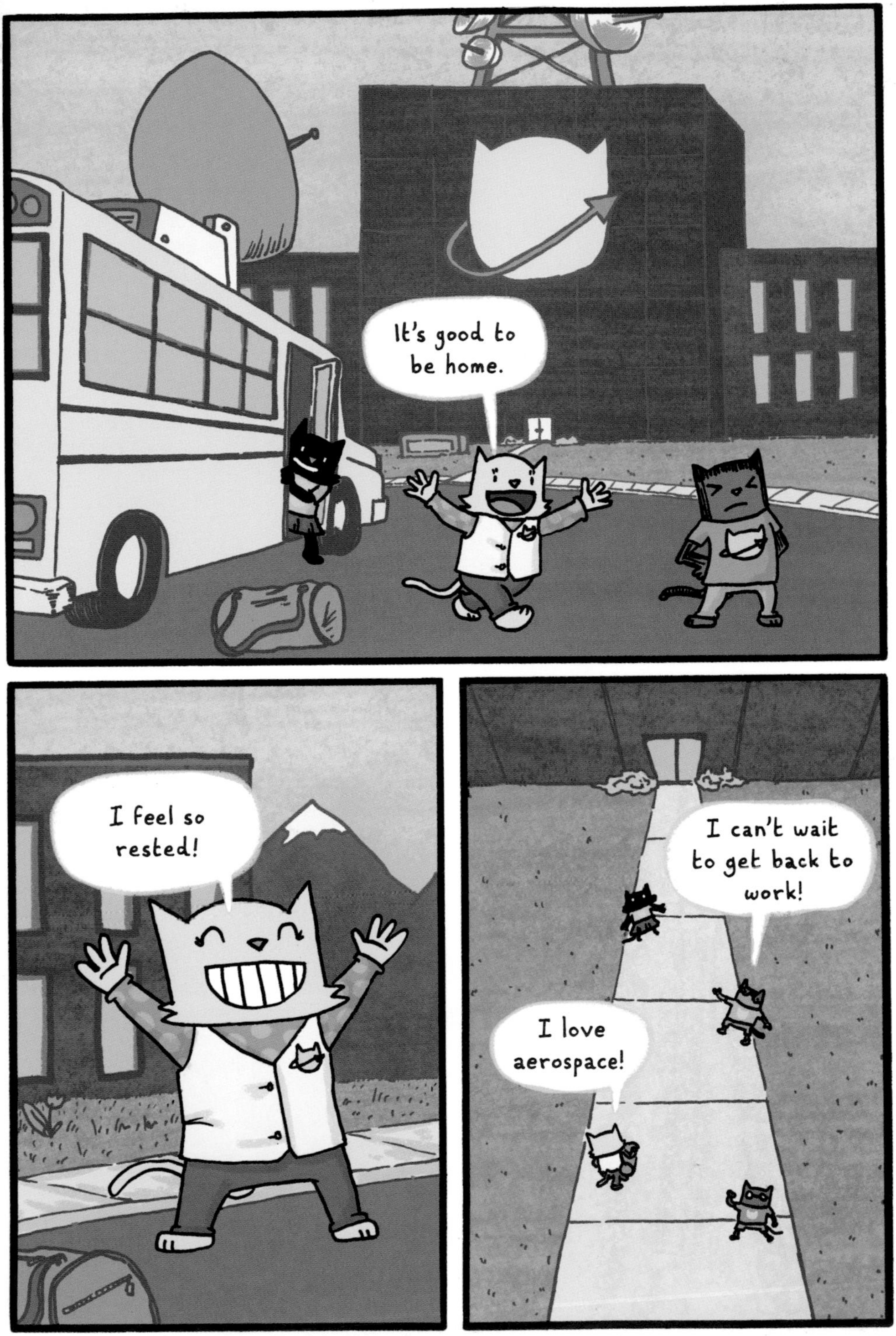
It's good to be home.
I feel so rested!
I can't wait to get back to work!
I love aerospace!

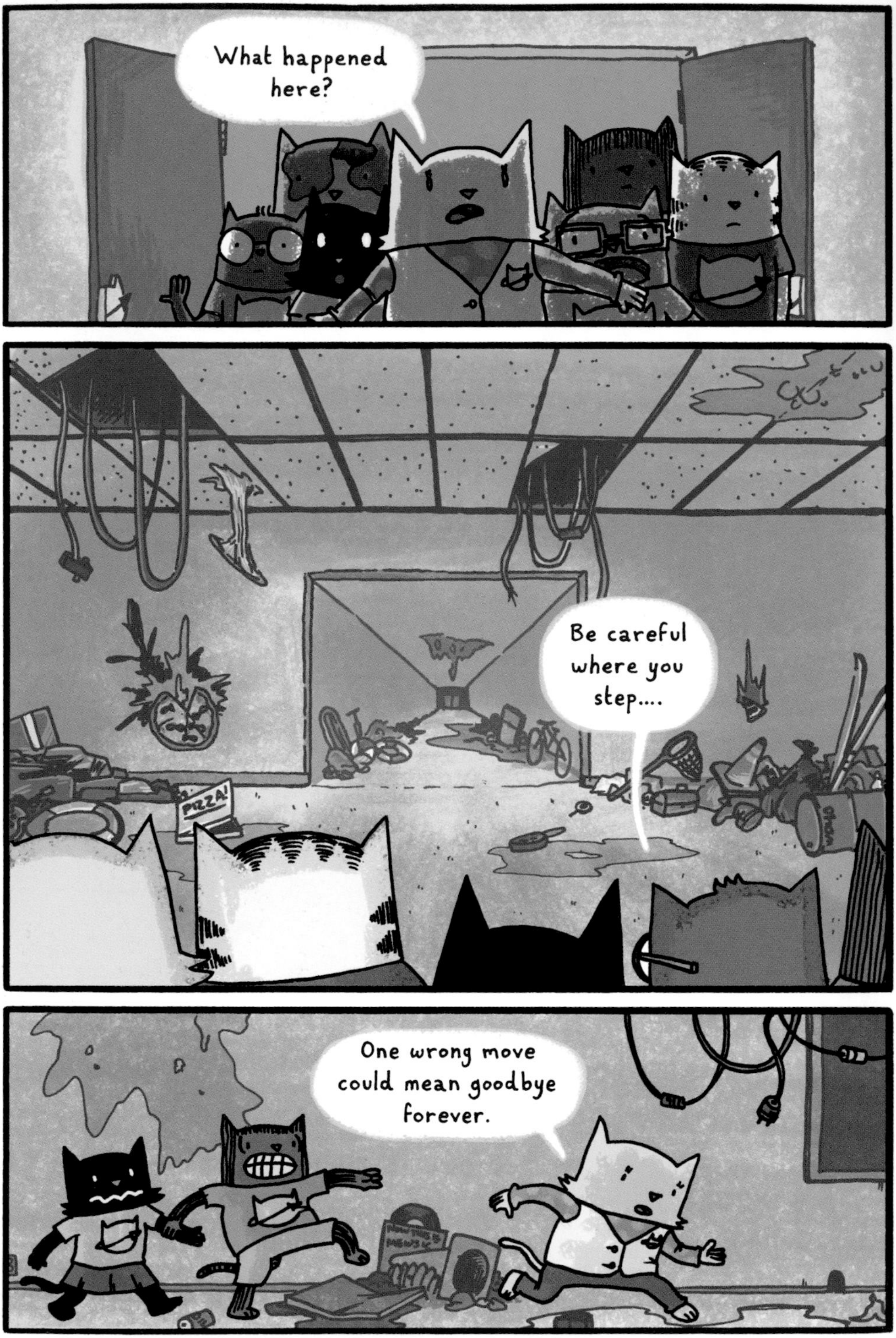
What happened here?
Be careful where you step....
PIZZA!
One wrong move could mean goodbye forever.

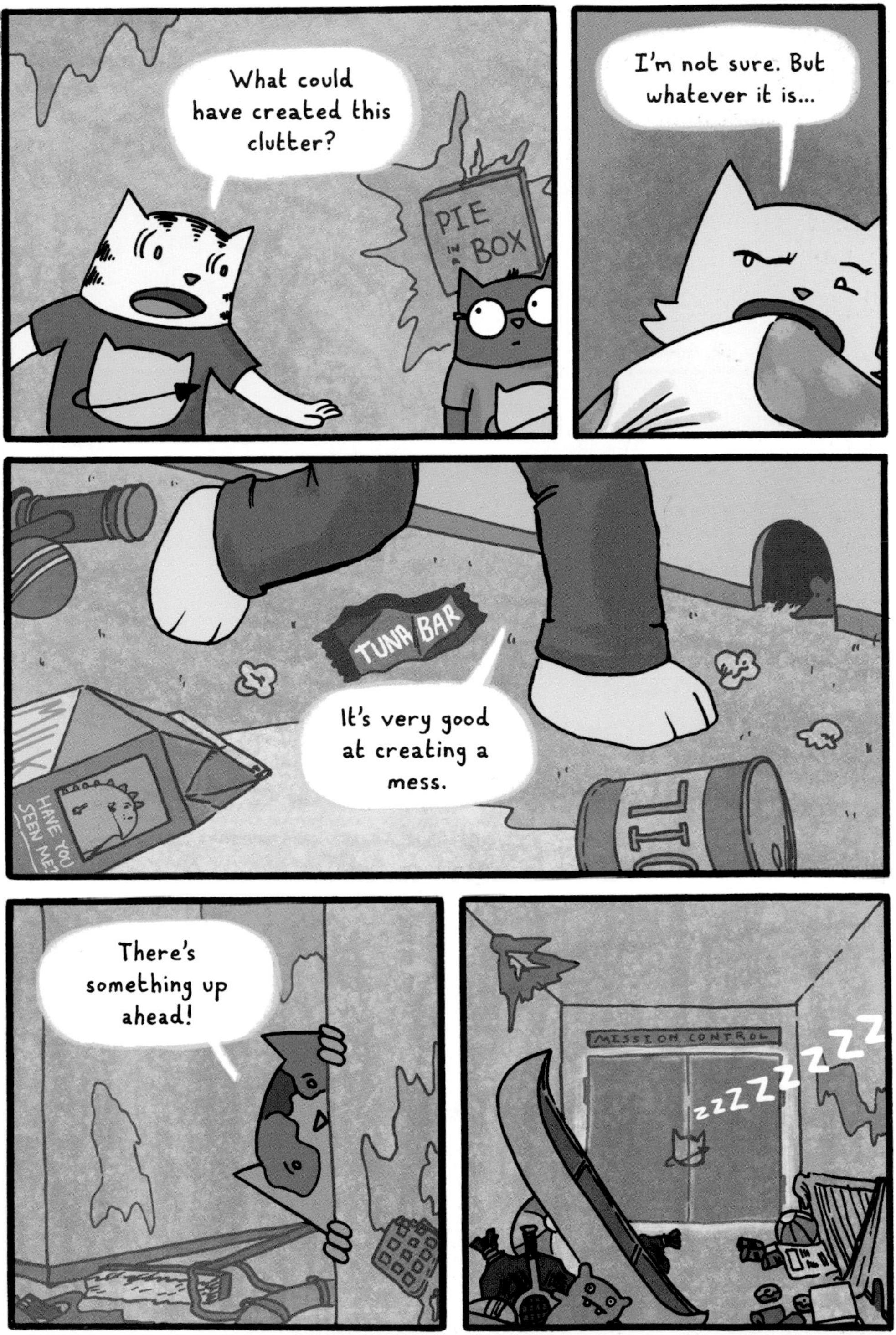
What could have created this clutter?
PIE IN A BOX
I'm not sure. But whatever it is...
TUNA BAR
MILK
HAVE YOU SEEN ME?
It's very good at creating a mess.
There's something up ahead!
MISSION CONTROL
zzZZZZZZZ

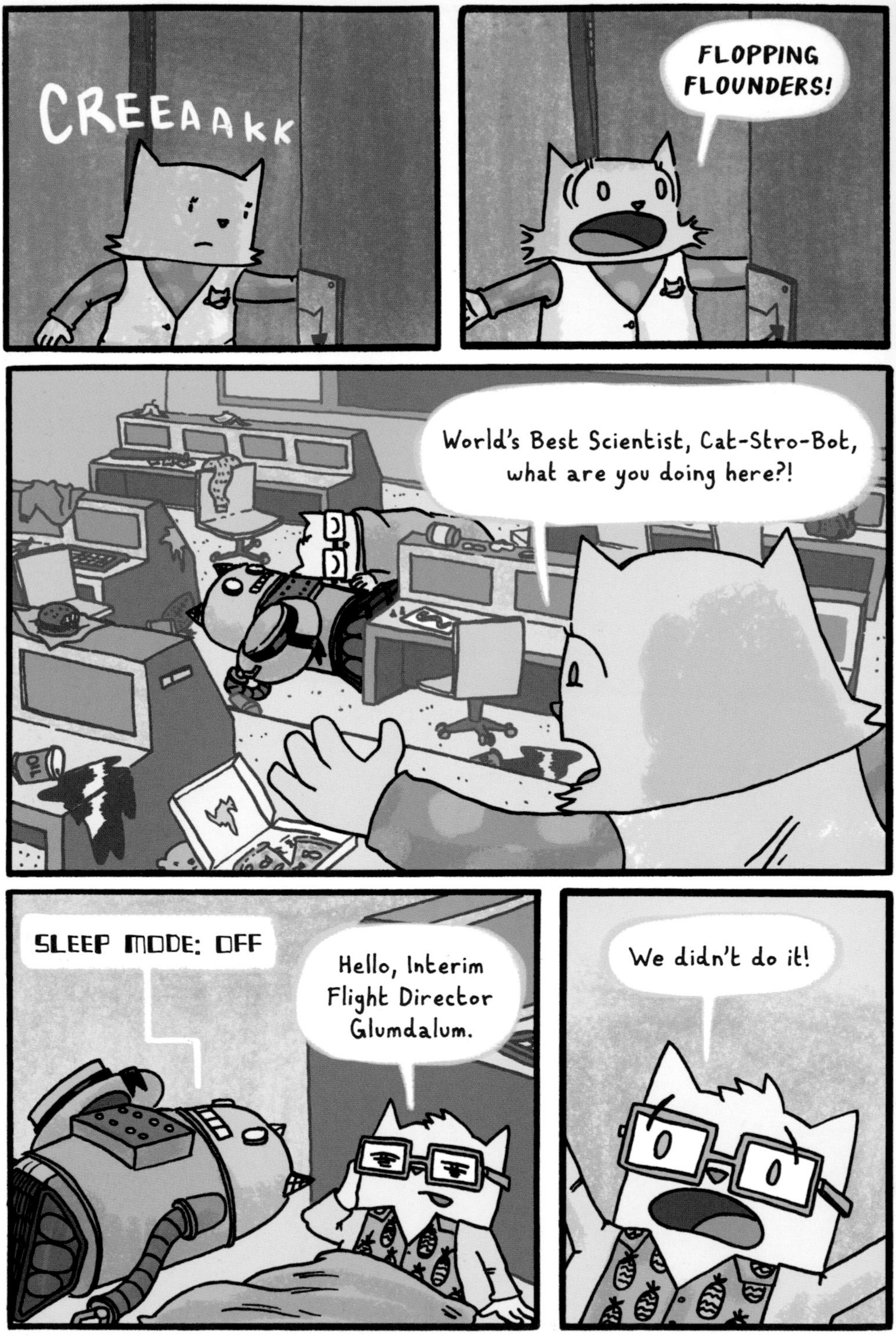
CREEAAKK
FLOPPING FLOUNDERS!
World's Best Scientist, Cat-Stro-Bot, what are you doing here?!
OIL
SLEEP MODE: OFF
Hello, Interim Flight Director Glumdalum.
We didn't do it!

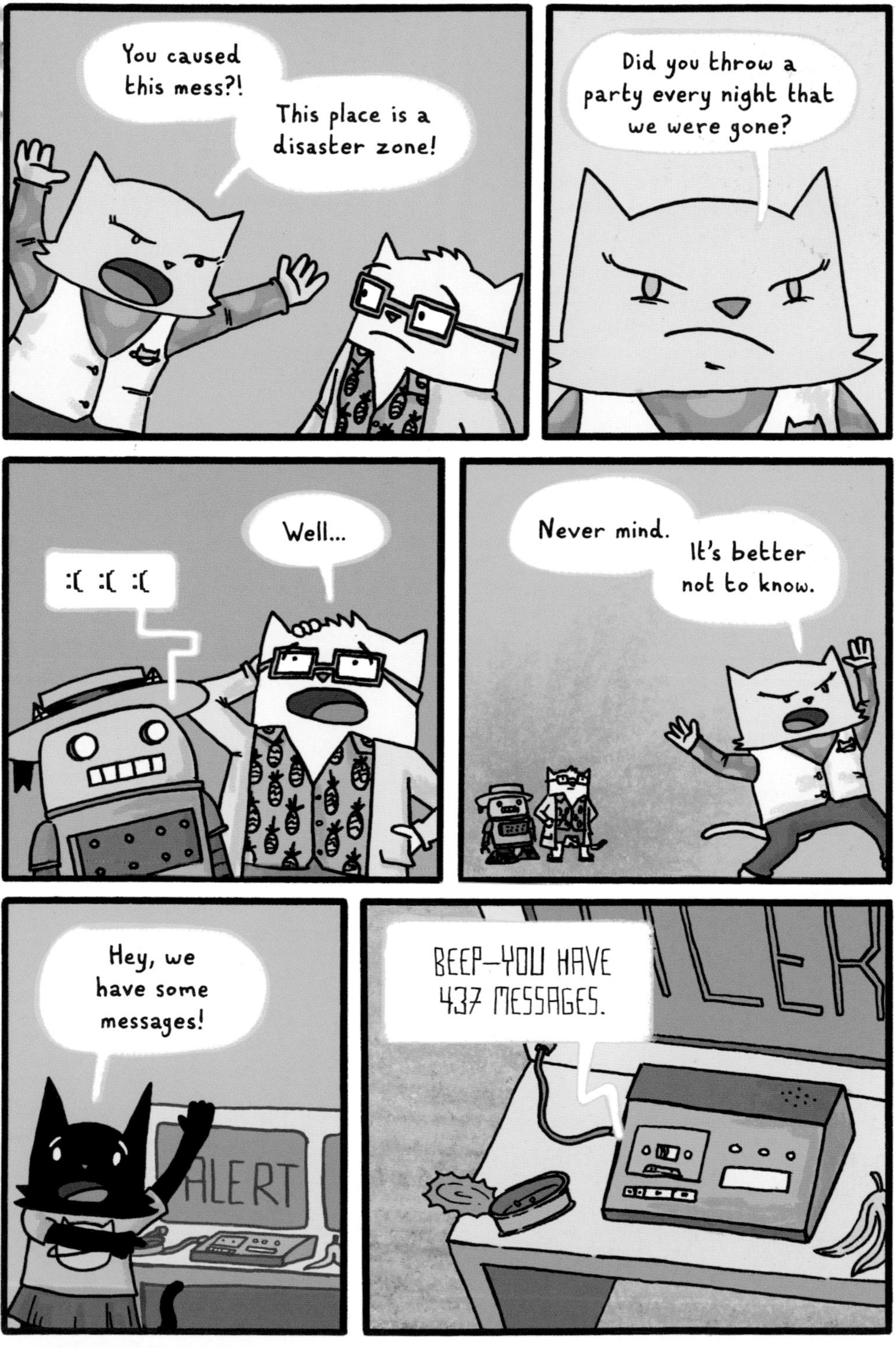

You caused this mess?!
This place is a disaster zone!
Did you throw a party every night that we were gone?
:(:(:(
Well...
Never mind.
It's better not to know.
Hey, we have some messages!
ALERT
BEEP—YOU HAVE 437 MESSAGES.

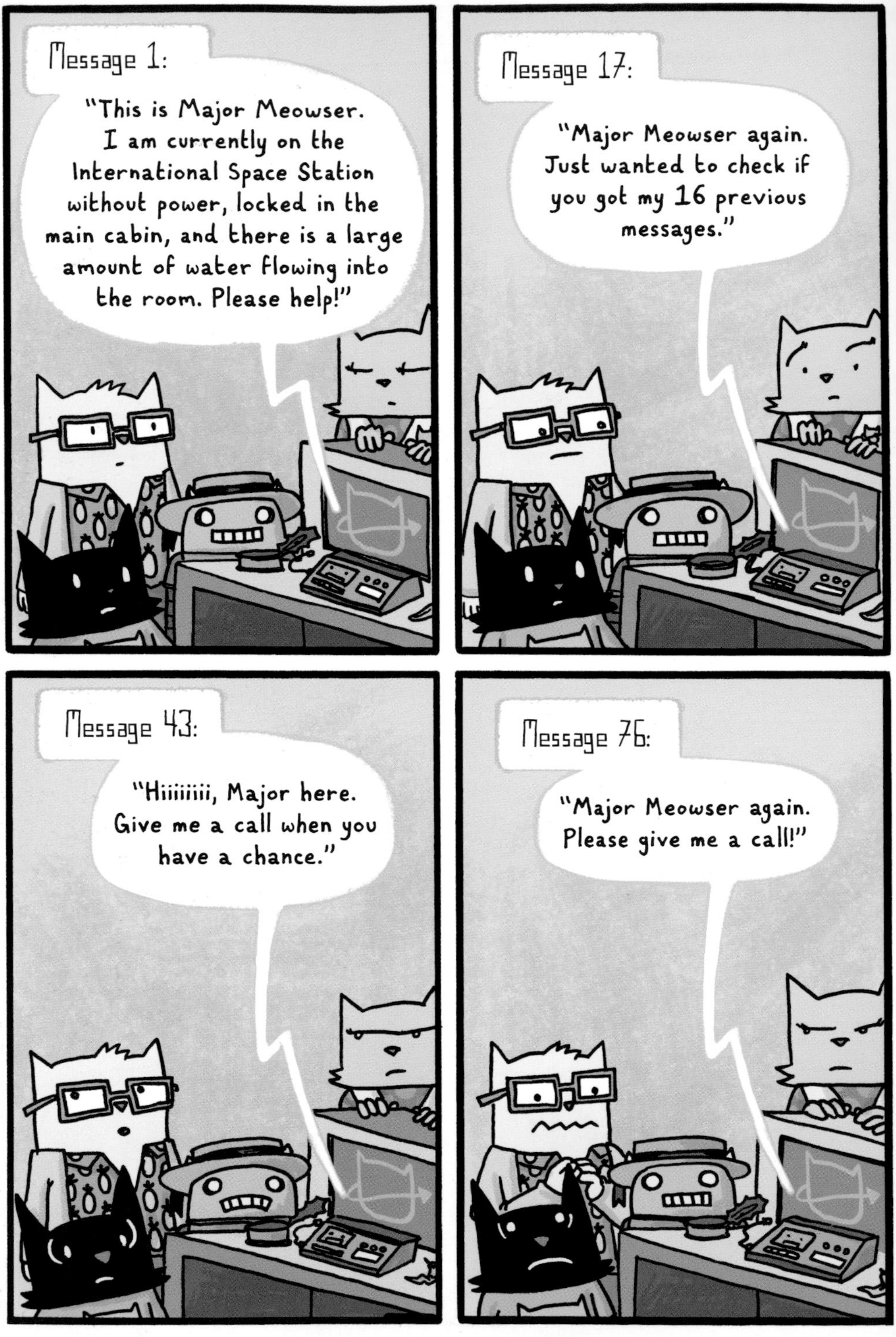
Message 1:
"This is Major Meowser. I am currently on the International Space Station without power, locked in the main cabin, and there is a large amount of water flowing into the room. Please help!"
Message 17:
"Major Meowser again. Just wanted to check if you got my 16 previous messages."
Message 43:
"Hiiiiiii, Major here. Give me a call when you have a chance."
Message 76:
"Major Meowser again. Please give me a call!"

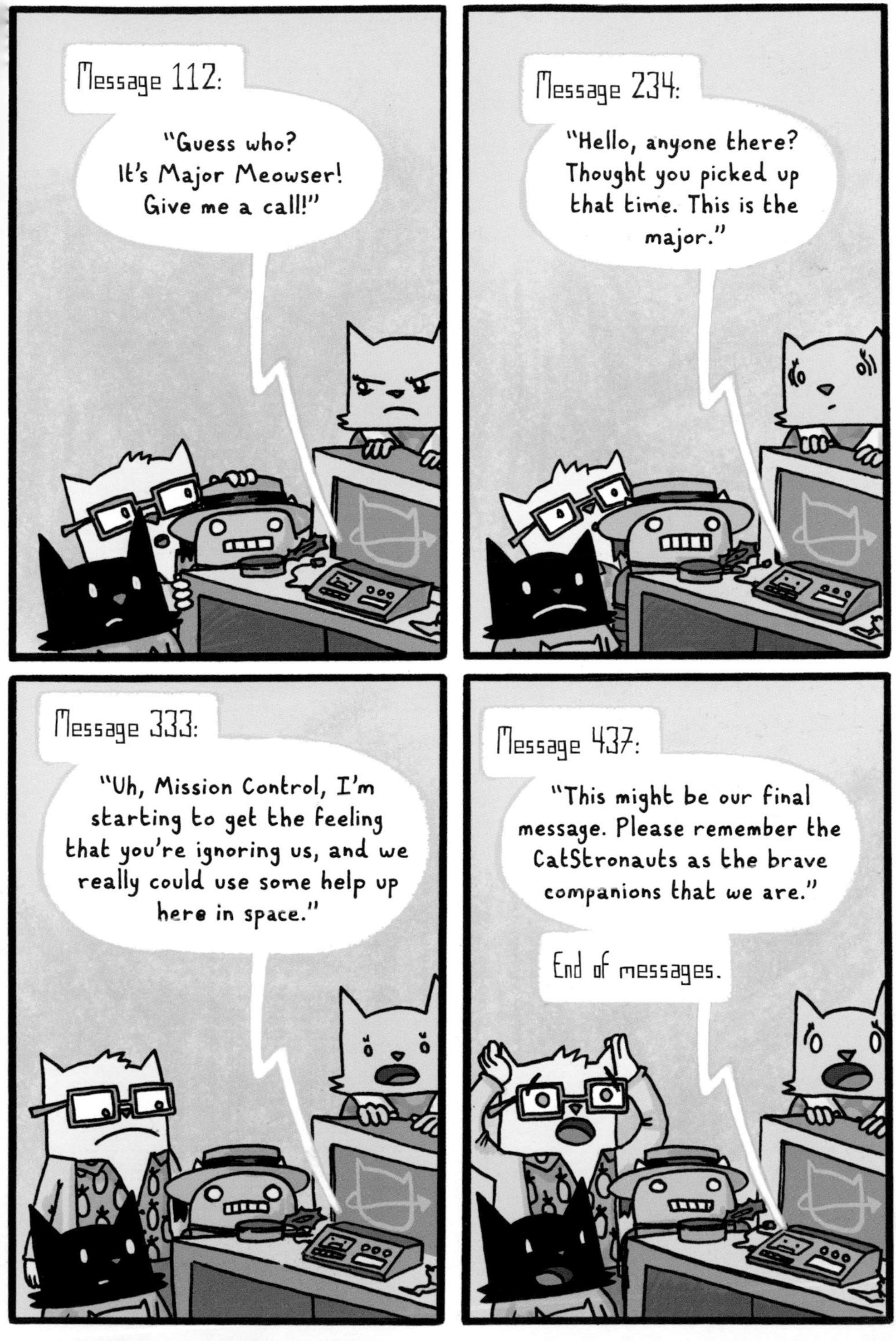
Message 112:
"Guess who? It's Major Meowser! Give me a call!"
Message 234:
"Hello, anyone there? Thought you picked up that time. This is the major."
Message 333:
"Uh, Mission Control, I'm starting to get the feeling that you're ignoring us, and we really could use some help up here in space."
Message 437:
"This might be our final message. Please remember the CatStronauts as the brave companions that we are."
End of messages.

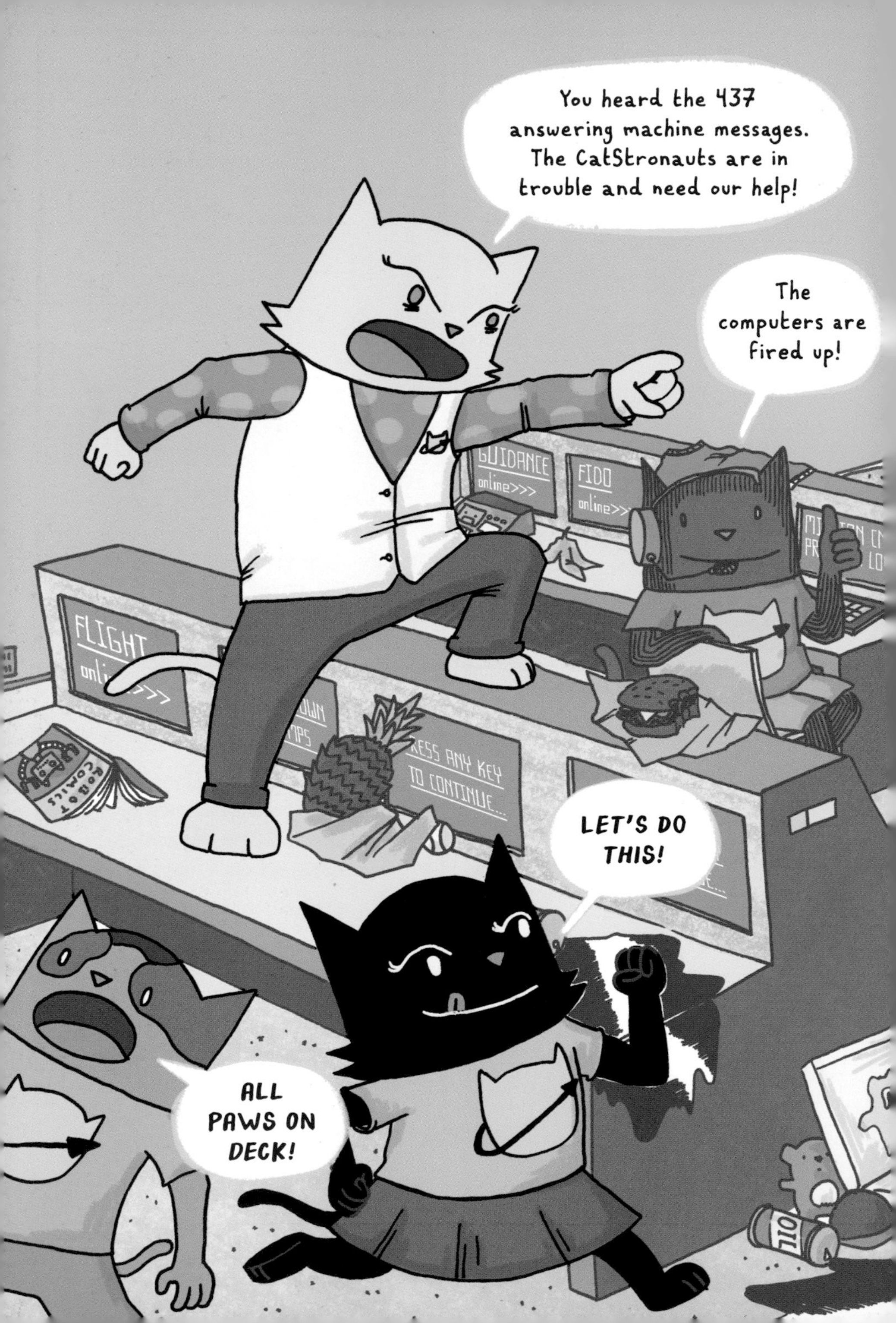
You heard the 437 answering machine messages. The CatStronauts are in trouble and need our help!
The computers are fired up!
GUIDANCE online>>>
FIDO online>>>
FLIGHT online>>>
PRESS ANY KEY TO CONTINUE...
ROBOT COMICS
LET'S DO THIS!
ALL PAWS ON DECK!
OIL

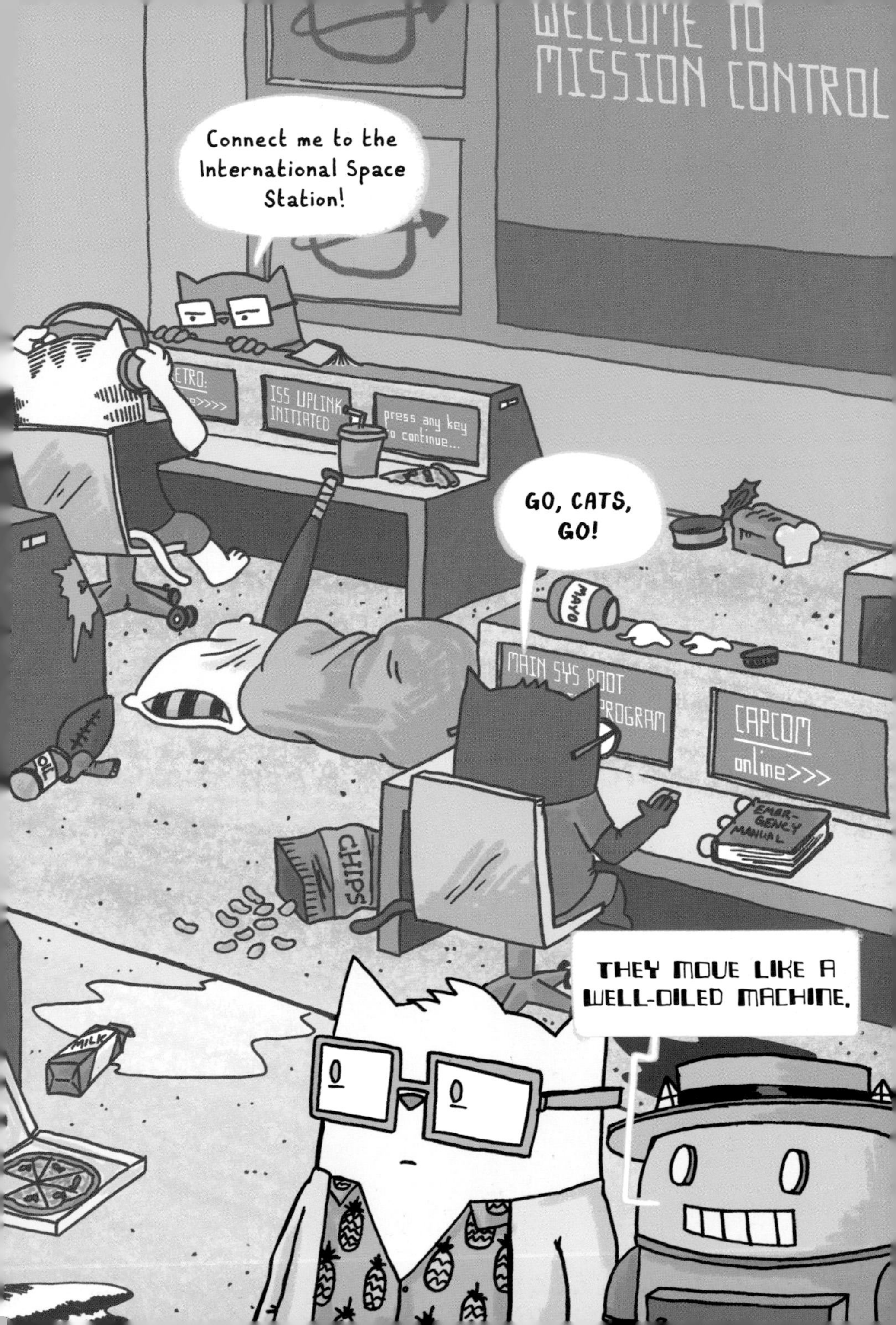

WELCOME TO MISSION CONTROL
Connect me to the International Space Station!
ISS UPLINK INITIATED
press any key to continue...
GO, CATS, GO!
MAYO
MAIN SYS ROOT
CAPCOM online>>>
EMER-GENCY MANUAL
CHIPS
OIL
MILK
THEY MOVE LIKE A WELL-OILED MACHINE.

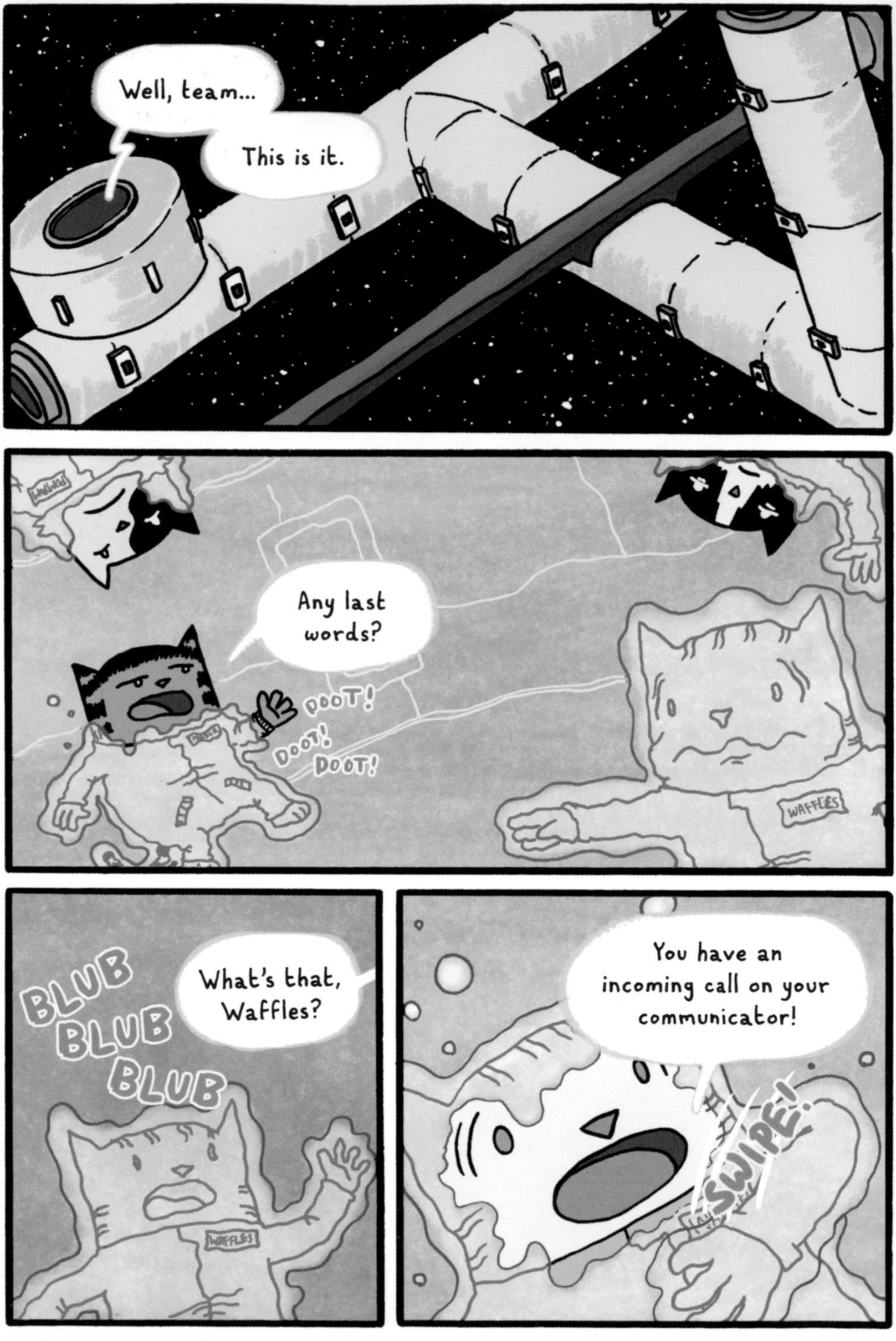
Well, team...
This is it.
Any last words?
DOOT!
DOOT!
DOOT!
WAFFLES
BLUB
BLUB
BLUB
What's that, Waffles?
WAFFLES
You have an incoming call on your communicator!
SWIPE!

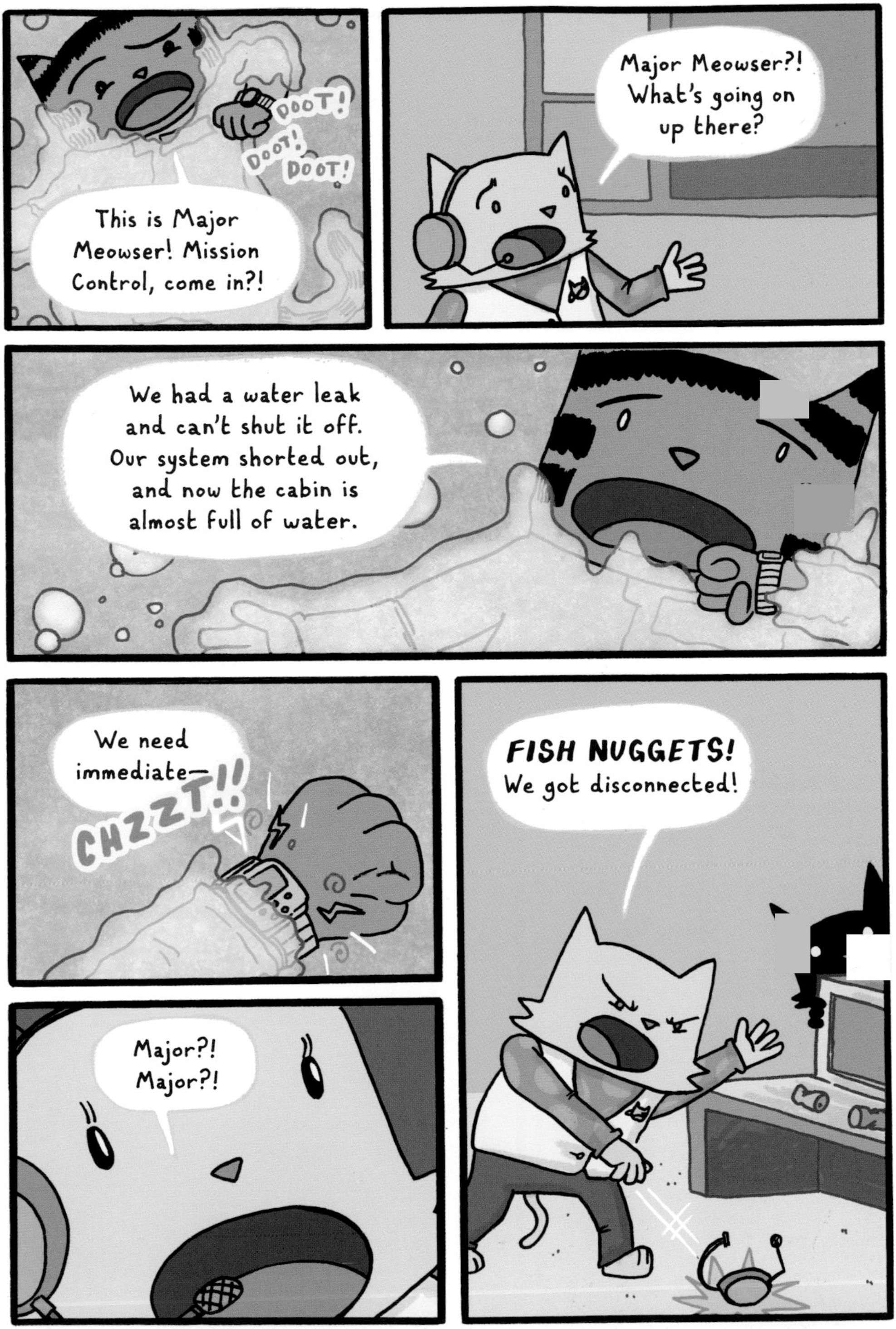
DOOT!
DOOT!
DOOT!
This is Major Meowser! Mission Control, come in?!
Major Meowser?! What's going on up there?
We had a water leak and can't shut it off. Our system shorted out, and now the cabin is almost full of water.
We need immediate—
CHZZT!!
FISH NUGGETS! We got disconnected!
Major?! Major?!

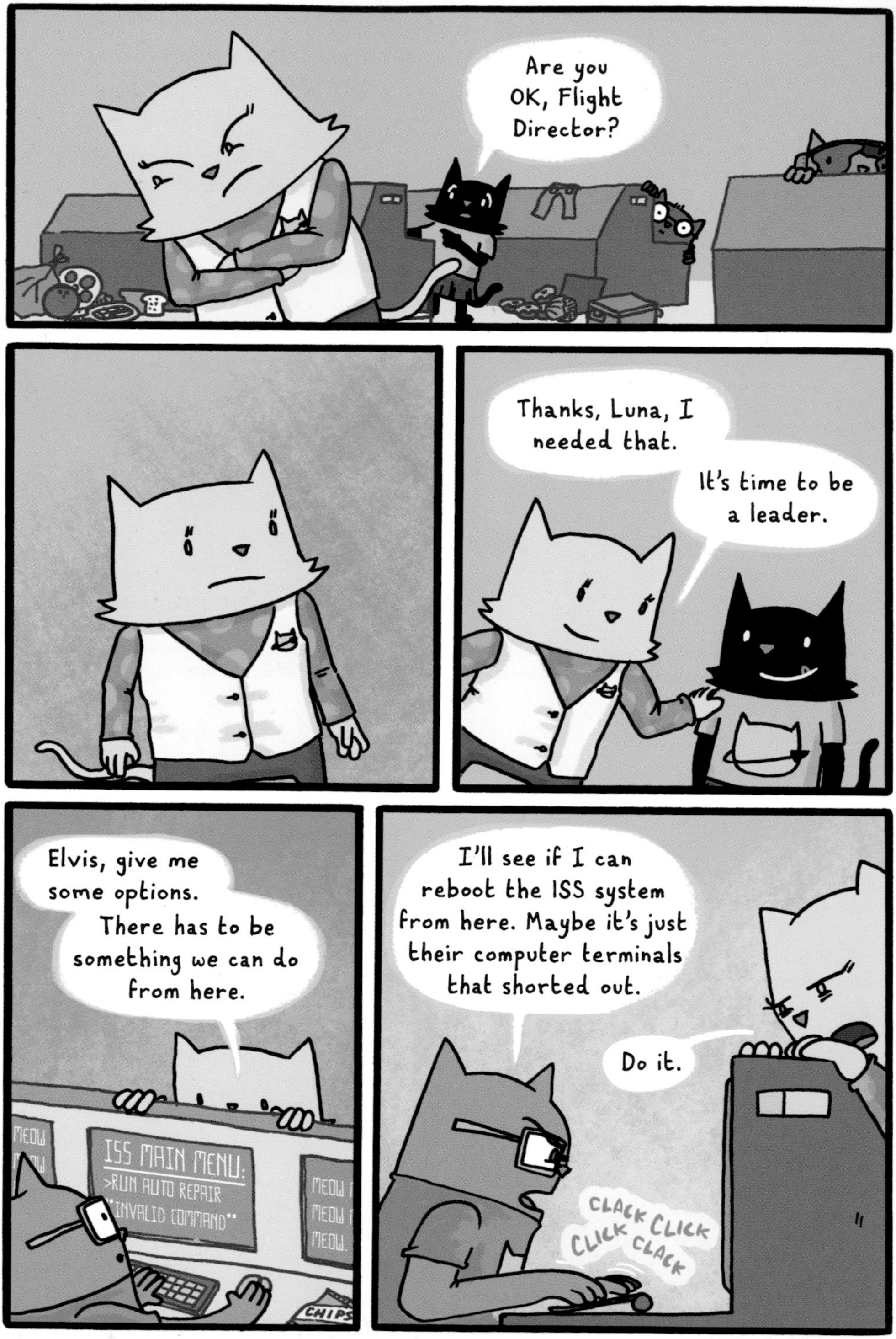
Are you OK, Flight Director?
Thanks, Luna, I needed that.
It's time to be a leader.
Elvis, give me some options.
There has to be something we can do from here.
ISS MAIN MENU:
>RUN AUTO REPAIR
INVALID COMMAND
CHIPS
I'll see if I can reboot the ISS system from here. Maybe it's just their computer terminals that shorted out.
Do it.
CLACK CLICK CLICK CLACK

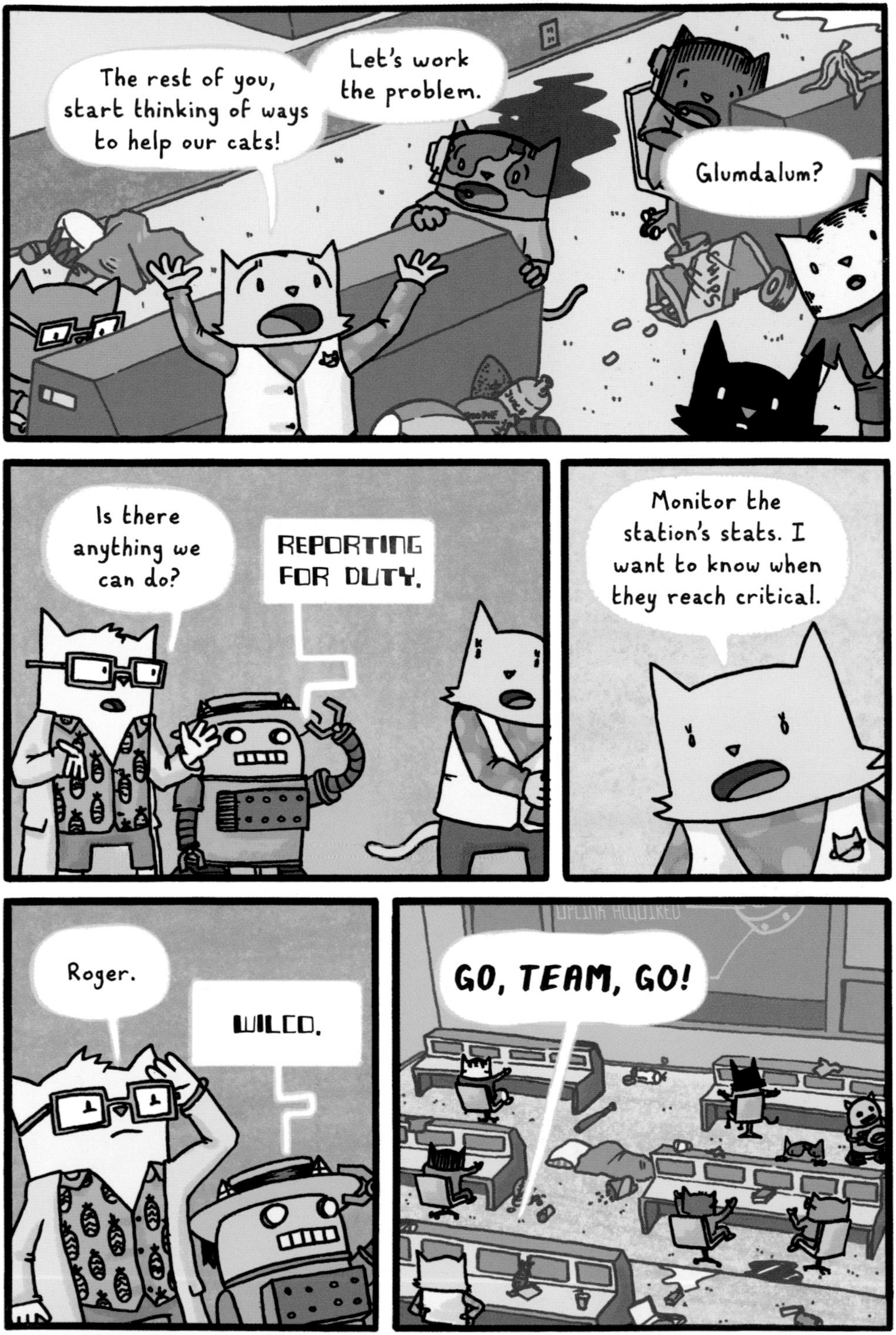
The rest of you, start thinking of ways to help our cats!
Let's work the problem.
Glumdalum?
Is there anything we can do?
REPORTING FOR DUTY.
Monitor the station's stats. I want to know when they reach critical.
Roger.
WILCO.
GO, TEAM, GO!

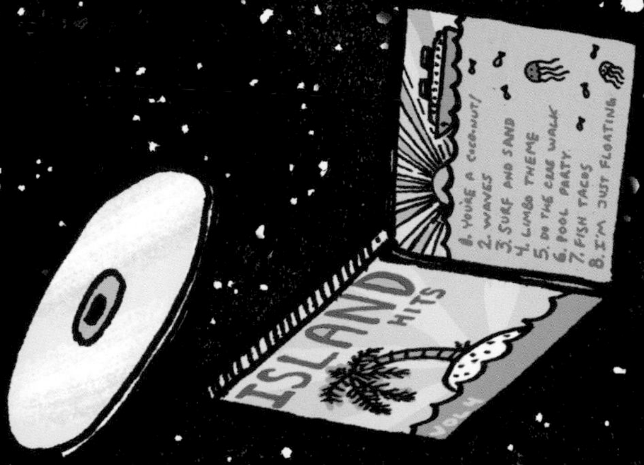
ISLAND
HITS
1. YOU'RE A COCONUT!
2. WAVES
3. SURF AND SAND
4. LIMBO THEME
5. DO THE CRAB WALK
6. POOL PARTY
7. FISH TACOS
8. I'M JUST FLOATING

CHAPTER 9

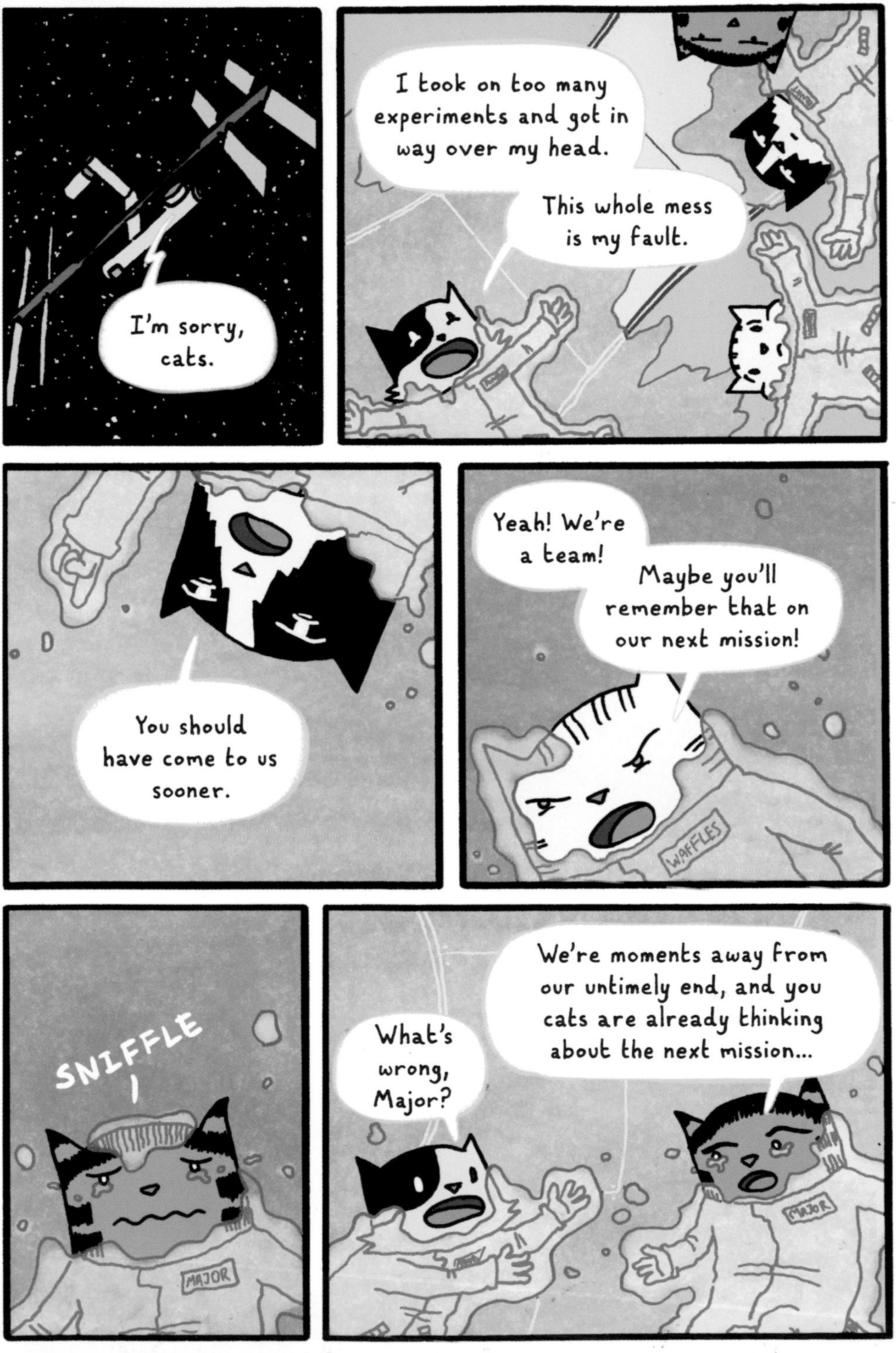
I'm sorry, cats.
I took on too many experiments and got in way over my head.
This whole mess is my fault.
You should have come to us sooner.
Yeah! We're a team!
Maybe you'll remember that on our next mission!
WAFFLES
SNIFFLE
MAJOR
What's wrong, Major?
We're moments away from our untimely end, and you cats are already thinking about the next mission...
MAJOR

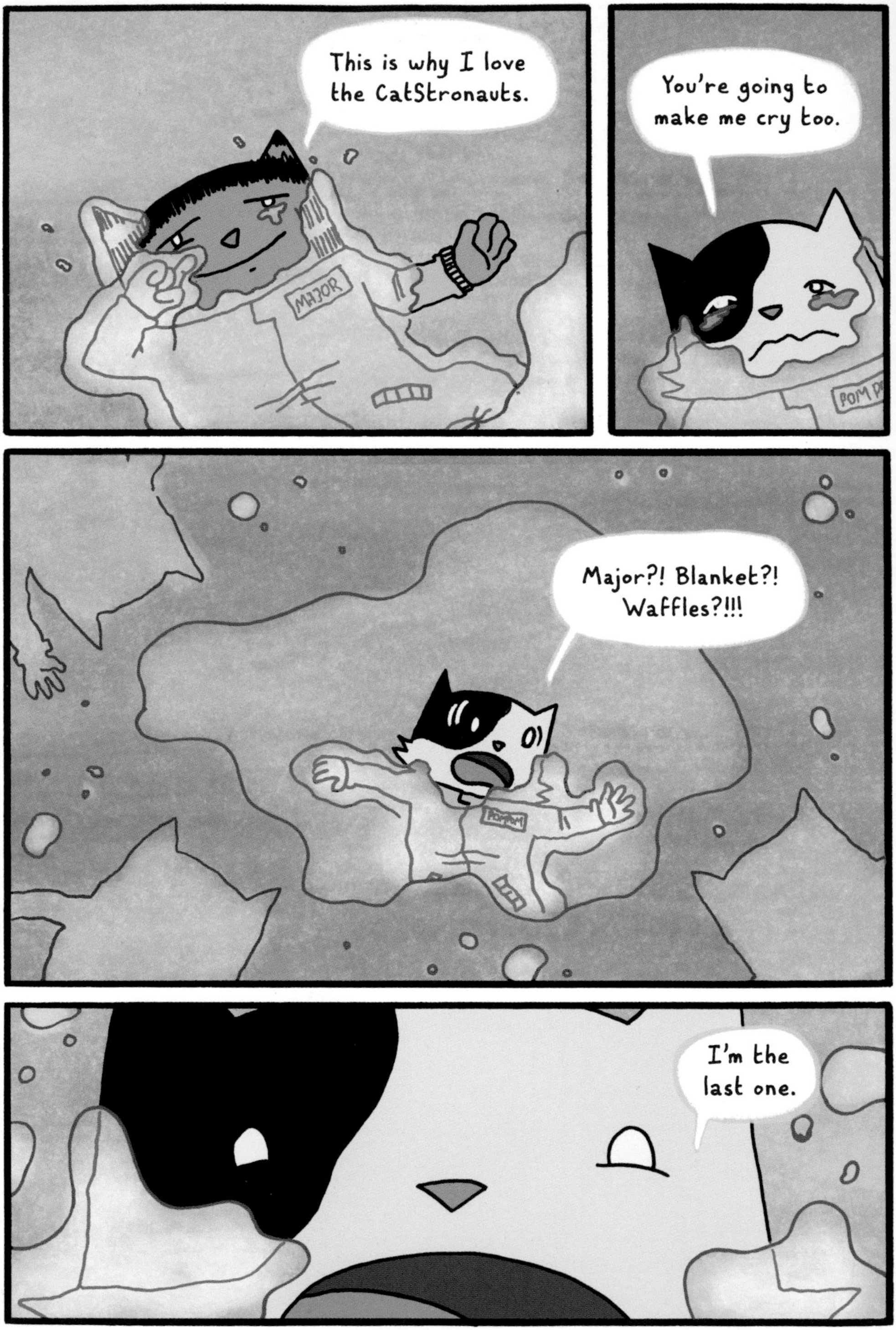
This is why I love the CatStronauts.
MAJOR
You're going to make me cry too.
POM PO
Major?! Blanket?! Waffles?!!!
POMPOM
I'm the last one.

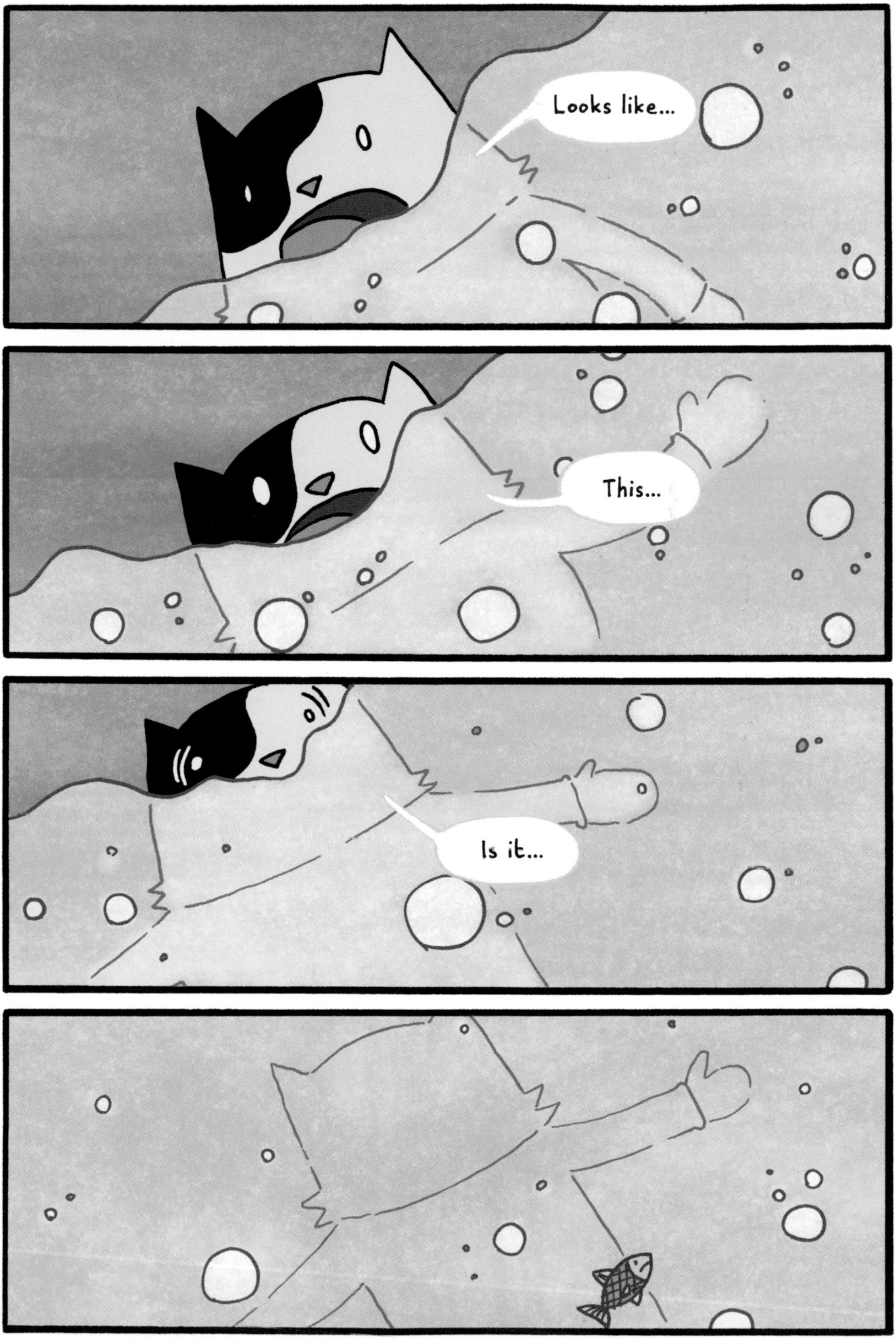
Looks like...
This...
Is it...

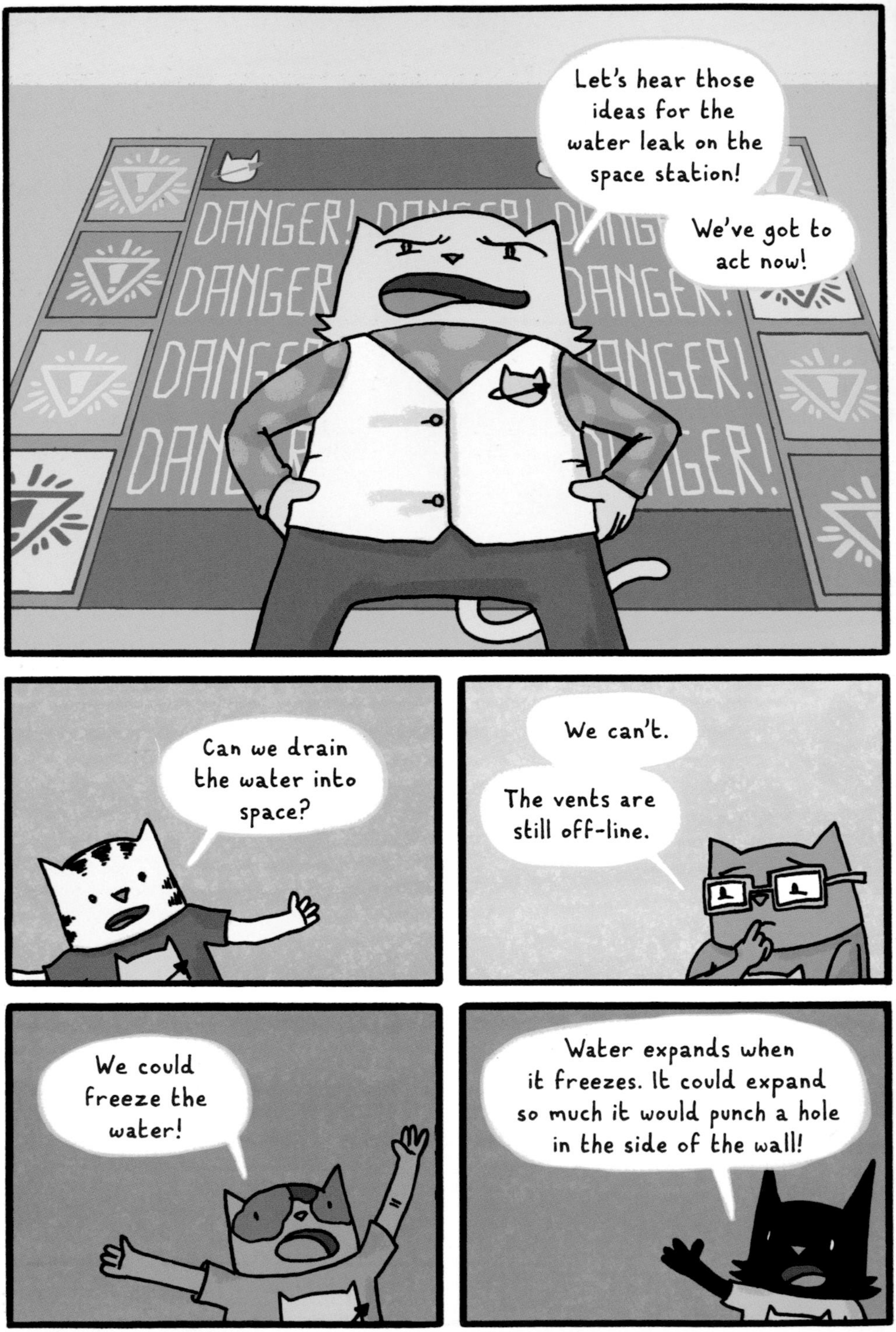
Let's hear those ideas for the water leak on the space station!
We've got to act now!
DANGER! DANGER! DANGER!
Can we drain the water into space?
We can't.
The vents are still off-line.
We could freeze the water!
Water expands when it freezes. It could expand so much it would punch a hole in the side of the wall!

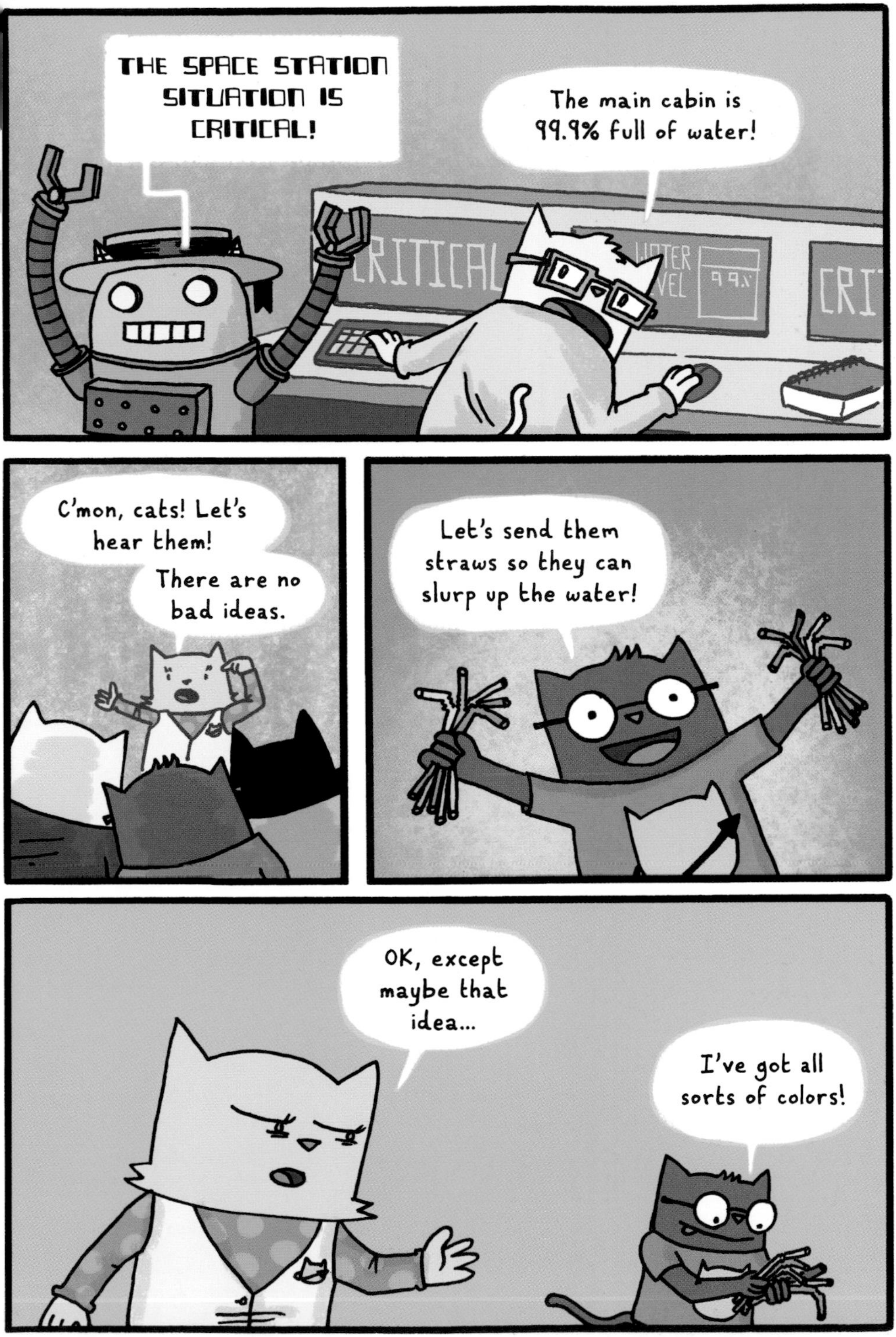
THE SPACE STATION SITUATION IS CRITICAL!
The main cabin is 99.9% full of water!
CRITICAL
CRIT
C'mon, cats! Let's hear them!
There are no bad ideas.
Let's send them straws so they can slurp up the water!
OK, except maybe that idea...
I've got all sorts of colors!

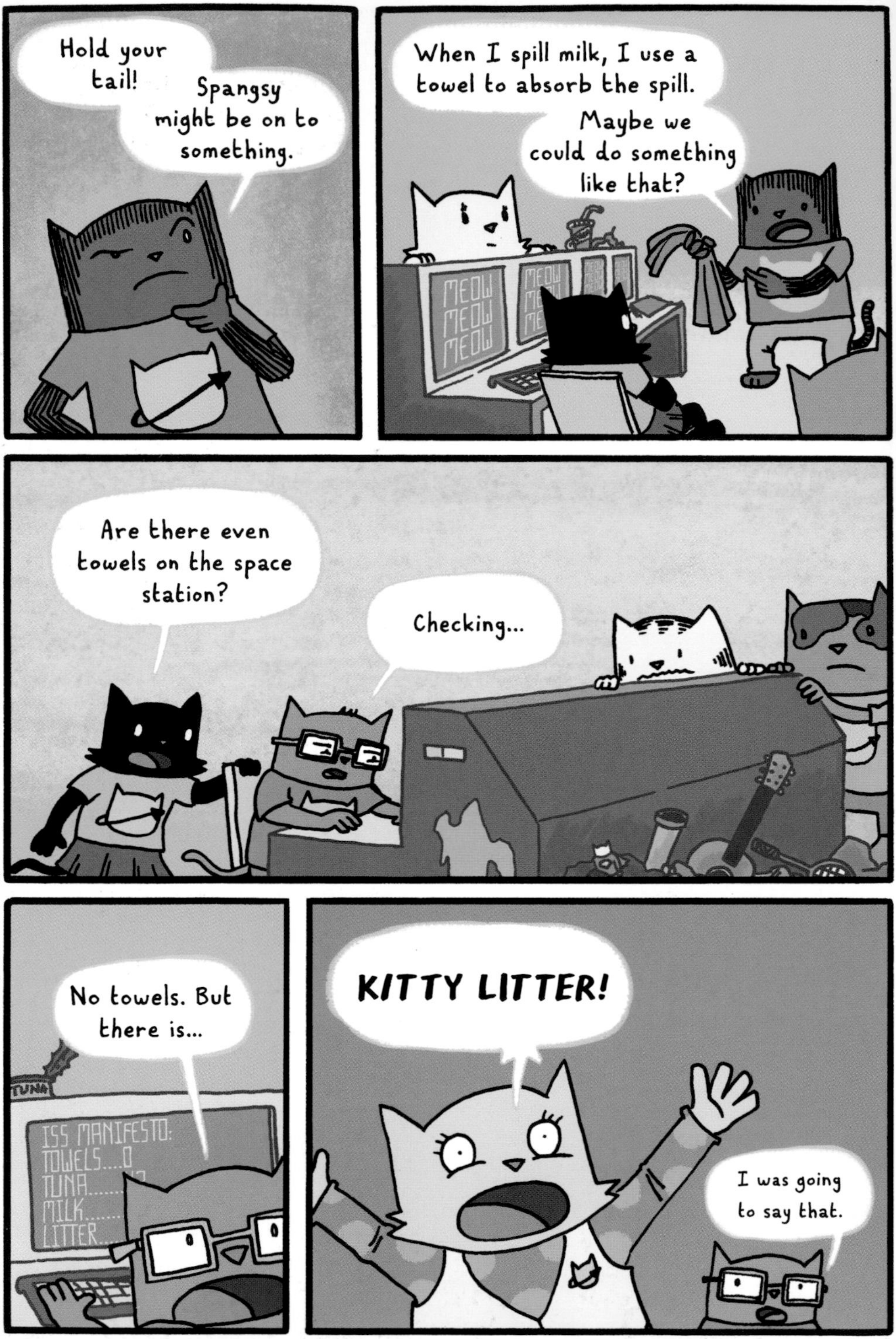

Hold your tail!
Spangsy might be on to something.
When I spill milk, I use a towel to absorb the spill.
Maybe we could do something like that?
MEOW MEOW MEOW
Are there even towels on the space station?
Checking...
No towels. But there is...
TUNA
ISS MANIFESTO:
TOWELS....0
TUNA......
MILK......
LITTER...
KITTY LITTER!
I was going to say that.

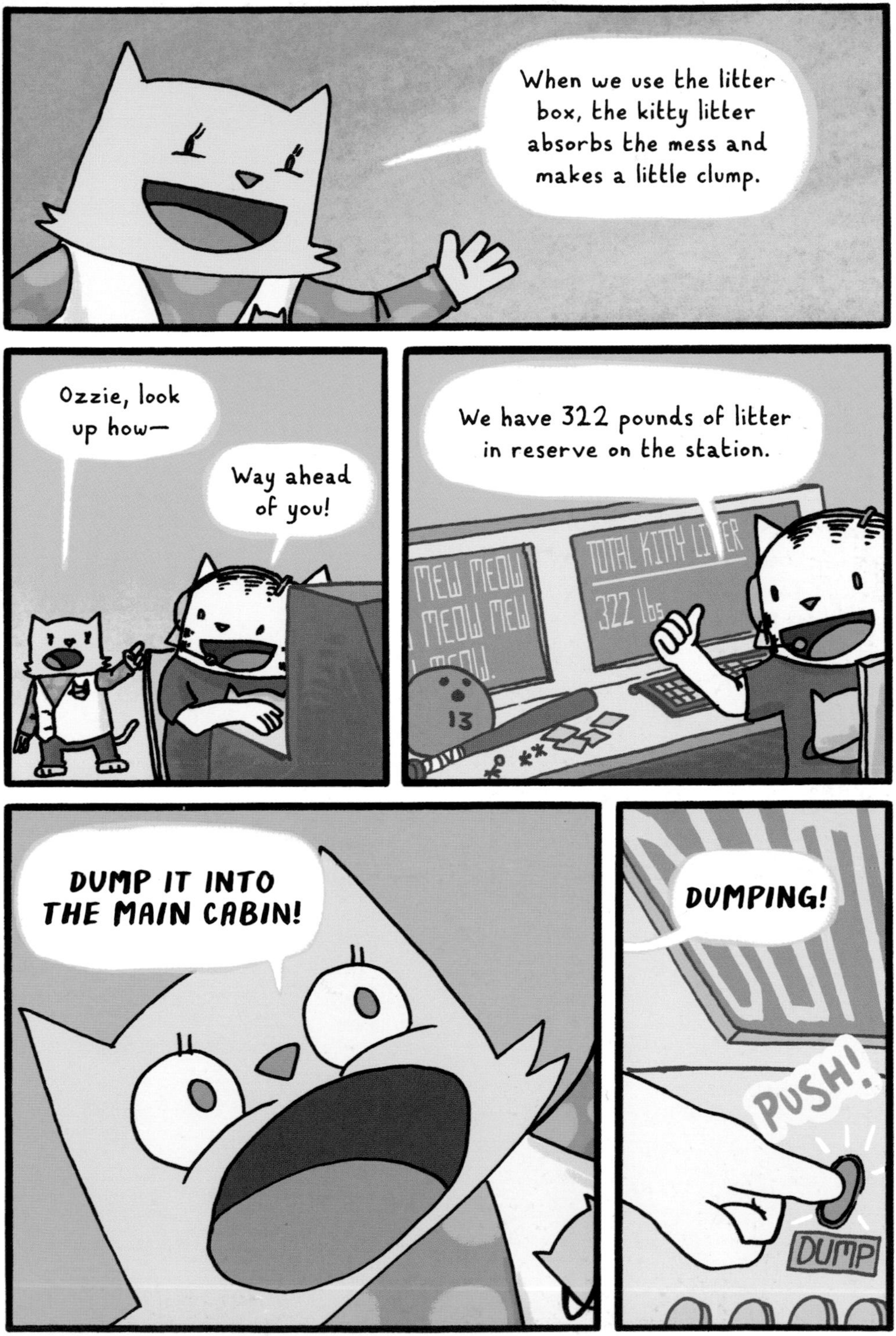
When we use the litter box, the kitty litter absorbs the mess and makes a little clump.
Ozzie, look up how—
Way ahead of you!
We have 322 pounds of litter in reserve on the station.
MEW MEOW MEOW MEW MEOW.
TOTAL KITTY LITTER
322 lbs
13
DUMP IT INTO THE MAIN CABIN!
DUMPING!
PUSH!
DUMP

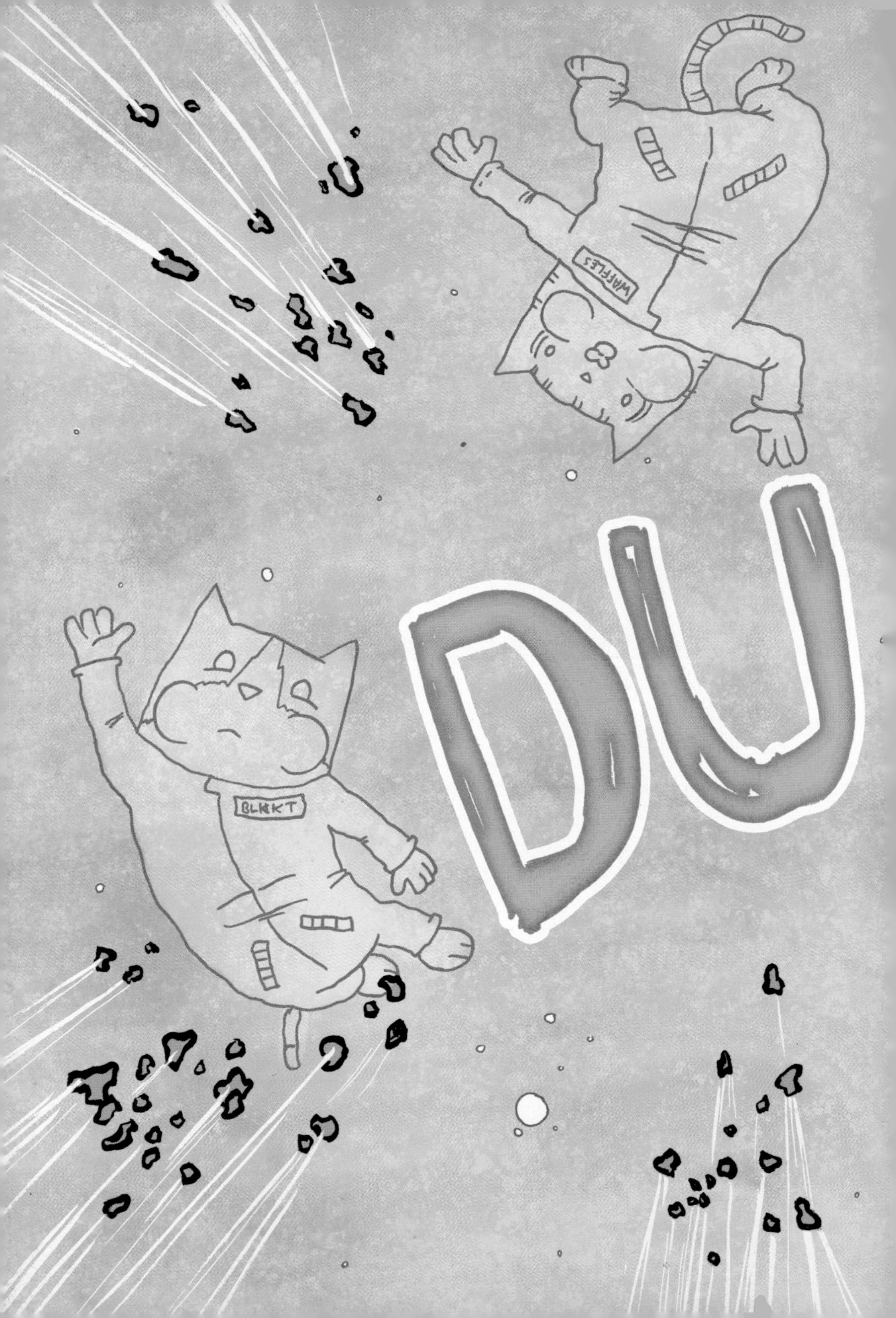
WAFFLES
DU

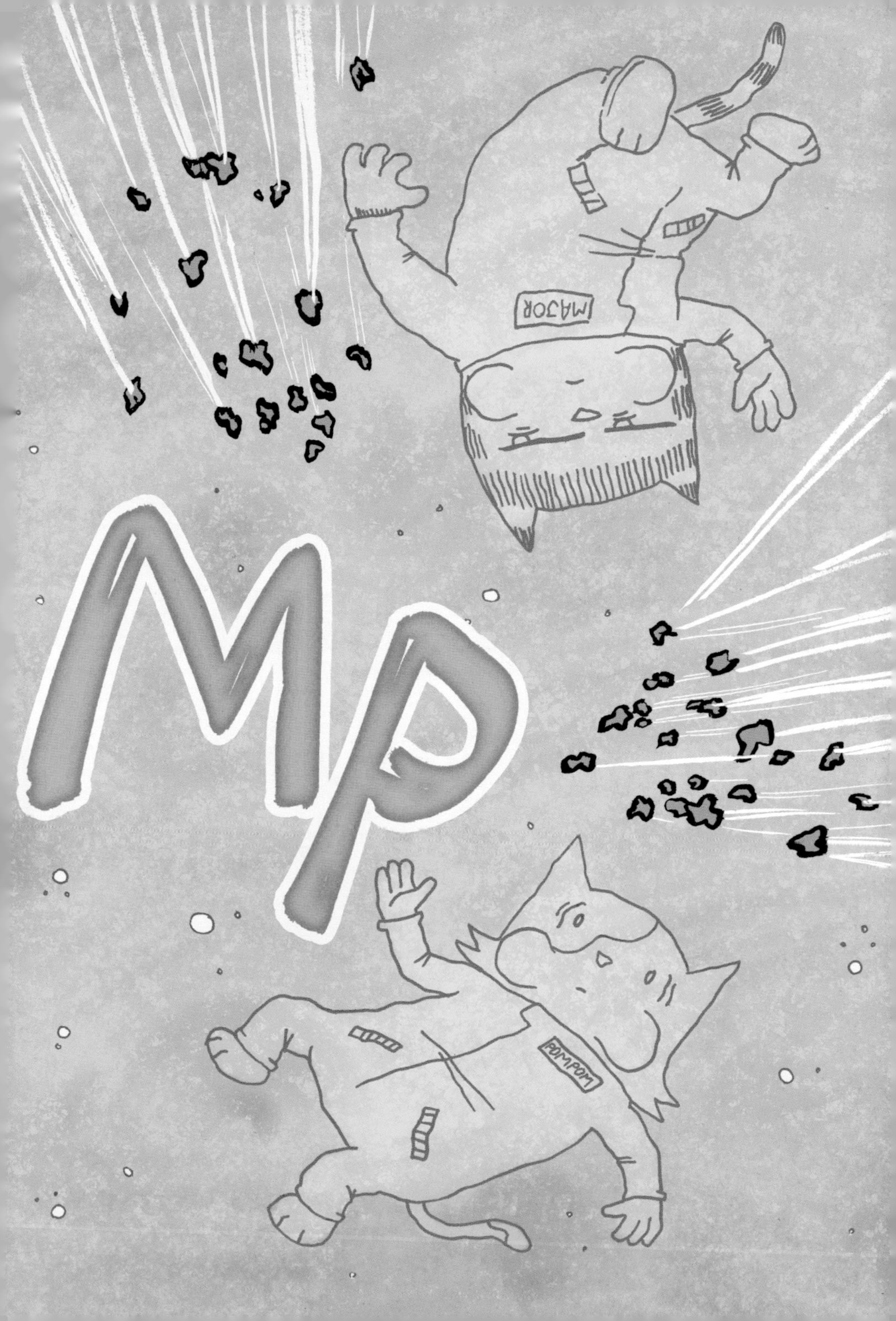
MAJOR
Mp
POMPOM

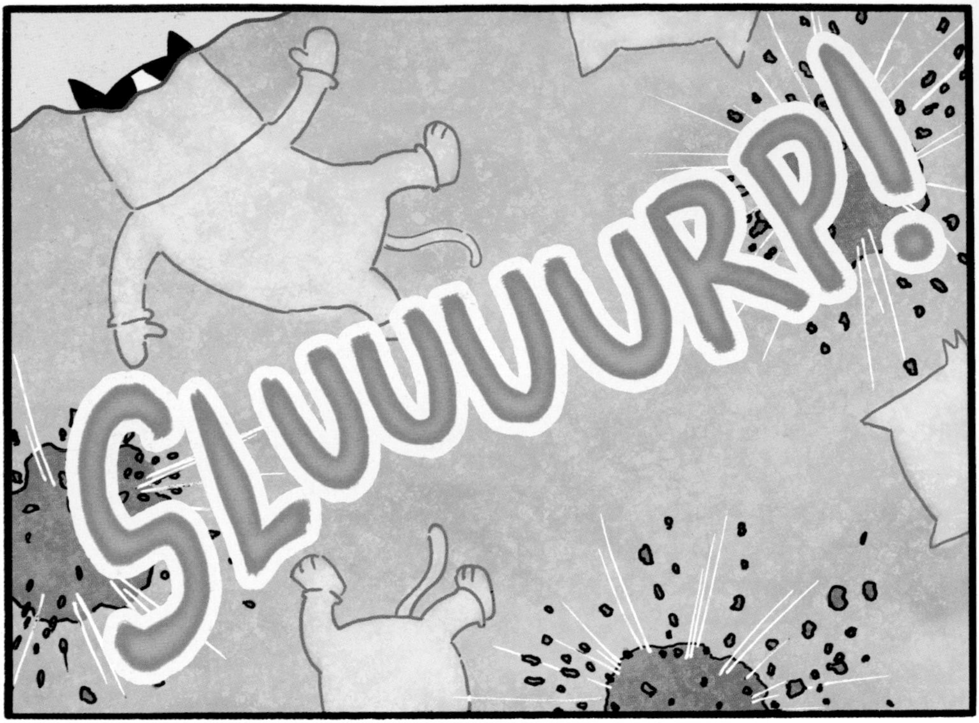
SLUUUURP!

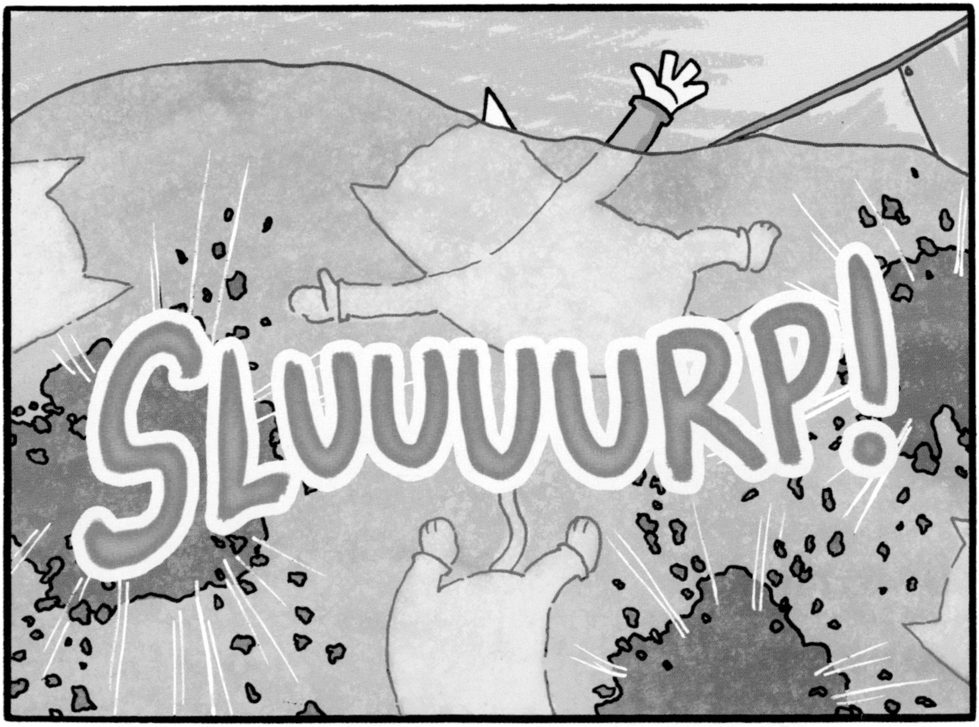
SLUUUURP!

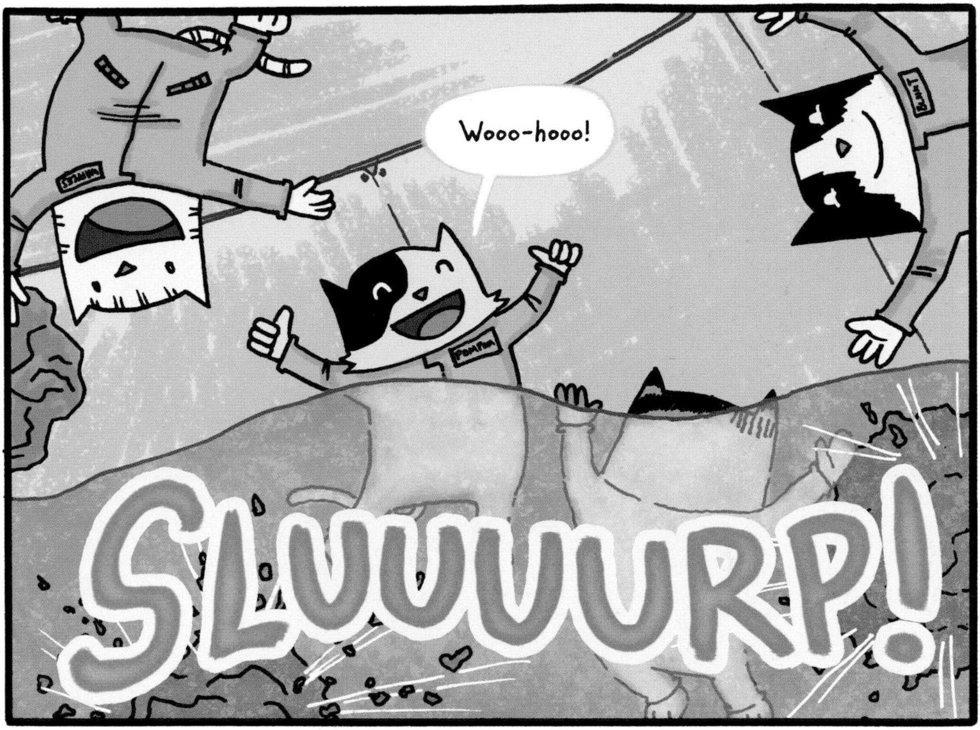
Wooo-hooo!
SLUUUURP!

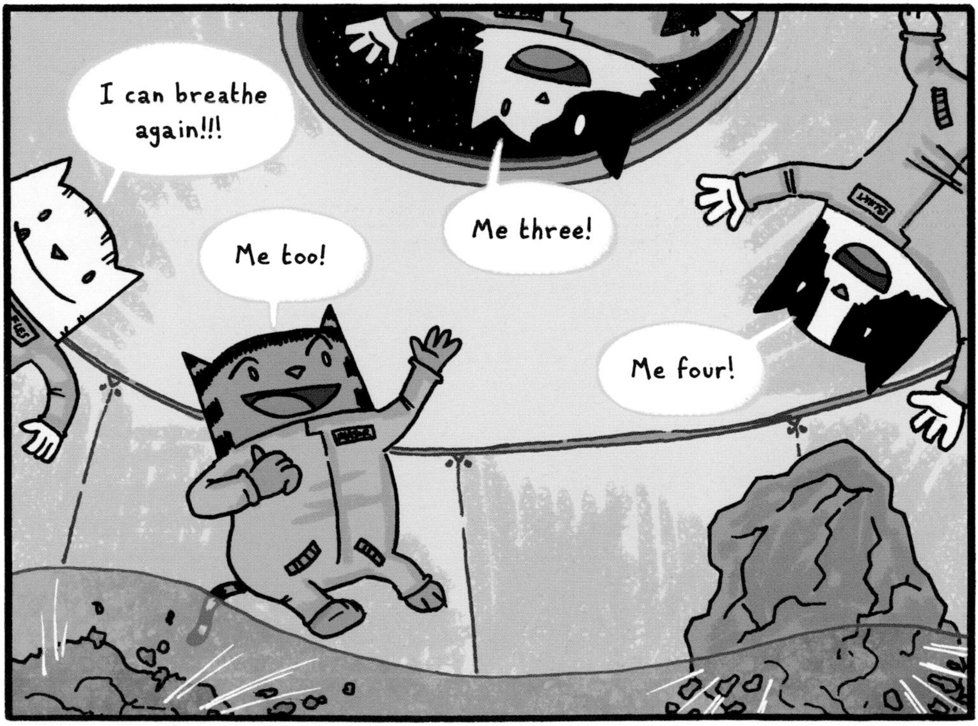
I can breathe again!!!
Me too!
Me three!
Me four!

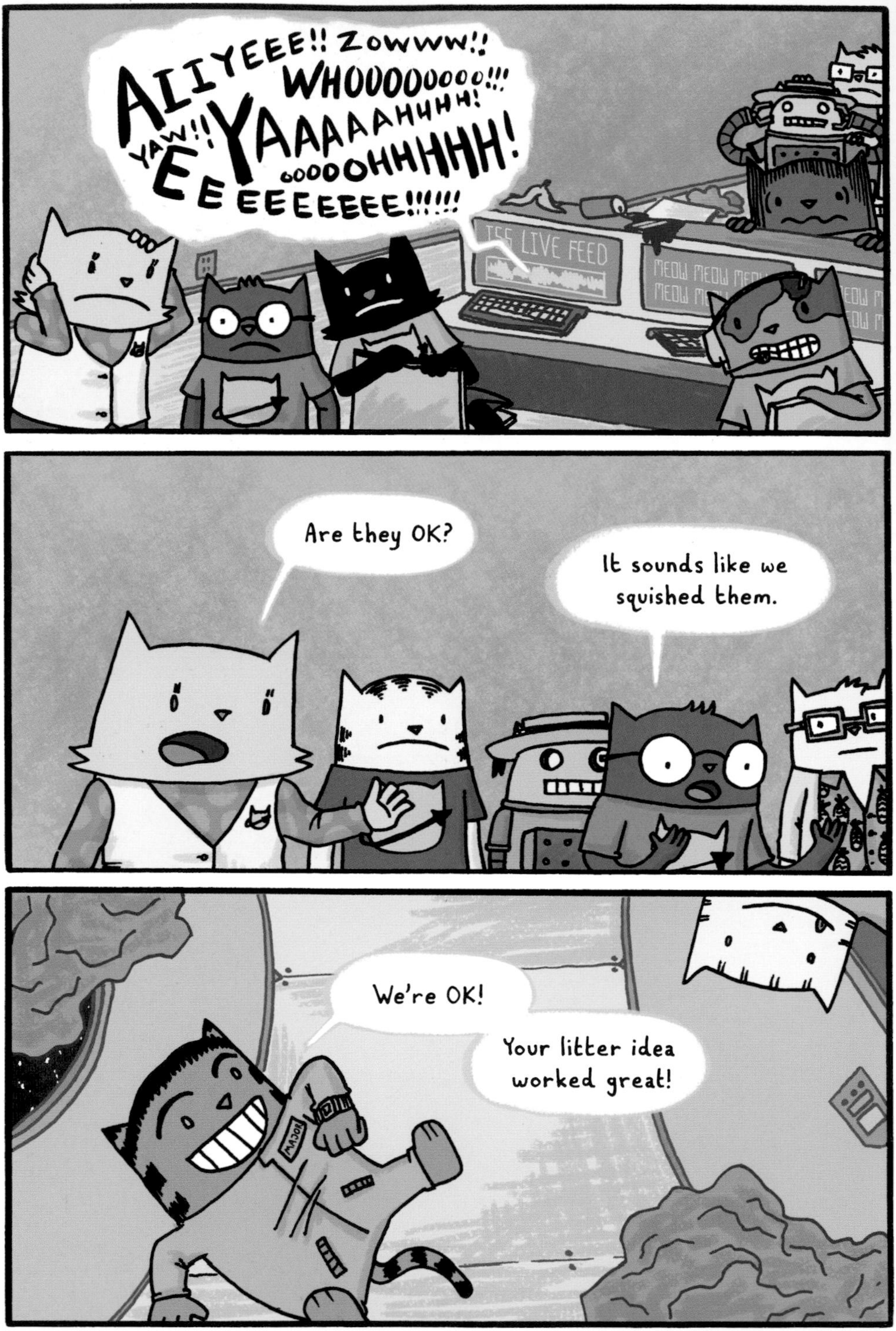
AIIYEEE!! ZOWWW!!
WHOOOOoooo!!!
YAW!!
YAAAAAHHHH!
ooooOHHHHH!
EEEEEEEEE!!!!!!
ISS LIVE FEED
Are they OK?
It sounds like we squished them.
We're OK!
Your litter idea worked great!
MAJOR

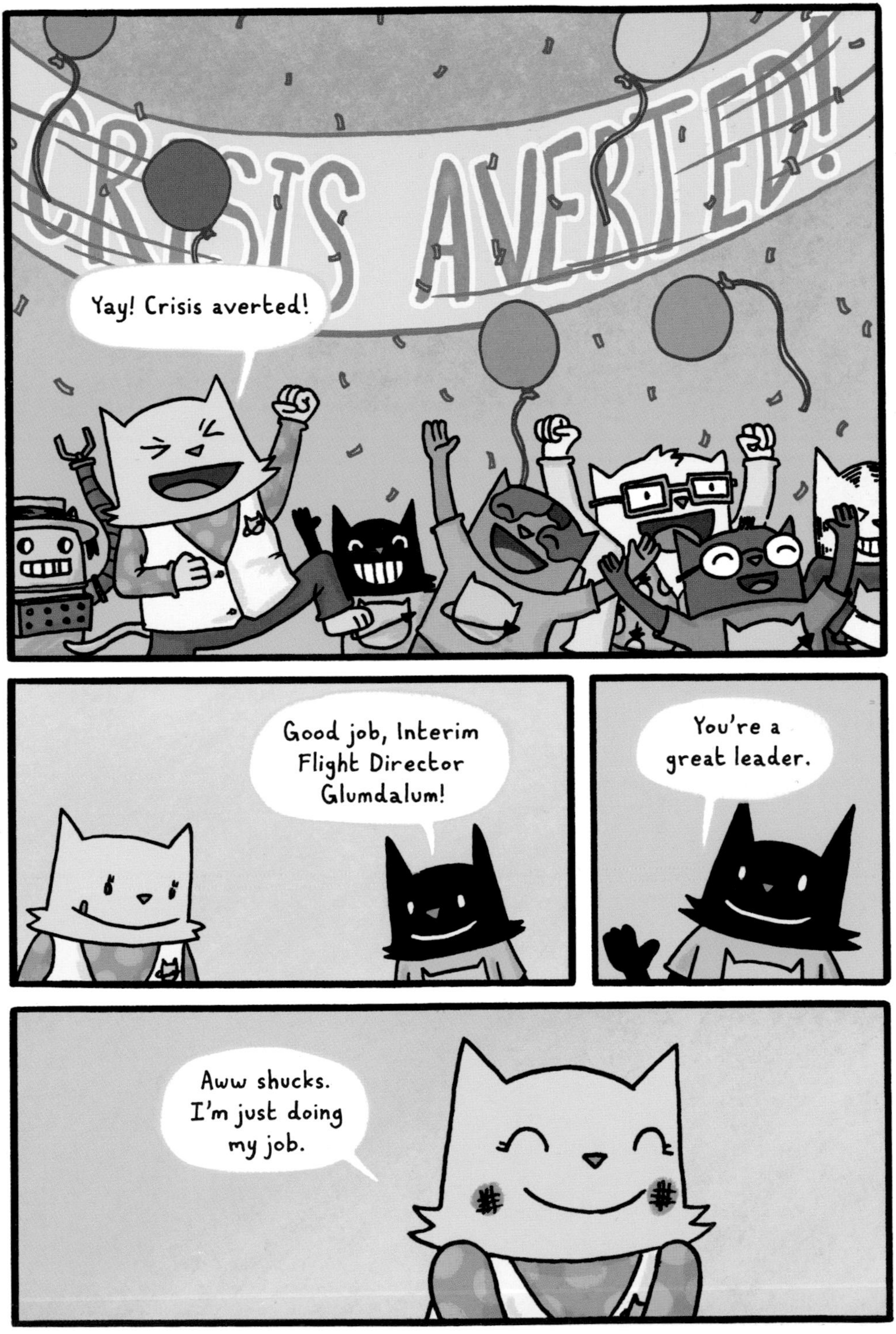
CRISIS AVERTED!
Yay! Crisis averted!
Good job, Interim Flight Director Glumdalum!
You're a great leader.
Aww shucks. I'm just doing my job.

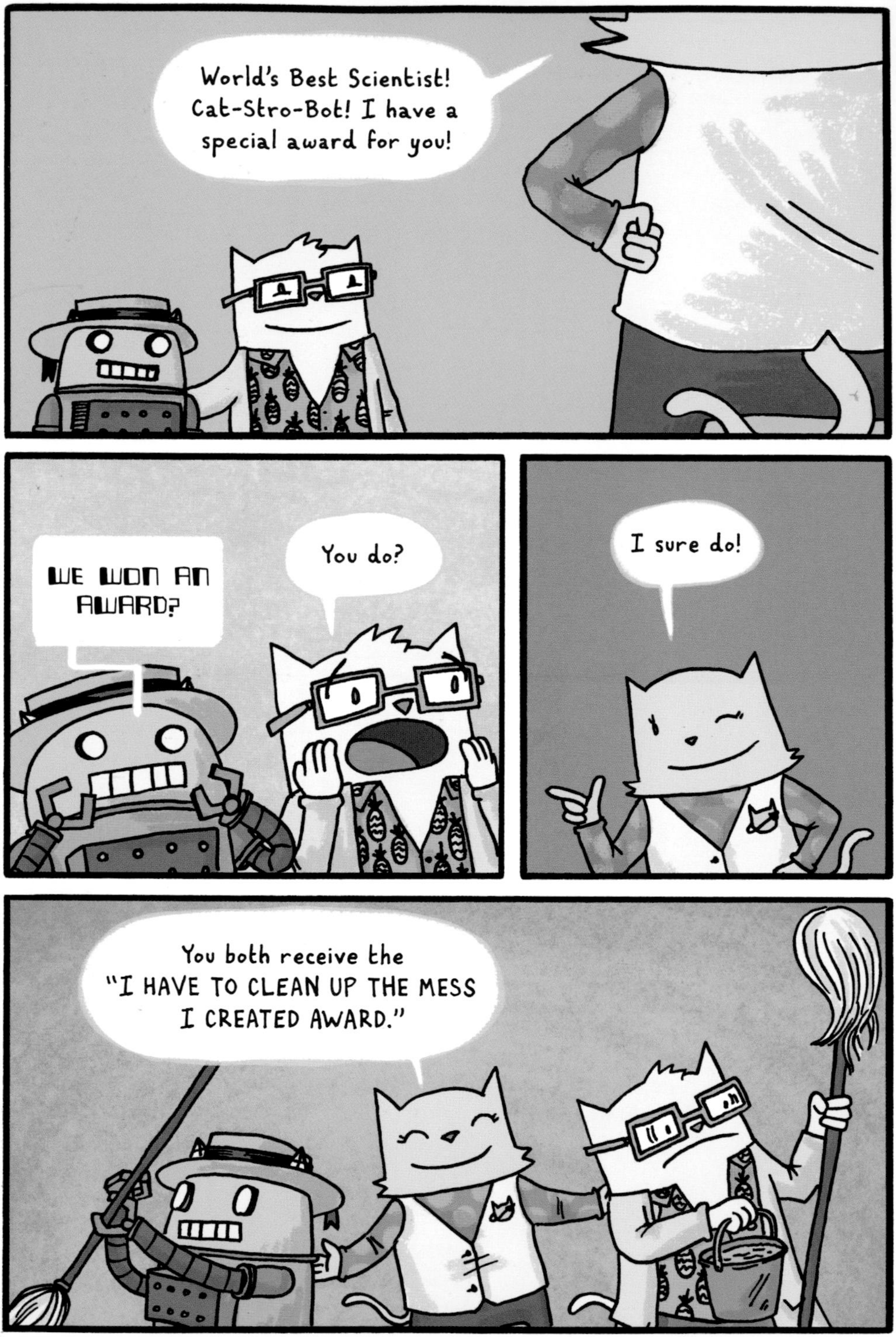
World's Best Scientist! Cat-Stro-Bot! I have a special award for you!
WE WON AN AWARD?
You do?
I sure do!
You both receive the "I HAVE TO CLEAN UP THE MESS I CREATED AWARD."

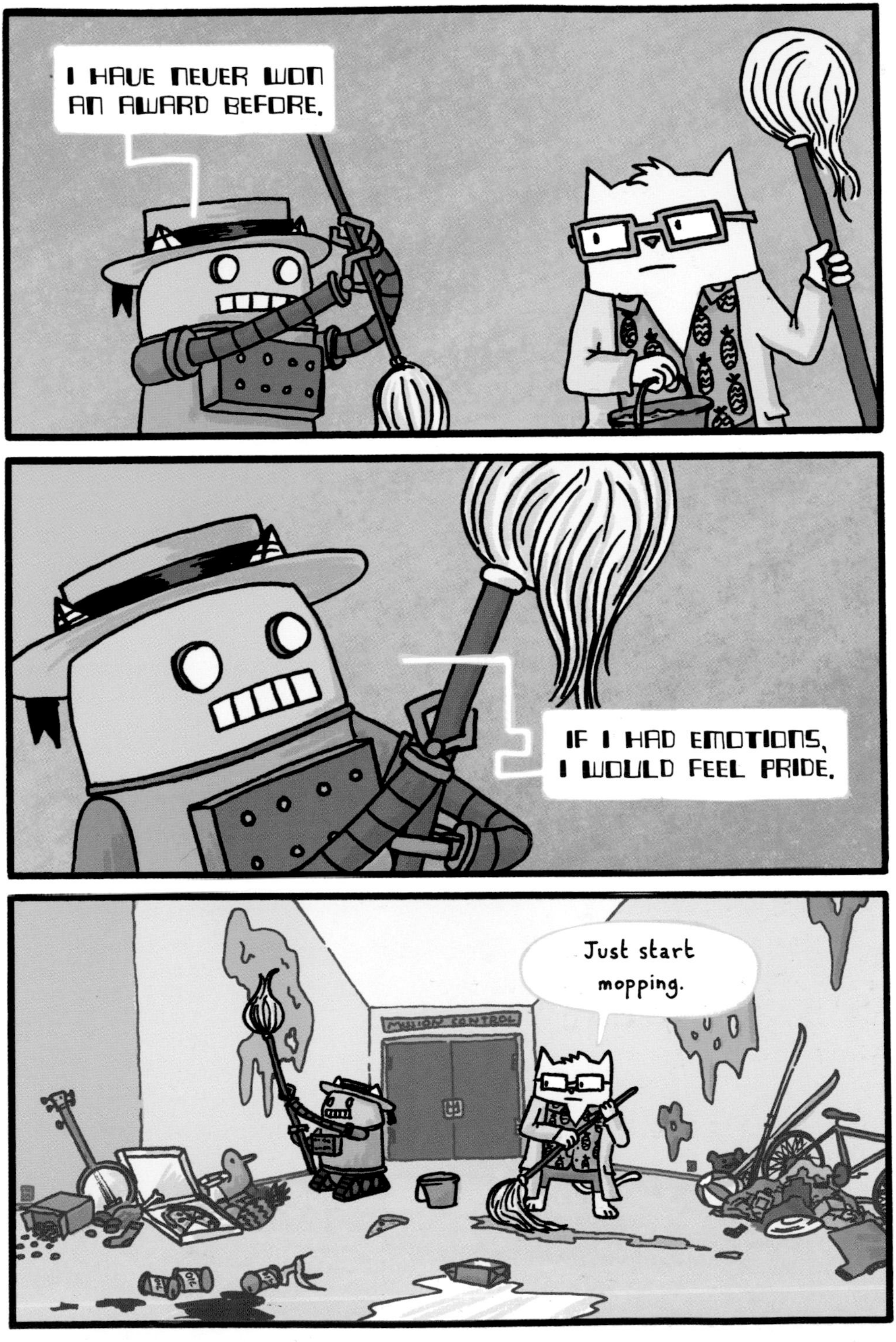
I HAVE NEVER WON AN AWARD BEFORE.
IF I HAD EMOTIONS, I WOULD FEEL PRIDE.
Just start mopping.
MISSION CONTROL

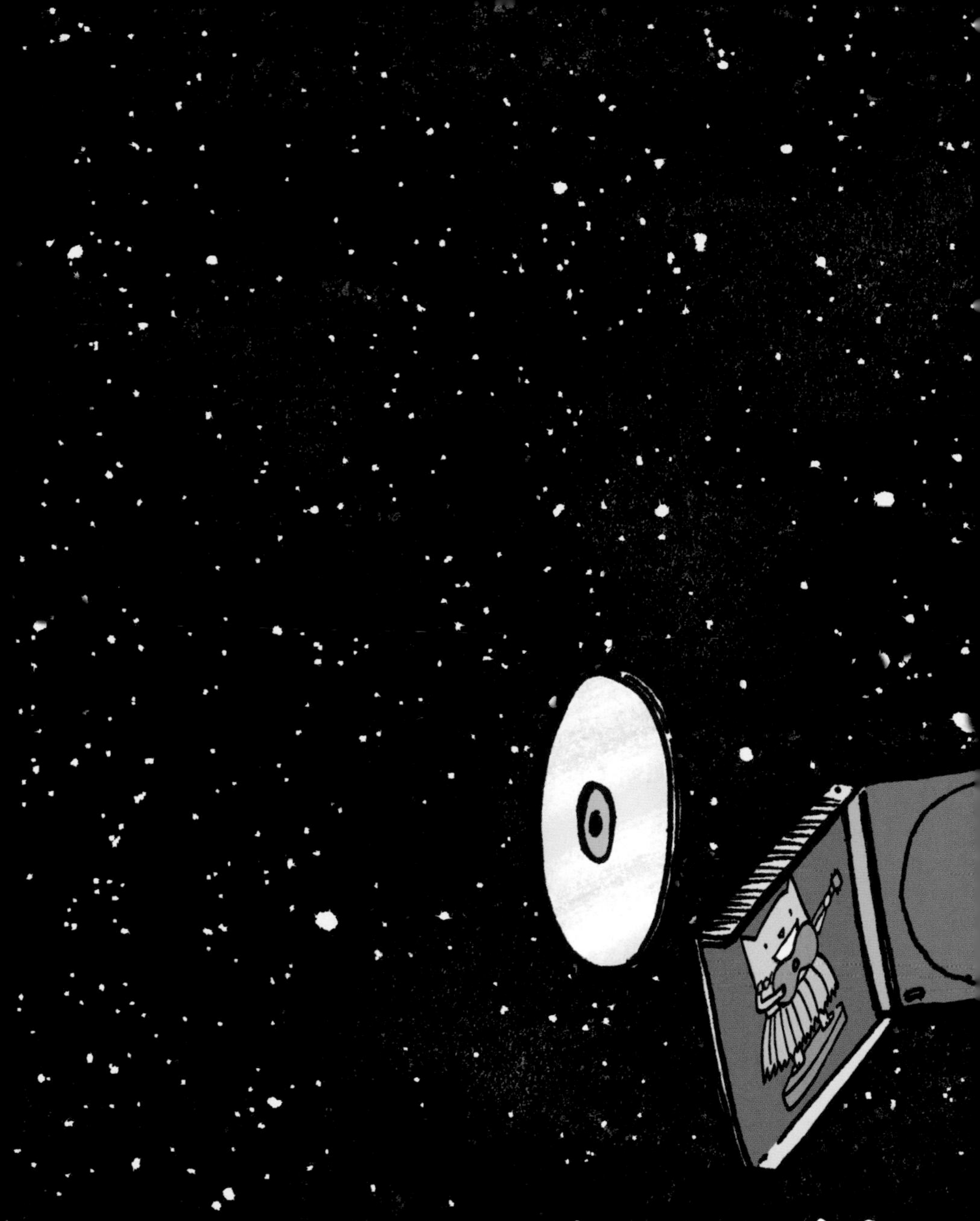

CHAPTER 10

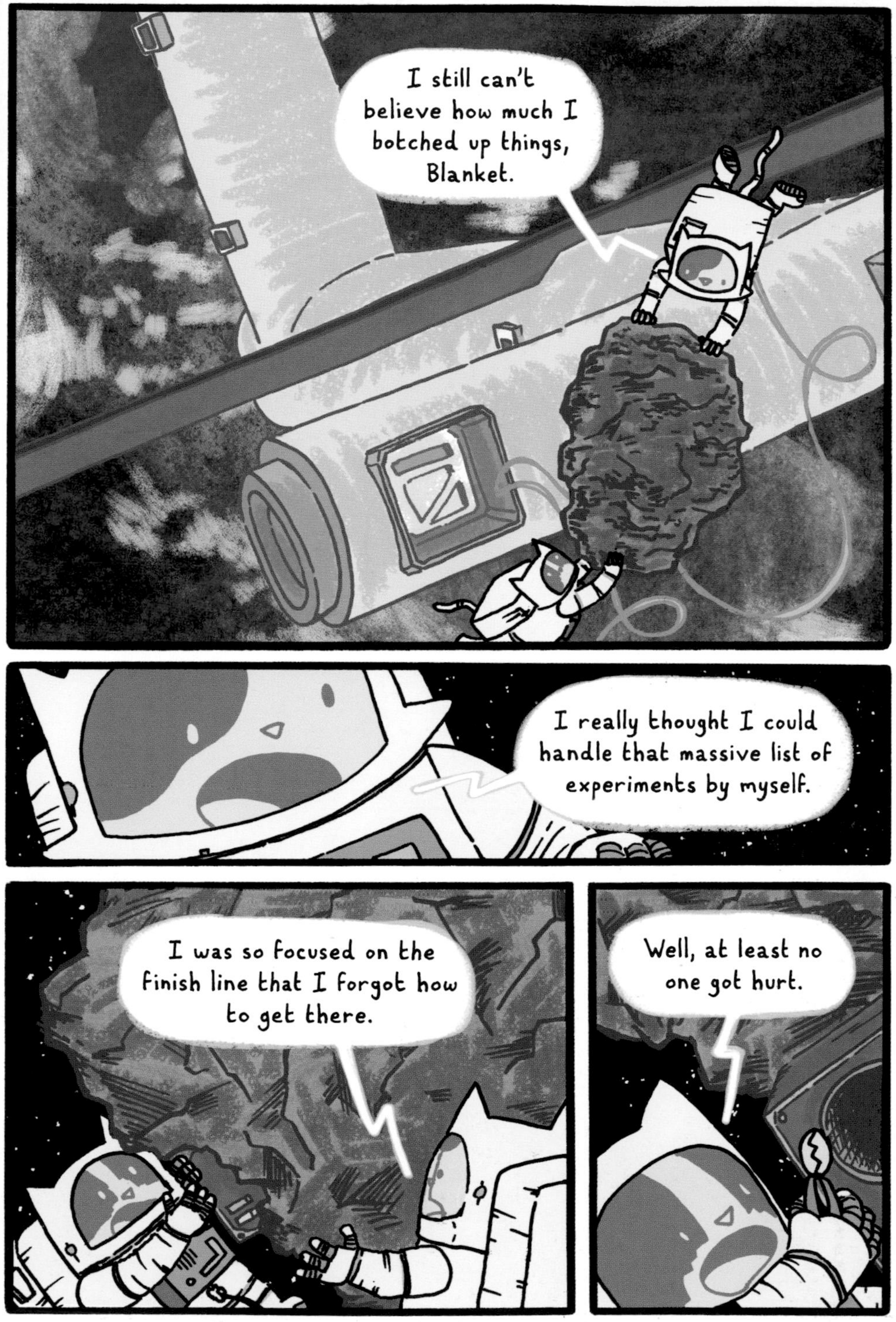
I still can't believe how much I botched up things, Blanket.
I really thought I could handle that massive list of experiments by myself.
I was so focused on the finish line that I forgot how to get there.
Well, at least no one got hurt.

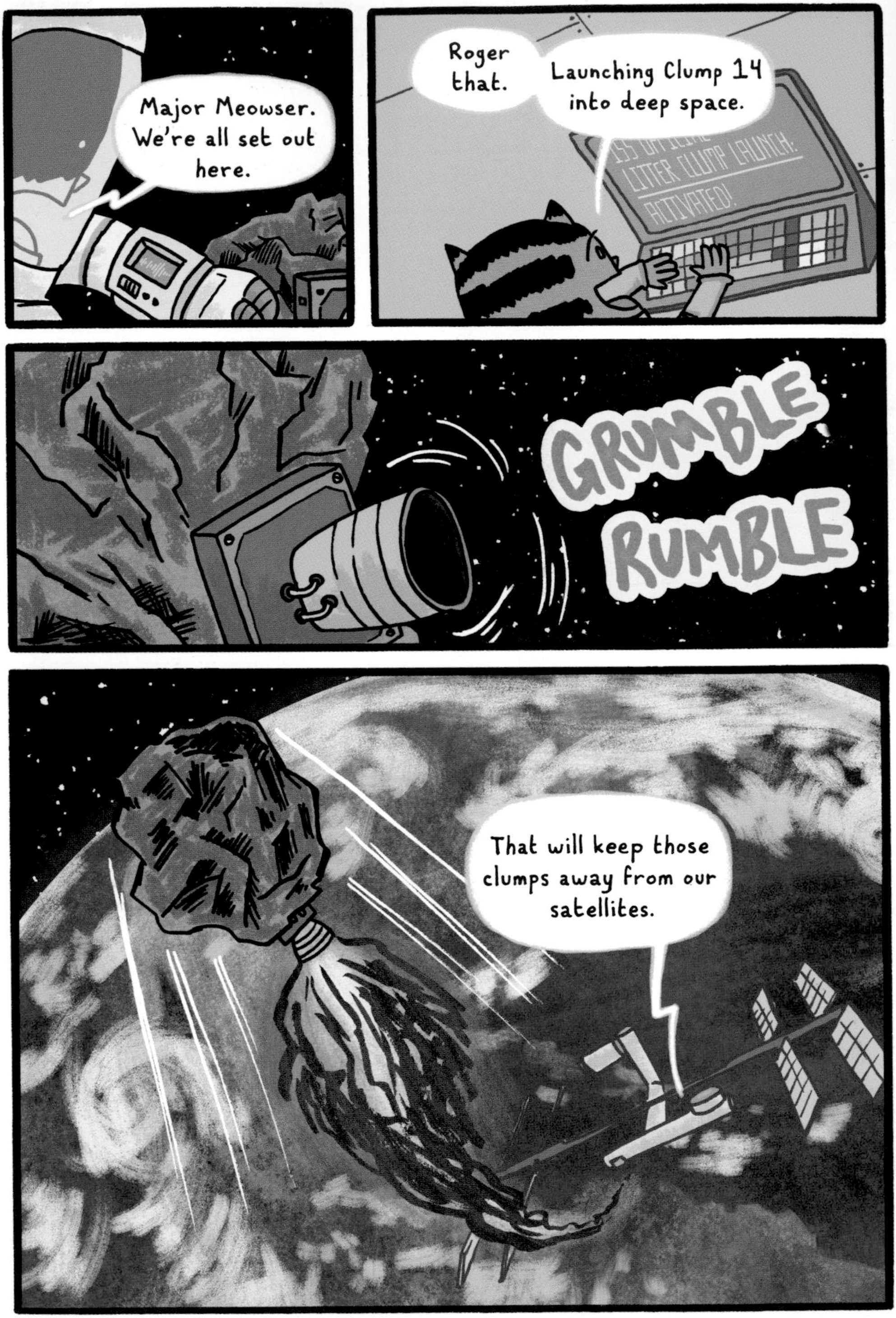
Major Meowser. We're all set out here.
Roger that.
Launching Clump 14 into deep space.
LITTER CLUMP LAUNCH:
ACTIVATED!
GRUMBLE
RUMBLE
That will keep those clumps away from our satellites.

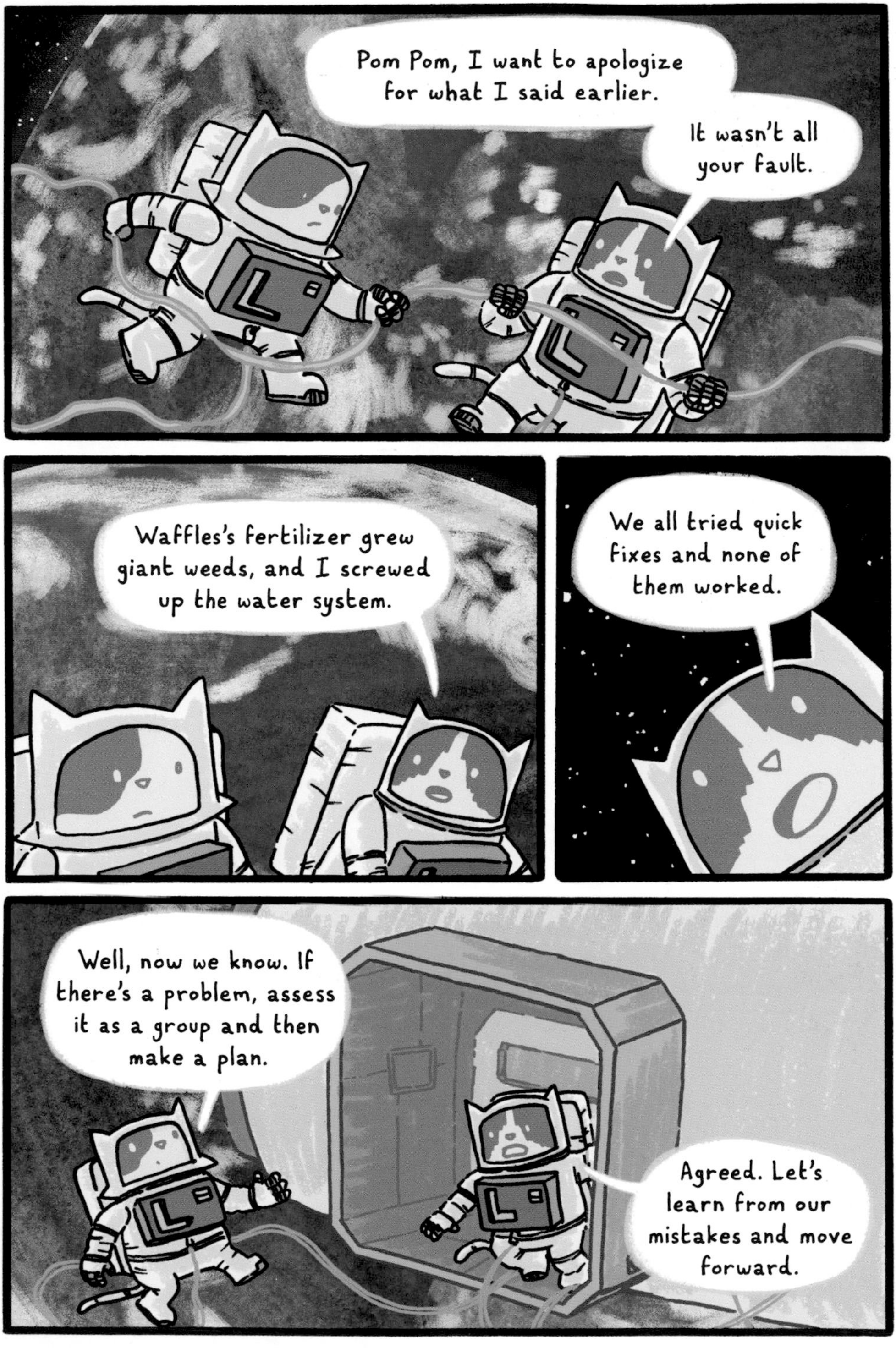
Pom Pom, I want to apologize for what I said earlier.
It wasn't all your fault.
Waffles's fertilizer grew giant weeds, and I screwed up the water system.
We all tried quick fixes and none of them worked.
Well, now we know. If there's a problem, assess it as a group and then make a plan.
Agreed. Let's learn from our mistakes and move forward.

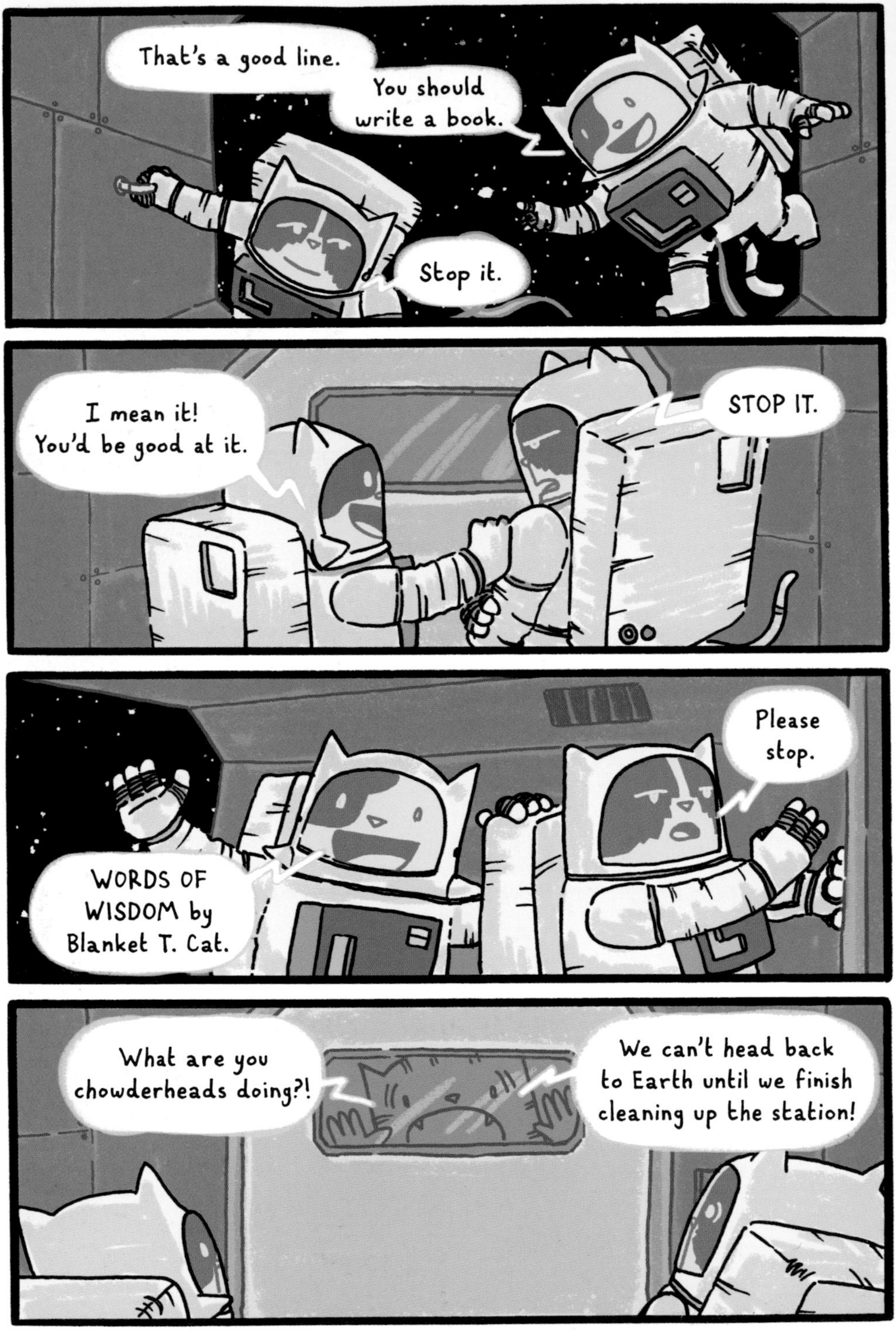

That's a good line.
You should write a book.
Stop it.
I mean it! You'd be good at it.
STOP IT.
Please stop.
WORDS OF WISDOM by Blanket T. Cat.
What are you chowderheads doing?!
We can't head back to Earth until we finish cleaning up the station!

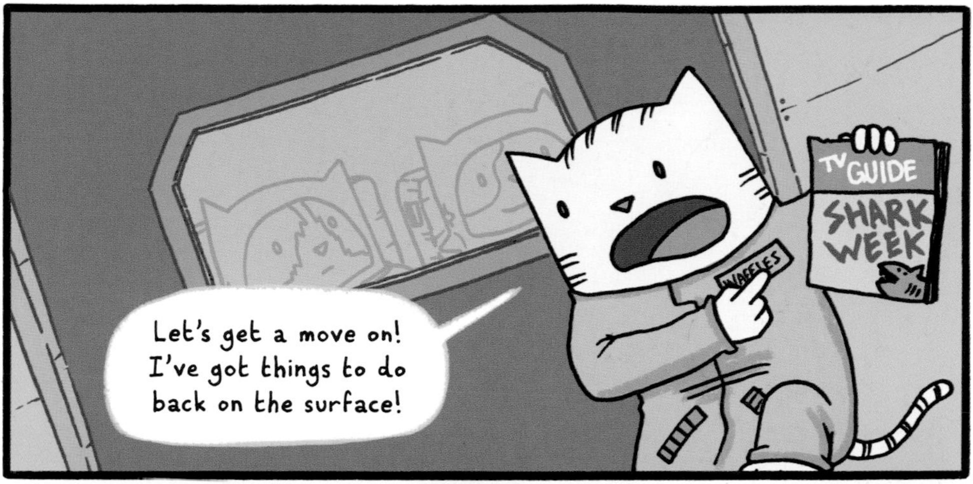
TV GUIDE
SHARK WEEK
WAFFLES
Let's get a move on! I've got things to do back on the surface!

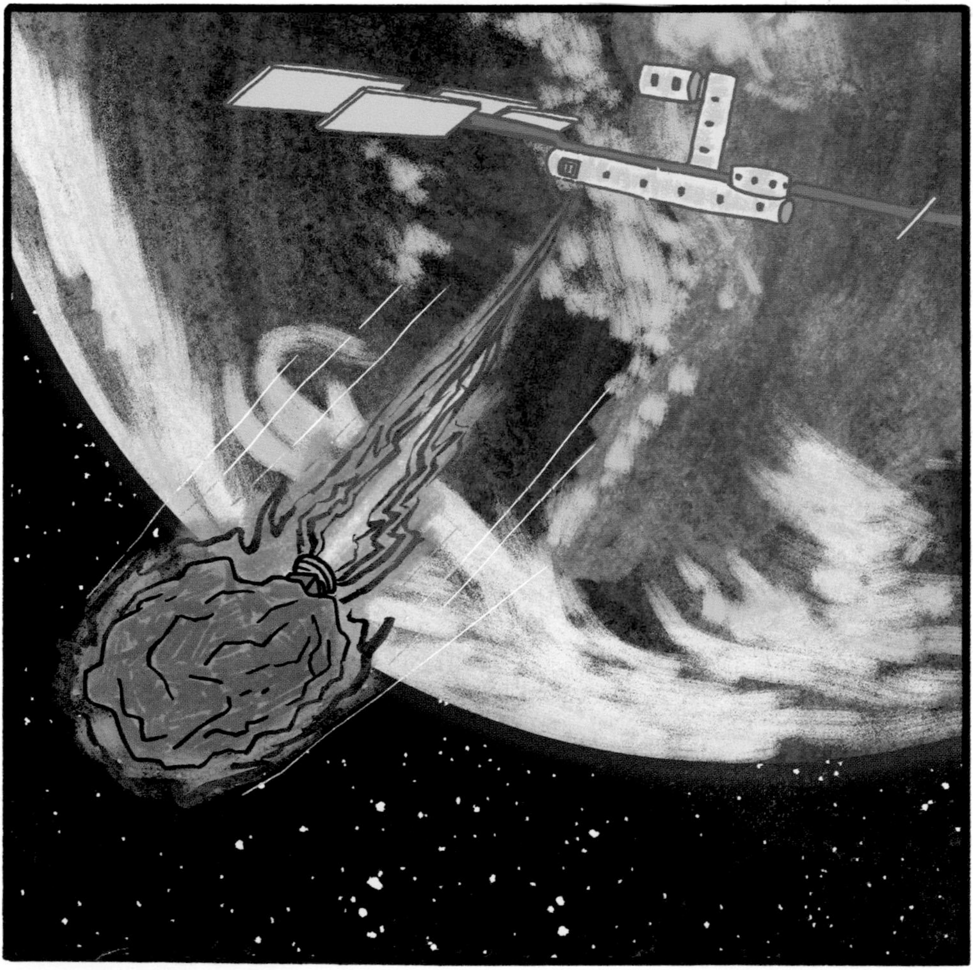

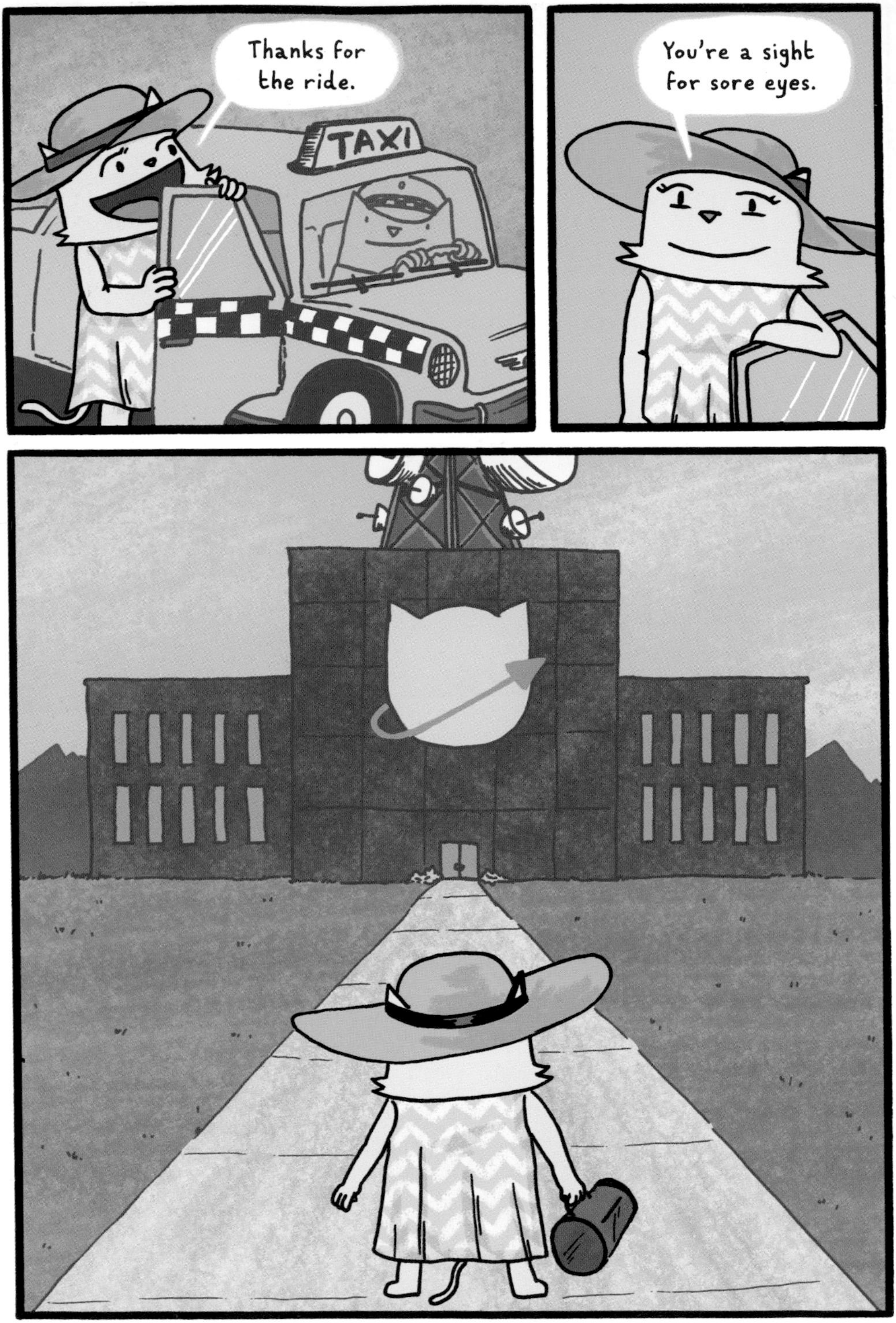
Thanks for the ride.
TAXI
You're a sight for sore eyes.

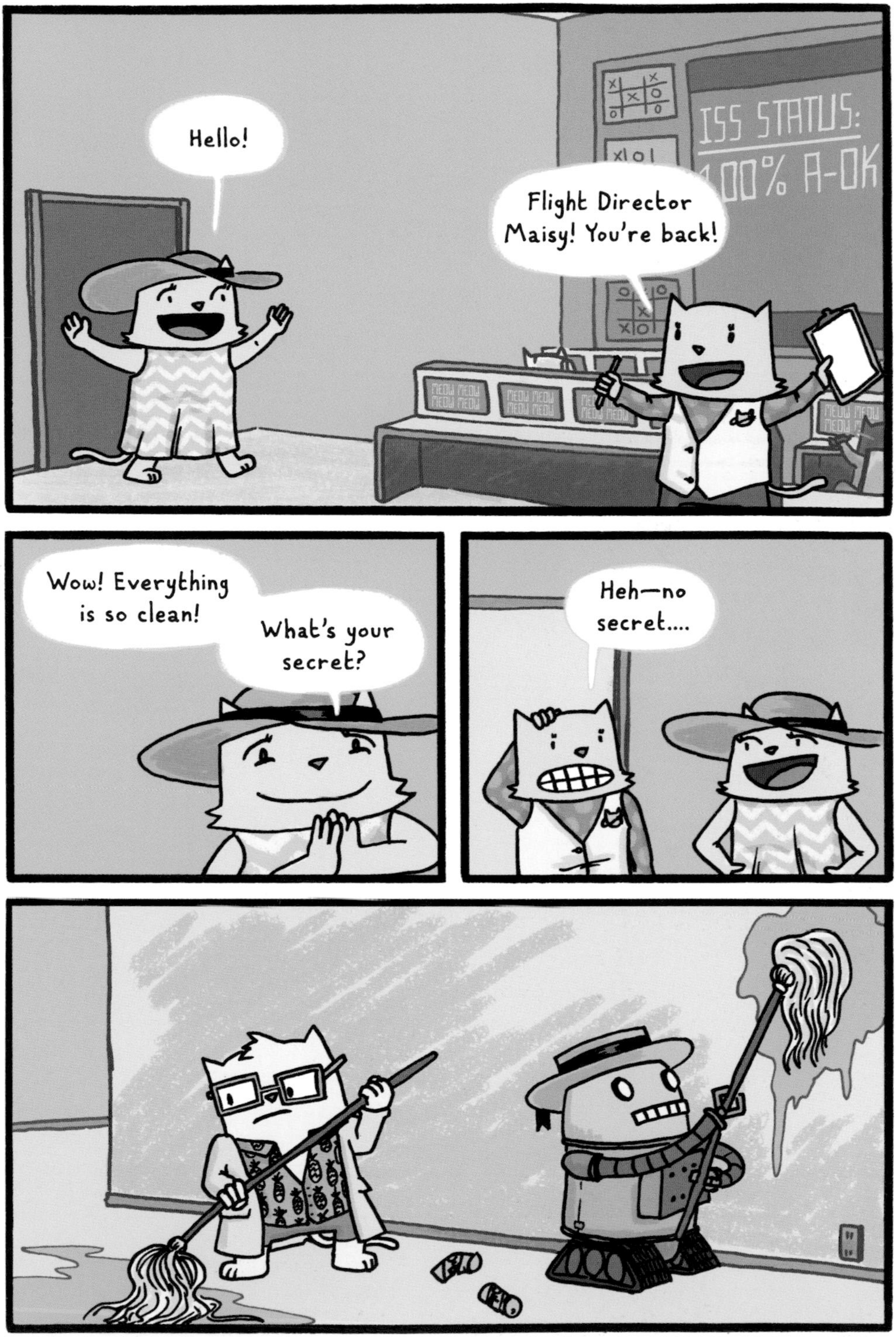
Hello!
ISS STATUS:
100% A-OK
Flight Director Maisy! You're back!
Wow! Everything is so clean!
What's your secret?
Heh—no secret....

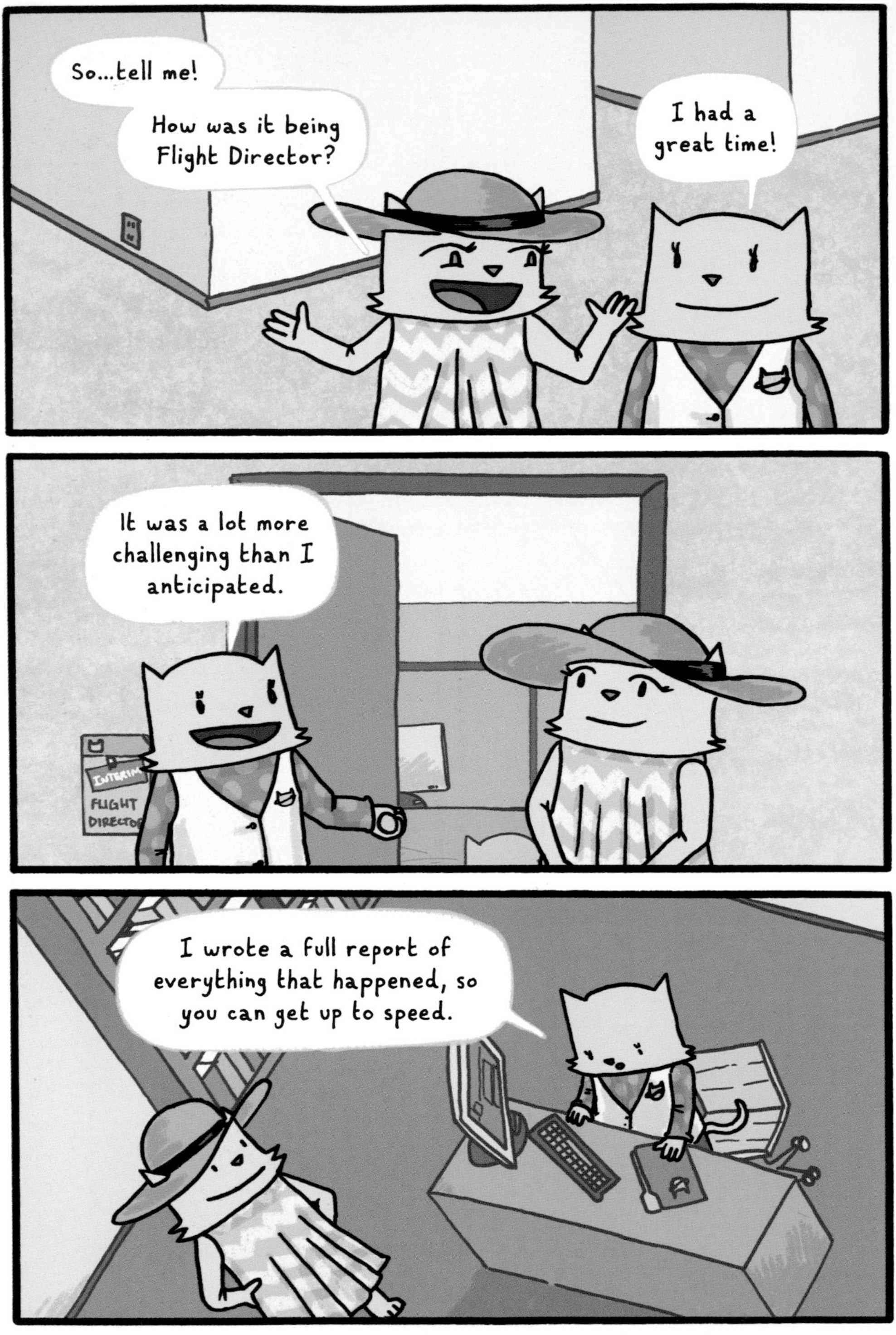
So...tell me!
How was it being Flight Director?
I had a great time!
It was a lot more challenging than I anticipated.
INTERIM
FLIGHT DIRECTOR
I wrote a full report of everything that happened, so you can get up to speed.

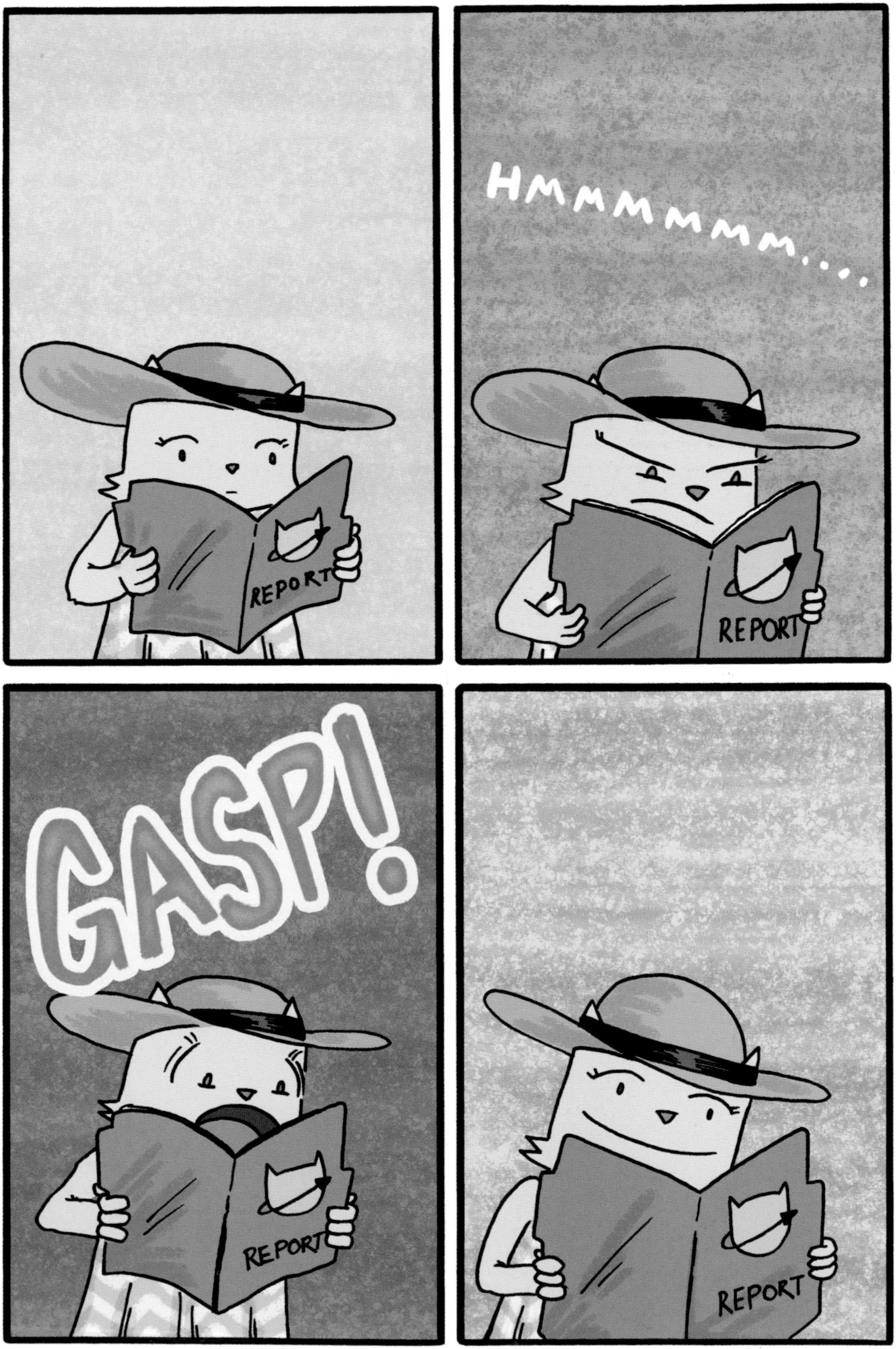
REPORT
HMMMMMM....
REPORT
GASP!
REPORT
REPORT

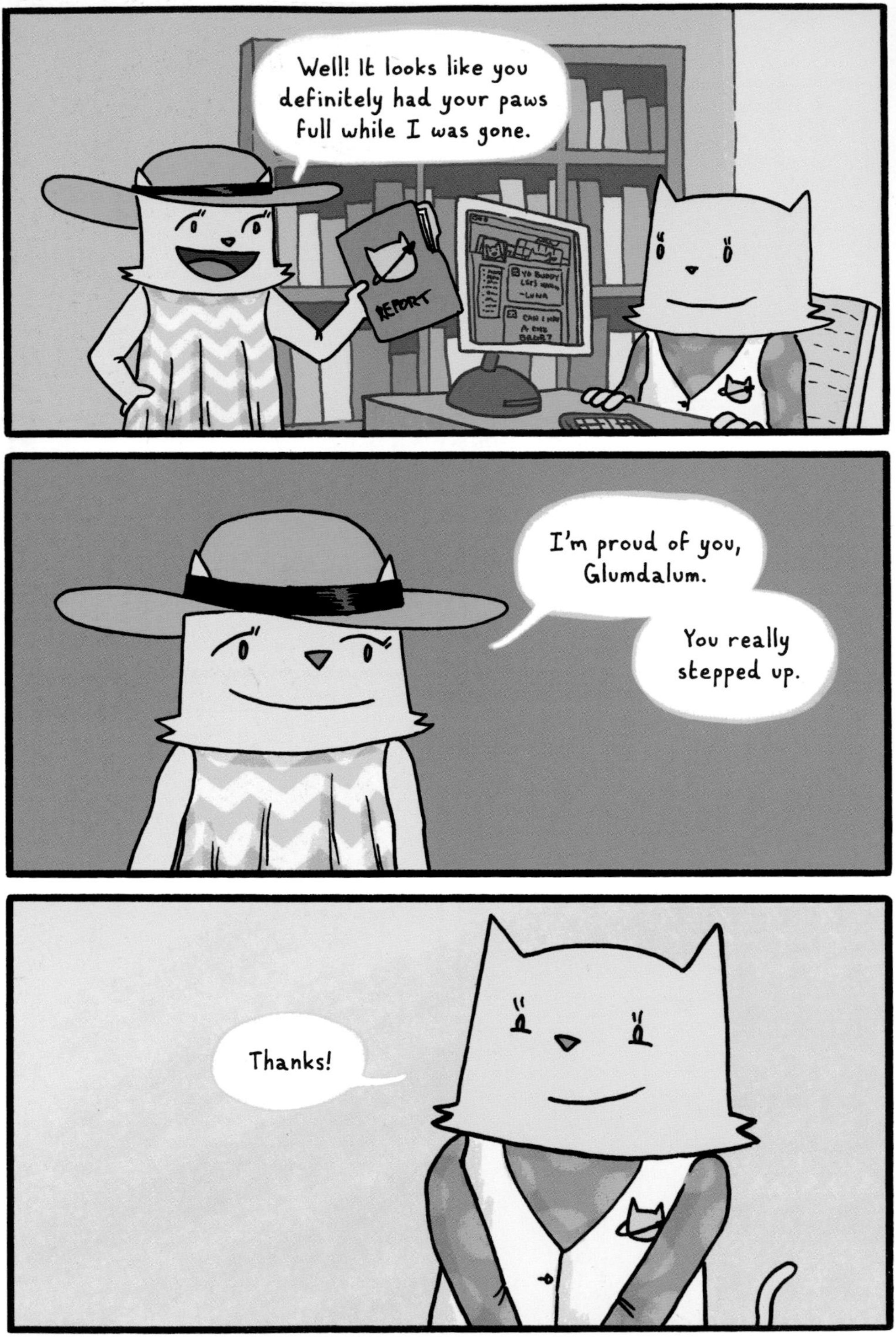
Well! It looks like you definitely had your paws full while I was gone.
REPORT
I'm proud of you, Glumdalum.
You really stepped up.
Thanks!

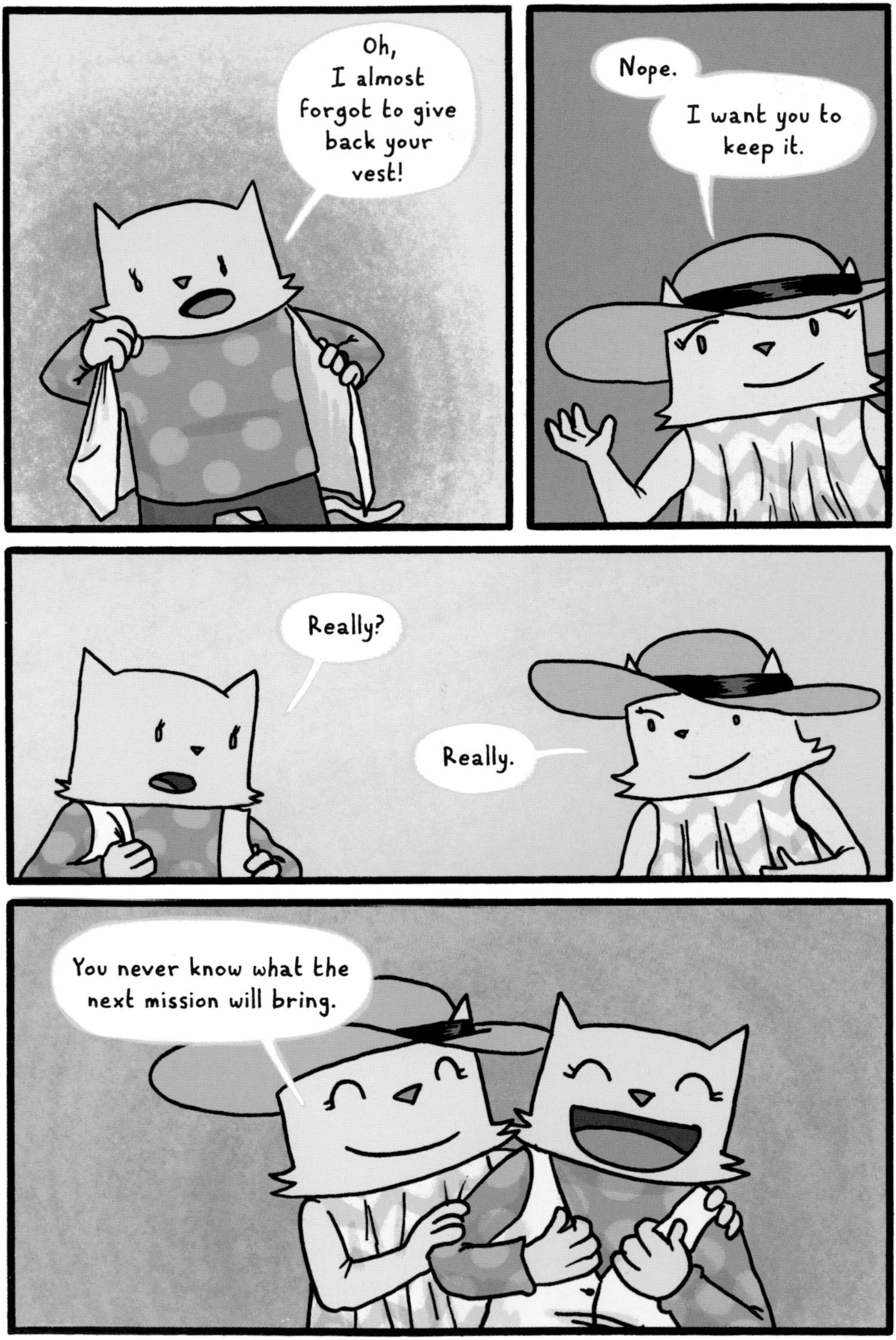
Oh, I almost forgot to give back your vest!
Nope.
I want you to keep it.
Really?
Really.
You never know what the next mission will bring.

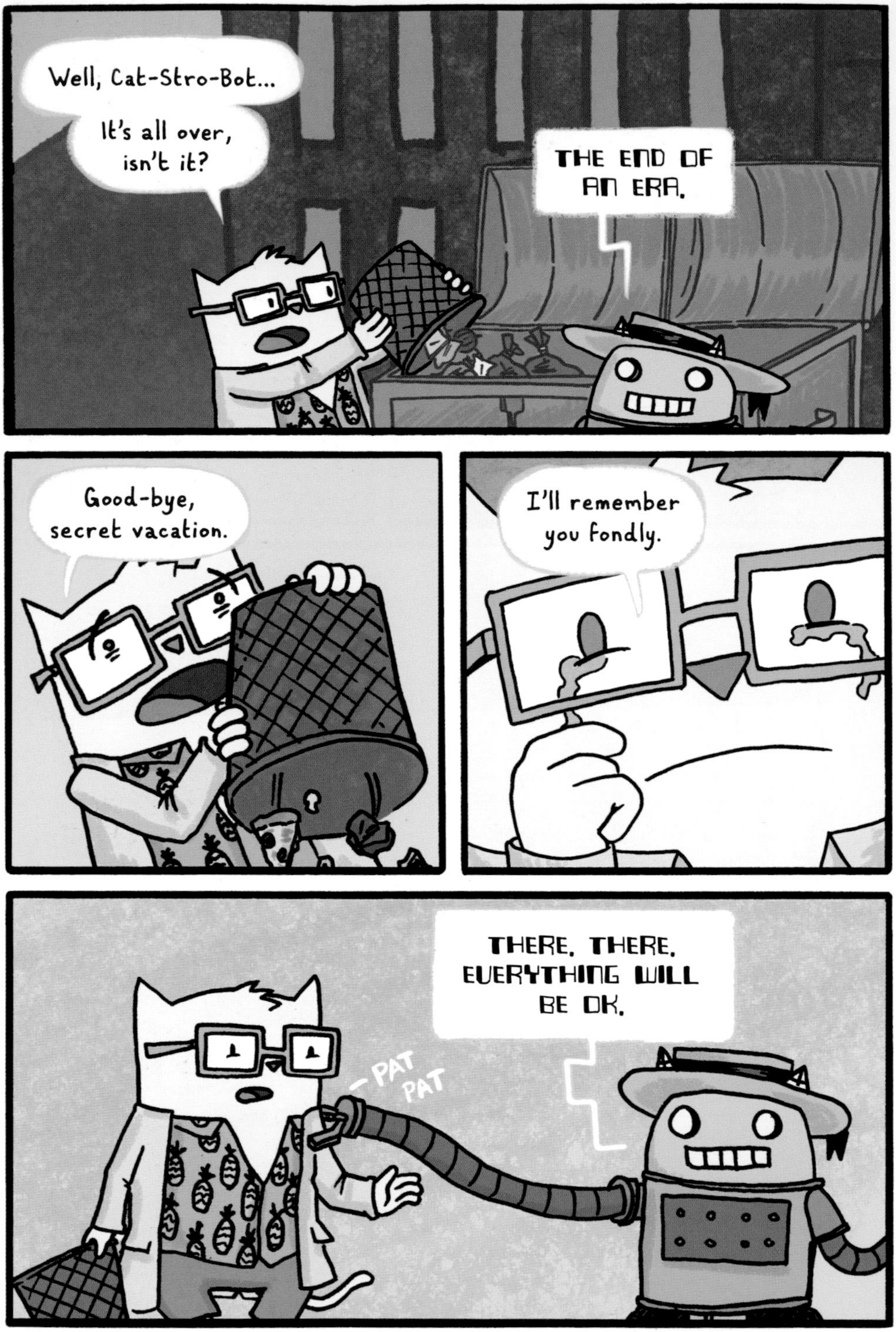
Well, Cat-Stro-Bot...
It's all over, isn't it?
THE END OF AN ERA.
Good-bye, secret vacation.
I'll remember you fondly.
THERE. THERE. EVERYTHING WILL BE OK.
PAT PAT

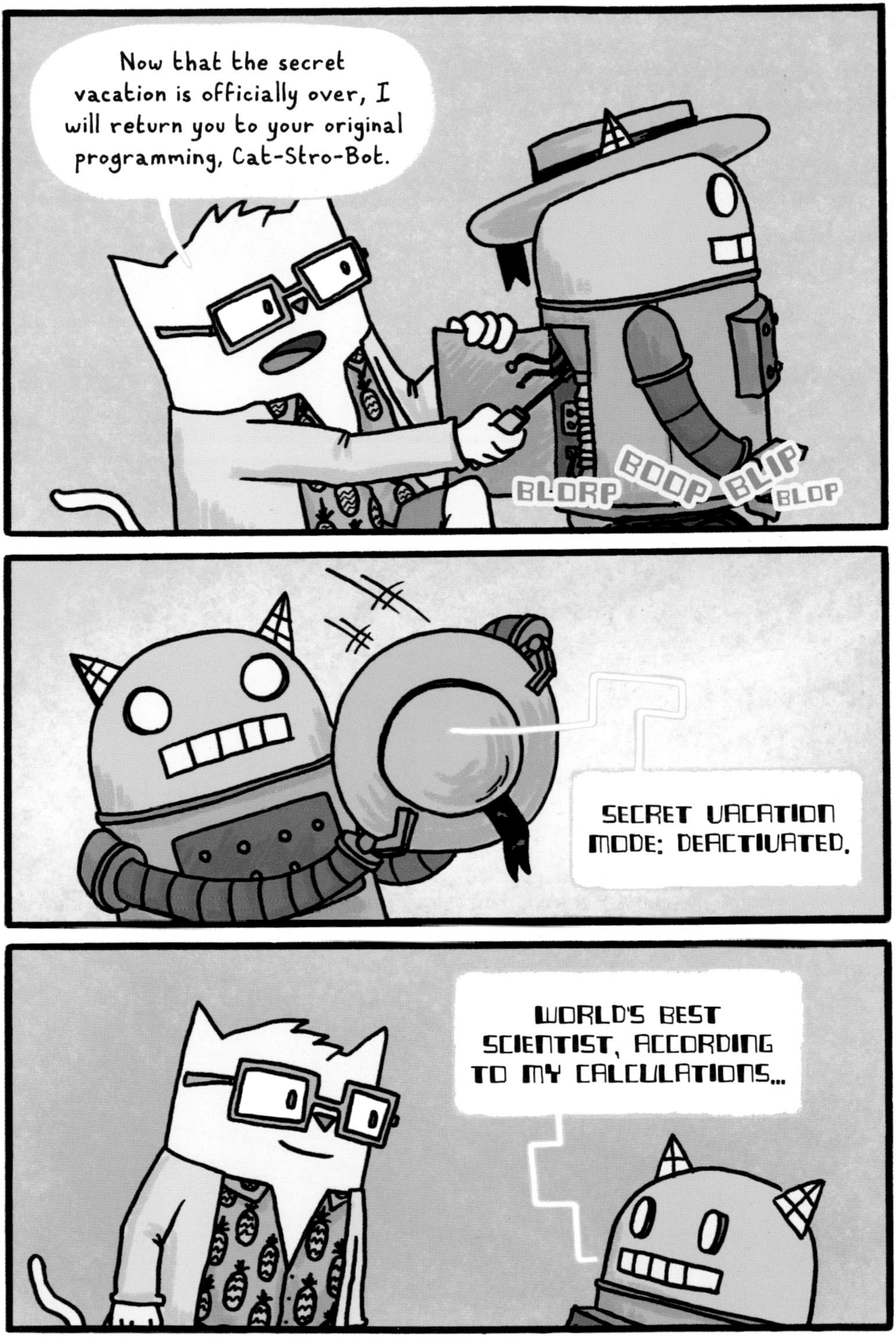
Now that the secret vacation is officially over, I will return you to your original programming, Cat-Stro-Bot.
BLORP
BOOP
BLIP
BLOP
SECRET VACATION MODE: DEACTIVATED.
WORLD'S BEST SCIENTIST, ACCORDING TO MY CALCULATIONS...

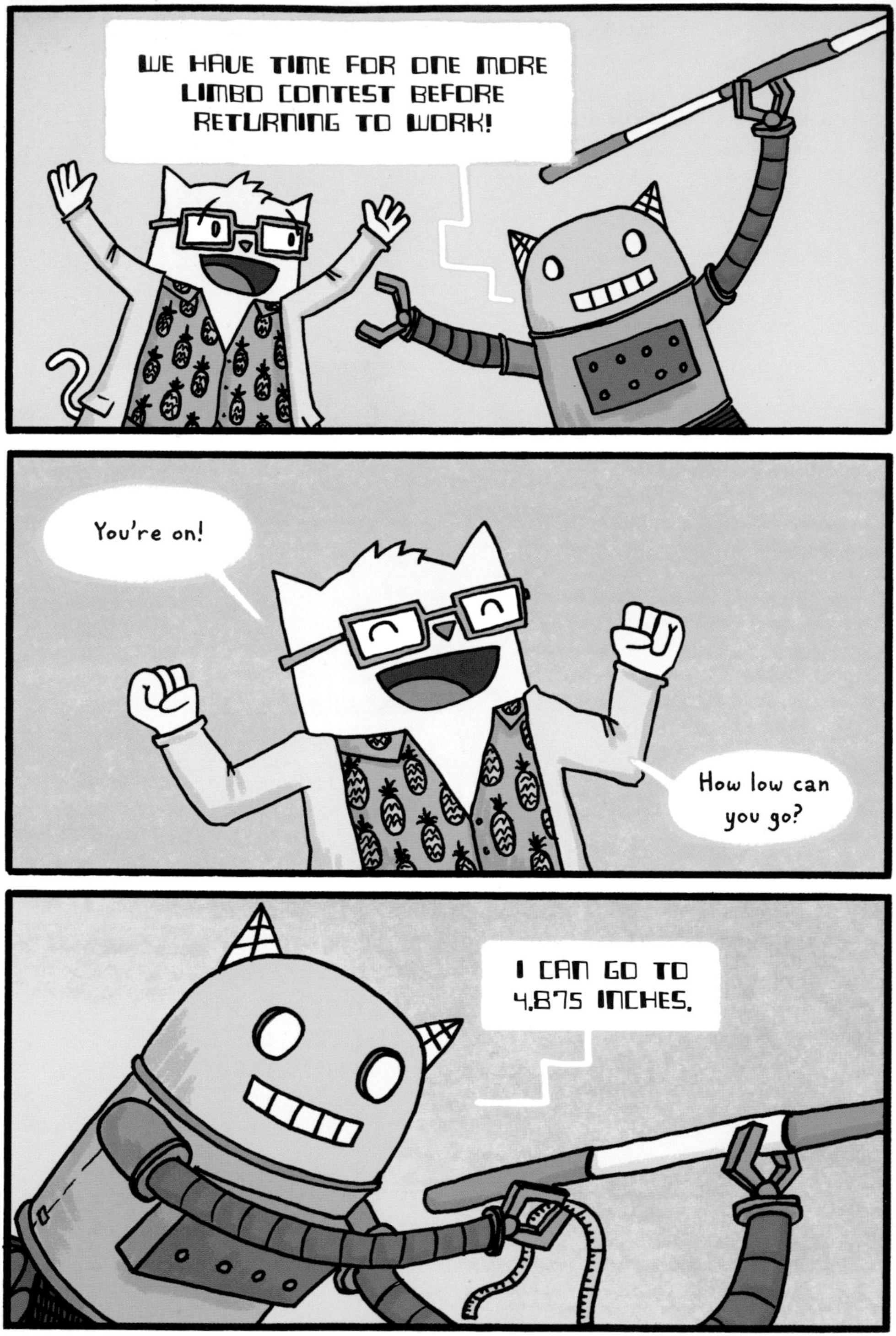
WE HAVE TIME FOR ONE MORE LIMBO CONTEST BEFORE RETURNING TO WORK!
You're on!
How low can you go?
I CAN GO TO 4.875 INCHES.

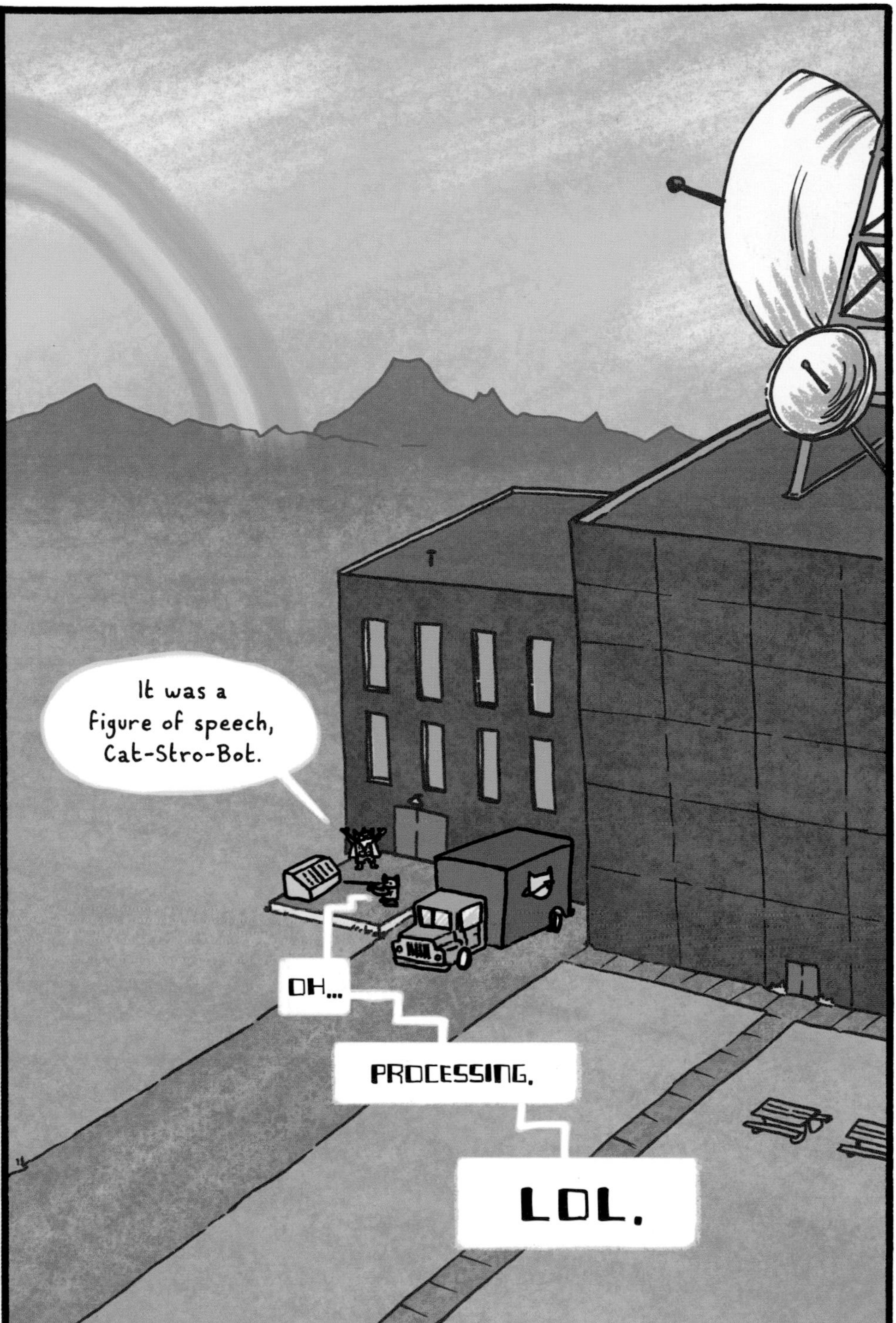
It was a figure of speech, Cat-Stro-Bot.
OH...
PROCESSING.
LOL.

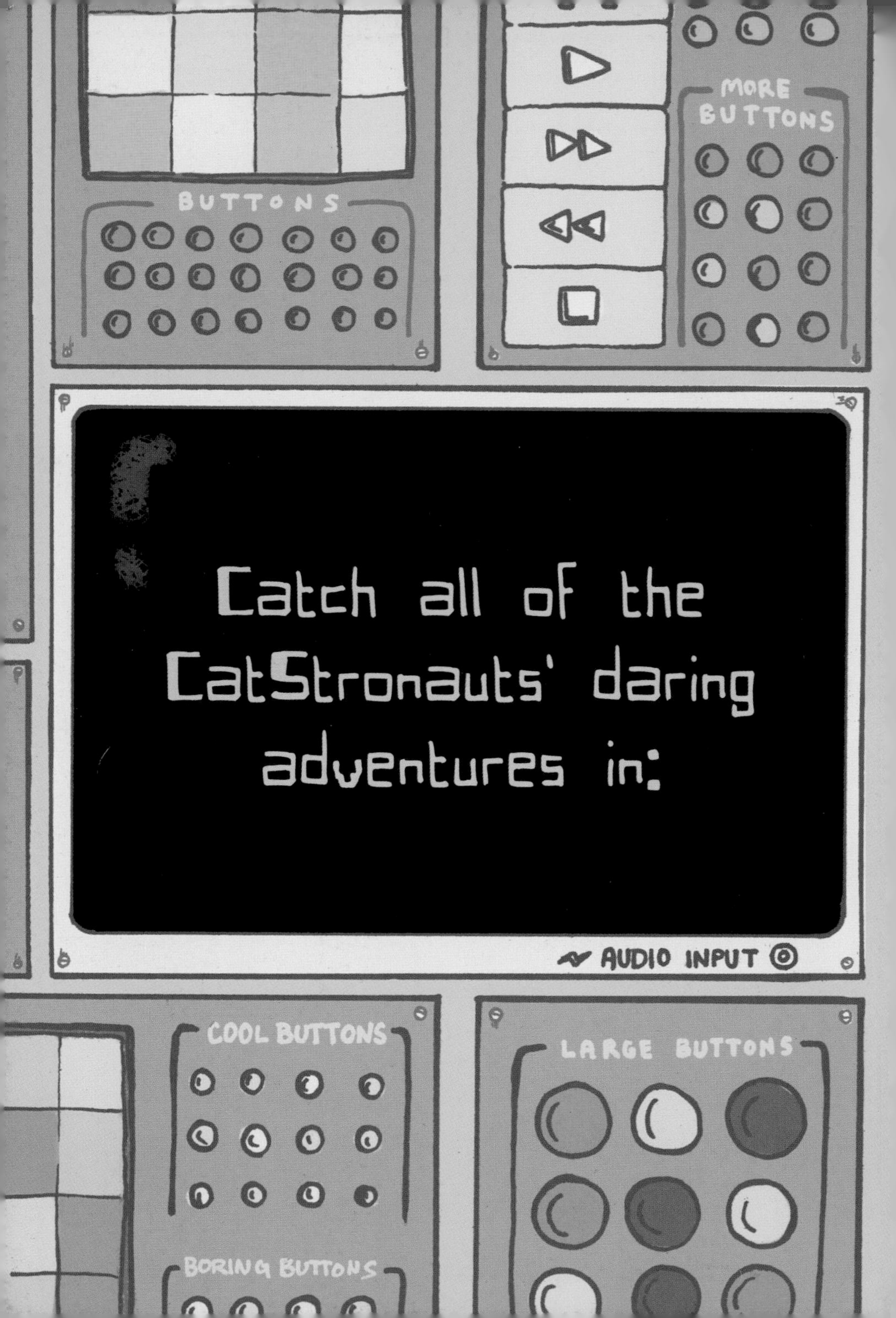
MORE BUTTONS
BUTTONS
Catch all of the CatStronauts' daring adventures in:
AUDIO INPUT
COOL BUTTONS
LARGE BUTTONS
BORING BUTTONS

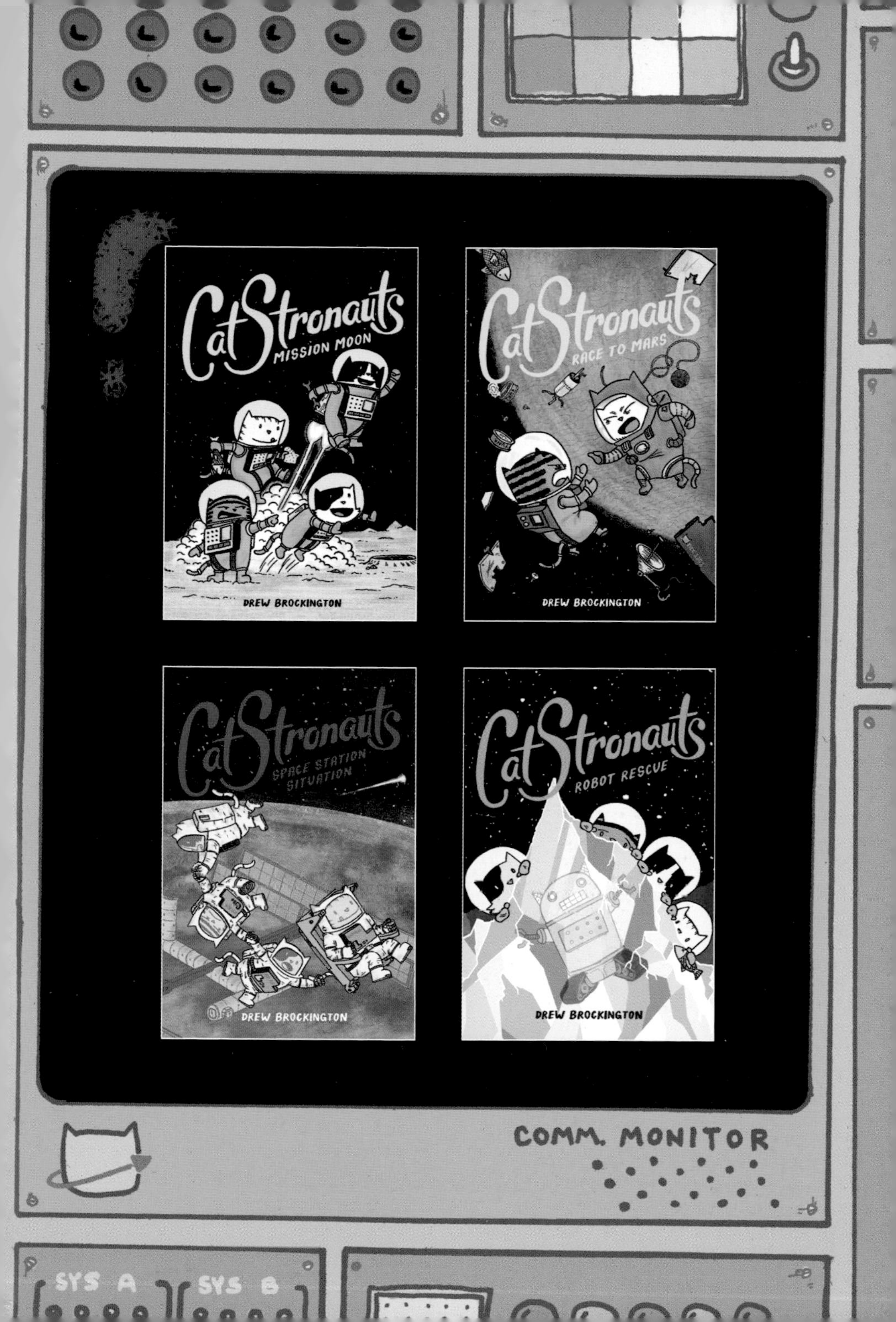
CatStronauts
MISSION MOON
DREW BROCKINGTON
CatStronauts
RACE TO MARS
DREW BROCKINGTON
CatStronauts
SPACE STATION SITUATION
DREW BROCKINGTON
CatStronauts
ROBOT RESCUE
DREW BROCKINGTON
COMM. MONITOR
SYS A
SYS B

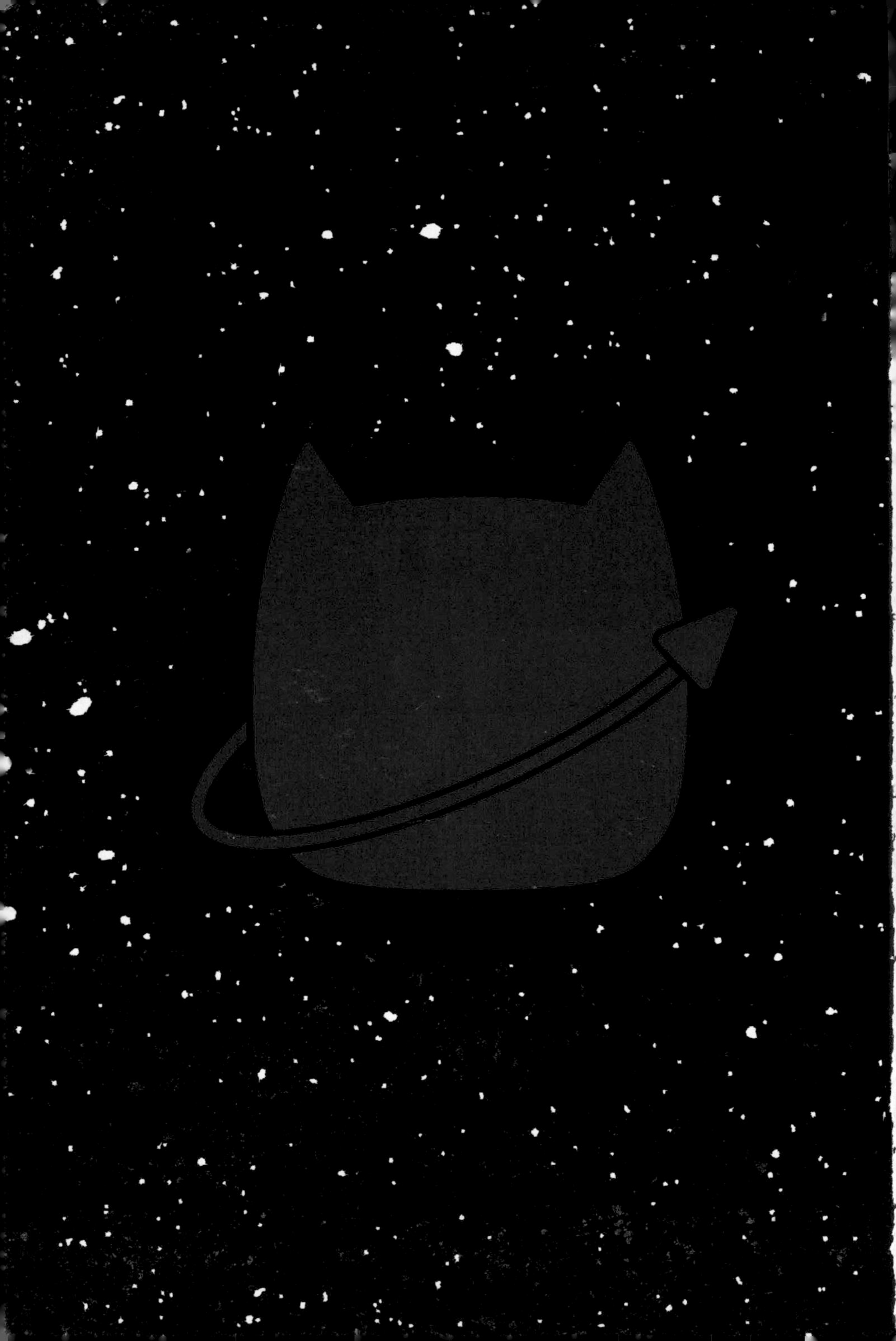

Cat scientists from COOKIE* have just finished building a new space garden module for the International Space Station and they need the CatStronauts' help installing it. While there, Pom Pom is excited to execute a few (hundred) experiments. Everything is going smoothly until...

...Pom Pom falls asleep, her plants die, and weeds start growing everywhere! Things get worse when the sprinklers turn on and the cabin starts filling with water. Plus, the cats back at Mission Control have accidentally abandoned the crew! With no cats around to help, will the CatStronauts ever get back to Earth?

*Center Of Obvious Knowledge and Interstellar Exploration

CAT-ASTROPHE HERE. HELP!
THE CATSTRONAUTS ARE IN A REAL PICKLE!

DON'T MISS:

CatStronauts
MISSION MOON
DREW BROCKINGTON

CatStronauts
RACE TO MARS
DREW BROCKINGTON

CatStronauts
SPACE STATION SITUATION
DREW BROCKINGTON

ROBOT RESCUE
DREW BROCKINGTON

$8.99 U.S. / $12.99 CAN.
ISBN 978-0-316-45126-0
50899
EAN
9 780316 451260

VISIT US AT LBYR.com

#CatStronauts

Printed in China

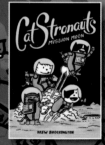

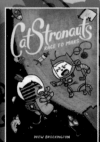

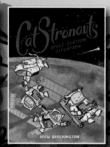

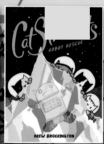